"*You're* not at all what I expected," Natalia said.

"Yeah, well, I'm not what I expected," Matthew returned grimly. "So what did you think you were going to find when you walked in here?"

"Either a smarmy two-bit rogue who is in this for the money or a nut-job who really believes he can rid people of demons."

Matthew half-smiled.

"You're not in it for the money," she admitted. "Any other man would have jumped at my offer and you turned it down flat. And Pastor Wiggins has been telling the press how you gave him a two-thousand-dollar check. You're not a nut-job either." She regarded him intently. "I'm not sure what you are, Matthew Gallow. But I'd like to find out."

She came over to stand in front of him and looked deep into his eyes, as though she were trying to see inside him.

"Do you really believe you saved that girl from a demon last night?"

By Margaret and Lizz Weis

FALLEN ANGEL
WARRIOR ANGEL

MARGARET AND LIZZ
WEIS

FALLEN
ANGEL

AVON
An Imprint of HarperCollinsPublishers

This is a work of fiction. Names, characters, places, and incidents are drawn from the author's imagination or are used fictitiously and are not to be construed as real. Any resemblance to actual events, locales, organizations, or persons, living or dead, is entirely coincidental.

AVON BOOKS
An Imprint of HarperCollins*Publishers*
10 East 53rd Street
New York, New York 10022-5299

Copyright © 2008 by Margaret Weis and Lizz Baldwin Weis
ISBN: 978-0-06-083333-6
www.avonromance.com

First Avon Books paperback printing: November 2008

Avon Trademark Reg. U.S. Pat. Off. and in Other Countries, Marca Registrada, Hecho en U.S.A.
HarperCollins® is a registered trademark of HarperCollins Publishers.

Printed in the U.S.A.

10 9 8 7 6 5 4 3 2 1

For David and for Natalie

Acknowledgments

We would like to thank our friend, theology scholar John Hefter, for his help and advice. We couldn't have exorcised those demons without you, John!

"Are not five sparrows sold for two
    farthings, and not one of them is
    forgotten before God?
But even the very hairs of your head are
    all numbered. Fear not therefore: ye are
    of more value than many sparrows."

Holy Bible, New Testament, Luke 12:6-7

FALLEN ANGEL

Chapter 1

Troy Beckman, late forties, church elder, solid, respectable, was jolted out of a sound sleep by the crack of shatter-
ing glass and screams.

He sat bolt upright in the bed. The room was dark, and
he experienced the panicky feeling of not knowing where
he was. He looked around at the room, what he could see
of it by the faint green glow of the clock, and it wasn't
familiar. He looked in the bed next to him and saw his
wife, Laura.

Good, he thought. *Love Laura.*

Then it came back to him. Beverly Hills. The Four Seasons Hotel. California.

Earthquake. Maybe it was an earthquake.

But, if so, wouldn't there be an alarm or something?

He heard more noise. Laughing and hooting and shrieking. Then a large splash, followed by wild cheering.

Troy relaxed. Not an earthquake. Just a party.

He looked at the clock. Four thirty. The fog of sleep

cleared. He was here for the weekend—a minivacation. No kids. Time alone with Laura in a luxury hotel, visiting Universal Studios, going shopping on Rodeo Drive, eating a fabulous dinner.

Not being jolted out of bed in the middle of the night.

"Troy, what are you doing up? What is that noise?" Laura was peering at him over the covers, still half-asleep.

Troy trudged over to the window to see what was going on. He parted the curtain to the French doors and watched something large and bulky sail past his balcony.

"I could be wrong, dear, but I think someone's throwing furniture into the pool."

"Oh," said Laura, and after a moment, "Why?"

"I have no idea."

Troy watched a lamp hurtle past his window. It landed in the water with a loud splash. He opened the sliding glass door, stepped out onto his balcony, and peered up. Cigarette butts and beer bottles were now falling like rain. Looking down, he saw a couch, a mattress, an armchair, and now a lamp in the swimming pool. He also saw lights going on all over the hotel, and he heard footsteps, violent knocking, and loud voices outside the room.

"Ms. Ashley. Hotel Security," said a deep male voice. He did not sound happy.

"Troy! Tell them to be quiet!" Laura said, and pulled a pillow over her head.

Troy put on a fluffy white bathrobe, compliments of the hotel, slid off the bolt, opened the door a crack, and looked out into the hall.

In the doorway opposite, a woman, maybe late twenties, stood blinking irately at the two men.

"Do you know what time it is?" she demanded. "It's four thirty in the goddam morning!"

Even at this hour, still half-asleep himself, Troy noted

that she was a remarkable-looking woman. Her waist-length hair was a rich brown color, highlighted by golden strands and adorned by a pure white streak that ran from a peak in her forehead. Her hazel eyes were large, with a golden glint lurking in the depths, a glint that seemed to imply she was secretly laughing at all the world. She had pulled on a gray hoodie over a T-shirt and large, striped pajama bottoms decorated with—oddly—penguins. She had shoved her feet into a pair of black, high-top tennis shoes. The undone laces trailed after her.

"Ms. Ashley—" the man began.

"Ms. Ashley?" she interrupted. "Oh, I'm sorry, Ms. Ashley died. I've called the morgue." The woman gestured vaguely back into her room.

"What?" The security man went goggle-eyed.

"She's stringing you," said his partner. "Don't be such a sap."

"Oh, all right, I'm Natalia Ashley," she admitted, adding, with a sigh, "I always try saying I'm dead, but it never works. Some night it will, and I'll get some sleep."

"You're Mr. Cain's manager?"

"Yes," she said, exasperated, "So, look, guys, I know you want tickets to the next show in Vegas, but I'm sorry, it's sold out. I can get autographs for you, but that's all. Now, g'night." She started to shut the door.

"Ms. Ashley," the man said in stern tones. "The hotel manager has called the police, and they're on the way. We're pressing charges."

"What? Why?"

"Don't you know what's been going on? The hotel is in an uproar. How could you not hear this racket? Are you deaf?"

"I am a little, actually," Natalia replied. "I stood too close to the amplifiers at a Nirvana concert back in '92."

She was interrupted by the sound of wild laughter and another splash.

"I heard that," she said.

"That," said the security guard grimly, "is Mr. Cain."

"No!" Natalia blinked at them. "The party ended at 2:00 A.M., and Cain went straight to bed—"

"Well, he didn't stay there. He's trashing his suite."

"You must have some other rock star," said Natalia firmly. "I heard Aerosmith was in town."

"It is not Aerosmith. Aerosmith are gentlemen."

The woman stared at the two men as though hoping they'd change their minds, but they merely looked grim and resolute.

"Shit," she muttered. "Wait a minute."

The woman disappeared into her room. When she returned, still in her penguin pajama bottoms, she had a cell phone in her hand and an earpiece in her ear.

As she accompanied the men, she glanced over at Troy and gave him a lopsided smile of apology. "Lots of commotion, huh? I'm terribly sorry. Cain doesn't usually behave like this. Must be all the excitement of the start of his tour.

"Sorry about all the noise, folks!" she said, speaking contritely to the other guests standing about the hallway in their fluffy white Four Seasons bathrobes. "But, hey," she added, with a shrug and a grin, "it's only rock and roll . . ."

She disappeared with the security men into the elevator.

Troy closed the door and went back to bed.

Cain the rock star. Cain the international sensation. Cain the pop-culture phenomenon. Troy wasn't much up on modern music, but even *he'd* heard of Cain. His kids were huge fans.

Wait until he told them. Mother and I were in the same

hotel with Cain when he was arrested by the police for throwing a mattress in the swimming pool. I actually saw Cain standing on the balcony with a lamp in his hand, he would add.

Who says we're old fogies? Troy thought triumphantly as he lay down on his bed and tried to go back to sleep.

As the elevator ascended smoothly and silently—no elevator music, gotta love four-star hotels—to the penthouse level, Natalia tried talking to the security guards, hoping to find out what damage Cain had done. They both stood in stony silence, however, refusing to answer her questions. She sighed and, noticing that her Chuck Taylors were untied, bent down to tie them. Can't have the manager of the number one rock-and-roll star in the world tripping over her shoelaces and falling flat on her face in front of the night manager.

Natalia missed the music, so hummed a few bars of "Girl From Ipanema" just to make herself feel at home.

The doors opened. The guards, flanking her, marched her down the hall.

"Dead man walking," she quipped, but the guards didn't laugh.

They rounded a corner, and there was the night manager, standing inside the doorway to Cain's room. At least Natalia assumed he was the manager by the fact that he was the one in the suit talking into the walkie-talkie. The air reeked of gin. The floor outside the penthouse was littered with broken glass.

"I'm Natalia Ashley, sir. What seems to be the problem?" she asked.

"Ms. Ashley—"

A nearly empty bottle of Jack Daniel's came flying out the door and smashed against the wall, missing the manager by six inches. Natalia and the manger both ducked to avoid the glass and booze ricocheting off the wall.

"Hell, I missed!" came a slurred voice from inside.

"As you can see," the manager said through gritted teeth, wiping Jack Daniel's from his face, "Mr. Cain and his friends are causing a disturbance. We've been inundated with complaints from the other guests."

"I'm sorry, sir. I really am. He's never done anything like this before. I think he's upset because the reaction from fans to his new show was . . . well . . . lukewarm. And for a show billed as the Descent into Hell, warm is bad."

Natalia stopped, eyed the manager. "You're not interested in that, are you?"

He grimly shook his head.

Natalia sighed. "Okay, look, if you'll move Cain to another room, I'll put a stop to the partying. No need to involve the police."

"Ms. Ashley, look in there!" The manager was red-faced, furious. "Mr. Cain has been throwing the hotel furniture into the swimming pool! The police are on their way."

Natalia stared at the hotel manager in astonishment.

"He's been what?" She leaned around the door to look into the suite.

It was a wreck.

Clothes were strewn everywhere. There were burn holes in the carpet where cigarette butts had been extinguished. The floor was littered with broken bottles and smashed beer cans, crushed potato chips and cheesy puffs. The bedsheets had been sliced to ribbons, the stuffing knocked out of the pillows. Some guy lay passed out on the floor near the door. Natalia didn't recognize him. Another man was crouched behind an overturned armchair, armed with a supply of bottles, which he lobbed at the door whenever the manager's head appeared.

Natalia looked for Cain and finally saw him outside on the balcony with another guy and three women. None of them had much on in the way of clothing. Cain was wearing his underwear—red briefs—over which he'd put on a pair of black leather, metal-studded chaps, no shoes, and no shirt. His blonde hair was disheveled, standing straight up on his head. His eyes were glazed over. The women were wearing various articles of club clothing missing either the tops or bottoms. Natalia gave the women a quick once-over and was thankful to see none of them looked underage. Cain and his newfound buddies were holding the flat-screen television over the edge of the balcony.

"This machine is destroying humanity! To the depths of Hell—or in this case the swimming pool—with it!" Cain shouted, as the television sailed over the balcony.

Natalia winced as she heard it splash.

"Why did you do that?" the manager yelled from the door, not venturing into the room, wary of the bottle-thrower. "What the hell did you throw the TV out for?"

Cain peered around, finally found the manager, and tried to focus on him.

"Your damn hotel doesn't carry the History Channel," he called out, aggrieved. "I always watch the History Channel when I can't sleep. Damn Nazis. I hate Nazis."

He put his arms around two of the women and, leaning on each other, they staggered back into the room. The other guy was hanging over the balcony, puking.

"I hate Nazis, too," said the guy crouched behind the chair. He lobbed a Smirnoff vodka bottle in the general direction of the door, and the manager ducked again.

Natalia shook her head. "Cain *is* very fond of the History Channel."

"We have the History Channel," the manager stated icily.

Natalia decided it would be best not to debate that point. "I understand the damage is going to be extensive, Mr. uuuuh"—she looked at his name that was pinned to his jacket—Mr. Reynolds. If you'll tell me the amount, I'll write you a check—"

"No, Ms. Ashley, I don't think you *do* understand." The manager was grim. "We had our misgivings when we permitted Mr. Cain to stay here, but you assured us nothing like this would happen."

"And I assure you now, sir, this is the first time things have . . . er . . . gotten out of control."

That was true. The kickoff party had gotten pretty wild, but the madness had been restricted to the ballroom, and it had ended at 2:00 A.M., when the big-name guests had departed in their limos and Cain had retired to his penthouse suite and Natalia had gone to her bed. Apparently Cain had decided the party wasn't over. He'd done some wild things in the past, but this was the first time he had ever awakened an entire hotel full of people. She hoped this wasn't starting a trend.

True, he was disappointed by the fans' reaction to the show. So was she, and she didn't know what to do about it. The special effects were fabulous. It was Cain. He just wasn't connecting with the audience. It was as if he was playing for himself, shutting out the audience, and they knew it and resented it. Natalia couldn't understand what had gotten into Cain. This tour was the biggest thing to happen to him, to both of them. It was what they'd dreamed about back in the old days, when he was playing cheap clubs for beer money. And instead of being excited about it, he'd been nervous, depressed. She had counted on the show itself—the thrill of performing live before thousands—jolting him out of whatever funk he'd fallen into. Instead, it just seemed to have made things worse.

Natalia was hoping the manager had been bluffing about calling the police, then she heard the elevator ding, and four Los Angeles cops came rounding the corner. She had to face it. Cain was going to be hauled off to jail.

"Not only is Cain going to be arrested," the manager stated, "in the morning I will be speaking to the Four Seasons corporate head office, who will, I am sure, be consulting legal counsel. I would imagine the corporation will sue Mr. Cain's record label and anyone else they can find."

He glared at her. "You're his manager, damn it! Aren't you supposed to keep him under control? I hope your boss fires your ass!"

Natalia considered telling him that Cain was the owner of the record label, which meant Cain was her boss and that he paid her to run the asylum, not police the inmates. The truth would only make the manager angrier, so she let it go.

Natalia walked into the suite, passing one of the cops, who had the bottle-thrower in custody and was hauling him off down the hall. She looked into the room, hoping against hope that Cain wasn't doing anything stupid (make that stupid*er*), such as resisting arrest.

Cain was hissing like a snake at the police as they cuffed him. Two of the women were hanging on to him by the shoulders, pleading with the cops to let him go. One woman lay prostrate on the floor, sobbing and clinging to Cain's foot with both hands wrapped around his ankle.

Cain flashed the women a smile. "Don't worry, ladies, we'll get together again. Next time I'm back in Dallas . . ."

The police pulled Cain toward the door. Unable to free himself, he dragged the woman on the floor along with him until the cops finally tore her loose.

"Cain, I love you!" she wailed.

"Dallas . . ." mumbled one of the women, sagging down in a chair. "'S funny. I coulda sworn I was in LA . . ."

"Nat!" Cain yelled, catching sight of her and giving her the grin that made his fans swoon. "Nat, darling, where were you? We needed a referee for the mattress-hockey game!"

Natalia wasn't laughing. "Can I have a word with him, officers? It won't take long."

The police halted, still keeping a fast hold on Cain, who stared at her, grinning drunkenly. "I love the penguins, Nat," he slurred.

Natalia gazed at him, perplexed. "What's gotten into you, Cain? Why are you acting like this?" She lowered her voice, hoping to penetrate the alcoholic fog. "I know you. This isn't you." She gestured at the ruins.

Cain looked around, then he looked back at Natalia. His gaze lowered. He seemed almost ashamed, then suddenly he jerked his head back to leer at her.

"Why am I doing this? Because I can!" he boasted, and belched gin fumes at her. "Because I'm a star!"

"You weren't a star tonight," she told him bluntly. "You forgot half the lyrics, missed your mark twice, messed up your cues. I could forgive that—it's the first time we've done the show before an audience, after all. But it was like you weren't there, Cain! No, that's not quite right. It's like you were there, but you didn't give a damn about any of the rest of us—including your fans!"

He stared at her, trying to bring her into focus.

"Give a damn. Damnation," he said softly. "That's what it's about, Nat."

"If you say so." Natalia was too tired to argue. She waved her hand. "You can take him away now, officers. Enjoy your night in jail, Cain."

He seemed to perk up at this.

"Just make sure the photographers are out there," he called over his shoulder, as they dragged him away.

Natalia paused to consider this. Of course the photographers would be out there. Had he done this on purpose? Was this a publicity stunt? Cain certainly looked and smelled drunk, but it sounded to her as if some part of him was stone-cold sober. If so, where had that part of him come from? The Cain Natalia knew, the Cain who had hauled her out of that mosh pit and maybe saved her life three years ago, wouldn't have done anything like this.

Natalia turned to the police officers. "Where are you taking him? I need to know, so I can tell his lawyer."

"Ma'am, he's going to headquarters on Rexford," said a cop, as they hauled Cain out the door.

"Nat!" Cain yelled, laughing back at her over his bare shoulder. "I love those striped penguin jammies. Buy me twenty pair, will you?"

The police dragged him down the hall. Natalia followed them until she made sure they had Cain safely in the elevator. He gave her a last grin and shook his head, to get the hair out of his eyes so he'd look good in the pictures.

Natalia fiddled with her cell phone, thinking rapidly. She remembered Cain's agent saying once, *When you're handed lemons, make lemonade.*

She flipped open her cell and hit speed dial. The phone rang and rang, then went to voice mail. Of course, Crandall would be asleep. Any normal person would be asleep. Natalia hit redial. Again with the voice mail.

"Damn it, wake up!" she told him.

She heard the phone pick up, then some fumbling as though he'd dropped it, then a groggy, "Huh?"

"Crandall. It's Natalia. Cain's being arrested. I want—"

"What?" Crandall had come wide-awake. "Arrested? God help us! He didn't . . . he didn't kill anyone, did he?"

"No, of course not, Crandall, don't be an idiot. We had the kickoff concert for the tour last night, and we held the party here. The party went well, but afterward, Cain threw some Four Seasons furniture into the swimming pool and woke up half the guests and now the cops are here and the hotel is probably going to sue us. So what I want you to do is— Would you stop swearing and listen?"

"I have every reason to swear," Crandall retorted. "I'm his public-relations agent! You were right to call me. We've got to keep this out of the press. I'll—"

"No," Natalia interrupted, "we don't want to keep it out. We want it in. The paparazzi have been camped outside the hotel all night, so we don't have to worry about them. But I don't want this just in the tabloids."

She drew in a deep breath. She didn't believe she was about to say what she was about to say. "I want Cain's arrest to make headlines in every newspaper from LA to Buffalo. I want this on CNN and the major TV networks and Fox— don't forget Fox, they'll eat this up. And AP and Reuters and C-Span and Bloomberg and anyone else you can think of—"

"Bloomberg?" Crandall was puzzled. "I think they only do financial news—"

"It was a joke, Crandall," Natalia said.

"I don't know how you can fucking joke at a time like this!" he shouted into the phone.

"It's either that, or I sit down and cry. Oh, yeah, and call his lawyer, will you?"

"Sure." Crandall sighed. "Right away. Why should I be the only one who's awake at this ungodly hour?"

Natalia thought this over. She'd finish out *her* sleep, at least.

"Call the lawyer in the morning," she said. "It won't hurt Cain to sleep it off in jail. Teach him a lesson. Tell

Parker he has to have Cain out on bail in time for his show in Las Vegas next week night, the Aladdin theater."

"But, Natalia—"

"They're taking him to Rexford. Love you, Crandall, bye!" she said wearily, and tapped her earpiece, ending the call.

She walked back to survey the damage in the hotel suite. She found the manager staring about gloomily. Natalia rounded up the drunken women and shoved them into one of the suite's bedrooms, then she shut the door and came back to the manager.

"Mr. Reynolds," said Natalia earnestly, "I personally want to apologize on behalf of Cain for this. High spirits. A little too much booze. I would like to make it up to the guests who were disturbed."

She recalled the man in the white bathrobe who was staying in the room across from hers. He'd kind of reminded her of her dad on his good days, when he was sober. How long had it been since she'd seen her father? Or even thought about him? Ten years maybe. He'd been a rotten dad. Her real father was rock and roll. Music was in her blood. Her grandfather, whom she'd adored, had been a Deadhead. He'd died when she was sixteen. After his funeral, she'd hopped a bus with a friend to follow a band, and she'd never looked back.

Natalia shook herself. Where had those memories come from? My God, she must be hallucinating! She'd heard that happened when you didn't get enough sleep. You started dreaming when you were wide-awake. With this tour to plan, she couldn't remember when she'd slept more than three hours at a stretch.

"I want to send a bottle of wine and a fruit basket to every guest in the hotel," Natalia said, dragging herself back to reality. "Would that help smooth things over?"

Reynolds looked at her, mystified. "I don't know how you stand it! He's an animal! Filthy, savage . . . One of those women had bite marks on her thigh!"

"He's never done this before," she repeated. "I don't know what got into him tonight."

She made arrangements for the wine and the fruit baskets, all in Cain's name. The guests would have them delivered to their rooms in the morning. She finally made it back to her room an hour later. Crawling into bed, she realized she was too wired to fall asleep. If Cain didn't get out of jail, she'd have to cancel his upcoming show, which was in a week. The show had been sold out for months. Rescheduling would be a nightmare, and Cain would be locked up in jail, where she couldn't throttle him.

What got into him? she asked herself again. *What is wrong with him? Maybe becoming an overnight sensation has gone to his head.*

"It won't happen to me," he had sworn to her long ago. "Stardom won't affect me. You won't catch me vomiting on stage like Tommy Lee or trashing hotel rooms."

And not only had he done it, she'd condoned his bad behavior by making certain he would be on every newscast this morning. He was number one all over the world. His concerts were sold-out. His videos were all over YouTube and MySpace. Tomorrow Jay Leno's people would be calling her and Larry King and *Saturday Night Live* and Colbert. Maybe even Wolf Blitzer . . .

That was all going to end and end fast if she didn't find some way to put some heat into the Hell tour. Some way to jolt Cain out of whatever funk he'd fallen into. Otherwise, instead of the Hell tour, it would be Tour from Hell.

Natalia flipped on the television, turned to NBC and the *Today Show.* There was Cain, showing off his handcuffs, mugging for the cameras. *Good Morning America.* Same thing. She switched to CNN, then to the Fox News Channel, and landed on a commercial—an advertisement for some new reality show. She had to wait through the commercial to see if Cain would be on. She watched impatiently, waiting for the news, then suddenly she forgot about the news. She jumped out of bed, walked over to stand in front of the TV.

It was as if Heaven and Fox cable news ("fair and balanced") were answering her prayers.

The reporter was doing an exposé on a priest who had created a sensation by traveling across the country performing exorcisms, driving demons out of people in front of a shocked and loving-it audience. Tonight Fox News was going to be there, live, filming the priest's show, prepared to expose him for the fraud and charlatan he was.

There was a close-up shot of the priest. Damn, the man was good-looking! Black hair, smoldering eyes, pale complexion, chiseled jaw. He looked the part! Fabulous under the lights, with flames shooting up all around him.

As Natalia began dialing the airline, she noticed her hands were shaking with excitement. She realized, suddenly, she didn't know where she was going.

"Where is he doing this exorcism?" she demanded of Fox. "What's the name of the damn town?"

They'd said it once, but she hadn't been paying attention.

"Tonight in Clarksville, Tennessee . . ." boomed the reporter.

"Thank you!" Natalia breathed. She kept punching numbers on the phone until a real, live person answered.

"American Airlines? I want a ticket for a flight today to whatever city is closest to a place called Clarksville, Tennessee . . ."

Chapter 2

$\mathcal{A}$ waitress in a yellow uniform whose name tag announced to an uncaring world that she was "Merle" deposited two mugs of coffee on the table. The mugs were made of ceramic with rounded rims and thick, hard-to-hold handles. Matthew's had a coffee-stained crack. Merle used a bit too much force, and the coffee sloshed over the edge, ran down the side, and made a puddle on the table. The waitress didn't care. She was busy with the usual supper crowd and was probably resentful that Matthew and his partner hadn't ordered anything except two coffees and a piece of pie.

"Thank you, Merle," Matthew said, smiling the smile that never failed to win them. "What's that short for—Merlene?"

"Merle is short for Merle," the waitress said, eyeing him suspiciously. Apparently his smile wasn't working today. The waitress walked off, drawling, "Merrrrleeeen," in disgust and muttering, "Sounds like some goddam Yankee name."

Matthew gave his partner a lopsided grin. "Off my game today, I guess."

Hannah didn't respond. She didn't even look at him, just sat staring at her coffee.

Merle—short for Merle—came back and tossed the pie onto the table. The plastic plate made a clatter as it hit, and Hannah flinched nervously. Matthew sopped up coffee with a wad of napkins and took a sip.

"Not bad," he said to Hannah. "You should try it."

"It's wretched," she told him. "It always is, places like this. You just don't taste it, that's all."

That was true. Far truer than she knew. Matthew didn't taste the coffee. Not anymore. He'd first drunk coffee where? Constantinople, he thought. The Ottoman Turks had introduced it there somewhere around the mid 1400s. Matthew had tasted coffee then, and he'd liked it a lot. He'd liked it still more later on when one of the popes had termed it the "devil's drink" for the effect it had on people.

But you drink something over and over and over again, centuries without end, and no matter what it is: coffee or tea, bourbon or Dom Pérignon, you stop tasting it. Matthew looked at the pie, which was advertised as peach and consisted of mostly peach-colored goo with maybe a slice of fruit that had happened to wander in, and he realized he hadn't tasted anything in a long, long time. It was all dust and ashes.

"Just like flirting with that waitress," Hannah went on. "I don't know why you even bother. You don't care."

True, as well. Matthew had stopped caring about the same time he'd stopped tasting coffee. Hannah didn't need to know that, however.

"Eat your pie," he told her. "And let's quit talking about me and discuss the job."

Hannah stuck a fork in her pie, carefully cut off the tip

and moved it to one side of her plate, then started in on the rest.

"Why the hell do you do that?" Matthew asked suddenly, irritated.

"Do what?" Hannah looked up.

"Cut off the end of the triangle and save it to eat last. You do it every goddam time."

"Yeah, and we've been together how long, and you're just now starting to wonder?" Hannah cast him an unhappy glance and threw down her fork. "If you must know, I make a wish."

"Huh?" Matthew stared.

"I make a wish. My mama said that if you cut off the tip of the pie and eat it last and make a wish, your wish will come true."

"So, has it?" Matthew tried the smile again.

Hannah sighed. "I spent last night in a room in a Motel 6 in Abilene, Texas, with a drunken con man, and tonight I'll be in a room in a Motel 6 somewhere in Tennessee with a drunken con man. What do you think?"

Matthew rubbed his eyes. He was tired, and he didn't need Hannah flaking out on him. The drive from Abilene had been a long one, and there hadn't been a whole lot to look at along the way. Not that he looked anymore. It was all the same. Every little town was the same. The inside of every motel room was the same, too. Clarksville or Constantinople. He'd spent his entire life on the road. Actually, he'd spent a good many lifetimes on the road. Always searching for something around the next bend.

It had turned out to be a long road. Too many bends. Leading nowhere.

He pulled a flask of bourbon from the pocket of his shabby suit coat and poured some into his coffee.

"Do you have to do that now? In public?" Hannah

demanded, shocked. She glanced around to see if anyone had noticed.

"Like you said, the coffee's wretched. Now finish up, so you can check into the motel. You lie low. I have to go look at the location tomorrow morning. They're supposed to be setting up the tent and building the stage. The pastor's going to meet me there at nine in the morning. He's all worked up over this TV thing."

Hannah shoved away the rest of the pie. She didn't eat the end she'd cut off, after all. Apparently if you didn't eat the whole piece, you didn't get to make a wish. Matthew tossed some money on the table, including a tip for Merle-short-for-nothing, and they left.

He opened the door to the Cadillac, started to climb in. Hannah's hand on his arm stopped him.

"I don't like this TV business, Matthew," she said unhappily. "I don't like it a lot."

He saw fear in her eyes. Her hand was cold and shaking. "What we're doing is fraud! And you're letting this TV crew film us doing it! They'll find out we're fakes, that we bilk people out of their money. They're bound to find out. We could go to jail!"

"Oh, come off it," Matthew snapped. "It's not fraud. It's entertainment. That's why the people put their money in the collection plates. No one who comes to see me really believes I'm exorcising demons."

"Yes, they do," Hannah insisted. "Some of them do."

"Then that's their problem. Not mine. If they're so gullible—"

"It's called faith, Matt!" Hannah said. She was in one of her self-righteous moods. "But you wouldn't know anything about that, would you?"

I did, Matthew thought. *I died for my faith once. But that's ancient history. And it's all over now.*

"It's not like you've never done anything shady in your life, Miss Holier-than-Thou," Matthew said impatiently.

Hannah's blue eyes opened wide. "I never did," she said, almost crying. "Not until I met you."

Matthew looked at Hannah, with her sweet, baby-doll face; her sunny, fluffy blonde hair and her sunny, fluffy personality, and he realized, *Damn! If she doesn't actually believe what she's telling me!* He shook his head in exasperation mingled with admiration. *I guess it's what makes her such a good con artist.*

He had met Hannah in Los Angeles, a city that serves up a midnight buffet of out-of-work, desperate actresses, which is what he used in his work. Matthew had been there in search of a new partner. He tended to have a high turnover in partners. Few lasted very long. Some were just plain bad actresses, and he'd had to fire them. Others took off on their own; some looking for more money, some seeking kids and husbands, some just yearning for stability in their lives. They left for whatever reason, and Matthew drifted on.

Six months ago, he'd stumbled across Hannah, tending bar at a seedy place in the valley and conning lonely men to "liven up a dull night for me, honey" by playing bar dice or cards with her.

Hustling drunks in a bar was no life for such a talented girl. Hannah was too good. She could pick marks, and she didn't even know it, not until Matthew started coaching her. Most men took their losses good-naturedly, figuring it had been worth it just to spend time basking in the smiles of a pretty girl. But then came the night she ran across a mean drunk, who was also a sore loser. He pulled a knife on her. Matthew jumped the guy, wrestled him to the floor, took away the knife, and tossed the guy out onto the sidewalk.

Of course, after that, Hannah was in love. They all fell in love with Matthew. He was a handsome man. He had to be handsome—it was part of the act. He appeared to be in his early thirties, with black hair cut short in back and worn long in the front. The ragged black bangs set against his white complexion emphasized his mesmerizing blue eyes. Those eyes attracted women "like flies to dead meat" Hannah used to say jokingly.

Dead meat. That described him. Matthew was dead meat. He'd died inside, even if he couldn't die outside. He was going through the motions of living. He wasn't truly alive. Nothing touched him, nothing moved him, nothing affected him. That was why he drank. It numbed the numbness. You can't feel nothing if you can't feel anything.

Hannah latched on to him, claiming she was too shaken to go back to tending bar. He was in need of a partner, so they hit the road together. He made love to Hannah for the same reason he made love to most women—because she expected it of him and also (secretly) because he kept hoping that someday she would be the one to awaken some sort of feeling in him. That didn't happen. It never happened.

He was surprised Hannah hadn't left already. She no longer loved him. He wasn't even sure she still liked him very much. That was all right. He didn't like himself. So long as she did her job, and thus far, she was the best partner he'd ever had. She was so good he'd made more money than he had in years *and* attracted the attention of an investigative journalist from Fox, and now he was going to be in front of a nationwide audience.

Even though the reporter claimed to have an open mind, Matthew knew perfectly well the guy was out to expose him as a fraud. Matthew should have played it safe, refused to allow the guy to film the exorcism. Instead, Matthew had practically dared the reporter to try to catch him in the act. Sure it was dangerous. That's why he was doing it. He needed the danger, needed the challenge.

That was why he couldn't afford to have Hannah walk out on him before tomorrow night. He had to play nice.

"We'll talk it over in the car," he said. "People are starting to stare."

Hannah climbed in the car—an old beater of a Cadillac, brown and dusty and nondescript. Deliberately nondescript. He didn't want folks in the small towns taking notice. Hannah slammed shut the door and fastened her seat belt. She sat as far away from him as possible, her lower lip jutted out.

Matthew sighed. Hannah with the sulks. This was just all he needed! He decided it was probably nerves, stage fright. The best way to handle her was to be cool and professional.

Matthew managed a smile as he pulled out of the parking lot. "The TV people want to discredit me, so you'll need to be on your toes. Do it up right, but don't overdo it, if you know what I mean. You can't phone this one in, Hannah. You have to really sell it tonight."

Hannah wore an injured air. "You've been saying the same damn thing over and over to me since we left Abilene. I'll do what I need to, and I'll do it right." She cast him a disgusted glance. "It would help if *you* lay off the bourbon."

"It was just a sip—"

"Hey!" Hannah grabbed him. "That was a stop sign you just blew through!"

"Sorry," he muttered, "I didn't see it. It's getting dark."

She continued to nag him about drinking while driving. Thankfully, her motel was nearby. He pulled up some distance from the front door and waited for her to get out. When they were working the con, they never stayed in the same hotel, in case someone might see them. He looked at her expectantly, but she didn't move.

"You're a fake, Matthew, a phony."

Matthew smiled. "Tell me something I don't know, sweetheart."

"That reporter's going to find out the truth."

"He won't. I'm too good. You're too good. Now will you just get out of the damn car? I've got work to do."

"Oh, all right." She climbed out and slammed the door.

Matthew popped the trunk so she could get her luggage.

"I need the address," she said, coming up and tapping on the window. "And cab fare."

He was pretty sure he'd already given her cab fare. Twice. He didn't argue, however, but forked over another twenty. Just one more gig to go, he thought.

Hannah flounced off angrily into the motel. She was wearing jeans and a halter top and flip-flops. Tomorrow night she'd be wearing her "floozy" dress, something low-cut, split up the thigh, with high heels and too much makeup. That was her act, that the devil was inside her, making her lust after men and urging her to do horrible things with them. Afterward, she'd be on her knees sobbing her heart out and taking money from old ladies to help feed her "poor little hungry babies" at home, while Matthew was accepting donations to fund his "good work."

Then they'd split the money and take off in the Caddy, heading to the next little town, the next show.

Hannah came walking out of the office a few minutes later, her key in her hand. She didn't look at him but unlocked the door to her room, went inside, and shut it. He waited until he saw the light come on, then he drove off.

He wondered suddenly, uneasily, if he could trust her to go through with the act. He decided he could. Hannah wasn't the type to find herself stuck in Clarksville, Tennessee, with nothing but cab fare.

He drove to another motel a few miles away, parked the

Caddy, grabbed his luggage, and headed to the office to check in. No one looking at Matthew now would connect him with Father Gallow, exorcist. During the show, he wore an ankle-length black cassock, complete with white collar and gold cross. Now he had on a button-down shirt, rumpled trousers, and he carried a shabby suit coat slung over his shoulder. Motel managers took him to be a traveling salesman. In many ways, they were right.

"I sell hope to the weary, salvation to the sinners, and righteous piety to the wronged," Matthew said aloud to the parking lot, testing out the line to hear how it sounded. He might use that when the reporter interviewed him. "I sell the idea that there is a God and that God has the power, through me, to drive out evil. I turn the demon-possessed into kind and loving human beings."

Yes, it sounded fine. Too bad people didn't know God like Matthew knew God. He'd met God, up close and personal. God had cast off Matthew a long time ago. Cast him out of Heaven, cursed him, then forgotten about him.

Fine. Screw God, Matthew thought. *Screw his angels. Screw 'em all.*

Wait until they see me on TV tonight. Matthew grinned. Tonight was going to be a good night. He could feel it in his almost-two-thousand-year-old bones.

His room was basic: two double beds, one window, venetian blinds to shut out the lights of the parking lot, a curtain, two towels, a shower, TV, and phone. Matthew went through the usual routine. He found the remote, turned on the TV. He always turned on the TV. He didn't like the quiet. He tossed his suitcase onto the bed and opened it, pulled out his vestments and hung them up. He'd iron them tomorrow.

He took a shower, then wiped the steam off the mirror, studied himself. His face was his trademark, and he had to look good. He'd shaved this morning, but even so, his beard showed up as a bluish shadow on his pale skin. He took care to keep out of the sun. His pale complexion made him look otherworldly, ethereal. His eyes were what sold it. A Victorian preacher had once told Matthew those eyes of his could "see through the skin of a sinner to the soul beneath." His mother had claimed that when Matthew was a child, back in ancient Rome, his blue eyes were so unusual that people seeing him would make the sign against evil, ward themselves against his gaze.

He chuckled. With his wet bangs hanging over his eyes, he didn't look spiritual. He looked boyish, puckish, like he was about to do something bad.

"'I aim to misbehave,'" he said to his reflection. He'd heard that line in a movie once and considered it suitable to himself.

Matthew grabbed a towel and dried his face. He looked tired. He was tired. He was always tired. Wouldn't do for him to look tired tomorrow night. It was early evening, but day and night meant nothing to him anymore. After the first few thousand, they started to run together into a meaningless mishmash. He needed sleep. Sound sleep. Restful sleep. Dreamless sleep.

Dreamless. That was the catch. He used to pray for his sleep to be free of the tormenting dreams. That was back long ago when he still prayed, back before he'd realized that no one was listening. When he figured that out, he quit praying and started drinking. Sometimes, if he drank enough, he could drown the dreams.

Matthew dug out the flask from the pocket of his trousers, took a pull from it, then lay down on the bed in his underwear. Fortunately, the motel had cable TV, one of their selling points. He found the History Channel. Nothing like history to put you to sleep. He watched World War II and drank bourbon as the Allies were bombing Dresden and fires raged out of control . . .

The centurion came toward him, flaming torch in hand. Matthew was tied to a stake. His robes were soaked in oil. Faggots were piled around his feet. Not far from him, a friend, Antonius, was surrounded by swirling fire. His screams were horrible to hear. Matthew could smell the sickening odor of burning flesh. Antonius had no feet, now, only charred lumps. Yet he still lived. His flesh was bubbling. He screamed and screamed, then his screams died away in a horrible gurgling.

And Matthew was next. The centurion looked up at him and grinned, and said something about "Christian dogs" and lit the wood beneath his feet . . .

Matthew struggled to escape the fire. But there was no escape. The flames licked the soles of his feet. The pain was excruciating, and it would only get worse. Matthew tried to keep from screaming. He wouldn't give his tormentors the satisfaction. He began to pray, but his flesh was roasting now, and he couldn't help himself. He screamed . . .

The sound of pounding woke him.

Matthew gasped. His eyes flared open. He was not tied to a stake being burned alive. He was lying on a bed, bathed in sweat, in the darkness, and the guy next door was pounding on the wall. Matthew sat up. His heart was beating wildly, and it took long moments of deep breathing to calm himself, return his heart rate to normal.

That was a long time ago, he said to himself. They can't hurt you now.

Except they could . . .

"Damn you," he muttered, and there were tears in his eyes. "Damn you, stop it!" He raised himself up and yelled loudly, loud enough to be heard in heaven, "Stop it!"

"You stop it, you son of a bitch!" shouted the guy pounding on the wall. "Some of us are trying to sleep!"

"Sorry," Matthew muttered. He felt around in the darkness for the flask. Locating it, he picked it up with a trembling hand and put it to his lips.

"God damn you!" Matthew said. "God damn you, God." He laughed. That was funny somehow. "I'll show you. Tomorrow night I'm going to put on *my* act and it's going to be on television and the whole world will see it! There's gonna be rubber snakes and flash powder and . . . and I don't know what all. Make those yokels fall to their knees and praise You and it'll all be a con. Just like the great con You've got going. And then what will You do, God? Send Your angels to chastise me? To tell me I need to ask for forgiveness? Well, it's not going to happen."

Matthew shook his fist at the ceiling. "You can keep me down here forever, torture me with nightmares, and I'll never ask, never beg for Your forgiveness. Do you hear me. There'll be glaciers in Hell first!"

Matthew raised the flask to his lips again. The flask was empty. Not that it mattered. The bourbon made him drunk because he wanted to believe it made him drunk. Alcohol— like everything else in his existence—had no effect on him. Cursing, he flung the flask across the room.

He lay back down, but he was too upset and shaken to sleep. He turned on the TV, keeping the volume low, so as not to further offend his neighbor. He switched it to Fox, hoping to see one of the ads they were running about him.

Instead, it was film of some rock star being dragged off by the police.

"—Cain Lukosi was arrested early yesterday morning after a wild party at the Four Seasons Hotel in Beverly Hills. Cain, as he's known to his millions of fans, was charged with destruction of property and being drunk and disorderly. This is footage from outside the hotel."

Matthew watched, bemused. He knew nothing about

rock-and-roll music, couldn't care less. Hannah listened to something she called Classic Rock in the car; sometimes she even sang along. Matthew generally tried to tune it out until Hannah's off-key wailing started to grate on his nerves and he'd order her to shut off the damn radio.

Two cops were manhandling this Cain fellow, trying to get him into a squad car and being hindered in their task by photographers and reporters and a small but vocal army of fans. The rock star was wearing nothing but red briefs and leather chaps. His hands were cuffed behind his bare back. He had tattoos all up and down his arms, and a large tattoo on his shoulders that spread up to his neck. It looked like wings of some sort. Black wings.

Reporters were shouting out questions at him. The rock star grinned at his fans and answered with expletives that were bleeped out. His fans, who were dressed in black, with strange-colored hair, cheered him on, screaming and pumping their fists in the air.

When one of the cameramen came in close. Cain spit straight into the lens. Then he lunged at the cameramen, who stumbled backward, filming all the time.

The cops wrestled Cain back.

Cain was yelling and his fans were yelling and the bleeping was almost continual.

The announcer came back. "Cain Lukosi's going to jail on the morning after the kickoff last night in Los Angeles of his sold-out tour—aptly named, the 'Descent into Hell.' Let's hope he makes bail before the next show," said the chirpy blonde news anchor to her male counterpart. "Or there will be lots of disappointed fans in Vegas."

"Maybe not so disappointed," said her partner. "Judging from the reviews in this morning's papers, Cain's show could be renamed: 'Descent into Boredom'!"

They both laughed.

The shot went back to Cain, spitting at the camera.

How did that song go? The one about the good life of a rock star? Hannah was always singing it.

"'Money for nothin' and your chicks for free,'" Matthew mumbled. That didn't make any sense, but then neither did glaciers in Hell.

He fell back onto the bed, and this time he slept.

Chapter 3

$\mathcal{M}$atthew pulled the Cadillac into the parking lot of the River of Faith Church. He was dressed for the occasion, wearing his ankle-length black cassock, white collar, and golden cross. He walked around back to the cavernous trunk—one reason he drove the old Caddy. A large tent had been set up in a field not far from the church. Workmen were inside arranging folding chairs. He could see a stage, hope they remembered he'd need electricity. He hauled a large black trunk out of the back. Inside were floodlights, colored gels, his well-worn Bible, and a variety of props, among them a battery-powered snake that would slither out of Hannah's beehive wig.

The preacher, Pastor Wiggins, opened the door to the parsonage and ushered Matthew inside.

"Father Gallow, how nice finally to meet you. I've heard much about you, and I'm pleased that you will be joining the service tonight." Pastor Wiggins shook Matthew's hand. The pastor was a large man with a very bald head and a strong grip.

"I understand the Fox News people called you, Brother?" Matthew asked.

"Oh yes, they explained everything to me. They'll be here to set up the cameras shortly. The whole town has heard what's going on. Everyone's very excited. No one's talking about anything else. I think we'll have a full house. I even rented extra chairs." Pastor Wiggins smiled broadly. "We'll show these unbelievers, doubters, and mockers, the power of God tonight, won't we, Father?"

"That we will, Brother," said Matthew gravely. "If you don't mind, I'd like to go over a few things before the reporters arrive. I need to see the stage, set up my lights, check the sound levels, and all that."

"Yes, of course. I'll show you around. Then I'll tell you how I typically conduct my service, and we'll go over my introduction. Do you think they'll film my sermon?"

Matthew politely said he hoped they would. As he accompanied the pastor, he made a mental note to find time to slip away to call Hannah. He'd learned that if he didn't call her during the afternoon of a show, she'd call him, and those calls sometimes came at awkward moments. She never had anything important to say. She mostly called because she was insecure, and she needed him to pat her on the head and tell her everything was going to go fine. She always claimed she called because she wanted to make sure he was sober.

Sure enough, almost as though she was psychic, his cell phone rang. He looked at the number.

"Uh, Brother, would you excuse me a moment?" Matthew said. "It's my mother. She hasn't been feeling well."

"Let her know she will be in my prayers," said the pastor kindly.

"Yes, Brother, thank you," said Matthew, and he moved off to the back of the tent.

"Yeah, Hannah, what is it?" Matthew asked, striving for patience. "I'm here and I'm sober. The setup looks good. How are you? Did you sleep well? I told you—I'm sober!" He hung up.

I definitely have to cut her loose, Matthew thought wearily.

Natalia landed in the airport at Nashville, picked up her rental car, and drove north to Clarksville. She loved Nashville and would have been glad to have time to hang around, visit the Country Music Hall of Fame, maybe see who was playing at the Grand Ole Opry. She didn't have time for fun, however. She had a date with a preacher-man.

Arriving in Clarksville, she was going to stop to ask directions, then she saw the Fox News satellite truck parked near a small church dwarfed by an enormous white tent that had been set up in a nearby field. A large sign advertised: "THE AMAZING FATHER GALLOW . . .

". . . and his All-Star Angel Revue," Natalia added with a giggle, which wasn't what the sign said, of course. It said something about bringing the Power of God to the Benighted.

Natalia had trouble finding a parking place, and she had to walk about a half a mile back to the venue. Though the show didn't start for over an hour, crowds were already starting to assemble. The Fox News truck drew quite a few people, who loitered about, clearly hoping to get on camera. The Missionary Aid Society tent, selling homemade chili, pie, lemonade, and ice cream, was doing a brisk business. After eating two bowls of the best chili she'd ever tasted, Natalia stuffed a hundred-dollar bill into the donation box, for Karma, she thought to herself.

She returned a few phone calls, one from Cain's lawyer,

who said there would be no problem about bail; then, since there was nothing else to do, she headed for the tent to get a seat close to the stage.

She was enjoying the peaceful night, breathing in the perfume of fresh-mown grass, watching the reds and purples of the sunset spread across the sky, and thinking that life wasn't like this in LA or something to that effect, when a piercing shriek near her ear made her jump.

A teenage girl wearing too much eye shadow and a Cain T-shirt leaped at Natalia, grabbed hold of her arm.

"You're his manager!" the girl gasped.

"Who? What?" Natalia said, trying to pull away from the clutching fingers.

"You're Natalia Ashley, Cain's manager!" the girl squealed. "I read about you in *Rolling Stone*!"

Natalia cast a sideways look out of her eye. She was, unfortunately, near the Fox News truck. The reporter, hearing the commotion, was staring at her with interest.

Natalia shook her head. "I'm sorry to disappoint you, miss. You've mistaken me for someone else."

Thank goodness she'd had the brains to dress conservatively! She'd even bought a skirt for the occasion.

The girl let go of Natalia's arm, but she continued to stare at her intently.

"I'm sure you're her," she insisted.

Natalia smiled politely.

"Sorry," she said again, and walked off. The reporter was turning away.

The girl tagged after her. "I *know* you're Natalia Ashley . . ."

"Grace, darling," said a harassed-looking woman, probably the girl's mother, "don't be rude—"

The girl whirled on her. "Shut up, you stupid old bitch! What do you know?"

People were staring. The mother looked as though she was going to cry. Natalia, embarrassed and uncomfortable, hastened thankfully into the tent. She found a seat in the front row at the end of an aisle. She chose this location so she could make a quick and unobtrusive escape if this act turned out to be a flop. Unfortunately, the girl in the Cain T-shirt plunked herself down in a chair right behind Natalia. She could feel the girl's eyes boring into the back of her head. Natalia tried to ignore her by leafing through the hymnal that had been left on her seat.

She wondered why in God's name a little hooligan like Grace was even at a revival meeting. She was more the type to be out stealing cars. Natalia soon found out the answer. Grace said something in loud tones about having been paid to come to this fucking stupid place by her fucking stupid mother and, by God, Mom had better come through with the fucking cash, or there would be hell to pay and so forth.

Jeez, I hope all Cain's fans aren't rotten little monsters like that one, Natalia thought. *You can be a rebellious teen, sweetie, and still not be a jerk.*

Natalia had been a rebellious teen once herself, but she hoped she had at least remembered that other people have feelings. How was it that song from the rock musical about the counterculture *Hair* went?

Natalia hummed the words. "'How can people be so heartless? How can people be so cruel?'"

And that immediately conjured up the image of Cain's rampage—captured live by every major network. Natalia winced. He wasn't setting much of an example, and neither was she. Condoning bad behavior. Worse than that. Publicly condoning bad behavior, making a spectacle of it. Natalia soothed her guilty conscience by telling herself she was making the best of a bad situation. Turning a negative into a positive.

She just couldn't figure out what had come over him lately.

He was never going to do it again, Natalia vowed. No more hotel rooms, at least not for him. Cain would be spending the rest of the tour sleeping and/or boozing on the bus!

And Natalia would make certain that any interaction with the fans was all very tame and respectable. One of her ideas for promoting Cain's tour had been to run radio contests in the next few cities. The fans would answer trivia questions about Cain and the band. The winners would receive backstage passes to the concert and the chance to hang around with Cain and the band after the show. There would be press interviews, of course, and the thought of showcasing fans like obnoxious, foul-mouthed Grace gave Natalia cold chills. She'd have to screen the winners very carefully!

Natalia stole a glance at the poor mother, who was seated next to Grace. Tight-lipped, Mom perched on the edge of the chair. She looked grim and unhappy, but determined. Natalia wondered what had possessed Mom to bring the kid to a revival meeting. Did she hope Grace would find Jesus? Natalia thought that extremely unlikely, but she wished Mom the best.

Grace lit up a cigarette—to the ire of her neighbors— and kicked the back of Natalia's chair with her huge black boot.

"Lying bitch! I still think you're Cain's manager," she said loudly.

Natalia was tempted to pick up her folding chair and smash it over Grace's purple hair. Natalia controlled herself, however, and did her best to ignore the chair-kicking, the smoke-blowing, and the taunting. She was considering moving into the next seat, but that was taken by a buxom blonde with a baby-doll face who plunked herself down in the chair. The blonde was dressed in Frederick's finest, wearing what looked to be half the Avon catalog smeared over her face.

The blonde was jumpy and twitchy and the moment she sat down, she started muttering, holding a conversation with herself, or so it seemed from what Natalia could overhear. Behind her, Grace kicked Natalia's chair again. Natalia was beginning to wish she'd never come and was half-considering leaving when a man walked onto the stage and quietly took a seat. The word went around. The audience buzzed and whispered. This was Matthew Gallow—the exorcist.

Natalia stared, mesmerized. He'd looked good on the thirty-second spot, but that was nothing compared to seeing him in real life. He was . . . Natalia searched for words to describe him. Otherworldly. Ethereal. Dangerous. His pale complexion, the smoldering eyes set beneath dark brows, the black hair swept back from a face that was just saved from being "pretty" by intense eyes, a cleft chin, and square-cut jaw. He sat at his ease, not at all nervous despite the glare of the lights and the cameras and the sleek, loud-voiced reporter. The priest's feet were on the floor, his hands quietly folded in his lap. He was dressed in a full-length black cassock with a white collar and a gold cross suspended on a simple gold chain.

He exuded power. He sat unmoving, not saying a word. He sent his dark-eyed gaze around the tent, and a hush fell over the audience: an expectant, nervous silence. Even Grace seemed to feel its influence. At least she stopped swearing and kicking Natalia's chair.

Natalia pictured this man standing on the stage for Cain's final number, holding up the cross, exhorting him to change his ways, as flames and smoke twined about them.

The fans would freak!

If this guy's act equals his looks, we're in business! Natalia thought.

Another man, the pastor, walked up to the microphone. He started to speak, but he was too close to the microphone, and the resulting feedback squeal nearly deafened the audience.

A technician leaped onto the stage, fiddled with the microphone, gently reprimanded the pastor, then leaped off.

The show was about to begin.

Matthew was seated in a chair behind the lectern on the stage, waiting for Pastor Wiggins to finish his sermon. He looked out over the crowd. The tent was packed. Every seat was taken—including the extra chairs—and people were standing on the fringes. Pastor Wiggins was overjoyed. The Fox News reporter—who was apparently some sort of celebrity himself, because people went up to shake his hand and ask for his autograph—was on a chair in the front row, trying to pretend he was just one of the crowd. His cameraman was filming from the back. The reporter had been arrogant, smarmy. Though he'd claimed to have an open mind, "fair and balanced."

"I'm here with an open mind, Father Gallow," the reporter informed them. He'd won Pastor Wiggins's heart by promising to include at least part of the sermon in the broadcast.

Highly gratified, Pastor Wiggins threw himself into his work. At first the audience had been twitchy, turning around to look at the camera or craning their necks to see the reporter. Pastor Wiggins knew how to handle a crowd, however. He was a "blood and thunder, fire and brimstone" preacher, and soon all eyes were riveted on him. His subject for this evening was the battle between good and evil and how each and every one of the attendees that night was there because they were on the right side of this eternal war. They were all called to be soldiers in God's army, fighting the ultimate battle.

Matthew gave a wry smile. If only it were that clear, that black-and-white. He knew different. For thousands of years people had been fighting wars in the name of God, each side claiming God was on its side. The truth was, God didn't take sides. He just wanted mankind to get along, love each other and help each other through life—not kill each other and use His name to justify the slaughter.

People didn't want to hear that, though. They wanted to know that God loved them and that He hated their enemies.

Matthew brought himself up short. He shook his head, ridding himself of these thoughts. He wasn't here to take God's part. He was here to spit in God's eye.

After the communion service, Pastor Wiggins introduced Matthew, and he stood up amidst thunderous applause. He thanked the pastor, shook the man's hand to even more applause, then took his place in front of the congregation. He very carefully kept from looking at either the camera or the journalist.

Matthew remained deliberately silent. He did not try to speak over the noise, and eventually the audience fell into an uneasy silence. Still Matthew did not talk. He left his place behind the podium and walked off the stage. People were startled, but intrigued. Matthew began to walk around the tent. He walked in silence down the middle aisle of chairs, then walked clear to the back of the tent, still not uttering a word. The camera followed him, and so did the eyes of every person in the congregation. He would pause every now and then and stare directly at one person, as if searching the soul. This never failed to get a reaction. Women would sometimes burst into tears. Men would get nervous and avert their gazes. As he walked, he kept an eye out for Hannah. Finding her, he noted her position. She was at the end of a row toward the front, sitting next to a remarkably good-looking young woman. Now he had the audience in the palm of his hand. They watched, breathless with anticipation.

He walked back to the stage.

The people were silent, waiting.

Wow! thought Natalia. *Can this guy play a crowd!*

He's good. Really good. She was already thinking what salary she might offer him. There was only one problem. What if he was a true believer? What if he wasn't a showman but truly believed he had the power to cast out demons?

Natalia had simply assumed (undoubtedly like the Fox News reporter) that this guy was a charlatan, a fake, a phony. Now she wasn't so certain. Either he was a very good man or a very good bad man. She couldn't decide which. It made a difference. If he was a true believer, the odds were he wouldn't want to go touring with a rock band. And the odds were that she wouldn't want him.

And right now Natalia wanted him—for the band, of course.

Father Gallow's gaze swept over the crowd, paused here and there, lingering on one person or another. Natalia found herself hoping his gaze would linger on her. His eyes came to her, passed over her to rest on the buxom blonde.

"Oh, come now, Father!" muttered Natalia under her breath, half-amused and half-miffed. "She's not your type!"

The blonde quit muttering to herself and gazed back at Father Gallow. Was it Natalia's imagination or had a signal passed between the two of them? Father Gallow's eyes shifted away almost immediately. The blonde once more began twitching and muttering.

Natalia sat forward on the edge of her chair.

And now Matthew spoke.

"As I walked among you just now, I was thinking to myself, why are you here?" Matthew asked. "Are you all here to listen to me talk? No, I don't think you are. I looked in your eyes, some of you, and I noted your faces, and I thought to myself, 'Pastor Wiggins is right.' He told me you were good people—"

"Amen!" someone cried out.

Matthew raised his volume. "He said you have kind hearts and powerful souls—"

This won him several more "Amens."

"He told me that you are here to join me in the war against evil!"

Loud cheers and applause and cries of: "We are, Father! We're with you."

Matthew pretended not to hear. He was working himself into ecstasy. "He said that *you* are the soldiers on the front lines of this war! That none of you will allow evil to reign here! Not in this town, not in this holy place, not in your hearts!"

Wild cheering and applause.

Matthew paused, waited until the crowd hushed. They grew so quiet, he could have heard the fall of a feather.

Matthew's voice grew stern, hard.

"What I want to ask you tonight is—are you ready to get your hands dirty?"

"Yes!" people shouted.

"What?" Matthew shouted back. "I can't hear you? I asked if you were ready to get your hands dirty! Are you ready for the fight? Ready for the battle to begin? Are you ready to help me cast the devil out of the hearts of those who have unwittingly invited him inside?"

"Yes!" the crowd shouted in unison.

"I can see the devil!" Matthew cried out. "He's here tonight! Yes, right here. Maybe sitting next to you. I can see him! He's inside that young woman—"

Matthew was about to point at Hannah, who was about to go into her act. He would point at her. She would stare at him in shock and start to protest, then suddenly she would seem to be dragged to her feet by some invisible power. She would begin to scream and writhe about, battling this unseen force inside her. Matthew would ask some of the men to help him, and between them they would haul Hannah, kicking and screaming and swearing and frothing at the mouth, up onto the stage. Matthew would put her forcibly into a chair and bind her arms and proceed to "exorcise" her.

That's what was supposed to happen.

Before Matthew could proceed, the reporter stood up. He was a commanding presence, and Matthew instantly lost his audience.

"Excuse me for interrupting, Father Gallow," said the reporter. He spoke very respectfully, but Matthew could see the smug glint in the man's eye, and Matthew suddenly knew what was coming, and there wasn't a damn thing he could do to stop it.

"*We* have a woman here we'd like you to help," said the reporter. He turned to a woman seated next to him. "Stand up, Mrs. Swithenbank, and tell Father Gallow how your daughter, Grace, is possessed by demons."

The reporter gave Matthew a cunning grin. "And how you expect him to save her . . ."

Chapter 4

The reporter waved his hand, summoned his crew. "Let's get a microphone on Mrs. Swithenbank!"

Matthew was caught. He flicked a glance at Hannah, who was staring at him, asking him with a horrified look what she was supposed to do. How the hell did he know? He gave a very small shrug. Hannah was darting glances left and right, as though she was certain the cops were about to jump her. Terrified, she hunkered down in her seat. She was sure he was going to be exposed and her along with him.

Matthew ignored her. Hannah would be safe enough. He needed to think about himself. Number One. He remembered bitterly all the flattering phone calls from this reporter about this interview, how the guy wanted to show the nation the power of prayer. And Matthew had agreed to it, all the while thinking what a sucker this reporter was. But it was Matthew who had been suckered. The con man conned. He should have seen this coming. It was all so damn obvious.

Maybe if he'd kept his head out of the bourbon bottle, he would have.

Matthew cast an oblique glance at Hannah.

Who was no longer there.

She'd panicked, run off.

Oh, my God! He *is* a con man, Natalia realized as she watched the buxom blonde hightail it across the pasture. Amazing how fast that gal could run, given those high heels she was wearing.

I was right! Natalia thought. The two of them *had* exchanged looks before the show started. That blonde had been the fake Father's shill or plant or whatever the con artists called it. He would pretend not to know her, summon her up onstage. She would pretend to be possessed, pretend to be "saved." And the people would swallow it whole and fill the collection plates, and his pockets, with dollars.

But now his shill was gone, and Father Gallow was standing in front of millions of viewers with a real, live, honest-to-God problem on his hands.

Because, behind Natalia, Grace's mother was rising to her feet.

Matthew's gaze flicked over Hannah's empty chair. *Fine,* he thought bitterly, *one less problem to worry about.*

He blotted out everything else and turned his full attention to the woman. What happened to him now depended on her. He was pretty good at reading people. Not surprising. He'd been living among mortals for almost two thousand years now.

Mrs. Swithenbank was in her midforties, well dressed, wearing a tailored suit and lots of jewelry: gold earrings, a gold necklace, gold bracelet, and several diamond rings. Matthew wondered if she was a plant for the reporter, like

Hannah was for him, and he regarded her closely. Her face was pale and strained. Her eyes were red-rimmed. She twisted the rings on her fingers. She looked desperate and afraid.

Her fear is genuine, Matthew realized. *She's in trouble. Real trouble.*

"It's my daughter, Grace, Father Gallow," said Mrs. Swithenbank, speaking into the microphone as the camera fixed its glassy eye on her. "I think . . ." She gulped, then brought the words out in a rush, "I think she's possessed. I need you to help her, Father! I don't know where else to turn!"

"She's turned to you, Father Gallow," said the reporter. "But you're not a real priest at all, are you, Father? You're a phony, a fraud. You and your confederate—that young woman who just ran out of here so fast—dupe people with your act, then you take their money! Isn't that true, Father? Admit it. Don't lead this poor woman on!"

The reporter thrust the microphone into Matthew's face.

The woman clasped her hands. Her knuckles were white. She fixed Matthew with a pleading gaze, and he saw that *she* believed in him, even if the reporter didn't. She had forgotten all about reporters and microphones and cameras. She was begging for his help.

Matthew was angry. This reporter was here to expose him for a fraud. Fine, Matthew could take care of himself. But to do that, the reporter was making use of this unfortunate mother. He was exposing her to public humiliation and ridicule and crushing disappointment when she realized the truth—that Father Gallow was a fake, a sham.

Matthew gave the reporter a look that said plainly "this is war, brother," then turned his attention to the woman and her problem.

"Where is your daughter, Sister Swithenbank?"

"I'm here, jerk-off," called out a shrill voice.

A girl came swaggering in from one side of the tent. She was about fifteen, Matthew guessed. She was dressed all in black, with black baggy trousers and a T-shirt that had some word emblazoned on it (Matthew couldn't make it out in the glare of the lights). The letters were formed of red flames leaping up from the hemline. Her face was dead white, with bright red lips and a shaved head except for a purple Mohawk. Her eyes were smeared with black eye shadow and outlined in black eyeliner.

Men and women gasped in horror as she swaggered into the lights. Pastor Wiggins raised his hands and cried out for Jesus to save them. The girl hissed at Pastor Wiggins, and he recoiled as though she'd been an adder. A woman in the front row called out for God to have mercy, and the girl turned and spit on her. The woman screamed, as her companions clustered around her with tissues. The girl laughed out loud. She was enjoying this.

The brat doesn't need an exorcist, Matthew thought grimly. *What she needs is a good spanking.*

The woman was talking. "Please, Father Gallow, you have to save her. Grace was always a sweet girl. She was a good student, respectful and kind. Now look at her! She's possessed by the devil! I just know it! She's never acted badly until now. Just look at her! Tell me you'll save her."

"Are you really going to go through with this charade, Father Gallow?" the reporter demanded.

Matthew shoved the microphone out of his face. He would have liked to have shoved it down the man's throat, but that wouldn't help matters. He had to think how to salvage the situation. Of course, the girl wasn't possessed. Her only problem was that she was a rebellious teenager, here to embarrass Mommy, and Matthew couldn't very well call on Heaven to drive that out of her.

While her mother was pleading, and Matthew was thinking, dear little Grace was flipping off the pastor and shouting obscenities at the congregation. The girl was close enough to Matthew that he could now read the word on the girl's shirt: "CAIN." The name sounded vaguely familiar. Some rock star . . .

Matthew had an idea. If there was ever a time that called for the use of the heavenly powers that had been mistakenly left to him, this was it. He might be able to throw a good scare into this bratty kid—scare her straight, as the saying went—and wipe that smug, know-it-all grin off that reporter's face.

Step right up, folks, Matthew said, inwardly grinning, *it's showtime!*

He summoned the girl onto the stage. She came willingly, only too happy to show off how terribly evil she was.

"Sit down in the chair, young lady," he said, speaking gently.

Smirking for the cameras, Grace sauntered over to the chair. She plunked herself down, crossed her legs and her arms, and leered up at him.

"You're not afraid of me, are you, Grace?" Matthew asked, still keeping his voice gentle.

"Afraid of you? Hah!" The girl spit at him.

The audience gasped. Matthew calmly wiped his face and went on.

"I can help you." He looked out at the congregation. "I know I can help this child. Are all of you ready to pick up your weapons?"

Shouts of "We are, Father!" and "Amen!" Good. The audience was with him again. The reporter was talking, but Matthew ignored him. The mother was staring at him with tears in her eyes, her hands pressed over her mouth.

"Grace needs our help," Matthew shouted. "She needs all

of us to help cast the demon out of her. Now I'm going to place my hand on this sweet child's head, and I want all of you to pray. Pray with me."

Matthew stood behind the girl. He put his right hand on her head and closed his eyes. He started to raise his voice in an exhortation to God.

"Father—" he began, but his prayer was cut off.

Pain shot through his arm. It felt like his hand was on fire. Matthew's eyes flared open. He stared in shock so great that for a moment the pain didn't register.

Flames, blue and orange, swirled around his hand as it rested on the girl's head. The flames began to spread, but not to Grace. She remained untouched. Matthew was on fire, but Grace's hair wasn't even smoldering. The flames were spreading, burning the sleeve of his cassock. He could smell burned flesh. He could see his hand withering in the fire, and he moaned in agony. The pain was so bad, he was afraid for a moment he was going to pass out.

He stayed on his feet, however, through sheer force of will, and also out of a grim determination to find out *what the hell was going on*? He'd meant to scare the girl, but right now he was the one who was scared.

He could hear people screaming and gasping. Some in the front row nearest the flames were scrambling out of their seats. Someone else was yelling about calling 911. The reporter was talking excitedly. Grace's mother was screaming. She jumped up onto the stage and ran toward Grace, trying to save her daughter from the flames.

"No!" Matthew gasped, teeth gritted against the pain. "Don't come close! Pastor, keep her away!"

"Look, dear lady," Pastor Wiggins cried, pointing a shaking finger. "The fire is not harming her!"

"Stay away from me, bitch!" Grace snarled, and lashed out her mother, clawing at her face.

The mother collapsed, sobbing, and Pastor Wiggins half led, half carried her to a chair.

A hand took hold of Matthew's hand and tried to wrench it off the girl's head. The hand was not Grace's hand. She was raving and clawing at the air. The hand was skeletal, misshapen—the hand of a creature of darkness, formed of evil, twisted and hideous. Fiery eyes glared at him in hatred.

A demon! Matthew realized. *Good God! The girl really is possessed!*

His first impulse was to turn and run, to get the hell out of this place. He didn't know what was going on. Maybe this was God's idea of a joke, a little payback. *I'll teach you to perform phony exorcisms, Matthew Gallow.*

Reporters and mothers and pastors be damned. Matthew had not signed on to wrestle real-live demons. He was about to wrench his hand free, leap off the stage, and make a run for it when he heard a voice, a young girl's voice. "Help me, Father! Please, help me! It's dark and horrible, and I'm afraid!"

Matthew looked at the girl helplessly.

This isn't my responsibility! Heaven is supposed to stop demons, not me. Not an angel Heaven had cast aside like so much garbage. Where is this girl's guardian angel?

The creature's dark wings enveloped Grace. Its clawed hands reached deep into her soul. The girl was alone, utterly alone. Matthew could feel it.

Alone except for Matthew Gallow, fallen angel, con man.

Matthew was angry clear through—angry at Heaven, angry at the reporter, angry at himself for having stumbled into this situation. He was angry and, deep inside, he was afraid. He hadn't felt fear like this since they'd tied him to that stake. He looked grimly at the demon.

"Let go of her," Matthew commanded, trying to keep the quiver out of his voice.

He must not have succeeded, for the demon only laughed and gibbered at him and pulled on Matthew's hand, trying to drag him down to Hell. Matthew felt himself starting to slip. A gaping pit opened up before his feet.

"Father! Please, save me!" the girl cried.

He had to save her. He had to save himself. The only way he knew how was to carry on with the exorcism rites, the rites that had all been a farce, a joke—up to now.

"Wine!" Matthew shouted. "Pour the communion wine on the flames!"

Despite the pain, he kept his hand where it was, on top of Grace's head. At the demon's urging, she was clawing at Matthew, spitting and hissing and slashing his flesh with her long nails, trying to force him to let loose. The fire burned him. Grace tore his flesh. The demon wrenched at him, trying to drag him under.

Still, Matthew kept hold. It was on the tip of his tongue to pray to God, ask for His help.

"I'll be damned first!" Matthew swore, and the thought came to him that he might very well be.

Pastor Wiggins had grabbed up the goblet of wine they had used for communion. His hand shaking, he dumped the wine over Grace's head.

The demon's hand shriveled when the wine touched it. The demon shrieked and snatched its hand away. The flames died. The wine dribbled down Grace's purple-streaked hair.

The demon let go of Matthew, but wasn't about to lose its prey. The demon folded its wings tight around Grace and began to prod her with its claws. She screamed and writhed in pain.

"Let her go!" her mother screamed. "Stop it! You're killing her!"

Even Pastor Wiggins looked doubtful.

"It's the demon!" Matthew gasped. He drew back his burned and bleeding hand. "Keep praying. We must keep praying for Grace's soul. And for mine," he muttered.

He made the sign of the cross and placed the two ends of the purple stole he wore onto the girl's shoulders.

"Grace!" he called to her. "I'm here. God is here. Be strong."

"Father, please!" she whimpered, her voice filled with panic.

The demon hovered near the girl. Its wings stirred. It knew what was coming and was gathering strength.

"Pray with me, Pastor," Matthew said, keeping his eyes fixed on the demon. "Pray with me, Mrs. Swithenbank. Pray with me, everyone! Lord hear us. Please give us the power to defeat this creature that has taken hold of Grace."

Matthew drew in a deep breath and began the rite. "'Saint Michael the Archangel, defend us in battle; be our defense against the wickedness and snares of the devil. May God rebuke him, we humbly pray. And do thou, O prince of the heavenly host, by the power of God thrust into hell Satan and all evil spirits who prowl about the world seeking the ruin of souls. Amen.'"

"Pastor, bring me my things, please." Matthew pointed to his case.

Pastor Wiggins hastily brought the closed case to Matthew. He placed his injured right hand on Grace's head. The demon tried to seize him, but Matthew's hand was still wet with the wine, and the demon couldn't take hold of him. With his left hand, Matthew opened the case. He drew out a crucifix—a very old crucifix, given to him long ago by a dear friend. He hung the crucifix around his neck. Then he drew out a small velvet sack. From the sack he took a small, very old, ornate glass box. Inside the box was a bone—a finger bone of St. Francis, or at least that's what the Jesuit had told him when he'd given it to Matthew a few hundred years earlier.

Matthew had not really believed it was the bone of a saint. He'd kept it as a curiosity, found that it came in handy for his work. He prayed now as he hadn't prayed in centuries that this bone was the real thing.

In a few seconds, he had his answer.

The demon snarled in fury. A generator exploded with a blinding flash. The lights went out, plunging the tent into darkness. Women screamed. Men called out in alarm. Children started to cry. The crowd was on the verge of panic. Matthew couldn't lose them. He needed them, needed their help.

"Don't be afraid. This is the devil's work!" Matthew shouted. "He wants you to run and hide. He wants us to leave him and let him keep Grace. But we're not going to leave, are we?"

Matthew placed the relic on the floor near Grace's feet. He kept his hand on Grace's head. "Pray with me!" Matthew began to chant in Latin. *"'Ab omni hoste visibili et invisibili et ubíque in hoc sáeculo liberetur.'"* He chanted the phrase three times, one each for the Father, the Son, and the Holy Spirit. "'From every enemy both visible and invisible and everywhere in this lifetime be freed.'"

Light, radiant and holy, spread over Matthew. Pastor Wiggins had lit the altar candles. Cringing, the demon snarled and averted its eyes. The creature wasn't defeated yet, however. It still kept fast hold of Grace.

Matthew reached out and took hold of the demon's hand.

"Let her go!" he said in low voice. "Let her go!"

The demon squealed in pain and gnashed its teeth and snatched back its hand. Its wings lifted. The demon vanished. Matthew trembled in relief, thinking the battle was over.

Suddenly Grace began to shake, then she opened her mouth wide. Lurid red light shot out from inside her, poured out of her mouth, beamed out of her eyes. The demon hadn't left. He had taken shelter inside Grace! The girl began to speak, but it wasn't her voice. It was the demon's voice, a hideous growl.

"This vessel is weak. And you, imposter priest, are even weaker. If you want this battle, I will bring it to you."

Matthew's Latin was a little weak, but he understood. He was exhausted; the pain of his burns was excruciating. He had to keep fighting, however. This was personal now—between him and Satan.

Matthew grabbed hold of Grace with both hands. "She is a child of God," he told the demon. "You can't have her!"

Grace went into convulsions. She pitched sideways off the chair, began rolling around on the stage. People leaped to their feet standing, trying to see. The reporter was shouting something about a backup generator. Grace's mother was having hysterics. Pastor Wiggins, God bless him, was praying at the top of his lungs. Matthew knelt, took hold of Grace and held her in his arms, held her fast.

Grace vomited black bile. Matthew recited the prayer to St. Michael over and over again. The girl retched again. A black shadowy form flew out from Grace's mouth. A hot, sulfurous wind blew through the tent, blowing out the candles. The shadow was deeper, darker than night. It spread over the heads of the congregation. Grace coughed and retched again. Then she opened her eyes and looked up at him.

Tears began to stream down her face, smearing the black eyeliner. "Mama," she cried, choking. "Mama, where are you?"

The shadow surrounded her, loath to give up.

"I'm here, Grace!" her mother cried. Crawling across the stage, she clasped her daughter in her arms.

The shadow swirled around them both, swirled angrily around Matthew, as he slumped on the stage.

And then the demon was gone.

Grace and her mother clung to each other, sobbing.

Matthew staggered to his feet. The crowd was silent, hushed, awed.

Matthew tried to take a step. He tried to speak, but the stage was tilting beneath his feet. The tent started to spin around and around, then the night seemed to crash down on top of him.

He collapsed, and the darkness closed over him.

The moment Father Gallow hit the stage, pandemonium broke out. Some people leaped to their feet, cheering and shouting and calling on the glory of God. Others slid out of their chairs to the ground, sobbing and praying. Pastor Wiggins was bending over Father Gallow, yelling for help. A small crowd gathered around Grace and her mother, offering their prayers and comfort.

Natalia sat in her seat, too stunned to move.

She knew a lot about special effects and their workings, and she'd never seen or heard of anything like that. It had all been so realistic! The demonic light, the black bile, the exploding generator. His hands on fire, the look of pain on his face. And she'd actually smelled his skin burning!

I have to have him! Natalia determined. *No matter how much money he wants, he can have it.*

Several men had picked up Father Gallow and were gently and reverently carrying him off the stage and out of the tent.

Natalia jumped up from her chair to join the large group of people that had gathered around Grace and her mother. Most were offering prayers and comfort, some were unabashedly gawking. The Fox reporter arrived, shouldering his way through the crowd, shoving his microphone at both mother and daughter, shouting questions. Natalia loitered on the outskirts, watching, waiting to see what they would say. She expected them to be eager to give the interview— millions were watching, after all. If the camera could just get another close-up shot of the Cain T-shirt Grace was wearing . . .

To Natalia's astonishment, both mother and daughter shunned the reporter. Averting their faces, they raised their hands, seemingly trying to escape the glare of the lights. Seeing this, several men in the crowd converged on the reporter and told him sternly to get out. The reporter became belligerent. Hearing the commotion, Pastor Wiggins left Father Gallow and, fearing trouble, gathered up his ushers and hurried over to calm the situation. He put his arm protectively around both mother and daughter and, as the ushers cleared a path, led them out of the tent.

Natalia found herself standing near the exit. Mother and daughter passed right by her. Grace glanced up, caught sight of Natalia.

"Oh, ma'am," said Grace tearfully, "I'm so sorry I was rude to you. Please forgive me!"

"Yes, of course," said Natalia, looking after them in astonishment.

Grace seemed genuinely contrite. She also seemed like a different girl.

Either she was a remarkably talented actress or . . .

"Oh, don't be ridiculous!" Natalia told herself with a laugh.

The refreshment tent was doing a brisk business, everyone feeling in need of something strong to recover from the shock. Since the strongest thing they had on the menu was lemonade, Natalia bought a large glass and sat down to drink it and ponder how and when it would be best to approach Father Gallow and persuade him to join a rock band.

Chapter 5

$\mathcal{W}$illiam was comfortably seated in front of the television in his living room, munching on popcorn and getting ready to call in a vote for his favorite singer. He was just about to dial when the phone rang. William cast an agonized look at the phone number flashing across the screen, at the young woman who was belting out one of his favorite songs. The phone continued to ring. Sighing, William answered.

"Hello? Oh, Derek! You got my message! How good to hear from you, my boy! How is Rachel? Wonderful, wonderful. You're back from your vacation? No, no I'm not in Chicago anymore. I've been promoted. I'm an Archangel now. Thank you. I couldn't have done it without you. But the promotion meant I had to relocate. Corporate headquarters. Cincinnati. I have no idea why. Yes, my boy, if I'm ever in Chicago, I'll be sure to look you up. My love to Rachel. I'm glad you two are doing well."

Smiling broadly, pleased for his two friends, William hung up the phone and started again to dial. The phone rang.

William groaned.

"Hello, yes!" He sat up straight and quickly hit the mute button. "Oh, uh, yes, sir. Am I watching television? Well, as a matter of fact, I was watching C-Span. Fox News? Uh, no. I never watch that particular network. Conservative bias. Yes, sir." William sighed. "I'll change channels right away. Right, sir. I'll call you back."

William hung up and hurried to his chair. His show had ended, and he had no idea who'd been eliminated.

"I really must get TIVO," he muttered as he switched channels.

The Fox News reporter was extremely excited, shouting into the microphone. "Never seen anything like it! Flames shooting out of a girl's head! Exploding generators! Shadowy wings! Vomiting bile. Is this Father Gallow for real? Or is it all smoke and mirrors? We do the reporting. You be the judge. Let's rerun that tape."

William watched.

"Oh, dear," he murmured, shaking his head. "Oh, dear, oh dear, oh dear . . ."

Sighing, he walked over to the phone and dialed a number. "There's no doubt, sir," he said. "It's him. Yes, sir. I'm leaving this instant."

Bright light, wondrous light poured down Matthew. He was back in Heaven and he was overwhelmed with joy. He opened his eyes, eager to look once more upon the beautiful, radiant countenance of God . . .

He opened his eyes and looked upon Pastor Wiggins.

Matthew shut his eyes. The light shining down on him was from a ceiling light. He shoved away the feeling of bitter disappointment, replacing it, as he always did, with anger—righteous anger. He tried to sit up.

"You should rest, Father," Pastor Wiggins said solicitously, laying a restraining hand on Matthew's shoulder. "How are you feeling?"

Like hell, Matthew wanted to say bitterly, but the good pastor would be shocked at his language.

"Would you like some water?" the pastor asked.

What Matthew really wanted was bourbon, but that would also shock the good pastor. He gave an inward sigh. The show must go on.

He opened his eyes and managed a wan smile. He drank a sip of water and leaned back against the pillows. He was lying on a couch in a room he recognized as the pastor's office. Someone had draped a blanket over him, and his hands were neatly bandaged. Matthew stared down at his hands. Memory returned, and he shuddered.

"You must be in terrible pain," said Pastor Wiggins. His voice sounded shaky. "One of my aides tended to you. Fourth-year medical student. The paramedics are on the way—"

"No paramedics," said Matthew, sitting up.

Pastor Wiggins looked concerned. "Those burns are serious—"

Matthew shook his head. "God will heal me," he said firmly.

That much was true, though his healing wasn't due to God's blessing so much as His curse. Beneath the bandages, Matthew's flesh had already started to regenerate. He couldn't have paramedics seeing that!

"I admire your faith, Father," said Pastor Wiggins, "but Our Lord gave us doctors for a reason—"

There was a knock on the door.

"I won't have them," said Matthew, and he swung his feet off the couch. "And I won't talk to that reporter either. I suppose he's been around asking for an interview?"

"Yes, he was here. I didn't let him inside. I have the door

locked and two of the ushers standing guard." Pastor Wiggins walked over to the door. Opening it a crack, he said, "Father Gallow isn't seeing anyone."

The usher said something and handed something inside. Pastor Wiggins took it, shut the door, and locked it.

Matthew's head throbbed. There was a buzzing in his ears, and that glaring light overhead wasn't helping. He lowered his head into his bandaged hands. He felt awful, as if that demon had won, claimed his body, turned it inside out, and left his insides exposed to the hell fires to shrivel up and rot away. That might have been his fate. He'd come close. Too damn close.

What happened out there? Matthew wondered, shuddering. He knew demons existed, just as he knew angels existed—he was formerly one of them. An angel, not a demon. But demons weren't supposed to be running around loose, stealing the souls of teenage girls. Demons were confined to Hell, kept there by God's holy warriors, who fought the eternal battle against them in Purgatory.

"Father Gallow," said Pastor Wiggins, his voice seeming to come from a great distance. "I've been informed that one of your own brethren is here to see you. A Father William."

Matthew kept his head in his hands, his eyes closed against the light. "I'm really not up to visitors, Pastor. If I could just be alone a little while. I would like to rest and pray. Extend my apologies . . ."

"Of course," said the pastor. "Certainly. I'll leave you—"

"Hello? Hello?" came a cheerful voice. "Pastor Wiggins? Father Gallow?"

A middle-aged priest with a cheerful, benign face pushed open the door and proceeded to walk inside. "I knocked. I guess you didn't hear me."

Pastor Wiggins stared at him in astonishment.

"But that door was locked!" he exclaimed. "I locked it myself!"

"Was it now?" The priest regarded the door handle in bemusement. "I think you must be mistaken. I turned the knob, and the door opened right up. I'm Father William," he added, smiling and extending his hand. "Sorry if I'm intruding—"

"Well, you are a bit, Father. It's just that Father Gallow isn't feeling well," the pastor explained. He shook hands, then took hold of the priest's shoulder and tried to lead him off. "I was just leaving myself—"

Father William neatly slipped out from under the pastor's grasp and walked over to stand in front of Matthew.

Matthew knew he was there, but he kept his head lowered, pretending he didn't.

"We should really discuss what happened tonight, Brother," said Father William in gentle tones.

Matthew was starting to lose patience. He lifted his head.

"Look, Father," he said testily, "I don't feel up to talking right—"

His words dried up. He stared at Father William, clad in his somber clerical garb, and Matthew's throat closed. His mouth went dry.

The beautiful, radiant light shone on him again, beaming from the beatific face, white robes, and feathery white wings of an archangel. The image lasted for the splitting of a split second, and then Father William—middle-aged, benign face and all—was back.

Matthew could only stare.

"Pastor Wiggins," said Father William, turning to him, "that reporter is trying to force his way into the building—"

Shouts could be heard, as well as what sounded like men scuffling. Pastor Wiggins hurried out of the room.

William walked over, locked the door.

Outside, Matthew could hear Pastor Wiggins's blood-and-thunder voice. "I will not tolerate such violence in a House of the Lord, sir!"

Matthew finally recovered his wits. "What the hell are you doing here?" he demanded. Fists clenched, he reared up off the couch, confronting the archangel. "No one asked you to come."

"Ah," said William, and he looked sad. "Are you sure about that, Matthew?"

"Damn sure," said Matthew surlily.

"It's a been a long time since—" William paused.

Matthew snorted. "Since they tossed me out of Heaven! Banished me to Earth to endure this wretched existence, day after day, year after year, century after century. Banished me here, then forgot about me!"

"We didn't forget about you, Matthew," William said. "You know we never forget one of ours." He waved his hand heavenward. "There is that quote from the Bible about numbering the hairs of your head and falling sparrows and all that. We remember you very well."

Matthew snorted and sat back down. The sudden movement had made him dizzy. His head felt like it was going to split apart.

"Let me see if I have all the facts," said William ruminatively. "You were born in A.D. 36 in Rome, son of a wealthy wine merchant. You inherited the business at his death, and you were quite good at it. You married a Christian woman and you converted to her religion. The Roman citizenry pretty much left you and your fellow Christians alone until A.D. 64." William sighed and shook his head. "The year of that terrible fire.

"The fire started in some shops near the Circus Maximus. It spread from there, flames raging through the city of two million people. The fire burned for six days, was finally brought under control, only to break out again. When it was over, ten of Rome's fourteen districts were in ruins. We have no idea how many hundreds died."

Matthew could see the flames shooting high into the sky. He could see the smoke billowing over the city, smell it, taste it. He wondered why he was letting this old fool ramble on, why he didn't tell him to shut up. Instead, Matthew listened. He knew what was coming, yet he listened anyway. Maybe it was like poking at an aching tooth. There was something oddly pleasurable about the pain.

"Fires were nothing unusual in Rome in those days, where every single house had a cooking fire, but this one was suspicious. The Emperor Nero had long wanted to rebuild Rome to suit his own design, and now he had a reason to do it. Too many people were openly blaming him, however. A rumor started that he played his fiddle while Rome burned, though that could never be proven. He needed a scapegoat and he found it—this new religious sect that had been causing a certain amount of trouble in the city.

"As chance would have it, many Christians such as you had businesses and dwellings on the side of the river across from where the fire started. Your property and your lives were spared. Nero sent in his legions and began to round up Christians."

William's voice grew gentle. "Christians were persecuted, tortured, put to death in the most cruel manner." He paused, then said quietly, "I am told that Nero actually had people tied to stakes in the gardens of his palace. Then they were doused in oil and set ablaze, their living bodies used as torches to light his ungodly revels. Is that true?"

"Stop it," cried Matthew savagely. "Just stop it!"

"When the soldiers came, you gave yourself up to them. You did this so that your wife and your children had time to escape. The soldiers brutalized you, tortured you, trying to force you to tell them where your family fled, but you never said a word. In the end, you died in the flames, in terrible agony. You died a martyr's death."

William sighed again, sighed more deeply. "You see, *we* don't forget, Matthew. We keep hoping *you'll* remember."

"Remember what?" Matthew blinked away his tears and jumped up off the coach again. "Remember the rotten way God treated me?"

William spread his hands. "You thought you were wiser, better, smarter than God, Matthew. You were argumentative, rebellious. Frankly, you were a pain in the butt. Mind you, son," the archangel admitted, "I've done a bit of rebelling in my time. The good Lord knows we're not all saints. But you took it too far."

William regarded Matthew sadly, gravely. "You sought to undermine God's authority, turn others against Him. You were fortunate God in His wisdom and mercy saw into your heart. He saw that this was the sin of pride, of arrogance. He knew you had no evil intent. Otherwise, it would have been the same with you as it was for Lucifer and his bunch. As it was, God gave you a chance to find redemption—"

"Speaking of Lucifer," Matthew said bitingly, deciding it was time to change the subject, "looks like you boys really screwed up! How did that demon get hold of that poor girl? Where was her guardian angel? Decide to take the night off? Go bar-hopping?"

William winced.

"I guess you . . . um . . . didn't get the e-mail," he said.

"E-mail?" Matthew stared at him. "What e-mail?"

William thrust his hands in his pockets and began to wander around the room. He finally sat down in the office chair behind Pastor Wiggins's desk. Here he rummaged about the objects on the pastor's desk until an electric pencil sharpener caught his eye. William picked up a pencil, stuck it in, and watched as the machine whirred and crackled. Pleased, he took hold of another pencil, started to stick it in.

Matthew's hand slammed down over his.

"Tell me what's going on! All these years I've been performing exorcisms and never once encountered a real, live, honest-to-God, fire-and-brimstone-breathing demon! What the hell happened?"

"Ah, yes," said William, looking up. "Your exorcisms. We've been meaning to have a talk with you. Not quite kosher, you see." He looked quite severe. "Do you really need to earn a living conning people out of their money by pretending to rid nubile blonde women of demons?"

"I thought you angels would be pleased," said Matthew caustically. "After all, I'm spreading God's word."

"For your own profit," William replied sternly.

"What else do you suggest I do to earn a living?"

"I don't know," William replied earnestly, "but it seems to me after two thousand years—" He paused, embarrassed.

"After two thousand years of existence—I won't say life—I would have learned a trade?" Matthew gave a bitter laugh. "Two thousand years, give or take a few. God is real creative, isn't He? I'm cursed by something that every other person on Earth would give anything to possess. Most would consider my curse a blessing. I get to live forever. Good old Matthew Gallow. Been alive for two thousand years. And looks like he'll live two thousand more."

He slammed his hands on the desk. "Unless some fucking demon kills me like almost happened tonight! Tell me, old man. Tell me what's going on!"

"Stop swearing. And keep your voice down," William said mildly. He stuck another pencil into the machine, listened to it whir. He seemed lost in thought, kept the pencil in there so long that when he finally pulled it out, there wasn't much left.

"To be perfectly honest, Matthew," he said finally, "we didn't tell you because we didn't think you'd care."

The angel looked up at Matthew. "Don't mistake me, son. We're very glad you *do* care. You saved that child's soul tonight. We are proud of you."

Matthew snorted and turned away.

"As much as you'd like to deny it, there is good in you, Matthew Gallow," William continued. "Unfortunately, you're putting yourself and all of us in danger."

"Yeah, right," said Matthew. "Just another goddam ploy to get me down on my knees, begging forgiveness."

"No ploy, I'm afraid. I almost wish it were. I'll do my best to explain. As you know, Satan has long sought to gain direct access to mankind. He hopes by perverting men to his evil cause, he will at last be able to conquer Heaven, depose God. Our warriors in Purgatory have fought valiantly for years to keep the fiends confined to Hell. Sadly, however, some of them fell victim to Satan's whisperings. They permitted some of Hell's most powerful archdemons to cross over, materialize on Earth. They are now working to throw the world into chaos. I just foiled an attempt, with the help of an angel warrior and a very brave young woman, to stop the demons from disrupting the world financial markets."

William mopped his forehead with his sleeve. "It was touch and go there for a while, let me tell you. Where was I? Oh, yes. You know that every human has a guardian angel—generally either a friend or relative who has passed on and cares enough about the person to volunteer for the duty. Unfortunately, the archdemons have found a way to slay the guardians."

"Impossible," Matthew said shortly.

William was regarding him shrewdly. "You just said you feared the demon was going to kill you. You're an angel. You're immortal. Yet you were afraid you were going to die."

Matthew had nothing to say to do that. He didn't believe what William was telling him, but he couldn't very well deny it either.

"Heaven is working desperately to try to foil Satan, stop his demons, save humanity," William went on. "We have agents in place all around the world. Our entire operation is carefully planned. We can't have a loose cannon rolling about the deck. You'll end up bashing a hole in the side of the ship, and we'll go down with all hands."

"Enough with the nautical metaphors," Matthew sneered.

"I was always a fan of Horatio Hornblower," William said, smiling. His smile faded. He began tapping on the desk with what was left of the pencil. "You have to stop these exorcisms, Matthew. You really must. You're venturing into deep, dark water, and you're going to end up over your head. You could throw our entire operation into jeopardy. It is not exaggerating to say you could place all mankind in very grave danger."

"And just how I am supposed to make a living?" Matthew demanded.

"You are talented, Matthew. Some might say a bit too talented," William added dryly. "You could do anything you want."

The archangel was right, of course. Matthew could do

anything he wanted. Truth was, in his long life, he'd done most of it already. He liked performing the exorcisms. He liked the adulation of the crowd. He liked the excitement, the thrill, the mischief. He liked being a little bit bad. But there was something more to it than that, something he didn't often admit. He liked talking to people about God. Matthew justified this to himself by claiming he was doing it just to irritate God, poke at Him with a sharp stick. But deep down Matthew knew better. He liked to think he was making a difference in people's lives—even if he did profit by it.

"If you don't care about the fate of mankind," said William gravely, "you might consider your own fate."

Matthew couldn't help but shiver. He didn't believe all this crap about demons taking over the world and killing angels. Well, let's rephrase that. He guessed he had to believe it. William wasn't lying—archangels don't lie. But Heaven might well be using this emergency to try to herd their lost sheep back to the fold.

Matthew slumped down on the couch, put his aching head in his hands, and closed his eyes.

"Just get out," he muttered.

He felt a hand on his shoulder, strong and warm. "You're like Frankenstein's monster," said William.

Matthew raised his head. "Frankenstein's monster? What the hell is that supposed to mean?"

"I suppose Lazarus *would* be a more suitable example," said William ruefully. "But I'm so extremely fond of that movie."

"I have no idea what you're talking about," Matthew said wearily.

"You're alive, Matthew," said William. "You were dead inside, and now you've been jolted back to life. And I think that like Lazarus and the poor monster, you're going to have a very hard time dealing with that fact," he added gently. "If you need help, you know where to turn."

He fumbled around in a pocket of his trousers, drew something out, and placed it in Matthew's hand.

It was a white feather.

"Is this supposed to be funny?" Matthew demanded.

William glanced down. "Oops, no. Sorry. My mistake. I mistakenly put my pants into the dryer with my down comforter. This is what I meant to give you."

He handed Matthew a card. There was nothing on it but a phone number.

"Call anytime, day or night," said William, then added wistfully, "Though if you could work around 'Passions . . .'"

Matthew tore up the card, tossed the pieces on the floor.

William watched, smiled. "You can't get rid of me that easily, I'm afraid," he said cheerfully.

Matthew snorted. William walked over to the door, passed his hand over the door handle. There was a loud click. The door unlocked and swung open.

Grace's mother flew in, sending William stumbling back against the wall. Startled, Matthew rose to his feet. The mother ran over to him, flung her arms around his neck, and hung on to him.

"Thank you, Father! Thank you! I have my baby back again!"

Grace was standing behind her. The girl was pale and shaken, but she was smiling.

"Thank God, not me," said Matthew. "I was but the humble vessel." He stole a sly glance at William.

"I do," said Mrs. Swithenbank. "I will."

She let loose of Matthew. Wiping her eyes and brushing back her hair, she walked over to the desk and began to rummage around in her purse. Her daughter kept close to her, and every so often they would each stop to smile at the other. Mrs. Swithenbank drew out her checkbook. Picking up a pen from the desk, she scribbled on the check, then tore it out of the checkbook and handed it to Matthew.

"Here," she said. "This is for you."

"Really, ma'am, I can't accept that," Matthew protested. The check was for two thousand dollars.

"To help in your ministry," the woman said fervently, and she pressed it on him. "Who do I make it out to?"

"Just leave it blank," said Matthew, and he took the check.

The woman and her daughter left the room hand in hand.

"You know what I think, William?" Matthew said. "I think this time Heaven has screwed up royally. God should have listened to me."

"God is always listening, Matthew," said William.

Matthew snorted. Folding up the check, he drew out his wallet, opened it up.

There was the card with the phone number.

Matthew looked up, about to make a scathing remark, but he saw it would be wasted. William was gone.

Matthew stood a moment, thinking things over. He thrust the wallet back in his pocket, put the blank check in an envelope, and addressed it to Pastor Wiggins. He tossed it down on the pastor's desk.

"Lazarus, is it?" Matthew muttered. "I'll show them."

"Pastor Wiggins," he called out. "I'm feeling much better now. I'll be glad to talk to that reporter."

Chapter 6

*A*fter his interview with the reporter, a weary Matthew refused Pastor Wiggins's kind invitation to spend the night at his house, saying that he really needed to be alone to commune with God, though what Matthew really needed after this disastrous night was a chance to commune with a bourbon bottle. The pastor sent him off with kind words and a blessing. Feeling he had earned it, Matthew splurged and picked up a bottle of his favorite, Knob Creek, on his way back to the motel. He carried it into the motel room and thankfully shut the door behind him, figuring he was shutting it on what had happened that night.

He got ice, then poured himself a drink and called Hannah's cell phone. It went straight to voice mail. He tried the motel, only to discover she'd checked out. He left a message on her voice mail, knowing she'd never call him back. She had been scared out of her wits. He couldn't very well blame her.

As soon as hung up, his cell phone rang. He looked at the number, didn't recognize it. The thought came to him that it was Archangel William. Probably thought of a few more sermons. Matthew shut off his cell phone. He'd no sooner done that when the phone in his room started to ring. He yanked out the plug.

And then reaction hit.

He broke out in a sweat and started to shake uncontrollably. The shakes were so bad that when he went to the sink to pour himself another drink, he missed the glass and ended up sloshing half the expensive bourbon over the counter. When someone outside slammed a car door, Matthew jumped at the noise and damn near dropped the bottle.

His heart was racing. He gasped for air, as though there weren't enough in the motel room. He splashed water on his face and tried to calm himself, but he had to admit it—his nerves were shot.

How ironic. He'd done this for the thrill of it. He hadn't counted on things being quite so thrilling!

Matthew bit his lip, clenched his hands into fists, dug his nails into his flesh.

Face it, brother. You're scared, he told himself.

Scared of what? Nothing can hurt you? You're immortal.

Except that demon *had* hurt him. Matthew looked down at his hands, and he could feel again the excruciating pain. Not only had it hurt him, the damn thing had nearly killed him! Impossible? Not now, apparently. If he believed William (and how could he not believe an archangel?), Satan had found a way to destroy celestial beings like Matthew.

Matthew leaned on the sink and stared at his reflection in the mirror. He was a mess. His eyes were wide and staring and red-rimmed. His hair draggled over his face. His cheeks were flushed as though he had a fever. His lip bled where he'd bitten it. He wiped away the blood, stared at himself, demanding answers.

What the hell was wrong with him?

And then he understood.

He felt pain. He felt fear. He felt Grace's terror. He felt the mother's anguish, and he felt pity. He felt anger.

He . . . felt.

Like conjugating a verb:

I feel. I felt. I am feeling. I have felt.

Except Matthew hadn't felt anything. Not in a long, long time.

Feeling had returned to Matthew, and it hurt, like the pain of life returning to frostbitten fingers.

He recalled a quote from his old friend Samuel Johnson. "When a man knows he is to be hanged in a fortnight, it concentrates his mind wonderfully."

Matthew was like the rich kid with a playroom full of toys. He was bored by all of them. Now he was the child who has only one toy. Now the toy meant something to him.

Which was, of course, what that decrepit old archangel had meant when William had likened Matthew to Frankenstein's monster and Lazarus.

Because he'd almost died again, Matthew Gallow had come to life.

And he wasn't at all sure he liked it.

Now he remembered why he'd stopped living all those years ago. Being alive meant being hurt. Matthew drank down the bourbon he'd managed to get in the glass. Funny. In the past, he'd drunk bourbon to try to feel something. Now, he was drinking to try to dull the feelings!

He finished off what was left of the glass, but the bourbon didn't help much. He was so pumped full of adrenaline he burned it off. He sat up in bed, twitchy and jumpy, and stared into the darkness, wondering what to do with this newfound life of his. He'd been very pleased with himself that night, defying the archangel, insisting that he was going ahead with his exorcisms; Heaven be damned!

But now when he thought about doing an exorcism again, he heard Grace's terrified cries and the demon's terrible laughter. He saw his hands on fire and felt the pain and smelled his own burning flesh.

Matthew's gut shriveled, his mouth went dry. He broke out in a cold sweat and was damn near sick to his stomach. How could he summon up the nerve to perform another exorcism?

Not only that, he'd have to find a new partner. How could he take a chance? Satan might throw in a ringer on him. As for more bookings, that wouldn't be a problem. Every revival meeting would be clamoring to have Matthew Gallow perform exorcisms. But after what they'd seen on TV tonight, they'd be expecting hellfire and brimstone, not flash powder and rubber snakes. And when he didn't deliver, they'd start to suspect he was a con man.

Except he wasn't a con man. Or rather, he was, but he wasn't. He could now perform real exorcisms. He could take on a demon and defeat him. Unfortunately, the next round, it might be the demon who won.

Matthew groaned inwardly and shook his head. What had he gotten himself into?

"I should have listened to Hannah," he muttered.

And the moment he said that, he realized he was in deep shit.

He sat down on the bed, propped himself up on flat pillows against the headboard, the glass of bourbon in his hand, and tried to think of some way out of all this.

He was still thinking when he fell asleep.

Matthew woke with a start. Sunlight glared through the cracks of the blinds. He blinked his gummy eyes and wondered for a moment where he was. Then he remembered, and he was sorry he did. He hadn't thought of any solution to his problems, and, to add to them, he had fallen asleep sitting up, and his neck was stiff, and his back hurt.

And he was hungry. Matthew couldn't remember the last time he'd felt hungry—really hungry. Hungry as in wanting scrambled eggs and bacon, hash browns and biscuits and gravy, coffee and orange juice.

Hash browns. Crispy brown on the outside with lots of salt, nice and soft on the inside. Funny, he'd never really thought about the taste of hash browns before. He tried to concentrate on his major worries, but he couldn't seem to take his mind off hash browns. With ketchup.

His mouth watered. His stomach growled.

Matthew rose stiffly from bed and promptly stepped on the empty plastic cup that had rolled off the bed and onto the floor. The plastic cracked, cutting into the bottom of his foot. He swore, kicked the cup, and headed to the shower. He stood in the hot water a long time, letting it run over his head and shoulders, reveling in the warmth. Throwing on a clean shirt and jeans, he grabbed the keys to the Caddy and opened the door to his motel room.

"There he is!" a voice yelled, and the next thing Matthew knew, he was nearly trampled by an onslaught of reporters, all of them shoving microphones at him, shouting questions.

"Father Gallow! Do you believe Satan walks among us? Did you really say he was President Bush?"

"Father Gallow, you're not listed in the Catholic Registry of priests. What is your response to those who claim you're a fake?"

"Father Gallow, is it true that you once tried to exorcise Ozzy Osbourne?"

There must have been twenty reporters surrounding him. The parking lot was filled with satellite trucks and cars. Curious onlookers hovered on the outskirts. Matthew stared at them in bewilderment. Overwhelmed by the din, he had no idea what to do or say. But, since they were all talking at once, it didn't seem likely he could get a word in anyway. Damn it, he just wanted to eat breakfast. He muttered something about having no comment and politely tried to edge his way through the crowd. The reporters jammed around him, pressed him back against the door. Now Matthew was starting to get angry. A microphone hit him in the jaw. He clenched his fist, ready to hit back, when a young woman came out of nowhere, popped up in front of him.

"Open the door. Go back into the room," she ordered Matthew in a low voice.

She turned to face the cameras.

"I'm sorry, guys," she said in a tone that cut through the shouting. "Father Gallow has no comment this morning. The Father may be holding a press conference later this afternoon. I'll let you know when and where."

The reporters were yelling questions at the woman, wanting to know who she was. She smiled and nodded and kept close to Matthew, who was fumbling with the key. Finally, the door opened. Matthew stumbled into his room. Some of the reporters tried to muscle their way in, but the young woman used her body to block the door.

"Who are you?" the reporters kept yelling.

"Father Gallow's spokesperson," the young woman shouted, and dove into the room after him.

They both threw themselves against the door and slammed it shut, catching someone's hand in it to judge by the swearing. Once the door was locked, the young woman turned to smile at Matthew, who was mopping his forehead and staring at her in astonishment.

She was striking, with an enigmatic smile like a Madonna, with large, lovely eyes. Her hair was long, brownish gold in color, accentuated by a white streak that framed her face.

"Thank you," he said. He kept staring at her, couldn't take his eyes off her. "Excuse me for asking, ma'am, but who the hell are you?"

The young woman threw back her head and laughed. Her laughter was like champagne in Matthew's blood: bubbly and intoxicating. She held out her hand and introduced herself.

"Natalia Ashley. Your spokesperson," she added, and the Madonna smile twisted into an impish grin. "And you are Father Gallow. Should I call you Father or do you have a first name?"

Utterly charmed, completely confused, not quite knowing what else to do, Matthew took her hand in his. Her grip was firm and warm. The young woman didn't let go, however. She kept hold of his hand in hers, was inspecting it.

"My, my, Father! That was a rapid recovery," she remarked.

Matthew snatched his hand from hers.

"The name's Matthew. And I think you better leave now," he said coolly. "Go join your friends out there."

"Don't be mad," said Natalia. "Forgive me. I'm not a reporter. Truly."

"Then who are you?" Matthew persisted.

Natalia peered out the window through a crack in the blind. "They're not going anywhere anytime soon, you know. It's just that I'm so curious," she continued, letting the blind drop and turning back to him. "I've seen lots of special effects, but never anything like those you performed last night! I could have sworn your hands were withering in the flames! You should be in the hospital with third-degree burns, not swilling booze in a cheap motel."

She sat down on the edge of the bed, made herself at home. "I assume you were wearing some sort of asbestos gloves. They looked quite natural. And the smell!" She wrinkled her nose. "How did you manage to fake the smell of burning skin?"

Matthew cracked the blind, peered out. She was right. No one was going anywhere, including himself. He looked back grimly at the young woman.

"I was sitting next to your shill last night," she added. "That's what you con artists call them, right? Shills? The blonde who ran off . . ."

"That's where I've seen you," he said, remembering the extremely good-looking young woman sitting near Hannah.

"You *did* notice me!" Natalia was pleased. "I was thinking I'd lost my touch. I guess you haven't heard from the blonde, huh? She left you high and dry to face the music alone?"

"Look," said Matthew, exasperated and confused, "thanks for helping me out of that jam, Miss, but—"

"Speaking of jam, have you had breakfast?" Natalia asked brightly. "I'll bet not. I haven't either. It took me quite a while to track you down. I had to talk hard to convince that nice Pastor Wiggins to give me your cell-phone number. Which reminds me, he may ask you about your sick mother. I couldn't think of anything else on the spur of the moment. I tried calling you. I was going to warn you about all the press coming after you"—she gestured toward the parking lot—"but your phone went straight to voice mail. I'm starving. Are you? We should really get something to eat."

She opened her purse, reached in, took out a card, wrote down something on the back, and handed it to Matthew. The front of the card was fiery red orange with the word: "Cain" emblazoned in flames. Other than that, it said simply:

Natalia Ashley. Manager.

He stared down at it. "I'm sorry, Miss Ashley, but I don't get it. Who is this Cain? Who are you? Why are you here?"

Natalia was amazed. "You know. Cain. *The* Cain, the rock star? The rock star everyone is talking about!" She spread her hands. "You *must* know. Your teenage shill was wearing his T-shirt last night. That girl is an amazing actress, by the way. Really convincing. I thought the woman who played Mom was a bit over the top, but that's neither here nor there. The point is, Mr. Gallow, I want to hire you."

"Hire me?" Matthew repeated, feeling dazed. He was having trouble keeping up with her. "Hire me for what?"

"I want you to perform your exorcism act during Cain's show. Live. Onstage. At the end of the show, when Cain does his famous song, 'Possession.'" She sat forward eagerly. "You see, my idea is that you accuse Cain of being possessed by demons. You rush onto the stage, wearing your black priest getup, and throw holy water on him or whatever it is you do and try to drive out the demon. Flames shoot up all around. If you can put in that business where your hands catch fire, the audience would freak—"

"It's not an act," said Matthew flatly. He leaned back

against the wall, rubbed his eyes. He was tired and hungry and screwed. He just wanted to be left alone to contemplate how truly screwed he was.

Natalia was amused. "Oh, come now! I was sitting next to the blonde, remember? And the demon-possessed girl and her quote/unquote 'mom' were sitting right behind me. I saw the looks you exchanged with them. Turn my card over. You'll find the money I'm willing to pay you on the back."

Matthew turned the card over. He stared at the figure. It took him a moment to count all the "0's," then he had to do it three times. When he finally figured it out, he looked up at Natalia in shocked amazement.

"You can't be serious!"

"Oh, but I am," she answered calmly. She frowned. "Isn't that enough? Let's say another fifty thousand . . ."

Matthew shook his head. He held on to the card, looked back down at the figure. The numbers blurred together. He rubbed his eyes again. This woman was lovely, charming, sparkling, intelligent. He liked her. He wanted to get to know her better. Too bad she had chosen this particular screwed-up moment to walk into his screwed-up life. He wanted to be alone. To figure out these new and painful sensations. Truth be told, he wanted to be alone so that he could get rid of these new and painful sensations.

"You're right. The blonde was my partner," Matthew said. "My only partner. She ran off because she was afraid that Fox reporter was going to expose us. And you're right about something else. The exorcisms *are* cons. Or rather, they *were* cons—until last night. Last night was real. I never saw that girl, Grace, or her mother before in my life. As for the rest of what happened, I can't explain it."

He handed the card back to her. "Thanks anyway."

Natalia absently took the card. She regarded Matthew intently, frowning and tapping the card against her chin.

"You're not at all what I expected," she said.

"Yeah, well, I'm not what I expected," Matthew returned grimly. "So what did *you* think you were going to find when you walked in here?"

Natalia rose from the bed and walked over to look inside Matthew's suitcase. His black cassock lay there, neatly folded, along with his Bible and the gold cross. She ran her hand over the black fabric of the cassock, glanced back at Matthew.

"Either a smarmy two-bit rogue who is in this for the money or a nut-job who really believes he can rid people of demons."

Matthew half smiled.

"You're not in it for the money," she admitted. "Any other man would have jumped at my offer, and you turned it down flat. And Pastor Wiggins has been telling the press how you gave him a two-thousand-dollar check. You're not a nut-job either." She regarded him intently. "I'm not sure what you are, Matthew Gallow. But I'd like to find out."

She came over to stand in front of him, looked deep into his eyes as though she were trying to see inside him.

"Do you really believe you saved that girl from a demon last night?"

Matthew could smell her perfume. He could see that her hazel eyes had gold flecks. Maybe that was why they sparkled in the light. He'd read about eyes that sparkled but never actually seen any until now. And he noted that she had unusually long eyelashes and a smattering of freckles on her nose.

"I don't know what happened last night," he answered. He shook his head. "I can't explain it."

"Well, at least you're honest," she said. "I like that in a con artist. Look, if you want the job, I still want to hire you." Natalia tucked the card back into his pocket.

Matthew shook his head. "You don't understand—" He stopped talking because, for one, he wasn't certain he understood, and, for two, she wasn't paying attention to him. She was talking on her cell phone.

"Al! Good morning! I need you to call whoever it is you call in Nashville and have them send a limo to this address." Natalia gave the name of the motel and its location. "In addition to the limo, I want you to hire four rent-a-cops to ride shotgun. Big guys. The bigger the better. They may have to use some muscle."

Natalia grimaced. "No, not fans. Reporters, yeah. They're camped out in front of the motel, and my friend and I are trapped inside. The fake priest?" She glanced at Matthew. "Yes, I think it's going to work out. Which reminds me. I want you to—" She lowered her voice to a confidential murmur, walked over to the far side of the room. She spoke for a few more moments, then added in a normal tone, "Oh, and I'll need someone to pick up my rental car. Thanks, Al. See you soon. Bye."

Natalia snapped the phone shut. "All set," she announced, coming back to join Matthew. "The limo will pick me up in about an hour or so, depending on how long it takes Al to round up security."

She looked at Matthew directly. "So. Are you coming with me or staying here in tabloid TV hell?"

Matthew didn't answer immediately. He peered again through a chink in the blind. The satellite trucks were still parked in the lot. Another one had driven up while they were talking. The reporters were standing around in knots, talking and drinking coffee. Some were on their phones. One was interviewing the owner of the motel. Cars were parking along the interstate, with people getting out and traipsing over to see what was going on.

Matthew turned back to Natalia.

"That's blackmail," he said.

She grinned. "Yeah. I know. Tell me, Father, will I be eternally damned for blackmailing a fake priest?"

Matthew sighed and ran his hand through his hair. He stared around at the walls of the motel room. He'd never noticed before how small it was. How small they were. All the motel rooms of all the Inn-B-Tween motels. He felt suddenly trapped.

Natalia's grin faded. She rested her hand on his arm, gave it a friendly pat. "Forget the blackmail, Matthew. I'll get you out of here. Whether you agree to work for me or not."

She cast a sidelong glance back at the black cassock.

"Is that all your luggage?"

"Yes," Matthew said. His life after two thousand years—shoved in a duffel bag and a briefcase.

"You travel light." Natalia grinned. "Like Henry Rollins."

Matthew wondered who the hell Henry Rollins was. Natalia kept her hand on his arm. Not caressing. Not a come-on. Just warm and reassuring.

The sudden thought came to him that he would like to kiss her. Not kiss her perfunctorily, kiss her because she expected him to kiss her. He wanted to kiss her because her lips were soft and sweetly curved, because she wasn't wearing lipstick, because her perfume and the scent of her made his blood tingle. He wanted to kiss her because she was alive, and he was alive. Because for him there were once more such things in this world as hot, crispy hash browns.

Her lips parted. She stepped a little closer to him. The gold flecks in her eyes shimmered.

"You know, this partnership will be perfect," she said.

"What?" Matthew asked, taken aback.

"You claim to drive out demons. Cain claims to have sold his soul to the devil," Natalia stated.

Natalia gave Matthew's arm another friendly pat. She walked over to the bed, flung herself down, and made herself comfortable. Picking up the remote, she switched on the TV.

"Is Denny's okay for breakfast?" she asked, settling back against the pillows. "I love their hash browns!"

$\mathcal{I}$f Matthew had any doubts about Natalia's being who she claimed to be, they were settled the moment he and she emerged from the motel room. The reporters no longer called out "Father Gallow!" They called out, "Natalia! Why are you here? Do you know this man? Does this have anything to do with Cain's being arrested?"

Four large security guards had cleared a path from the door to the waiting limo. Natalia crawled inside the limo, followed quickly by Matthew.

"I knew they'd figure out who I was eventually," Natalia said, scooting across the seat to make room.

Reporters surrounded the limo, tapping on the glass, taking pictures though the glass was so dark it was unlikely they'd get any good shots. Once Natalia and Matthew were safely inside, the security guards piled into a car behind them. The limo driver floored it, and they took off, almost running over some of the members of the press.

"The gossip columns will be speculating about this for

days!" Natalia said happily, and she squeezed Matthew's hand. "You're already good for business."

"I haven't said I'd work for you yet," Matthew pointed out.

"That's true. I'll give you until we're finished with breakfast to decide," said Natalia. "But let me point out some of the advantages. You think that's the end of the hounding?"

She jerked a thumb over her shoulder at the press corps, some of whom were jumping into cars in an attempt to follow them.

"Forget it. You're a celebrity now, Matthew. The press will be hot on your trail. You won't be able to go anywhere without them dogging your steps, calling you on the phone, interrupting your meals, snapping pictures of you in the john with your pants down. And how do you think you'll go back to conning people at cozy little revival meetings after this?"

Matthew had already asked himself that question, and he already knew the answer.

"But if I start touring with a rock band," he pointed out, "won't that make my problems worse? I'll be even more of a celebrity."

"You will," Natalia agreed. "But there will be benefits. I can offer you security guards and private limos, a certain amount of privacy and, of course, an excellent salary. And there's no long-term commitment. Cain's tour only lasts for a few months, and once the tour's over, you'll be free to do whatever you want."

"You make a good case," Matthew admitted. "I'll think it over." He paused, then said, "So what's this about Cain's thinking he's sold his soul to the devil?"

"Oh, it was just a publicity stunt," said Natalia, laughing. "I don't know how much you know about Cain—"

Matthew shook his head. "I never heard of him before I saw him on the news the other night."

Natalia grimaced. "Yeah, well, it all started when Cain became an overnight success. Literally. He was playing crappy little bars for beer money, then one night he uploaded a video of his song, 'Damnation' onto YouTube, and by the next night there were something like a million hits on it."

Natalia eyed Matthew. "You have no clue what I'm talking about, do you?"

Matthew shrugged. "I don't even own a computer. Hannah was into all that stuff, though. She used to talk about YouTube . . . I think . . ."

"Hannah. She was the blonde. Was she your girlfriend?" Natalia asked with interest.

Matthew stared at her, then looked away.

"I'm guessing she wasn't," Natalia continued. "You don't seem all that broken up about her leaving. Anyway, because of the YouTube business, Cain made the news. We held a press conference. A reporter asked him how he became an overnight success, and Cain said the reason was because he'd sold his soul to the devil. Which all started with Robert Johnson."

"Robert who?" Matthew was having difficulty keeping up.

"Robert Johnson was a blues singer in the thirties," Natalia answered. "According to legend, he took his guitar to a crossroads at midnight. There he met the devil, who tuned his guitar for him in exchange for his soul. After that meeting, Robert Johnson went on to become one of the all-time great blues guitarists. He died when he was really young and no one knows much about him and thus the legend. Cain just picked up on it. Of course, like Doc McGhee says, 'Overnight success is a great way of destroying a band.' I'm trying to make sure that doesn't happen."

"Who's Doc McGhee? Cain's physician?" Matthew asked.

"No, of course not!" Natalia said, laughing again. She seemed to find Matthew incredibly amusing. "Doc McGhee. The manager for Motley Crue and Kiss. He wrote what he calls: 'Ten Golden Rules' for running a rock band. I'm trying my best to follow them. And it's not easy."

She sighed. The golden flecks left her eyes, and Matthew thought that was a shame.

"I'll be honest with you, Matthew," Natalia said seriously. "The tour isn't going well. Cain was a flop on opening night. I don't understand it. I've seen him play his heart out for fifty bucks in some nowhere bar, and the night he performs for a sold-out crowd in the Hollywood Bowl in LA, he plays like his heart was in San Francisco. Or maybe Cleveland. The audience knew he wasn't into it, and they sat on their hands. When an artist doesn't feel the love coming from the fans, he can't give it back. So Cain went from bad to worse. His final number, 'Possession,' is the one the kids come to see. It went over like a punk show at the Republican National Convention. That night he got stinking drunk and trashed a hotel room and landed in jail."

She spread her hands. "I managed to turn lemons into lemonade. I kept his name in the news, but it wasn't for the right reason. It was: 'Cain Goes to Jail' when it should have been 'Cain Goes Platinum.'"

"And how do I fit in?" Matthew asked.

"I haven't thought it all through yet, but my plan is to announce that the famous exorcist, Father Gallow, has decided to try to save Cain from Satan. You'll fail, of course. I hope you don't mind that?" Natalia asked, seeming concerned.

"No, I don't," Matthew answered.

"It's just . . ." Natalia hesitated. "You seem to take all this seriously. And yet, you admitted you were conning people. I don't understand you."

"I don't understand myself," said Matthew, giving her a reassuring smile.

Natalia was going to say something else, but her phone buzzed. It had been buzzing almost continuously, but she'd always looked to see who was calling, then sent it to voice mail. This time she said, "I have to take this." She began talking to someone about Cain and court dates.

Matthew watched the scenery slide by the window and thought things over. He had to admit it seemed the ideal solution to his problems. *I do my act, and that's just what it is—an act. No more burning flesh, no more demons trying to drag me off to hell. And no more doddering old archangels preaching at me! I make tons of money. Do practically no work. Live it up. And after that, I go back . . .*

To what? he asked himself.

Not drinking bourbon in Inn-B-Tween motels, Matthew answered himself.

So now you'll be drinking bourbon in the Hilton. What's the difference?

Matthew told himself to shut up.

"I'll take the job," he said, when Natalia ended her phone call.

Her eyes lit up, the gold flecks glittered. "I'm so glad!" she said. She put her hand over his and squeezed it impulsively. "I really am. I think you're going to be a hit."

He returned her smile and the hand squeeze. She looked at him. He looked at her, their hands touching . . .

He drew back, took out his flask.

"You haven't had breakfast yet," she protested. She eyed him. "Do you need that stuff?"

"I don't need it," Matthew said. "I like it."

He felt uncomfortable and ended up putting the flask back in his pocket.

Natalia smiled. "Thanks. It's just that my parents—"

Her phone rang again. She looked at the number. "It's Cain. He's out on bail. I have to take this." She answered, then covered the receiver, and said softly, "I haven't told him anything about you yet. Oh, here's Denny's! Good. I'm famished. Hi, Cain!" she said loudly. "Did you have fun in jail? Yeah, well maybe you won't do anything stupid like that again. Where am I?"

She peered out the window. "At a Denny's near Nashville. I'll explain later. I've got some exciting news for you. No, I can't go into it now. I'm starving. See you soon. Behave yourself. Bye!"

The limo pulled up in front of Denny's, arousing the curiosity of the customers, who all turned to stare. Fortunately, no one recognized either Natalia or Matthew, and they settled into a booth. Natalia ordered a Grand Slam and Matthew made it two. He smiled at the waitress and she smiled back and kept bringing him more coffee.

And Natalia was right. These were the best hash browns he'd tasted in all of his many lives.

Chapter 8

"*I* don't want to spring you on Cain yet," Natalia had told Matthew at the airport. "I need a couple of days to explain everything to him. His next show is in Vegas. Here's your ticket—first class. And I've made reservations for you at the Bellagio. And here's some money for expenses. Meanwhile, I'll have the contracts drawn up, ready for you to sign."

"Is Cain likely to have a problem with this?" Matthew had asked.

"Oh, no," Natalia had lied glibly.

The truth was, Natalia was certain Cain *would* have a problem with bringing Father Gallow into the show. A huge problem, in fact. Cain had become a bit of a prima donna since he'd made it big. His inflated ego had already opened a rift between him and the band members. He'd made it clear that there was only one star on this tour, and that star was Cain. He would not react at all well to the thought of sharing the spotlight with the exorcist.

Natalia would just have to convince Cain this was in his

best interest. She and Cain went back a long way together. Hopefully, she could handle him.

She rejoined the band in LA. Thankfully, the police had released Cain in time to take the bus to his second show of the tour in Las Vegas. They hit the highway the next day.

Once they were on the road, Natalia tried to talk to Cain, but he insisted that he was too tired. He hadn't been able to sleep a wink in jail. Though it was only midmorning, he went to bed, promising to talk to Natalia when he woke up.

Natalia sat cross-legged on the sofa in the bus, her Mac laptop in her lap. She should really be concentrating on her upcoming discussion with Cain, but she couldn't concentrate on that. All she could think about was Matthew Gallow.

The video of the exorcism was all over YouTube. She watched it again and again and still found it baffling. When the camera zoomed in on the priest, Natalia hit stop, froze the frame. Matthew's face was livid, glistening with sweat, and drawn with pain. Yet his eyes shone with a strange light. Holy fervor was one way to describe it. Good acting was another.

Natalia stared at him long and hard.

"Who are you, Matthew Gallow?" she asked the picture.

The picture had no answer. And neither did anyone else. Natalia had searched high and low for information on this man. She had even called in a few favors from people who had access to files ordinary people couldn't access. They hadn't found anything about him either. No birth certificate. No social security number. No driver's licenses. No passport. No credit cards. No credit reports. No bank accounts. Never filed a tax return. No police record. He wasn't listed in the Catholic Registry of priests. No surprise there. But the rest of it was a mystery.

Matthew Gallow didn't exist.

"Fascinating," as Mr. Spock would have said to Captain Kirk with a quirk of his slanted eyebrow.

All right, so Matthew Gallow wasn't his real name. Cain wasn't Cain's real name either. But you could find information about Cain. It had been Natalia's experience that you could find info about anyone if you looked hard enough. An exception might be if they were in the Witness Protection program. But even then, Natalia had heard about high-school reunion-planning goons tracking down people who fondly imagined they'd left all that behind.

This man, whoever he was, intrigued Natalia. Handsome, mysterious, he was a bundle of contradictions. He was a cheat and a liar, but he was honest about being a cheat and a liar. He was hardened and cynical, and at the same time confused and vulnerable.

He seemed at times oddly bewildered by life, like a man who has been jolted out of a long sleep. Natalia had never seen anyone eat breakfast with so much relish. Matthew wolfed down two helpings of hash browns, kept raving about great they tasted.

It was Denny's, for God's sake!

He found her attractive. That much was apparent in the warmth in his blue eyes, in his quiet smile, in the way he touched her hand, let his hand linger on hers. She found herself getting flushed and tingly whenever she remembered that moment. Yet at the same time, he was reserved, withdrawn. A man who lived very much inside himself. She had the feeling he only ever gave a small part of himself to any woman, a part that was ready-made, came right off the rack. The real man, the man beneath the black cassock, was locked up deep inside.

"No," Natalia said softly, changing her mind, "the real man is right here."

She tapped the image captured on the compluter screen.

Ah, well, she thought, brightening as she began answering a pile of e-mail and fan requests. He'll have to give me his social security number when he signs the contract. Then I'll have him!

She turned on her iPod, hummed to the music as the miles rolled by. The bus was plush, the best money could buy. Cain had given Natalia carte blanche. Only the best all the way, he'd told her. There were two buses—one for the band and the roadies and one for Cain and herself. Her bus had four bunks, one for Al, their driver, one for herself, and two more in case any guests or reporters traveled with them. Cain had his own bedroom in the back.

Natalia's bunk was comfortable and cozy, and when she crawled inside, stretched out, put in her earplugs, it felt like home. The rocking of the bus soothed her, sent her straight to sleep. In the morning, she would wake up to find herself in a new city, each one different than the one before.

People thought it was about the money she was making. How little they knew! It was about the music. Her grandfather had taught her that. Woof had been a Deadhead, taken her to concerts before she could walk. They'd spent a lot of time on the road, Nat and Woof. She looked back on those days as some of the happiest of her life. She couldn't imagine a desk job where she stared at the same four walls, did the same routine day in and day out. Not for her the hamster-in-a-cage existence.

She had a bank account, but couldn't tell you how much was in it. Her accountant took care of it, paid the taxes, did whatever it was people did with money. She had bought an apartment in LA, which she'd seen exactly twice. She was currently allowing an old derelict friend of her grandfather's to crash there. She liked buying clothes and shoes and jewelry, but she couldn't buy a lot because there wasn't room for a huge wardrobe on the bus.

She had blown some of her money on decorating the bus, and she'd enjoyed that. She had it done all in wood with black trim. There was a table with benches, a couch, three lounge chairs, a TV, wireless Internet, game consoles (for Cain), full bathroom, shower (Natalia's treat for herself), and, of course, a stereo system.

When they were on the road, Natalia spent most of her time seated in the front of the bus at the "dining room" table, her laptop open, answering e-mails and talking on the phone. Sometimes she would sit up in the big captain's chair in front with Al the driver, chatting with him and watching the world go by.

Al was in his early forties, dark hair, with an unfailingly cheerful attitude. He had a wife and adopted son back in Wisconsin—he adored them both—and a designer cat. He kept pictures of the wife, the kid, and the cat on the console in front of him.

Natalia liked Al. He was professional, trustworthy. She had met him when she and Cain had been performing at Alpine Valley in Wisconsin. Al had been their limo driver. She'd been so impressed with him, she'd hired him on the spot.

She was singing along to Beck's "Loser" when a hand on her shoulder made her jump.

Cain stood there in nothing but his underwear, yawning and rubbing his head with his hand.

He was saying something to her.

Natalia took out the earplugs. "What?"

"You wanted to talk to me about something?" he repeated.

"Oh, yes, right," she said. "Let's go back to your room. I want you to see something."

"It better not be any fucking lecture about me going to prison," he said sullenly.

Natalia quirked an eyebrow. "It was your own fault," she pointed out.

He muttered something it was probably just as well she couldn't hear and stomped back to his room. He flung himself on the bed, arms crossed over his chest, and glared at her from beneath a mass of tousled hair.

Natalia sat down, put on her sympathetic face.

"Look, Cain, I know you've been worried about how the concert went the other night—"

Cain shrugged. "What are you talking about? I thought it went fine."

Nat stared at him in astonishment. "You did?"

"Yeah." He frowned. "Why? Didn't you?"

Natalia gave a wry smile. "If you call fans getting up and walking out during the last number, then I guess you could say it went fine—"

Cain bounded out of bed. "They didn't!" he cried angrily.

"They did, too. Maybe you couldn't see it because of the lights, but you must have heard the deafening silence in place of applause. Look," she added in mollifying tones, "I'm not saying it's your fault. I'm saying it's mine. The setting, the special effects, it's just not working."

Cain regarded her warily a moment, then he sat back down on the bed. "Yeah, you're right, Nat. It is your fault. So what are you going to do about it?"

Natalia bit her tongue. The old Cain, the Cain she'd known for years, the Cain who had been her friend, would have never talked like that to her. She had to make allowances. He was a star now. Millions adored him. That must be putting a lot of stress on him. It was her job to make things smooth for him.

"I have an idea," she said. "I want you to see something."

She spent a few moments syncing her computer to his TV. Cain's bedroom was posh. It had a large-screen TV, DVD player, Wii, and surround-sound stereo, and a cabinet stocked with his video games and all of his favorite movies, most of them horror flicks.

Natalia perched on the edge of the bed.

She tapped on the TV remote control, hit the Play button.

A reporter was walking into a tent, saying something about an "old-fashioned tent revival meeting." She fast-forwarded through the reporter and stopped when he came to footage of a priest standing in front of an audience with his hand on a girl's head.

"She's wearing one of your T-shirts," Natalia said to Cain. "Great publicity."

The priest's hand suddenly burst into flames. The reporter was shouting something, then the screen went dark. The reporter came back on to say that there'd been some sort of technical difficulty. He went on to describe how the priest had claimed to have driven a demon out of the girl.

"Wow!" said Cain, impressed. "That was something. I wonder how he did that without setting the kid's hair on fire. So what was your idea?" He grinned at her suddenly, and, for a moment, the old Cain was back. "You want to set my hair on fire?"

"I did the other night," Natalia said, grinning back at him. "Seriously, though, my idea is to hire this Father Gallow to exorcise you during the final act. This will really wind up the show with a bang, not to mention all the publicity. We use pyrotechnics. Have flames shoot up to simulate the fires of hell. We have a trapdoor, and it looks as if you're starting to get pulled down to eternal damnation—"

Cain's face contorted. He went livid with rage.

"What made you say that? Why did you say that?" he shouted furiously, and he leaped out of bed. Bounding over to stand in front of her, he screamed right in her face.

"Why did you say that?"

Natalia had never been so shocked in her life.

"Don't yell at me! And get out of my space!" She stood and shoved him back.

To her astonishment, Cain took a swing at her.

Natalia recalled number 10 of Doc McGhee's golden rules on managing a rock band: *If all else fails, punch someone.*

Cain was off-balance from the swaying of the bus, and his swing missed by a mile. Natalia had grown accustomed to taking care of herself over the years. A girl had to, if she toured with the bands. Planting her feet firmly, Natalia balled up her fist and nailed Cain squarely on the jaw.

"You don't hit me," she said to him as he fell back on the bed. "No one hits me!" Her knuckles hurt like hell. She sucked on them.

Cain sat up. Blood dribbled down his chin.

Al was yelling from the front, "Natalia! What's going on? Is everything all right back there?"

"Is it, Cain?" Natalia demanded tersely.

In answer, he picked up the Wii and hurled it into the TV screen and shouted, "You're not hiring some fuckin' priest to take over my act!"

"Al!" Natalia shouted. "Pull over!"

Al was already slowing the bus down. Natalia glanced out a window, saw they were heading for an exit. Cain stood wiping blood off his chin and blinking dazedly at the remains of his TV set. The floor was covered with broken glass.

"You're barefoot," said Natalia coldly, turning to leave the room. "Watch where you step."

"Natalia," Cain said, mumbling through his swollen lip, "I'm sorry—"

"Fuck off," she said, and she stomped out of the bedroom.

Al was pulling the bus into a combination gas station and snack shop. He cast her a worried glance. "You okay?"

"Yeah, fine." Natalia slumped down in a chair at the table. She was startled to find she was shaking. "Cain tried to hit me." She couldn't get over the shock.

"I'll have a little talk with him," Al said grimly as he pulled the bus into the back of the station. Al wasn't a big guy, but he was tough and wiry. Cain wouldn't stand a chance. "What's he strung out on?"

"That's just it," said Natalia, perplexed. "He's cold, stone sober. He just . . . went berserk. For no reason."

The bedroom door opened, and Cain came out. His lip was swollen and he was still wiping off blood. He'd put on a T-shirt and jeans and his Doc Martens, no socks. His blonde hair flopped into his face, making him look like a little boy. He wouldn't meet Natalia's eye.

"Hey, uh, Al, next time we pass a mall, could we stop at a Best Buy? My TV's . . . uh . . . busted," Cain said half-defiant, half-ashamed.

"You don't hit Natalia, you little prick," Al said, his fist clenched. "I don't care if you are the world's biggest rock star, you don't hit women. And you don't go trashing my bus while we're doing seventy miles per hour down the highway!"

"I didn't hit her. I missed," Cain said, trying to be funny. "She was the one who hit me. You landed a good one, Natalia." He touched his lip gingerly. "I hope I can still sing tomorrow night."

"Put some ice on it," said Natalia. "You'll be all right."

She rose from the table. "I'm going into the store. You want anything?"

"I want to get off this fuckin' bus," Cain said. "Please, Nat. The store isn't that busy. No mobs of adoring fans." He tried to grin and winced.

"Do what you want." Natalia walked off the bus.

Al cast Cain a warning glance and left the bus, as well, going inside to get coffee, then chatting with the driver of the band bus, which had pulled in behind them. A couple of the roadies came out, laughing and joking. The band members remained inside, probably watching old *Kung Fu* reruns.

Inside the store, Natalia went on her customary search for unsweetened tea. "Why is it," she asked the lady behind the counter, "that they take tea that has no calories and dump tons of sugar in it to sweeten it up, then, because people don't want the calories, they take out half the sugar and call it 'diet,' only diet tea still has calories and regular tea doesn't. Does this make any sense?"

"Is that really Cain?" the lady asked, awed. "The rock star?"

"In the flesh," said Natalia.

"Son of a bitch," said the lady, awed, staring at him. "And he's using my restroom."

Natalia looked around, startled. The restrooms were out-side. One of the roadies who traveled with them—a guy named Burl—had asked for the key, and now he and Cain and another of the road crew were heading for the restroom. Natalia frowned. Women went to the restroom in packs. She'd never known men to do it, and she didn't like it. Cain's bus had a perfectly good restroom, undoubtedly cleaner than the one here. Why was he using this restroom?

As for the two crew members who were with him, Natalia didn't know much about them. Usually the bands hired roadies in every venue they played, and that's what she normally did, except for these two—John and Burl. Since they handled the pyrotechnics, Cain had insisted they travel with the band. The pyrotechnics were state-of-the-art and perfectly safe—if you knew what you were doing. It made sense to keep the same two guys who worked with them constantly, and Natalia had agreed, though she thought it odd that Cain would make such a big deal about it. Mostly he didn't pay attention to anything onstage. Natalia wondered uneasily if the two were helping Cain get drugs.

She did her best to keep Cain clean and off the hard stuff and hallucinogens. To quote her old friend Doc McGhee on rock-and-roll management: "Their personal life is your livelihood. If their personal life gets out of control, you have to step in."

Natalia didn't use any drugs herself.

Been there, tried that, didn't like it.

She liked being in control, and she'd soon learned that drugs take away your brain and hand it over to some football player who drop-kicks it into the next county. As for Cain, she'd seen him on drugs and she didn't like that either. He turned into a sodden, sloppy mess who was out of it for days afterward. Back in the day when they were first getting started, she and Cain had talked about rock stars who ruin their lives with drugs.

The Cain she once knew didn't like taking drugs—the Cain who had been a brilliant young guitar player with a knack for writing music and making his own knockout videos. It had been her idea to put his videos up on YouTube. They'd been a phenomenon, made Cain an overnight success, and apparently completely changed him.

Natalia paid for her bottle of green tea and hurried outside in time to see the two crew members and Cain disappear into the restroom. Natalia went over, jiggled the door handle. It was locked.

She pounded on the door and yelled out, "You ladies better be gossiping about your dates last night and not doing any funny stuff in there!"

Cain's muffled voice came through the door. "All right Mommy, we're being good."

"Yeah, right," she muttered.

She stood there with her ear plastered against the door. The voices were low and muffled. She could only hear snippets of what they were saying. She thought she heard one of the roadies say, ". . . she show you the video of the priest?"

More mumbling, then Cain saying, "I told her no fuckin' way. I'm the star."

"You are, kid, you remember that," said the roadie, adding, "She doesn't appreciate you."

"Maybe you should get rid of her," said the other roadie in a low growl.

"No," said Cain. "She'll do what I say."

Natalia was so shocked she almost dropped her tea. She was seething with anger. They were two goddam roadies! Bought and paid for. How dare they suggest to Cain that he get rid of her?

Hearing the toilet flush and someone walking toward the door, Natalia wondered what to do. Her impulse was to fire their asses on the spot, but they were union and they'd fight it and she couldn't prove anything. It was her word against theirs. There would be a row and probably another scene with Cain, and no pyrotechnics crew. Her skin burning, she turned and stalked off. She'd be keeping a close eye on those two.

And how, she wondered suddenly, could two roadies possibly know about her seeing Father Gallow? And why would they even care? And since when was Cain such buddies with these guys? That answer was relatively simple. They flattered him, sucked up to him. No one else was his friend these days. The guys in the band were barely on speaking terms with him.

Still, Natalia found it all very peculiar. Feeling in need of sustenance, she went back to the store for a bag of trail mix and a bag of popcorn. Armed with reasonably healthy carbohydrates, she returned to the bus to sit at the table, eating popcorn and waiting for Cain. The roadies returned to their bus.

Cain went into the store, bought cheese and peanut butter crackers, and signed an autograph for the giggling and over-awed girl at the cash register.

Cain was the last person to board.

"Let's rock and roll," he said cheerfully. "Oh, and don't forget to stop at Best Buy, Al, my man. Like I said, I need a new TV."

Al shot him a baleful glance. Cain pretended he didn't see it.

Natalia eyed him suspiciously.

"Don't worry, Nat. I didn't shoot up or anything," he said. "I'll piss in a cup if you want me to."

He paused on his way back to his bedroom and rested his hand on her hand.

"I am sorry I tried to hit you," he said remorsefully, giving her hand a squeeze. "And I'm sorry I acted like a two-year-old. But no goddam exorcist is screwin' up my act, Nat. I'm serious. The act is fine the way it is. And it is my act. No changes. Okay?"

"I've already hired him, Cain," said Natalia flatly. "He'll be joining us in Vegas."

Cain stared at her. His face went taut, rigid. His eyes burned.

"He won't be part of the act that night. He'll need time to rehearse, and I want him to see the show, get a feel—"

"Fuck you," said Cain viciously.

Turning on his heel, he stomped back to his bedroom and slammed the door shut.

"And sweep up the broken glass!" Natalia yelled. "I'm sure as hell not going to do it."

All she heard in response was more swearing.

Chapter 9

$\mathcal{M}$atthew spent a couple of nights in a suite in the Bellagio hotel, compliments of Cain. Natalia called him several times, ostensibly just to chat, but in reality to check on him, make sure he hadn't blown town. He asked her how Cain had responded to the news he was joining the act. She replied that he'd been fine with it. No problems.

She called him when the bus rolled into town, said she'd have a limo pick him up, bring him to the theater. The buses were parked behind it, in the parking lot. She'd meet him in the theater.

Matthew had spent his days holed up in his hotel room. He'd tried going out into the street, only to discover that somehow the press had found out where he was and were lying in wait for him. He'd beat a hasty retreat back to his room. At least the food was excellent. And Natalia had sent him a box of chocolates as a gift. He found himself thinking a lot about her. He looked forward to her phone calls.

He was very much looking forward to seeing her again. Of all the women he'd known in his many lifetimes, he'd never met one quite like her.

She was champagne after years of drinking flat, stale water.

"The name's Matthew Gallow," he told the guard when he reached the theater.

The guard checked a list.

"Someone will be with you in a moment, sir. Put this on."

He handed Matthew a security tag. "You can wait in the seats inside."

Matthew had done some theater work in his checkered past. Hell, he'd done nearly every kind of work there was in his long lifetime, from coal miner to sous chef to insurance salesman. He had always liked the theater; always liked actors. They never cared who you were because they knew you weren't the real you anyway. Even the act was an act.

He found a seat in the twentieth row and sat there, watching people come and go. No one paid any attention to him. Lights flashed on, changed colors wildly, went out. A voice like that of God (if she'd been a woman) came booming through the empty theater saying something about the sound check.

An hour passed. He was watching some guys futzing around onstage and wondering if he should say something to someone, when a voice hailed him from the stage.

"Father Gallow!" Natalia called to him, then came running down the stairs and through the aisles to meet him. She extended her hand. "Good to see you again!"

She was wearing tight jeans and a sweaty T-shirt that read: The Clash. She was not wearing a bra, and he could see her breasts jiggle beneath the T-shirt. Bangle bracelets clashed on her wrists. Her fingernails were painted bright orange and her fingers glittered with rings. She even wore rings on her orange-painted toes.

Her smile was radiant. She smelled of some sort of perfume mingled with that faint musky odor that some women exude. Breathing in the fragrance, feeling the warm pressure of her hand in his, Matthew caught himself imagining what it would be like to slide his hand beneath the T-shirt, cup one of those small breasts . . .

He became aware of his thoughts and his feelings—especially his feelings. Desire. Infatuation. Admiration. Attraction. He'd thought such feelings were long-ago dead and gone for him. Or it might be more accurate to say he'd hoped such feelings were dead and gone. He had not cried at their funeral. Feeling nothing was better than feeling pain. Or so he'd thought. With the return of these feelings, he wasn't so sure. The touch of her hand again felt pretty damn good, sent tingling jolts of electricity through him.

She seemed to pulse with energy, as though her body was having trouble containing her spirit. He wondered what it would be like if her spirit burst free from confinement, and he caught his breath at the thought. She withdrew her hand, put her hands on her hips. Her breasts moved tantalizingly beneath her shirt. He focused on her face, looked into her hazel eyes and saw the flecks of gold.

"It's Matthew, remember?" he said, and he couldn't help himself from smiling. She made him want to smile.

"Is it?" she asked archly. "Is your name Matthew. I mean, your real name. I've done some research, you see, and you don't exist!"

"Actually, my real name is Gaius Marius," said Matthew coolly.

Natalia blinked. "That sounds . . . Roman. Like something out of Julius Caesar."

"Yes," said Matthew, looking around the theater.

"Did your parents have a thing for Roman names?" she asked.

"You could say that," Matthew replied. He looked back at her. "Matthew Gallow sounds a lot sexier. Don't you agree?"

"I do agree," said Natalia softly. Then she laughed, and added, "Cain's name isn't really Cain, you know. It's Rupert. Why someone would name a poor kid Rupert is beyond me, but that's parents for you."

She held up her iPhone, pointed it at him. "Hold still. Smile."

"What—"

Something clicked.

"I just took your picture," she said, and she showed it to him. She gave him an admiring look. "You're very photogenic, Matthew. You have wonderful eyes. The picture is for your security pass. I'll need photos for the press release. Do you have some head shots?"

"Head shots?" Matthew was baffled. "I'm not sure—"

"Don't sweat it. We'll do that tomorrow. Does anyone ever call you Matt?"

"No—"

"Thank God! Grab your luggage. I'll take you to the bus now. Introduce you to Cain." She paused, then stopped to look at him. Her eyes were clouded, the golden flecks gone.

"I have to be honest with you. There's a problem. Cain doesn't want you in the show."

Matthew felt like a punctured balloon, with all the air whistling out of him. He stared at her in dismay so great it was physically painful.

"Does this mean I'm fired?" he asked, his throat tight.

"No, absolutely not," she said firmly. "I still think you're what the show needs. I have to talk Cain into it, that's all. I'm hoping when he meets you—"

She let that trail off, forced a smile. "Don't worry. You'll still get paid—"

"It's not about the money, Natalia," he said.

A rosy flush suffused her cheeks. "I'm glad," she said a little breathlessly. "I mean"—she seemed confused—"it should be all about your art, shouldn't it?"

"The art of being a con man?" Matthew asked wryly.

Natalia regarded him frankly. "I like you—Gaius Marius. But you're right. That name just isn't you. Follow me."

Natalia began walking swiftly back toward the stage. Matthew had to react quickly to catch up with her.

"When is the show?" he asked her, only she wasn't listening to him. She was on the phone, talking through a gadget stuck on her ear.

"Yes, I've got a fix. Yes, Father Gallow. He's with me now, and if you'd shut up for five minutes, I could talk to him. The poor man's only just got here. No, Cain isn't happy about it. He's got to be talked into it, though. Or else we might as well cancel the rest of the tour. Ticket sales for the upcoming shows have plunged into the orchestra pit."

She ended that call only to answer another and another after that, moving all the while. Matthew followed Natalia through the maze of stairs, doors, and stagehands. She walked fast, graceful and lithe, bobbing and weaving and gliding. He tripped over cords, got tangled up in ropes, and blundered into crates. He breathed a sigh of relief when they exited the back of the theater.

Two buses, black and gray, with dark windows, were in the parking lot. Access to the parking lot was blocked by gates, and the area around the buses was further cordoned off with steel barricades. Security guards wanted to see their passes. Natalia grabbed Matthew's arm and hauled him into the secure zone. Not once did she cease moving, or seem to look to see where she was going, or stop talking on the phone.

"This is it," she said, walking up to the lead bus. "'Home again, home again, jiggety-jig.' Do you remember that scene from *Blade Runner*? All the mechanical dolls there to meet him. There's something after the 'jiggety-jig,' but I can never remember. Do you know?"

Matthew realized a beat later that she was actually talking to him and not to the phone. The phone's earpiece was still in her ear, but the light had gone off.

"I'm not much on poetry—" he began, when her phone rang again.

As the phone kept ringing, she spoke to him quickly, stringing the words together. "The show's tonight. I just want you to watch, get a feel for it. See how you'd fit in. I'd like to hear your ideas, suggestions. Hello, Nathan, thanks for returning my call. I was wondering—"

She banged on the bus door, which was locked. At her knock, the door hissed loudly and opened. Natalia ran up the stairs two at a time. Amazed at the size of the bus, Matthew followed her more slowly.

Natalia covered her earpiece with her hand, and said softly, "Al, Matthew. Matthew, Al."

"I'm the driver in case you're wondering," said Al, who had opened the bus door. The two men shook hands. "Welcome to the nuthouse. Sit anywhere."

"Thanks," said Matthew, and stared around in astonishment.

If he hadn't just walked into a bus, he would have thought he stepped into the living room of someone's home. Except this was plusher and more luxurious than any home Matthew had ever been in. Leather, polished wood, cut crystal, refrigerator, microwave, carpet, bathroom.

Al walked over to the sofa and stretched out. "Excuse me," he said. "I was driving all night. Our trip was delayed. We had to stop at a Best Buy to purchase a new TV for the child." He closed his eyes.

Matthew looked around in perplexity. There were children on the bus?

Natalia ended her phone call.

"He means Cain," she explained. "As for the bus, it's leased. It's not ours."

Matthew felt heat rush up the back of his neck to his face. He was embarrassed to be caught visibly gawking.

"Looks like it's ready to take off at any moment," he said. "Like a jet."

"Yeah, well, it's home." Natalia flung herself down comfortably on the sofa. Almost immediately, she bounded back up again. "Oh, Jesus, where are my manners? Oops!" She put her hand over her mouth. "Sorry about taking the Lord's name in vain. It just slipped out."

"I'm not a real priest," said Matthew. "Remember?"

"I shouldn't swear like that, though," she said. "It's a bad habit, especially now that we're going to have kids hanging around. Remind me to tell you about the contest."

She stood looking at him. "What was I going to say?"

"I don't know—"

Her phone was ringing again. She looked at the caller ID, sent it to voice mail.

"Oh, yeah, my manners. Would you like a drink? We have Coke, Mountain Dew, Snapple, Evian—"

Matthew could see rows of bottles in a cabinet and highball glasses on the counter.

"Bourbon," he said.

Natalia looked disappointed. "Are you sure you wouldn't rather have Snapple?"

"Fine," he said. He couldn't help but add, "It's okay for Cain to booze it up . . ."

Natalia sighed. "One drunk on the bus is all I can handle." She rummaged around in the fridge. "Let's just say I'm thankful Cain isn't doing worse."

Her phone buzzed. Natalia looked at the name, and this time she answered.

"Excuse me. This is private. Cain's lawyer." She handed a bottle to him, picked up a bottle of cold tea, and walked toward the back of the bus. Drawing aside some curtains, she crawled into a cubicle and drew the curtains closed after her.

Matthew surreptitiously drew out his flask, sneaked bourbon into the Snapple.

"Is she always on the phone?" he asked Al.

"Yeah, she's always on that goddam phone," said a man's gruff voice.

But it wasn't Al, who was asleep or appeared to be. The voice had come from behind Matthew.

He turned to see a middle-aged man seated on the far end of the same couch on which he was sitting. Matthew was startled. He could have sworn no one had been sitting there moments earlier. Where had this old guy come from?

He was an aging hippie with a weathered face, grizzled gray stubble, and long, iron gray hair that he wore in a braid down his back. He had a bandanna wrapped around his forehead and was wearing a tie-dyed T-shirt with "Free the Chicago Seven" printed on it. His faded blue jeans had holes in them. He was sitting with his arms crossed over his chest, glaring at Matthew balefully.

Though taken aback by the glare and the fact that the old hippie had apparently materialized out of thin air, Matthew politely introduced himself.

"Hello there, sir. I'm Matthew Gallow." He reached across the sofa to shake hands.

To his astonishment, the man shrieked and jumped off the couch. He began to pace around the bus, muttering to himself.

"Wait, wait, wait! Don't panic. That man *cannot* see you. It's the acid talkin'. That's it. A flashback."

Puzzled and more than a little disconcerted by this strange behavior, Matthew glanced toward the front of the bus, toward Al, to ask for an explanation. Al simply rolled over, however.

"So . . . uh . . . do you work for Cain, sir?" Matthew asked, hoping to find out who this character was.

The old hippie stopped pacing. He looked carefully around the bus. Seeing no one else in sight, he faced Matthew.

"Who're you talkin' to?" he demanded.

"You, sir," said Matthew.

"Damn!" The old guy staggered backward, clutching at the table for support. "You can see me? And hear me?"

"Well, yes," said Matthew.

He was starting to feel extremely uncomfortable, and he wished Natalia would come back. Was this some kind of joke they played on the new guy? He'd heard about drugged-up rock stars, and he knew he should have been prepared for this, but Natalia had seemed far too professional and in control to allow that sort of behavior. Who was this old dude anyway?

"This can't be happening," the old guy was muttering. "I musta made a mistake somewhere. Shit! I've been so damn careful! I wonder . . ."

All this time, the old guy had been darting glances at Matthew out of the corner of his eye. "There's something not right about you . . ."

He stopped, turned to face Matthew full on. The old guy's eyes narrowed, then flew open wide.

"Son of a bitch," he said, awed. "You're one of *them*! Why the disguise? You undercover? Hey, man!" He seemed suddenly put out, defiant. "You're not here to take me with you, are you? 'Cause I won't go. I've been with Natalia since she was sixteen and ran away from home. We're a team, the two of us. Can't split us up. We're like Simon and Garfunkle. Well, bad example there . . ."

Matthew had been trying to get in a word edgewise, and he finally succeeded. "Calm down, Old-timer. I'm just here for a job."

"A job?" The guy eyed him suspiciously. "I don't believe it. What kind of job does one of your kind get with a rock band?"

"Like I told Natalia, I'm not a real priest," said Matthew. "It's all an act. Excuse me a moment, will you? I have to use the facilities."

Matthew walked past the old hippie to the bathroom. He didn't really have to go. He wanted to put an end to this strange conversation. He hoped the guy would be gone by the time he came back, but when he returned, the old guy resumed his seat on the couch. The old fellow didn't say anything to him as Matthew walked past him, heading toward the front of the bus, but Matthew felt the old guy's eyes follow him.

"Say, who's the weird old man?" Matthew asked Al, who was once more awake and staring at him oddly.

"What weird old man?"

"The one—" Matthew stopped.

Everything the old man had said came back to him, hit Matthew a mental blow that literally rocked him back on his feet.

"You should sit down, Father," Al suggested. "You look like you've seen a ghost. Or lay off the sauce." He glanced pointedly at the pocket where Matthew kept his flask.

"Never mind," said Matthew. "Sorry I woke you."

Al shook his head and shut his eyes again.

Matthew took out his cell phone, put it up to his ear, and pretended to be talking to it.

"So, who do you think I am?" Matthew asked the old hippie.

"One of Heaven's finest. Here to arrest me. Oink, oink!" The old hippie gave with a high-pitched squeal. "Piggy, piggy, piggy!"

Matthew shook his head. "I'm not what you think."

The old hippie glared. "Hell, man, you're a fucking angel! Anyone can see that!"

"Not *anyone*," Matthew said with emphasis. "Only someone who's . . . passed over."

"The word is 'dead,'" said the old hippie. "No need to try to pretty it up. I keeled over eleven years ago at a Rolling Stones concert. Massive heart attack." The old man seemed rather proud of the fact. "Never did take care of myself. Life finally caught up with me. Wouldn't have minded going much except for the kid."

He glanced fondly in the direction of Natalia's cubicle.

"I'm her grandfather. Name's Woof. I couldn't see leavin' Natalia on her own. Her parents weren't for shit, so when your kind came to escort me through those pearly gates, I said 'no, thanks, fellas. I'll stick around here for a while.'"

He shrugged. "Heaven was beautiful and all that, but I guess I just got into the habit of livin'. It's a hard habit to break."

"I wouldn't know," Matthew muttered to himself. Aloud he said, "So you're a ghost . . ."

"And proud of it," returned the old hippie.

Chapter 10

*M*atthew was perplexed. He didn't know how to handle this bizarre situation. In all his years on Earth, one would think he'd have run into a ghost sooner or later, but he hadn't. He supposed he'd been lucky. Ghosts were lost souls who were still so strongly tied to this life that they couldn't leave it. Some ghosts were good, others evil. The reasons for their continuous existence were numerous and varied.

Damned spirits who had refused God's forgiveness were bound to the scene of a crime, forced to suffer in eternal torment for their crime until they finally repented. Some ghosts were victims of crimes who had turned from God to seek revenge. And there were ghosts like Woof, who still felt so protective of those they had loved they couldn't leave them. Despite what Woof thought, Heaven took a tolerant view of such benign spirits, knowing that sooner or later they would find their way home.

"Anyway, if you're here to drag me back, I'm not going—"

"Heaven's not in the business of dragging people anywhere," Matthew said. "Besides, I don't work for them."

Woof reared up, fists clenched. "If you're working for the dark side, you're not coming anywhere near Natalia—"

"I work . . . for myself," said Matthew.

Woof eyed him, then relaxed and slouched back down and put his feet up on the couch.

"Got tossed out, huh?"

"Frankly, it's none of your damn business," Matthew retorted.

"It might be," said the old hippie with a shrewd glance. "I saw the way you were looking at Natalia. You just watch out, Mister—"

"Gallow. Matthew Gallow. And why do they call you 'Woof'?" Matthew asked, not certain he'd heard right.

"'Woof, woof,'" said the old hippie, winking. "'That's my dog imitation.'"

Matthew stared blankly at him.

"'Woof, woof,'" Woof continued gleefully. "'That's my other dog imitation.'"

"Oh, uh, right . . ." Matthew said. He was beginning to wonder if Heaven might not have seen this guy coming . . .

"It's a quote from a movie," Woof explained. "'Always with them negative waves, Moriarty!' You know. Donald Sutherland. *Kelly's Heroes*. Clint Eastwood—"

"Ah, well, I don't go to movies much," Matthew replied.

"Too good for 'em, huh?" Woof looked disgusted.

"It's not that . . ."

Matthew was relieved to see Natalia returning.

"She doesn't know about me," Woof told Matthew in a loud whisper. "Don't say anything."

Before Matthew could respond, Natalia sat down on the sofa opposite. She gave him an apologetic smile. "Sorry about that. That damn phone. It's gotten worse since the tour started. I've shut it off for now.

"Where were we? I got your drink, didn't I? Do you want a refill? Anyway, I have a contract for you to sign. Let's go over it, see if you have any questions."

She drew out a sheaf of papers and set them down on the coffee table in front of him. "It's a standard contract for performers. I don't suppose you belong to the Actor's Guild?"

"No," Matthew replied.

She made a face. "That's too bad. You'll have to join. Can't go onstage unless you do. I'll take care of it. We'll pay your dues. As to the contract, it's long and very detailed, and you should read it, but here's the gist. We hire you to perform onstage with Cain. You do your act, and we'll pay you handsomely. You don't get paid for performances that you miss, whether it's due to illness or too much bourbon or whatever, and at the end of the tour you don't work for us anymore. You'll sign an agreement that you won't talk to the press about Cain, reveal any of our deep, dark secrets. If you do, we'll send in the wolverines to bite off your fingertips."

"'We're out of badgers,'" Woof snickered. "'Would you accept a wolverine in its place?'"

Matthew blinked, mystified. "I beg your pardon?"

Both Woof and Natalia were laughing. Matthew had no idea why. They both had the same laugh, hearty and boisterous, infectious. He felt like laughing himself, and he didn't even know what he was laughing about. Wolverines, badgers? It was all so absurd.

Natalia reached out impulsively, grabbed Matthew's hand, and squeezed. "You look confused. I'm sorry. I love quoting from movies and TV shows. My grandfather and I used to do it all the time. Don't you recognize that line about the wolverines? It's from *Saturday Night Live*."

"First season," Woof struck in helpfully. "John Belushi."

Matthew shook his head.

"I guess they didn't have a TV in the monastery, huh?" Natalia said in sympathy.

Matthew opened his mouth.

She grinned. "I know—you're not a priest! I was teasing."

She leaned back on the sofa and regarded him intently. "I'm very glad about that, by the way."

"About what?" Matthew asked, not sure what she meant.

"The fact that you're *not* a priest."

She reached over and gave his hand a gentle caress. His mouth went dry, his heartbeat quickened. Then she went back to glancing over the contract. Matthew was aware of Woof eyeing him balefully.

"Tell me about your grandfather," Matthew suggested.

"What?" Natalia looked up, startled. Then she smiled and seemed to melt. "My grandfather. What a great guy! I loved him better than anyone in the world. He mostly raised me, you see. My parents"—she grimaced—"well, let's just say they'd never be nominated for the *Leave it to Beaver* award. Woof lived with us—"

"His name was 'Woof'?" Matthew interrupted.

"That's what he called himself. The name came from a character in the musical *Hair*. Woof was a hippy. Turned on, tuned in, dropped out. He played the guitar, followed the Dead—"

She paused, looked quizzically at Matthew. "You *do* know about the Grateful Dead, don't you?"

"Yes," said Matthew, smiling. "'Come hear Uncle John's Band.'" He said a silent "thank you" to Hannah.

"Glad to see you're not entirely illiterate," Natalia said acerbically. "Anyway, Woof would take me out for long drives in his old beat-up van. We'd listen to the radio or his tapes, and he'd quiz me on the music. He'd make me tell him the name of the band, the lead singer, stuff like that. We'd sing along with the songs together, so I learned all the lyrics. He'd tell me stories about the band members. He knew them all, you see.

"At night, when things at home got bad, I'd slip into his room. We'd drown out the sounds of my parents getting screaming drunk and slapping each other around by turning the TV up real loud."

"That's why she's uptight about the bourbon," Woof remarked. "She used to lecture me on the weed, too. Wish I'd listened. I might be alive today."

Matthew tried to block out the old hippie's voice, concentrate on Natalia.

"We'd watched old movies," she was saying, "and shows like *WKRP, Andy Griffith, Saturday Night Live, The Beverly Hillbillies* . . .

"Woof died when I was sixteen," Natalia added, her eyes shimmering. "I couldn't bear it, I missed him so much. So I ran away from home to follow the bands. I never went back. And here I am."

She was quiet a moment, then said softly, "I still miss him. I'll hear a song he loved or I'll remember something— like that line about the wolverines—and, it's odd, but I have the feeling he's really close to me. I can almost hear his voice . . ."

She shrugged and went back to perusing the contract.

Matthew cast a sharp glance at Woof.

"No way, man!" he said earnestly. "She does *not* know I'm here!"

"Good thing," Matthew remarked.

"What's good?" Natalia looked up, startled. "I'm a little deaf, so you need to speak up—"

"He talks to himself," Al volunteered from the sofa. "Answers himself, too."

Natalia grinned.

"Do you really talk to yourself? I'm glad. Means you're as crazy as the rest of us. You'll get along much better that way. Now, back to the wolverines. Here's what you can say to the press. You can only speak for yourself, but I prefer that you do that through me. Promotional stuff is fine. I want you to give interviews, I'll arrange it—"

She stopped because Matthew was shaking his head. "I've had my fill of the press."

Natalia studied him, chewing on her lip. "Maybe you're right. Maybe we should keep you a question mark. The enigmatic and mysterious Father Gallow. I'll think about it. What else can I tell you?"

Matthew nodded. "You're saying I sleep here."

"Over there." Natalia pointed out a bunk. "My bunk's there, across from yours."

Matthew was pleased to hear that Natalia had her own bunk. He'd been afraid that she was sleeping with Cain.

"I don't care what you do in your off hours," Natalia added, "as long as you're in time for rehearsals and don't miss the bus when we're ready to pull out."

Just then the door to Cain's room opened, and Cain himself walked out. He was bare-chested, wearing pajama bottoms slung halfway down his hips, and rubbing sleep out of his eyes. His hair was in his face. He cast a bored glance around the bus. His gaze raked over Matthew without interest.

Natalia stood up, and so did Matthew. He noted that the moment Cain appeared, Woof rolled his eyes and retreated to the very farthest corner of the bus, where he began strumming an imaginary guitar and singing something about "blue-eyed groupies" and "the cover of *Rolling Stone*."

"Cain, this is Matthew Gallow," Natalia said quietly. "The exorcist I told you about. Matthew Gallow, Cain Lukosi."

Cain grunted and went to the sink. He poured himself some orange juice, grabbed a handful of tablets from a bottle on the counter, and swallowed them at a gulp.

"Why'd you let me drink so damn much last night?" He glared at Natalia accusingly.

"Not my job to look after you. I can hire a nanny if you want," she told him.

"Very funny." Cain grunted again and finished off the orange juice.

"Nice to meet you," Matthew said for lack of anything better.

"Whatever," Cain mumbled. He scratched himself and opened the refrigerator. "We got any waffles?"

Cain took a frozen waffle out of the box, stuck it in the toaster. He waited until it popped up, then grabbed it, wrapped it in a napkin, picked another carton of orange juice, and walked back to his bedroom. He slammed the door shut with his foot.

"Lead singers—assholes, all of 'em," Woof remarked. "Except Jerry Garcia. Great guy, Jerry. Now if I knew he was in Heaven, I might consider going . . ."

"He'll come around," Natalia said, adding cheerfully, "Tonight's show's going to be just as bad as LA—if not worse. He hasn't rehearsed once or even set foot on the stage. He knows I'm right. He just won't admit it."

"Whatever you say. You're the boss," Matthew said.

Natalia smiled at him. "I was thinking you and I could go over your act. I've been watching the videotapes. I have some ideas about staging, and I've done some preliminary work on it. I hope you don't mind, but it's a lot different from what you're used to—"

"Church revival tents?" Matthew interjected.

"I can show you now, if you want," Natalia said. She held out a pen. "After you sign your contract."

"Oh, uh, sure." Matthew signed and initialed everywhere she told him to. He didn't read it. He didn't bother. It didn't matter to him what it said. As strange and unlikely as it seemed, he felt like for a little while, at least, he'd found a home.

"You have to put in your social security number," she said, when Matthew started to hand her back the pen. "You do have one, don't you?"

Matthew hesitated, then, catching her grin, he said, "I have one that will get by."

Natalia rolled her eyes. "Belongs to a dead man, I suppose."

"Ha-ha!" Woof roared with laughter. "She's got you there, Angel Boy!"

Matthew wrote down what passed for his social security number.

"Al, you have the controls," said Natalia, as she and Matthew left the bus. "Lock up after us. Do you have any props you need, Father?"

Matthew grabbed the case that contained his Bible, purple sash, holy water, relics, and followed her off the bus. They headed back toward the theater. Natalia walked with a long stride, confident and energetic.

"Don't pay any attention to the way Cain behaves," she told Matthew. "He's very into himself. I think it's part of the act with him. He's always 'onstage' so to speak."

"I can work with him," Matthew said. "I've worked with worse." He thought this over, then added, "Though not much. Personally, I think he's a stuck-up little prick."

Natalia laughed. "Well, at least you're honest. I know it's hard to believe now, but Cain used to be a really great guy." She sighed. "He was fun to be around. We had lots of laughs. Fame changed him. Went to his head."

"He was in love with her," said Woof.

Matthew jumped. He hadn't realized the ghost had come with them.

"Natalia thought she was in love with him for a while," Woof continued. "Then she figured out she wasn't, thank goodness, and put an end to it. He took it hard. When he hit the charts, went platinum, I think he thought that was going to make her love him." Woof shook his grizzled head. "It didn't. So he turned into an asshole."

"Why do you stick with Cain?" Matthew asked, talking pointedly to Natalia.

He had to keep reminding himself not to talk to Woof. Natalia could neither hear nor see the ghost of her dead grandfather, and she would think he was truly loony if he began holding conversations with thin air. He didn't want to confirm the opinion Al the driver had of him.

They entered the theater and were once more in the tangle and confusion of backstage.

"The reason I stay with Cain is simple," Natalia said, but she didn't immediately answer. She switched on her phone and was listening to her voice mail messages.

"Well, for one thing, I'm making enough money to buy my own third-world country. Most people would think that was the reason, but it isn't. I spent months living on ramen noodles and ketchup packs I stole from restaurants just to get Cain started, and I enjoyed every minute of it. I'd go back to those days in a minute. Because, you see, my real love is the music. I've always loved the music.

"Add to that the fact that my job is never dull. I'm always on the move. I call the shots. Cain's success is my success. He wouldn't be Cain without me."

"Cain wouldn't be jack without her!" Woof muttered. "But try telling him that."

"It must be the same for you, Matthew," Natalia was

saying, as they walked onto the stage. "You're always on the move. No ties, no strings attached. No social security number."

"I'm just a rover," Matthew answered. "I don't like 'systems.' I don't like being in them or having to rely on them for anything. I make my own way in this world. I don't need someone telling me what to do and when to do it."

"So that's why they kicked you out of Heaven," Woof remarked.

Matthew forgot himself. "Just shut up, will you?"

Fortunately Natalia didn't notice. She was searching for a mark on the stage.

"You sound a lot like my grandfather," she remarked.

"Don't compare him to me!" Woof exclaimed, shocked. "He's not anything like me!"

Natalia moved closer to Matthew, looked into his eyes. "I think we're going to get along fine, Matthew Gallow." She clasped his hand, twined her slender fingers around his.

Her lips were tilted to him. Her eyes started to close. He was intoxicated, and he hadn't touched his bourbon. He drew near, bent low . . .

Her phone buzzed. She glanced at it.

"Damn! Cain's lawyer again. I've got to take this," she said, and she gave him a lopsided smile of apology and turned and walked away.

Matthew straightened, drew in a deep breath. He was disappointed and, yet, at the same time, relieved. As though someone had just pulled him back from jumping off a precipice. Things were happening much too fast. And he was having to contend with new and confusing feelings churning around inside him, especially his feelings for her. *Keep your hands in the air and no one gets hurt.* There was a good movie quote for you!

"That's funny," said Natalia. She was standing on the stage, staring at her phone with a puzzled frown. "You heard my phone buzz, right? The caller ID was the number for Cain's attorney. But when I answered, Parker wanted to know why I had called him! It was like my phone dialed itself. Weird."

Matthew looked up to see Woof grinning.

"So, where did we leave off?" Natalia asked with a smile. She moved in close again.

Matthew stepped back a pace. "You were . . . going to show me my blocking."

Natalia made a disappointed face. "Back to business then, eh, *Father*." She laid teasing emphasis on the word.

"I think it's better that way," he said gently. "We haven't known each other very long."

"Oh, well, I guess you're right," Natalia said with a shrug. She cast him a golden-flecked grin over her shoulder. "We *are* on tour, though. What happens on the bus stays on the bus. Still, we'll play it your way—for the time being at least, though I don't guarantee I won't sneak into your bunk at night. Now, here's what I was thinking. Cain will be playing the guitar here. You'll enter stage left—"

"Good man," Woof told Matthew. He rested an invisible hand on his shoulder. "You'd only end up hurting her in the end. Like in *The Bishop's Wife*—1947. Cary Grant's an angel and he's sent to Earth to help the bishop, who's played by David Niven, and Cary Grant meets Loretta Young—"

"That's one of the few movies I have seen." Matthew cut the ghost off tersely. "I know the story. The angel meets a human woman and falls in love with her."

He rounded on Woof, suddenly angry. "And how does that movie end, Old Man? How *can* it end? He's an angel. He'll live forever, while she'll grow old and die. He'll lose her the same way he's lost every human he's ever loved. That's the curse, you see. The curse of being immortal. Cary Grant's the one who gets hurt in that movie. Not Loretta Young. And his pain will last for eternity. It's easier just to quit loving."

"Were you talking to me?" Natalia asked, turning around.

Matthew shook his head. "I was rehearsing my lines."

She raised a skeptical eyebrow. "For the act? I thought I heard you say something about Cary Grant. Do you call on him for help?"

Matthew grinned. "Wasn't he the exorcist?"

"In the movie? No, that was Max von Sydow."

"I always get them mixed up," Matthew said easily, as he walked over to join her.

"Man!" Woof muttered as Matthew walked away, "You are one screwed-up angel!"

Chapter 11

The sound check was complete, the stage set, security on hand. Cain was going over some last-minute changes to the songs with the guys in the band—changes that no one liked, apparently, to judge by the raised voices. Natalia sighed and shook her head. She considered intervening, changed her mind. She would only make matters worse.

Cain was well aware Matthew was in the wings, there to watch the show. Natalia had argued, pleaded, cajoled, trying to urge Cain to allow Matthew's act in the show. All to no avail. She had assured Cain that Matthew was not out to grab the spotlight. Matthew had been in the glare of the spotlight and, unlike Cain, Matthew hadn't enjoyed it at all. He had assured Cain as much. Cain had refused even to listen. He was rude to Matthew, silent and sullen around Natalia. Now he was yelling at the guys in the band, who, having known him for years, were not the least bit in awe of him and were yelling right back.

"It's going to be a great show tonight," Natalia muttered.

Seriously, she hoped it was—for the sake of the fans. She hoped Cain would get it together, play his heart out. She didn't see that happening, though. Something was wrong with him these days. The stress of the tour, the fame, the pressure—maybe it was all too much. If only he would listen to her . . .

She left the control booth, where she had been going over the visuals—the video screen, lights, pyrotechnics, and went backstage to meet and greet the personalities who had come to watch the show and the contest winners. Cain's tour was being partially sponsored by local radio stations, who provided a guest DJ to introduce the main act. Natalia shook hands with the guy and made sure he was given the royal treatment.

Cain was the hottest thing on the planet right now. Natalia couldn't imagine his getting any hotter, but she could foresee him crashing and burning. Rock stars had been doing that since the beginning of time, or at least since Johnny Cash. Take Motley Crue, for example. They had been on the top of the music scene, ruled the charts, and thought they were invincible. They weren't. Drugs and booze landed them in the toilet and flushed their status along with it.

Natalia was working hard to make sure Cain didn't start weaving his way down that deadly path—for her own sake, as much as his. Most band managers lucked into their jobs—she had, though the way she looked at it, she'd made her own luck.

Some band managers went down with their bands and disappeared beneath the waves. Natalia was intent on showing the world that a good band manager could keep the ship afloat even if the deck was on fire and loose cannons were smashing through the hull. *Rolling Stone* magazine had already credited her with being "in part responsible" for Cain's success. If and when Cain self-destructed, she wanted the article to read: "Cain was a failure despite the best efforts of Natalia Ashley" not "because Natalia Ashley let Cain get out of control."

One of her ideas had been to hold contests on the local radio stations during the tour. The lucky winners were driven around in limos, given backstage passes, treated like rock stars themselves. After the concert, they would get to hang out with Cain. It had been Cain's idea to have the contests based on questions about the lyrics to his songs. He wrote all his own lyrics and took pride in them. He always made sure the thumping beat of the music didn't stomp all over the words, nor did he end up with word-mush. His lyrics were complex and symbolic. The fans would spend hours trying to decipher them, arguing about them in chat rooms and on blogs. They would search for clues to the meaning by watching his videos and buying his albums.

What surprised Natalia was that Cain was taking an active interest in the contest, even down to insisting on personally selecting the winners. They'd had a contest in LA, and now this one in Vegas. He'd read through the entries (or so he claimed; she was a little dubious about this) and given her a list of winners. When she'd asked out of curiosity just what these kids had done to win, Cain was a little vague. He had "liked their answers."

She had done the usual background checks on them. Tonight's winners were three boys and one girl. They were waiting for her backstage, and they were all so excited their eyes were almost bugging out of their heads. Natalia introduced herself and asked them a few questions: What did they like about Cain, etc. She took them to the backstage area where they could watch the concert and made certain they knew to stay out from under the feet of the stagehands. She pointed out the security guys, who would be there to keep an eye on them.

Matthew was here, as well, waiting to watch the show. He waved at her, and she waved back.

"Any questions?" she asked the kids.

"Yeah! Did Cain really throw a woman off of his hotel-room balcony?" one of the kids wanted to know.

"He threw furniture," Natalia answered. "Something he shouldn't have done. He knows he behaved badly, and he's very sorry about it."

"We heard he threw the woman off the balcony because she wanted to switch to the History Channel on TV," said the girl, brushing away Natalia's morality lecture.

"Actually Cain likes the History Channel," Natalia replied. "He majored in history in college."

The kids frowned, obviously disappointed. Natalia glanced at Matthew and grinned. She then checked the clock on her cell phone.

"Okay, guys. The show is going to start soon, and I need to get up to the sound booth. Do you have everything you need? Would you like something to drink?"

"Champagne," said one of the boys. He was a real charmer, with his Abercrombie jeans and sporting a Rolex. "Cristal, if you have it. If not"—he shrugged—"I'll settle for Dom Pérignon."

Natalia had to work hard to keep a straight face. Even though his mom could afford it—she was a well-known judge—what parent in her right mind bought a teenage kid a Rolex? "I'm glad you'll settle for Dom, because that's all we drink around here," said Natalia. "Now let's see some ID."

"I left it in my Porsche. I am twenty-one, though." The

young man gave her a smile that probably melted teenage girls into puddles. "Say, maybe you and I could go out after the show."

"You're seventeen, Rob," Natalia told him. "You go to Bonanza High School. You're on the track team."

The kid was taken aback. "How do you know that?"

"Remember that entry form you filled out? I did some checking. Part of my job. It was a nice try, though. There's soda in the fridge in the green room. Help yourselves."

Rob winked at her. "I'd still like to go out with you. I like older women."

Natalia winked back. "And I like older men, not boys." She cast a glance at Matthew to see if he'd heard. He must have, for he met her glance and smiled warmly. Her heart gave a little flutter.

Rob shrugged, cheerful in defeat and already making eyes at a young female stagehand.

Natalia watched them depart for the green room and thought back to her groupie days. Liquor had flowed like water backstage then. *Not* Dom Pérignon. More like Jack Daniel's. No questions asked. The record labels hadn't been scared of being sued like they were today. Natalia had participated in some wild shit back then. Fortunately, she'd just got her feet dirty. She hadn't sunk into it up to her neck like some. She'd known girls so enamored of the stars they'd let themselves be abused by the bands and roadies, who would pass them around, then throw them away like garbage.

Natalia'd had too much self-respect for that. Besides, it was the music she loved. She gave herself to the music, not to the bass player. She knew rock and roll, knew jazz and R&B, knew where it came from and where it was going. Because of that, the guys in the band had respected her and liked to have her around. If she had an affair with a band member, she kept it light, never badgered him to settle down, and made sure there were no hard feelings when it ended. The music was what mattered—that and the excitement of life on the road. Her mother had always claimed her side of the family had gypsy blood in their veins. Natalia believed it.

"Nice kid," said Natalia, going to join Matthew. "A little spoiled, perhaps, but not obnoxious about it. Are you okay? Do you need anything to eat or drink? Oh." She paused. "I see you've got something already."

Matthew secreted his flask, thrusting it back into the pocket of his blue jeans. "You might want to check on Cain. He came storming past, shouting that he wasn't going on."

"Oh, my God!" Natalia groaned and hurried off.

She wondered as she threaded her way through stagehands and props, heading back to the dressing rooms, if she should say something to Matthew about his drinking. She'd seen booze ruin so many lives—her parents' for starters. The family that drank together stayed together—if for no other reason than the fact that neither could find the door. Natalia decided, reluctantly, that it was really none of her business. At least not yet. If the drinking started to interfere with his work, that was another story. As yet, he didn't have any work to do.

She reached Cain's dressing room and found the door locked.

"Go away!" Cain shouted.

"You know I won't!" Natalia shouted back.

There was silence, then footsteps, then the door opened.

"What's this about you not going on?" she demanded.

Cain slouched sullenly back into his seat. He had not even started to put on his makeup.

"They hate me!" he muttered, staring at himself in the mirror. "The guys in the band hate me!"

Natalia sighed. She put her hands on his shoulders, started rubbing them, like a coach might massage the shoulders of a star athlete.

"No, they don't," she said quietly. "You can't start making changes in the music thirty minutes before the show, sweetie. Of course, that's going to upset them. It sounds good the way it is. Go with it."

"No it doesn't," said Cain suddenly. "You're right. The show stinks. But I won't have that priest involved!" He flung himself around, glared at her. "I won't!"

Natalia sighed. "I don't understand you. What's the big deal? Think of the publicity! Nothing like this has ever been done before by any rock star! Being exorcised onstage. It beats the hell out of biting off the heads of birds . . ."

"I know. It's not me, Nat," said Cain. "It's them. They don't want him." He flung himself out of his chair, began to pace nervously about the room. "They told me. Someone'll get hurt . . ."

Natalia eyed him narrowly. He was trembling all over. His face was pale, and he was sweating. He looked sick, feverish.

Natalia thought she recognized the symptoms. "Okay, Cain, where's your stash," she said grimly. "I know you've been shooting—"

Suddenly he clutched his gut, doubled over. "I gotta go . . ."

He dashed off to the small bathroom. She could hear the sounds of retching.

The sounds quit. The toilet flushed, but he didn't come out.

"Cain?" Natalia yelled, worried. "Are you all right?"

"Yeah, fine," he said, coming back into the room. He didn't look at her, kept his eyes averted. He sat down at the dressing table, began fumbling with the brushes.

"You're sure you're okay," Natalia said, concerned.

Cain gave a ghastly smile. "Just a touch of stage fright. Send in my makeup gal, will you? The cute one."

Natalia watched him for a few moments. He seemed okay. Lots of artists suffered from stage fright. Some never got over it. She'd never known Cain to be one of them, but then, he was under lots of pressure.

"Thirty minutes!" came the call.

Natalia left him. She sent in hair and makeup and his dresser, told them to hurry.

As she headed back out into the theater, to take her place on the soundboard, she recalled what Cain had said. They "didn't want the priest. People would get hurt."

That made no sense whatsoever. For one, Matthew wasn't even a real priest! She put it down to paranoid delusions. He must be on drugs again. Tomorrow she'd make some excuse to get him off the bus, then she and Al would search his bedroom, find out where he was hiding the stuff, and dump it.

The soundboard was on scaffolding that had been built in the middle of the theater, forty yards or so from the stage. From here, Natalia could look down on the crowd now starting to throng into the venue.

There were no seats on the ground level. Standing room only. The kids surged immediately to the front and staked out their spot for the show—the closer to the band, the better. Natalia had the set list in front of her, so she knew which songs would be played when. She put on a headset to hear the roadies and the cues for the stage effects.

A black curtain hung in front of the stage. The audience and Natalia waited with anticipation. It would have been hard to say who was more excited—her or the fans. This moment was the moment she lived for. The moment just before the curtain went up. The moment when her pulse raced and her heart throbbed and electric thrills shot all through her body. She had always hated it when bands kept their fans waiting. When that happened, the feeling of excitement drained out of her and left her empty.

For that reason, Natalia insisted that Cain appear on time, capture the audience when their enthusiasm was at its peak. And it was the reason she never used an opening act.

The radio DJ walked onto the stage, coming out from the wings. He stood in front of the curtain, which remained closed. Some in the crowd jumped out of their seats and started clapping.

"Thank you, thank you. My name is Big Mark Mancuso from KOMP, Everything That Rocks in Vegas! Tonight I am here to introduce"—he sucked in a breath and let it out in a roar—"Cain!"

The DJ was sucked offstage as though by some titantic force. Dead silence fell. Natalia could almost hear thousands of rapidly beating hearts, then the beat of a drum sounded, matching the rhythm. The crowd cheered and screamed. The black curtain was still down, but they knew Cain was behind it.

The drumming heartbeat slowed, then came to a halt. The crowd went quiet. A sudden blast of fire shot up from the stage, a wall of flame that leaped from the base of the stage and rose to about twenty feet in the air. The entire front row of concertgoers fell back, screaming in delight, moving away from the heat. The light was so intense that Natalia had to shield her eyes, and she'd known it was coming.

When the flame wall vanished, there was the band. The crowd freaked. A thin layer of smoke began to roll across the floor of the stage, spilling over onto the crowd.

Good, Natalia thought, the smoke is staying low. She had been afraid it might rise up and obscure the band. The special effects crew had assured her they would not let that happen, and so far they were as good as their word.

Now the guitar solo, one of the solos for which Cain was famous. As the music rose in tempo, Cain appeared, rising up through the bottom of the stage on a rotating platform. A huge video screen on a wall behind the stage provided a close-up view of Cain's face so that even the fans watching from the very back of the auditorium could see him.

Cain wore black leather pants with flames running up the sides and black-strapped leather boots. He had on a black T-shirt with the sleeves cut off that read: "God is Dead. Cain Lives!" They'd be doing a brisk business in T-shirt sales after the concert. Natalia made a mental note to see to it that the contest winners each received one.

The band joined in with Cain's guitar playing, and the show continued. Everything was going well. The smoke stayed low, and no one in the front row was coughing. Nothing had caught fire. And because nothing had caught fire, Natalia knew Cain would want to make the flame wall bigger. She'd have to find a politic way to turn down the request. Cain wanted everything to be over-the-top, and unless something got destroyed, he was convinced they weren't working hard enough.

"Sorry," she'd tell him. "Love to, but the insurance company won't cover it."

She was just starting to breathe a little easier when she suddenly realized that the band was playing one song, and Cain was playing something entirely different. The band stopped. Cain kept playing. The guys in the band stared at each other, then scrambled to catch up, coming in halfheartedly. They had been playing the right song. It was Cain who had screwed up. Either that, or he'd done it deliberately to show them who was boss.

After that, things went from bad to worse. The audience grew restive. There were hoots and whistles and jeers. The band was playing mechanically, as if they were windup toys, and what was sad was that it didn't much matter. Cain wasn't paying any attention to them anyway.

Natalia felt like she could vomit. She wanted it all to end, wondered for a moment if she should tell them to just bring down the curtain. That would only cause trouble. There would be fans who wanted their money back. She gritted her teeth and waited it out.

Two hours later, Cain was wrapping up the show.

No one left. The clapping and stamping started. Cain's hard-core fans wanted an encore. Natalia couldn't imagine why. Maybe they thought it was bound to get better.

Cain and the band were taking a five-minute break to get drinks and towel off, and after that they would return to play one of Cain's most popular songs. Except the band didn't return. Cain came out alone.

Natalia got on her mike, yelling for the stage manager, demanding to know what the hell was going on.

"There was some sort of trouble," the manager said. "Cain told the band to . . . well, you know."

Natalia put her head in her hands. The audience was uneasy, restive. They didn't know what was going on. Cain played a few chords. The song—a fast, hard-driving, metal number—sounded weak and lame without the band behind it.

Cain fumbled through the opening. The crowd began to hoot and jeer and clap—not in a good way. Some started throwing things on the stage at Cain, water bottles, ice, anything. Others in the crowd got angry and started shouting for them to shut up, and to stop throwing stuff on the front row. Some kids began pushing and shoving each other.

And then a grim voice came over her earphone.

"We got trouble!"

Chapter 12

*N*atalia looked down from her vantage point to see the crowd go insane. Three thousand kids suddenly started, for no reason, to beat the shit out of one another. Some of the kids surged toward the stage, began to climb up on it. Others were swarming into the bleachers and trying to break up the seats.

Natalia called for all available security to come to the stage. Her first thought was to protect Cain. She was about to order him to stop playing and get the hell out of there, then she realized pulling the plug might make the crowd even wilder. Natalia decided to clear the venue. This was officially out of control, a full-scale riot.

"Bring up the houselights!" she ordered.

The security detail was wading through kids, pulling out the worst offenders, but the frenzy was escalating. Natalia saw a girl get punched in the face. She remembered her own terrible experience when she'd been knocked unconscious. Her stomach churned.

Natalia was baffled. Nothing like this had ever happened before. The crowds had been noisy and done some dancing at Cain's concerts, but things had never spun out of control. And the riot had happened so fast, so unexpectedly, like someone had flipped a switch and made everyone go stupid.

Cain continued to play. His face was strained and tense. He didn't seem to know what else to do. Security guards were wrestling kids practically right in front of him. He backed up to keep clear of the melee and still kept playing. Natalia put in a call to the police.

"Send an army," she said.

If security did manage to herd the crowd outside, the rioting would spill out onto the street. Natalia had a feeling the cops were going to earn their pay this evening. A large donation to the local government and the policemen's pension fund would be in order.

Natalia could do nothing more except watch. Cops came flooding into the venue. The music stopped. Cain must have realized no one was listening to him. He stood onstage, the guitar in his hand, and he looked as though he were going to cry.

"Mike!" Natalia yelled into her radio. "Close the curtain! And get Cain off the stage and back into his dressing room!"

But before the curtain could come down, Cain gave a cry. "Hey! Stop! Don't you—"

He flung down his guitar and lurched forward. He was staring and pointing at her.

Natalia could hear the roadies shouting at each other over the radio. Then she felt what she thought was an earthquake. The scaffolding shook beneath her feet.

She looked down.

"What the—"

* * *

Matthew didn't know much about rock music. He'd never attended a single rock concert. But even he didn't need Woof's ghost to tell him he was watching a disaster. Matthew took a pull from his flask, secreted it back into his pocket. Anything to get through this. Matthew glanced at the contest winners. At least they were having fun.

"It's the start of the tour," he heard the kid with the Rolex say knowledgeably. "There are always a few glitches."

Fortunately, the stage manager had the presence of mind to hustle the kids into the green room before Cain came offstage and got into a screaming, swearing match with his band.

The band guys told Cain what he could do with himself and walked off. Cain glared after them, then picked up his guitar and walked back onstage alone. He began to play by himself. The audience didn't like it. The fans began to stomp their feet and jeer, and suddenly all hell broke loose.

Matthew didn't see how it started. Someone pushed someone who pushed someone else who lashed out with a fist and before you could say "Altamont," the fans were kicking, punching, and seemingly trying to kill each other.

"Damnation!" Woof swore.

The word seemed suitable. The houselights came on, and Matthew had a sudden vision of Dante's Inferno, demonic figures writhing in torment in Hell's pit. He'd seen mobs before, from the furious crowds storming the Bastille in Paris to soccer fans rampaging through the streets of Rome. He shook his head in sorrow and disgust and took another drink from his flask. He wondered, suddenly, where Natalia was. The last he'd seen of her, she'd gone backstage. He put his flask in his pocket and walked over to the stage manager, who was in radio contact with Natalia, intending to ask him where she was.

The stage manager was shouting into his radio and couldn't be bothered with Matthew. He waved him silent.

Cain had quit singing, mainly because no one was listening. He was staring, transfixed, at the melee. The stage manager yelled at Cain to start playing again, to try to calm everyone down. Then some fans started to climb up on the stage, and the manager began yelling at Cain to get the hell out of there.

Cain gave a wild cry.

"Natalia!" he screamed. "Look out!"

Throwing down his guitar, he ran toward the front of the stage.

"Stop him!" yelled the manager, and a couple of the stagehands dashed off in pursuit.

"Natalia! Where is she?" Matthew shouted, trying to make himself heard over the chaos.

Woof had gone quite pale, if that was possible for a ghost. He pointed a shaking finger. "Out there! On top of the scaffolding!"

Matthew could see Natalia now. She was perched on top of the scaffold at least fifteen feet above the floor. Kids were surging around the scaffolding, which looked as if it was made out of Tinkertoys. It had begun to rock perilously.

Cain was trying to get to her. The stage manager sent the stagehands to get him. They hustled him—protesting and fighting—offstage.

Matthew started to leave the wings, to try to reach her, and was nearly brained when the heavy curtain came thundering down almost on top of him. He fought his way out of the smothering fabric and came out onstage. He stared out at the scaffolding, which was rocking back and forth.

"Woof! How can I reach her?" he demanded.

"You're the angel!" Woof yelled back. "Don't you have wings or something?"

"Do you see any wings?" Matthew cried furiously.

Woof glared at him, then said, "This way!" He set off at a lope and guided Matthew through the tangle of ropes and sets and curtains to stairs that led off the stage and down into the aisles.

Matthew ran down the stairs and onto the floor of the theater. It was like falling into an ocean whipped by storm winds, except he had fallen into an ocean of humans gone insane. He floundered his way through the pushing, swearing, screaming, shoving, clawing, spitting mob. He was more than once swept off his feet. He lost sight of Natalia and had no idea where he was. He could see nothing but contorted faces, flailing bodies, and flying fists. Right when Woof might have been useful, the ghost had vanished.

Suddenly the crowd in front of Matthew parted, rather like the Red Sea at the coming of Moses. Kids ceased fighting and began climbing over the seats. Matthew wondered what had happened, then he realized they were trying to get away from one of the biggest guys Matthew had ever seen. The guy must have been six-foot-five and weighed three hundred pounds and none of that was flab. He wore the uniform of a security guard. Scowling, he came charging straight at Matthew, who was one of the few left in the vicinity.

Matthew grabbed his security pass and waved it at the guy.

"Kimo!" he shouted, reading the guy's name off a plastic tag. "They're in trouble." He pointed at the rocking scaffolding.

Kimo turned to look. Fortunately, the big man had brains as well as brawn. He didn't stop to ask questions. He turned around, began heading in that direction, wading through the crowd, with Matthew close on his heels.

They made good time. When people didn't get out of Kimo's way, he coolly picked them up and tossed them aside. Matthew was close enough now that he could see a group of kids swarming beneath the scaffolding, deliberately trying to bring it down. Natalia and another person were trapped on the platform high above them. A narrow metal-rung ladder led off the platform, but with the way it was swaying and rocking, climbing down would be perilous.

Natalia's face was pale. She was scared, but she wasn't panicking. An agonized Woof hovered near her, helpless to protect her. Natalia's hands gripped the railing, trying to keep her balance as the scaffolding rocked back and forth. She was yelling down at the kids to stop before they killed someone. Her voice was swallowed up by the shrieks and cries, however. No one could hear her. Matthew wondered if the kids even knew anyone was up there.

Kimo continued plowing through the mob, hurling bodies left and right. When they reached the scaffolding, Kimo gave a great, full-chested roar, a bellow that seemed to shake the walls. The kids turned around, saw Kimo coming, his broad face twisted in scowling rage. The kids fell over themselves trying to get away. Kimo caught a few by the scruff of their necks and helped them along.

The mob had been dispersed, but the scaffolding continued to shake. Matthew plunged into the shadows beneath it, and there he saw an astounding sight, like something out of one of his more demented nightmares.

Two strange-looking beings, with ugly, wizened bodies and fiery red eyes, had hold of one of the legs of the scaffolding and appeared to be dismantling it, tearing it apart with their bare hands. The scaffolding was not as flimsy as it had first seemed to Matthew. The intricate construct of steel poles, pins, and rods was solid, well built. But the construct could not withstand the superhuman strength of the two who were ripping the scaffolding apart, prying out bolts and pins, tearing down the steel poles.

Matthew skidded to a standstill. Unable to believe what he was seeing, he closed his eyes, opened them again, and the demonic creatures were gone. He was looking instead at two men—big guys, wearing Cain T-shirts and blue jeans.

He yelled, "Hey!" and lunged toward them.

The two guys turned at his shout. They stared at him wide-eyed, apparently as wildly amazed to see him as he had been to see them. Whoever they were, they bolted at the sight of him and vanished into the mob.

He looked up above. The scaffolding was sagging perilously, about ready to collapse with him underneath it. He didn't give a damn about himself. The whole damn theater could fall down on top of him, and he might end up with a throbbing headache. His concern was for Natalia.

Matthew grabbed hold of Kimo's arm and pointed. Again, Kimo didn't ask questions. He saw the danger and knew what Matthew was silently asking of him. The big man grabbed hold of the collapsing leg, wrapped his arms around it, stabilizing it at least temporarily.

Matthew raced out from under and looked up at Natalia.

"It's going to collapse!" he shouted. "You have to come down!"

Natalia was white-faced, but still in control. She turned to the guy who was up there with her. They seemed locked in a brief argument, but then she shoved him bodily toward the ladder. The guy came down fast, hand over hand, obviously accustomed to racing up and down scaffolding.

The platform gave a lurch. Natalia gasped and held on. She was terrified of staying, but even more terrified of climbing down the ladder.

Kimo was still holding on to the scaffolding. His face had gone red with the exertion, his big shoulders trembled.

"I can't hold it much longer!" Kimo gasped.

"Natalia!" Matthew shouted, keeping his tone calm, level. "You have to climb down now." He positioned himself at the bottom of the ladder. "Look at me! Don't look at anything else."

Woof was beside her, hovering around her, urging her to climb the ladder. Natalia bit her lip. Then, drawing in a deep breath, keeping her gaze fixed on Matthew, she put her foot on the first rung, and started to climb down. She was about halfway down when Kimo gave a bellow. The scaffolding began to collapse. He let go and dove for cover. Natalia screamed. She lost her hold and fell.

Matthew caught her and dragged her to the floor, shielding her with his body as the scaffolding came crashing down all around them.

Matthew grunted as he felt something hit him on the back and something else smash into his head. He didn't think much about it. He was afraid he was crushing Natalia, and he tried to shift his weight off her as much as possible.

A dust-choked calm settled over the theater. Matthew waited a few seconds until things quit falling on top of him, then he cautiously raised his head.

He breathed a sigh of relief. The platform had canted sideways, with the result that most of the scaffolding, the platform, and the sound equipment had come crashing down into the middle of a section of seats off to his left. He would have had some explaining to do if it had fallen down on top of him. He hoped to heaven no one had been sitting in those seats.

He picked up a couple of steel poles and shoved them aside, then knelt to see to Natalia.

"Don't move," he cautioned, bending over her.

"I'm okay," she said, ignoring his warning and sitting up. "No, really, I am. Nothing hurts. No blood. No broken bones. Are you all right?" she asked worriedly.

"Fine," said Matthew, giving her a reassuring smile. "Just a little shaken up, that's all."

"Is anyone else hurt?" Natalia asked anxiously. She clutched at Matthew in desperation. "Tell me no one else is hurt!"

A couple of aisles over, Kimo was rising up out of the rubble, calmly tossing aside steel poles and brushing off the dust. The soundman came crawling out from a row of seats. He was bleeding from a cut on the head, but otherwise seemed okay. Woof sat slumped in a seat. He had gone quite white and was mopping his face with his bandanna. The ghost looked worse than any of the living.

Guards and police were arriving on the scene, shoving aside pieces of the scaffolding and peering underneath it, calling out to see if anyone was under there, if anyone needed help. Paramedics with their equipment came charging down the aisles.

Matthew tried to keep Natalia from standing up until the paramedics checked her out. She insisted she was okay, however. Seeing he couldn't stop her, he assisted her to her feet.

"Take it easy," he cautioned. "Here, you're shivering. Put on my jacket."

She tried several times to put her arm in a sleeve, but she was shaking so that she kept missing. Finally, Matthew caught hold of her hand, thrust it into a sleeve. He was starting to button it, when she suddenly flung her arms around him and buried her face in his chest.

"You saved my life!" Natalia said in muffled tones.

He could feel her trembling, and he held her close, patting her back, stroking her hair, doing whatever he could to soothe her.

"Cain saw you were in danger," said Matthew. "And see that big guy over there? His name's Kimo. He saved you."

"But you threw yourself on top of me." Natalia lifted her head, looked up at him with frightened eyes. "You could have been killed!"

"Yeah, right," Woof muttered, but he grinned as he said it. He continued mopping his face. "You did good, Angel Boy. Saved my little girl. I owe you big-time."

"I remember the time when I was in the mosh pit," Natalia was saying, shivering, "and Cain—"

She gave a gasp and pulled away from Matthew.

"My God! Cain! I'd forgotten about him. Is he safe?"

"Don't worry about that jerk," Woof told her. "This was his fault. He damn near got us all killed. Asshole."

Matthew wondered about that. He might have agreed with Woof, except that Matthew kept seeing, quite vividly, those two demonic figures beneath the scaffolding. Had he really seen demons or had it all been a delusion—his bourbon-soaked mind playing tricks on him. He had been thinking of the pits of Hell only moments before. Perhaps he'd projected the image onto the horrible scene in front of him. Whether or not those two men were demons from Hell or demons who crawled out of his bourbon bottle, Matthew was in no doubt about one thing—the two had deliberately sabotaged the scaffolding.

"I have to find out about Cain! Where's my phone?" Natalia fumbled in her pocket. Her phone was not there. She glanced confusedly about the floor.

"Cain's safe," Matthew assured her. "I saw the stage-hands hustle him backstage. Same with those kids, the contest winners. They're okay, too."

"Thank God!" Natalia whispered. Then she shuddered and covered her face with her hands. "Oh, God! This is awful!"

"I know," Matthew murmured, taking hold of her again, drawing her close. "You're safe now. It's all over. Try not to think about it."

"I wish I could!" she said miserably. "But that's not possible. I have to . . . call . . . someone . . . I can't find my phone. Where's my phone?" She started to pull away.

"You don't have to call anyone or do anything now," Matthew said firmly, keeping hold of her. "You've had a shock. You need to take care of yourself. Time enough for all that later."

But even as he said those comforting words, he saw a couple of policemen talking to Kimo. The big man pointed to where the scaffolding had been standing, telling what he'd seen. Matthew wondered what Kimo was saying to them.

"I guess you're right," Natalia said, sighing.

She sagged against him, rested her head against his chest. He held on to her, continued to comfort her.

A policeman came toward them, climbing over the wreckage. "You two okay? There's an ambulance waiting."

"You should have a doctor check you out," Matthew said to Natalia.

She shook her head, nestled closer against him. "No, just hold me a moment or two longer. Then I do have to go to work. Ambulances!" Natalia shuddered. "I hope no one got hurt! Do you think anyone did?"

"I don't know," Matthew answered somberly. "It was pretty chaotic there for a while."

"Did anyone get hurt, officer?" Natalia asked faintly. "I'm Natalia Ashley. I'm Cain's manager."

The policeman shook his head. "Some bruises, a twisted ankle, a few fat lips, and a concussion, but so far as I know, that's the extent of the injuries. Fortunately, no one was in those seats when that scaffolding came down. Your security team did a good job of clearing everyone out before the riot got too far out of hand."

"Thank goodness!" Natalia breathed.

"Ms. Ashley," said the policeman deferentially, "I'm going to need a statement. I'd also like to speak to Mr. Cain . . ."

"Of course." Natalia drew away from Matthew. "You should go to bed," she advised him. "Get some sleep."

"What about you?" he asked.

Natalia sighed bleakly. "I'm in for a long night."

Leaning near him, she kissed him on the cheek.

"Thank you, Matthew Gallow," she said softly, looking at him with soft, tear-shimmering eyes.

She joined the policeman, and the two walked down the aisle, heading backstage. At that moment, something buzzed at Matthew's feet. Natalia's phone. Matthew stepped on it, crushed it. The buzzing ceased.

Woof chuckled. "You're not half-bad, Angel Boy."

The ghost heaved himself to his feet. Looking around, he shook his head in disgust. "Too damn many cops. I'm heading over to the bus, maybe smoke a joint or two with the guys in the band, calm my shattered nerves. Too much excitement for an old dude like me. Why don't you come along, Angel Boy?"

"Stop calling me that!" Matthew said. He would have said more, but at that moment a policeman approached them, and Woof departed with precipitous haste.

"Excuse me, Mr. Gallow," said the policeman, after taking down his name, "that gentleman over there says you were under the scaffolding with him. Could I ask you what you saw, sir?"

"It was all very confusing," said Matthew vaguely. "Kids flailing about underneath—"

"According to that security guard, he saw two adult

males under the scaffolding. It looked to him as if they were deliberately ripping it apart. Did you see anything like that?"

"I'm not sure. There were lots of people under the scaffolding," Matthew answered with an apologetic smile. "Sorry I can't be of more help."

"Could you describe anyone?"

Red eyes, slavering mouths, fangs, clawed hands and feet, batlike wings, misshapen, twisted bodies . . .

Matthew shook his head. If he told them what he'd seen—or what he'd imagined he'd seen—he'd be the one they locked up.

"If you remember anything more, give us a call," said the policeman, and he walked off.

Matthew stood a moment, brooding, then, catching sight of Kimo, he walked over to have a talk with the big man.

"I want to thank you for what you did, Mr. uh . . . I didn't catch your last name."

"Kimo," said the big man. He had a large lump on his forehead and a jagged cut on his arm, but he was otherwise all right. "Everyone calls me Kimo."

Matthew held out his hand. "Thank you. You saved my life and Ms. Ashley's."

Kimo shrugged his massive shoulders in embarrassment. His face went red. He shook Matthew's hand, engulfing it in a massive fist.

"It was nothin'. Glad I could help. Hell of a dustup, wasn't it?" Kimo added, obviously trying to shift the subject away from his heroics.

"You could say that," Matthew answered wryly. "The cop asked me what happened under the scaffolding. He said you told them you saw two guys—"

"Yeah," Kimo nodded his head. "Two guys takin' the damn scaffolding apart." His face scrunched up in a scowl.

"I know this sounds crazy, but they looked to me like two of Cain's roadies!"

"Two of Cain's who?" Matthew asked.

"Roadies. You know. Guys who work for the band. They all wear those Cain T-shirts."

Kimo was right, Matthew realized. He was trying to remember where he'd seen those T-shirts before. Several of the guys backstage were wearing them.

"Doesn't make much sense, does it?" Kimo said.

Matthew had to admit it didn't.

"Still," Kimo went on, with another shrug, "I guess some lunatic could get his hands on one of those T-shirts if he wanted to. Coulda been anybody, really. People are fucked up, you know."

"Yeah, I know," Matthew agreed. "Who are these guys? These 'roadies'?"

"Local guys hired by the band to handle the lights, the props, the sound—all that sort of thing. Maybe one of them has a grudge against Cain."

"So you think this was local?" Matthew asked.

"Yeah," said Kimo, then he shrugged again. "But what do I know?"

Matthew felt relieved. They were leaving Vegas in the morning. Hopefully, he was leaving behind the demons, as well. All his demons.

"I'm sure Ms. Ashley will want to thank you, Kimo. I told her what you did. You should stop by, see her before we go."

"Aw, it was nothin'," Kimo muttered, flushing again. He looked pleased, however. "I'm just glad everyone's okay."

Matthew stood in the aisles, wondering what to do with himself. The police were swarming over the crime scene, stretching yellow tape around the seats. The theater manager was trailing anxiously after them, asking how long this would take, saying they had another show tomorrow night.

Matthew thought about going backstage to find Natalia. Then he reflected that she would probably be with Cain, and Matthew didn't particularly relish the idea of being around the "asshole" tonight.

He put his hand in his pocket, reaching for his flask. He took hold of it, then let go. Instead, he pulled out his cell phone. He flipped the phone open, pressed the key for "Contacts."

There was the number Archangel William had given him.

Matthew started to dial, then abruptly hit "End."

What would he say? That he'd seen two demons ripping apart the scaffolding at a rock concert?

Yeah, right.

Matthew slipped the phone back in his pocket and walked up the aisle, heading for the exit.

He was worn-out, physically and emotionally drained. And, back on the bus, a bottle of Jim Beam was calling his name.

Chapter 13

Still shaken, shivering from the cold, Natalia hugged Matthew's jacket around her as she made her way backstage. Someone—she didn't know who—thrust a bottle of cold water into her hand. She took a moment to sit down on a coil of rope, drink the water gratefully, and calm herself. The first order of business was to put the frightening events out of her mind. She didn't have time to deal with the trauma now. Save that for later, when she could fall apart in private.

Instead, she concentrated on Matthew, on how wonderful he had been standing below that shaking scaffolding, holding his hands out to her, urging her to come down, his voice calm and reassuring, catching her when she fell. She recalled the warmth of his embrace, how safe and secure she had felt in his arms. He'd been kind, gentle, reassuring. She wished she was back there in his arms, wished he was holding her now, protecting her from the unpleasantness that lay ahead.

"No such luck." She sighed as she rose to her feet and started off to deal with the situation.

This was her job, after all. This was what she'd signed up for—not only the good, but also the bad and the ugly. This definitely fell in the latter two categories. She thought wearily of everything she had to do: phoning Cain's attorney, phoning the press agent, phoning hospitals to check on the injured . . .

Which reminded her that the first thing she needed to do was find a phone!

She made her way back to the dressing-room area. The guys in the band had already gone back to the bus. One of the stagehands told her he thought Cain was still here. She was walking down the hall, heading toward his dressing room, when she saw the door open. To her astonishment, two roadies walked out. She was startled and troubled to note that they were the same two who'd gone with him into the bathroom while on the road.

"Hey, you guys shouldn't be back here," Natalia said sternly, approaching the two. "Don't you have jobs to do?"

The two halted.

"Yes, ma'am," said one. "We just wanted to check on Cain."

"Make sure he was okay, ma'am," added the other. "See if there was anything he needed."

Such as what? Dope? Natalia thought, but didn't say. She didn't like these two guys, didn't like the way they were always hanging around Cain. She would have liked to fire them, but she hadn't caught them doing anything wrong, and the last thing she needed at the moment was trouble with their union.

"Thank you," she said coldly. "Now get back to work. We have to be packed up and ready to leave tomorrow morning for San Francisco."

"Yes, ma'am," said the two, and they went on their way, though she noted they took their time about it.

She would have liked to say something to Cain about it, but now was not the time. He would be extremely upset over what had happened, rattled and unnerved. He would blame himself. Perhaps he might want to cancel the rest of the tour! She couldn't allow that. She would need to be strong, reassuring, restore his self-confidence. This was a onetime thing, an aberration, she would tell him.

Natalia paused to gather up her courage before she went inside. She knocked, but there was no answer. Frightened, she thrust open the door.

"Cain?" she called as she hurried inside.

He'd apparently just come from the shower, for his hair was still dripping wet, and he had a twisted-up towel around his neck. He was wearing a pair of skinny black jeans.

"Hey, Nat," he said, calmly toweling his hair. He grinned at her shamefacedly. "Kind of a bust tonight, wasn't it?"

Natalia gawked at him, speechless.

"Where are the kids?" he asked. "The ones who won the contest? And the pizzas? You know I'm always starving after a show. How did it look from out front? Were the flames tall enough? Was there video?"

He sat down in the chair in front of the mirror, began to comb out his hair.

Natalia sputtered a moment before she could find her voice.

"Yes, the flames were tall enough. Yes, there's video for you to watch. Did you know there was a fuckin' riot?" she yelled at him. "Did you know the scaffolding came crashing down with me on it? People could have been killed! I could have been killed!"

Cain shrugged. "The boys told me you were okay and that no one was seriously hurt. I checked on that, called the police myself. Aren't you proud of me? The boys told me it was a real rager."

Natalia felt her legs give way. She sank down in the nearest chair. Here she'd been worried that he'd be upset. Now she was the one who was upset because he wasn't. She was about to yell at him again when it occurred to her he might be putting on an act, covering up his real feelings, perhaps for her sake. She decided just to go along with him.

"You're going to leave by the back way," she told him wearily. "I don't want you anywhere near the press. Not until I've had a chance to write up a formal statement about how sorry you are, etc."

"Am I?" Cain asked.

"Are you what?"

"Sorry. The riot will be headline news in the morning—"

"The wrong sort of headline!" Natalia lost her cool and began raving. "Parents won't let kids go to a show where they might get trampled to death! There will be cancellations, not to mention lawsuits. Our insurance and security costs will go—"

"—through the stratosphere—" Cain finished. "I know. I understand. Look, Nat, just tell the press we've tightened security and we're taking steps to make sure nothing like this will happen again."

"And what steps would those be?" Natalia asked sarcastically.

"I had an idea. If we bring in that priest-fellow you hired to do the fake exorcism, the spectacle would keep the fans entertained, stop them from beating up on each other." His reflection smiled at her from the mirror.

Natalia stared at him in amazement.

"You mean . . . now you *want* Father Gallow to go on with the act?"

"I've got an absolutely radical idea about how to play this with him. You get him all rehearsed in time for the next show, then leave everything to me."

"I . . . I . . ." Natalia stopped, then started over. "What made you change your mind?"

Cain didn't answer. He turned away, tossed the comb on the dressing table, and, grabbing a shirt, pulled it over his head.

"Cain, did you hear me?" Natalia asked.

He emerged from the shirt, blinked. "No, did you say something?"

"Yes. What made you change your mind about the exorcism?"

He shrugged. "Like I said," he told her, tugging down the shirt, "I had this idea about how to work it."

She knew there was more to it than this. She couldn't imagine what, though, and since he was doing what she wanted, she let it drop.

"Fine," she said. "Matthew and I will go over the act with you tomorrow—"

Cain shook back his wet hair. "You don't need me. I'm going to the green room. Have the contest kids meet me there. And bring the pizzas. Pepperoni and mushroom with extra cheese."

He started to walk past her. Natalia stopped him. Grabbing his arms, she forced him to face her, look her in the eye. He was pale and tense. His muscles twitched nervously. This show of bravado was all an act. Underneath that brazen exterior was a frightened little boy.

"Cain," said Natalia gently, "I can send the kids home. In fact, it would probably be better if I did . . . You go get some sleep."

He gave her a phony smile and shook her off. Pulling out his cell phone, he showed her the time. "It's not even eleven o'clock yet. I couldn't sleep. Too hyper. And I have to eat. We don't want to disappoint these kids, after all. Just an hour, Nat. I'll eat, schmooze with the kids, drink a beer or two, that'll be it. An early night."

Natalia was still dubious, but she reflected that sending him off to meet with the contest winners might be a good idea after all. The kids would keep Cain occupied, and she'd post security guards to make sure there was no more trouble.

"Okay," Natalia said and, on impulse, she gave him a hug. "I'm glad you're all right."

Cain stiffened in her embrace, then he suddenly relaxed and hugged her back, hugged her tight.

"I was really worried about you, Nat," he said, and his voice trembled. "When I saw you up there, saw the scaffolding shaking . . ."

She felt him shudder.

Natalia patted him on the back. "It's okay. Everything's okay. Cain." She added, after a moment, "I can't breathe . . ."

"Sorry." He let go.

Natalia sucked in air, then said, "Could I borrow your cell phone? I lost mine, and I need to make some calls."

"Lawyers." Cain grimaced. "Sure." He handed over his iPhone.

Natalia escorted him to the green room, where she told the crew to bring in pizzas with beer for Cain and Cokes for the kids. She made certain the kids had all called their parents, who must have heard about the riot, to tell them they were all right. Rolex Kid's mother wanted him home immediately, but he pleaded and begged and at last received permission to stay. He grinned as he hung up. Apparently he was accustomed to getting his own way.

Natalia hung around the green room for a moment to

make sure Cain was all right. He seemed fine. He ate pizza and showed the kids his guitars and his tattoos and his "battle" wounds as he liked to call them, though his scars weren't from any battle but from stupid things he had done, like falling through a plate-glass window when he was drunk, trying to walk on hot coals, messing around with his pet alligators.

The kids were having a great time. Cain was on his best behavior, not drinking to excess. Security was on hand. Natalia decided she could leave them for a little while, go make her phone calls.

"The limo will be here to pick you up in an hour," Natalia told the kids, then she went back to Cain's dressing room. Her first order of business was to send for Kimo, the security guard. She thanked him gratefully and was amused to see the big guy blush.

"Would you like a job with the band?" she asked him on impulse, the idea coming to her suddenly. "Cain needs a personal bodyguard. Your duties would be—"

"I'll take the job, ma'am," he said at once.

"I haven't told you your salary—"

"Whatever you pay me will be fine, ma'am," he said.

She'd have to find room for him, but she was thinking of hiring another bus anyway. She'd move Kimo into the third bus, along with the roadies. After Kimo left, a big grin on his face, she locked herself in Cain's dressing room and went to work.

She was about to dial Mr. Parker's number when she noticed that Cain had received several voice mails. Cain rarely bothered answering voice mail. She was always all over him about that. Sometimes calls came in from important people or from his agent, wanting to set up appearances on *The Tonight Show* or Letterman. He needed to return these calls or else have her return them for him. She usually went through his calls with him, but in the hassle of getting the show going, she'd forgotten. She glanced at the list of callers. Two from his agent. Several listed as "Unknown." One name, the most recent caller, jumped out at her.

Burl.

An unusual name. Natalia had heard it before. She tried to think where. Of course. One of those roadies was named Burl. She frowned down at the name. What was he doing calling Cain? Especially right after the concert . . .

Cain had answered that particular voice mail, but he hadn't bothered to delete it.

Natalia frowned down at the name. She hated like hell to be spying on Cain. Then the thought occurred to her that if Burl was offering to supply Cain with drugs, she'd have the excuse she needed to fire his ass.

Cain's welfare was her responsibility.

She played the voice mail message.

"Cain, this is Burl. The situation's changed. We need to keep this Father Gallow around. Tell Natalia you've decided that you want him in the show. I'll explain later."

Natalia stared blankly at the phone. She couldn't believe it. She played the message again, and it said the same thing the second time that it had the first.

So that's why Cain wanted to put Father Gallow in the act—because Burl the Roadie told him to!

Did that make any kind of sense?

Bewildered, Natalia could do nothing for long moments except stare dazedly at the phone, as though it might be able to offer an explanation. When the phone suddenly rang—Cain's ringtone was set to the creepy theme song from the movie *Halloween*—Natalia nearly leaped through the ceiling.

She let the call go to voice mail and pondered what to do. Confront Cain? She'd have to admit to spying on him, and while ordinarily he would have brushed that off, she had the feeling he would get really angry about this.

Something strange was going on between him and these two roadies. She had no idea what it could be. Blackmail? That's what it sounded like. But what did that have to do with Matthew Gallow? Was he in on it? But how could that be? She'd hired those two roadies months ago, long before she'd ever heard of Father Gallow.

Confused notions such as these swirled about in her admittedly shell-shocked brain. She finally realized she'd been sitting here for thirty minutes, wasting time speculating on this bizarre mystery when she had far more urgent and important work to do.

I won't ask Cain, Natalia decided. I won't upset him. But I will ask Matthew.

Once she'd made that decision, she put in a call to Cain's attorney to find out just how much trouble they were in.

Chapter 14

"What do you think of the special effects?" Natalia asked.

She and Matthew had spent the past three hours working on his act. They were in the Fillmore Auditorium in San Francisco. A week had passed since the disastrous show in Las Vegas. They'd been on the road for a day and in San Francisco for the rest, and during that time, Natalia and Cain's lawyers had managed to move news of the riot from screaming headlines on the front pages of the nation's newspapers to a couple of columns in the Entertainment section.

Fortunately, no one had been seriously injured. Cain had made a very contrite and humble public apology. Natalia had assured the fans that they were hiring extra security and that they were changing the act, dropping mysterious hints about what they had planned. Some people had demanded refunds, but any tickets people turned in were immediately snapped up. Cain had kept a low profile, staying on the bus and playing video games and watching the History Channel.

Natalia and her new phone had seemed permanently joined together. She even slept with her Bluetooth headpiece in her ear. Matthew had lounged about on the bus, chatting with Al, watching the country roll by, or drinking Snapple mixed with bourbon (when Natalia wasn't looking) and listening to Woof's tales of life on the road during the sixties. Whenever Matthew had found himself getting too interested in what the ghost of the old hippie had to say, he had gone off to lie down in his bunk.

Sometimes he and Natalia had found a few moments together to talk, usually while she was taking a break to eat something. He enjoyed these moments. She was warm, exciting, funny, unpredictable, volatile—alive. And she made him feel alive. Very much alive. He'd find himself lying in his bunk, imagining what it would be like to take her in his arms, kiss her, caress her breasts, feel her legs wrap around his . . . At such times, he was glad there was a shower on the bus.

He knew, guessed, or hoped Natalia was starting to feel the same about him. She liked to walk while she was on the phone ("It's the only exercise I get!" she said to him), and whenever she was on a call, she would pace up and down the narrow aisle on the bus. Every time she passed him, she seemed to somehow brush against him, nudging his shoulder with her hip, touching his leg with hers. Once the bus had given a lurch as Al swerved to avoid a deer, and Natalia had ended up in Matthew's lap.

"Drop in anytime," he had quipped.

"I will," she had promised.

She had lingered another moment, just to let him know she wasn't eager to leave, before getting up to answer another call.

This morning Matthew was preparing for the act's debut tomorrow night. He and Natalia had run through the special effects, with her standing in for Cain. ("Cain's not much for rehearsals," she had said in apology.) At the end, both were exhausted and sweating. Even Woof looked tired, and he hadn't done anything except jump up in alarm when Natalia came a little too close to the flames shooting up out of the stage. Otherwise, he lounged, playing his air guitar or playing pranks on Matthew, such as suddenly shifting a piece of scenery so that Matthew tripped over it or jostling Matthew's elbow so that he dumped Coke in his lap. Apparently Woof wasn't going to let a little inconvenience such as being dead get in the way of his fun.

"The effects are pretty damn amazing," Matthew told Natalia, in answer to her question, and he meant it.

"Just remember to watch for your mark, and don't get too close to the fire," Natalia warned, adding teasingly, "You wouldn't be nearly as handsome with your eyebrows singed off."

"Trust me! I'll remember," Matthew promised, as he wiped the sweat from his forehead. The heat from the flames was intense.

He hesitated a moment, then said, "Natalia, there is something I feel we should talk about."

"Yes, what's that?" Natalia asked absently, typing a text message into her phone.

"When I do an exorcism, I generally win," Matthew said quietly.

Natalia sent her message, then looked up. "Uh?"

"I usually cast out the demon," Matthew explained. "Send it back to where it came from. In this instance, when I try to exorcise the supposed demon from Cain, I lose."

Natalia frowned at him, perhaps trying to figure out

if he was serious or not. Matthew wasn't sure himself. He had not meant to say that, couldn't imagine why he'd brought it up. Someone might think he actually gave a damn.

"Look, we discussed this once, back when I first hired you."

"We did?"

"Well, at least I mentioned it, and you didn't seem to have a problem with it. The fact is, it's all an act," Natalia said. "You do realize that, don't you? All for fun. I mean, I can understand where the churchgoing crowd would demand their money back if the demon chased *you* out of the revival tent. But our audience loves Cain, and they want to see him win."

"In other words," said Matthew slowly, "you want them to believe that Cain is truly possessed by Satan."

"That's what the song's about," Natalia explained patiently. "The name of it is 'Possession.' Of course, it's all a metaphor. Cain isn't saying he's possessed by the devil. He's saying he's possessed by the music, like all creative people are possessed by their art. The song is about how the artist has to make sacrifices for his art. His art is his passion. Cain is saying in the song that like Robert Johnson, he'd go to the crossroads, sell his soul to the devil, all for the music."

Matthew thought it over. She was right. He could understand the metaphor. He could understand Cain. Even envy him. Matthew couldn't remember when he'd felt passionate about anything.

No, wait. That wasn't true. He'd felt passionate about saving Grace from the demon. And what had he done about it? He'd been so damn scared he'd run away to join the circus. Hiding in a world of make-believe. Those flames had been the fires of Hell—not the *Pyroflare 3600: De-*

signed to Produce Astounding Effects and Meet or Exceed All Safety Requirements.

"Matthew," said Natalia abruptly, "can I ask you something?"

"Anything," he said, smiling.

"The night of the riot, Cain loaned me his phone. I couldn't find mine, remember?"

Woof—lying stretched out on a stack of pallets—gave a ghostly snort. Matthew remembered, all right. He remembered crunching her phone underfoot.

"Anyway," Natalia went on, a faint flush staining her cheeks, "while I was using Cain's phone, I noticed he had some voice mail messages. He's really bad about returning calls, and so I was checking them when I noticed there was one from Burl."

She regarded Matthew intently as she said this, as though she expected a reaction.

"Unusual name, Burl," he said, simply because she was waiting for him to say something.

"Yes, it is. That's why I noticed it. Because I know only one Burl, and he's one of the roadies who travels with us."

Natalia cast a sidelong glance into the wings. "He's the one standing by the control panel. He handles the pyrotechnics. The big tough-looking guy in the Cain T-shirt."

Matthew looked where she indicated, and he stiffened. He did know Burl, though not by name. He'd seen him before. Standing beneath the scaffolding.

"So that's Burl," Matthew remarked, eyeing the man who was just a man. No wings, no fangs, no flaming eyes. Just an overweight guy in a Cain T-shirt that had coffee and sweat stains down the front.

"You do know him?" Natalia said.

Matthew shook his head. "I've seen him around, that's all. I didn't know his name or that he was a roadie."

At that moment, almost as if he knew they were talking about him, Burl turned to face them.

"You gonna need to rehearse any more today, Ms. Ashley?" he yelled.

"No, you guys can take a break!" she called out.

Burl and the other man who handled the pyrotechnics waved their hands in response and sauntered off. Matthew had seen the other guy before, too. He had also been standing beneath the scaffolding.

"I didn't know roadies traveled with the band," Matthew said, trying to sound casual. "I thought they were guys you hired locally."

"Most of them are. Burl and John, the pyro guys, travel with us," Natalia answered. "They have special training and licenses for that type of work. Cain insisted we use them, said he didn't want an incident like the tragedy that happened at the Great White show in 2003. I had to agree with him. It made sense."

She eyed Matthew. "You're sure you don't know Burl from somewhere?"

Matthew shook his head. "Sorry. Can't help you."

Natalia sighed. "I was really hoping you would. That's the only way this makes sense! You see, Burl left a message for Cain on his phone. The message was about you. Burl told Cain to bring you into the act. I was wondering if you knew why he would tell Cain to do that?"

Woof bounded up off the pallets and drifted over to stand beside Matthew. "I don't like the sounds of this, Angel Boy. Cain's an asshole, but he's not stupid. And why do I get the feeling you're not telling my little girl the truth? What the heck is going on here?"

Matthew shrugged. "Like I said, I don't know this Burl. Do you really think that's why Cain changed his mind about me? Because this guy Burl told him to?"

Natalia sighed again. "Sounds crazy, doesn't it. Cain won't listen to me—his manager and friend—but he takes the advice of some roadie he's known for maybe a month."

"What did this Burl say about me exactly?" asked Matthew. "Do you remember?"

"It's not like I could forget. I've been playing the message over and over in my head, trying to figure it out. He said: 'The situation's changed. We need to keep this Father Gallow around. Tell Natalia you've decided that you want him in the show.'"

The situation's changed. *What situation? Because I saw that they were demons? But how would they know that? And what difference would it make to them anyway? I'm just a guy, just an actor.*

"You're looking awfully serious," said Natalia. "Should I be worried?"

"I'm mainly confused. I've just been trying to think of some connection between the two of us," Matthew said. "Sorry, I can't come up with anything."

"Oh, well. It's probably nothing. Rock stars do crazy things. They're a superstitious bunch. Like baseball players who won't change their socks if the team's on a winning streak. There was a rock star who wouldn't go onstage if he couldn't have his favorite brand of potato chips to munch on in his dressing room. Maybe Cain thinks this Burl brings him luck or something."

"Possibly," Matthew agreed, and decided it was time to change the subject. "Will I get another chance to rehearse tomorrow? I'm still not feeling really sure of myself."

"We can run through it in the morning if you want, though I don't think you need to. You've got it down cold."

"Cold my ass!" he said with a grin. He was still sweating.

Natalia laughed. "That reminds me. The only stage effect I couldn't figure out how to reproduce was that bit where that girl's head went up in flames yet she didn't get burned. You have to tell me how you did that. Mainly for my own curiosity, of course. I could never convince Cain to go along with it. I know better than even to try. He's in love with his hair. We have to fly in his own personal stylist from LA to wherever we are on the road when he wants it trimmed. Still, just for me, I'd like to know."

Matthew quit grinning. He'd told Natalia back in the motel that the exorcism of the demon from Grace had been real. Of course, Natalia hadn't believed him. He hadn't really expected her to, had he? Yes, to be honest, he had. Or at least, he'd hoped she would. He'd been too damn close to nearly losing his life *and* his soul! He'd been an emotional wreck, and he needed someone to believe in him, if only so he could believe in himself.

They hadn't talked about that night since. He wished she hadn't brought it up.

"I'm sorry, Matthew," said Natalia, seeing his expression darken. "Did I say something wrong? Oh, my God! I did, didn't I! You said the hellfire part was real. It's just . . . hard for me to wrap my mind around that . . ."

"I know," he said. "Let's just call it a trade secret and leave it at that."

Natalia was interested. "Do exorcists have trade secrets like magicians?"

"I'm saying I have *my* secrets," he said. "And I need to keep them. This job won't last forever. Someday I'll be back in the Inn-B-Tween motel in some little town, doing my act for a bunch of true believers sitting on folding chairs . . ."

He heard the bitterness creep in his voice, but he couldn't help it. Someday he would be back on the road. A year from now. Fifty years. A hundred years. Long after Natalia was dead and forgotten by everyone except Matthew Gallow, who still carried around the sound of her laughter in his heart. Natalia would be hard to forget. All the more reason to keep from letting himself fall in love with her. The last thing he needed was another hundred years of pain. He'd been through that more times than he liked to remember. How many graves had he stood on, wept over? Wives, lovers. They'd grown old together. He could pretend to age with the best of them. They'd died, and he'd gone on living and living and living and inside he was dying and dying and dying.

Finally, he'd put a stop to it. He kept women at arm's length, didn't let them get inside him. Some punk girl with gold-flecked eyes wasn't going to cause him to lie awake nights with an aching heart.

Natalia made a soft sound and put her hand on his arm. Her hazel eyes were luminous with sympathy.

"But all that's changed now, Matthew," Natalia told him softly. "You don't have to go back to that life. You're making lots of money on this tour," she continued, talking to him even though her phone was buzzing. "You can buy a house, settle down . . ."

"I will if you will," Matthew quipped to lighten the mood. This had definitely gotten way too serious. "I'm guessing you're making lots of money. How many houses do you own?"

"You're a rat, Matthew Gallow!" Natalia doubled her fist, turned her pat into a punch on his arm. "Here you go and make me feel all sorry for you, then you take a jab at me. Keep your damn secrets then. And I'll have you know I own my very own apartment in LA."

"Yeah, and when was the last time you were in that apartment?" Matthew challenged. "I'll bet you've sublet it."

She stuck out her tongue at him and finally answered

her buzzing phone. "Hello, Al? You're breaking up. What? CNN? I'm nowhere near a TV. I've been roasting myself and the good father in the fires of Hell. Cain? What about him? Al, I can't hear you— Wait. Let me find better reception. I'll call you right back."

She hurried toward the wings, with Woof traipsing along behind her. Someone shut down the stage lights, leaving Matthew alone in semidarkness. The stage door was open, letting in sunlight. He could see Natalia silhouetted in the open doorway, talking on the phone.

He remained onstage, thinking about the act. He should probably be thinking about Burl and the other guy, because that had the potential to be a lot more serious, but Matthew shoved them out of his mind. Thinking about the possibilities made him uncomfortable, and he was feeling overwhelmed as it was. There was so much to remember—his cue, finding his mark, not turning his back to the audience. He'd done his act a thousand times. He could do it in his sleep. He'd never done it under blinding lights with rock music pounding in his ears ("You should wear earplugs," Natalia advised.) and fire shooting up out of the stage and fans screaming ("You'll have your own groupies," Natalia predicted.) and Cain dressed all in black leather, spewing blood from his mouth, and shrieking and gyrating and playing his guitar while Matthew screamed Latin at him. ("So that Latin's the real deal, is it?" Natalia asked, impressed.)

And what about Cain? Was he any sort of actor at all? Did it even really matter? Matthew had the feeling it didn't. Cain would do whatever he damn well pleased, and Matthew would have to go along with it.

I'll need my wits about me, he was thinking, when the stage door slammed shut suddenly, cutting off the daylight and plunging him into darkness. He stood still a moment to allow his eyes time to adjust, then began to grope his way toward the wings. He hoped like hell he didn't fall off the stage into the orchestra pit.

When he blundered into a curtain, he guessed he'd reached the wings. He could see light coming through a crack beneath the stage door. That led him toward the door. He opened it and blinked in the bright sunshine, startled to find it was only midafternoon. It could have been midnight, for all he knew. He'd completely lost track of time.

He left the theater and headed for the bus, planning to have a drink or three and lie down. He was halfway across the parking lot when he realized he'd left his briefcase back on-stage. Considering that the briefcase held the only objects in the world he truly valued, he turned back to retrieve it. He didn't know how to turn on the stage lights, and that meant he had to grope his way backstage again in the dark. He knew his way around a little better now, however, and he propped the door open to provide at least a little sunlight. He found his case where he'd left it by the curtain and was walking back to the door when he heard two men talking.

"I don't see why we can't go through with the original plan and get rid of him," said one in grumbling tones.

"Because the higher-ups think he's onto us. We need to know how much he knows and if he's told anyone. This is too important to screw up."

"Why don't we just shut down operations?"

"We can't. It's gone too far. Our job is to keep an eye on him. The big boys will take it from there."

"Where've we heard *that* before . . ."

The two walked off.

Matthew recognized the voice. It belonged to the roadie called Burl. What were they talking about? Who had they been going to get rid of? Cain? Had they planned to murder him? Was that why they'd sabotaged the scaffolding? No, that didn't make any sense. Cain wasn't on the scaffolding.

They didn't need to kill Cain to "get rid" of Cain, Matthew realized. If people had been killed in the fall of the scaffolding the concert tour would have been canceled.

But now, "plans had changed." The only plan that had changed that Matthew could see was Burl telling Cain to use Matthew in the act. *Because the higher-ups think he's onto us. We need to know how much he knows and if he's told anyone.*

Who were these higher-ups? Record label executives? Promoters?

Matthew didn't know that much about the business. And maybe it didn't have anything to do with the music business anyway. Maybe they were talking about drug deals. That would seem to make more sense. Maybe they'd been supplying Cain with dope, and he'd threatened to turn them in and they were blackmailing him. . . .

Matthew wondered if he should tell Natalia.

Pondering what to do—if anything—he walked back to the bus door and had lifted his hand for the knock that would alert Al, when he was startled to find the door unlocked. He was about to enter, when the door whipped open and Natalia burst out.

"Cain, thank God!" she cried, then she saw it was Matthew. Her face fell. "Oh, it's you. Have you seen Cain?"

"No. What's happened?" Matthew asked, alarmed. "What's the matter?"

"There's been a murder!" She gasped for air and seemed to be having trouble breathing. "And Cain's involved!"

Chapter 15

"Cain! Murdered?" Matthew stared at her. He had the wild thought that the roadies had succeeded.

"Naw," said Woof, who was lounging in the seat next to Al in the front of the bus. "No such luck."

"What happened?" Matthew asked, relieved. "What's going on?"

Natalia didn't answer. Her face was pale, even to her lips, her eyes wide and frightened. She kept hitting redial on her phone or trying to. She continually missed because her hands were shaking.

"Come on, Cain!" she pleaded. "Answer, damn it!"

She ended up talking to his voice mail. Keeping her voice deliberately calm and soothing, she said, "Cain, I know this is bad, but it's not your fault. It's just a stupid coincidence. Call me back so we can talk about it."

Natalia hung up, then ran her hands through her hair and stared bleakly around the parking lot. "That's all I can do." She looked over to the security fence. Reporters were swarming around it, trying to find a way past the guards. One of the reporters spotted her and yelled a question, then they were all shouting.

Natalia grabbed Matthew and dragged him inside the bus. Al shut and locked the door after them.

Natalia's phone buzzed. She looked at the number and, seeing it wasn't Cain, let it go to voice mail.

"Should I call the cops?" Al asked tensely.

"Yes. No!" Natalia said, changing her mind in an instant. "He may have been smoking something or snorting something . . ."

"He wasn't," Al said. "I keep an eye on him when you're not here, you know. And he and I had been working on the bike together. Cain was upset when he rushed past me, not stoned. I wouldn't have let him get on the chopper if he was high. You know that."

Natalia groaned. "I can't believe he rode his chopper! He's probably got thirty paparazzi chasing after him—"

"Not a chance." Al gave a grim chuckle. "Cain peeled out of here on his bike so fast he caught them all napping. He was wearing his helmet with the black face guard, so I'm not sure they even knew it was him. A few jumped in their cars and took off, but he was long gone by that time. Do you have any idea where he'd go?"

"Not a clue," she answered despondently. "He doesn't know this city, and neither do I."

The two stared at each other bleakly.

"Is there anything I can do?" Matthew asked, hoping once more to find out what was going on.

"Say a prayer, Father," Natalia answered.

She saw his startled look, and added, "Sorry. Bad joke."

Slumping down on the couch, she sat there, doing nothing except stare at her phone, willing Cain to call. Al remarked that there might be a news chopper chasing him, and he turned on the small TV in the front of the bus. Woof was stretched out in a chair with his feet on the dashboard. When Matthew finally gave up and looked to the ghost for an explanation, Woof rolled his eyes.

"Stupid, self-absorbed asshole," he muttered. "It's all about him."

"I'll just . . . go take a walk," Matthew said, feeling that he was in the way.

"No, don't," Natalia said quickly. She reached out and grabbed his hand. "The press would be all over you."

Matthew sat down.

"Like it or not, you're one of us now," she added with a lopsided smile.

"So it's all right if you tell me what happened," Matthew said.

"Of course! I'm sorry. Somehow I thought you were here when the news came." Natalia sighed. "As you know, we have this contest running on the local radio stations in every city we play. The winners watch the show from backstage, meet Cain, hang out with him—"

"I remember." Matthew nodded. "The contest winners were there the night of the riot—"

"There must have been a full moon that night," Natalia said grimly. She drew in a deep breath. "Anyway, do you remember one of the contest winners? A seventeen-year-old kid? He was good-looking, a charmer. He wore a Rolex. He even asked me out. He wanted to drink champagne . . ."

She blinked back tears, couldn't go on.

Al picked up the story. "It seems last night this kid murdered his mom, then killed himself."

"Good God!" Matthew exclaimed. He remembered the kid—a handsome young man, easygoing, laughed a lot.

"The mother was a high-powered Federal judge. They found her body, with him lying beside her."

"But what does Cain have to do with it?" Matthew asked.

"The kid was wearing a Cain T-shirt," Al responded.

"It was covered in blood . . ." Natalia put her hand over her mouth, closed her eyes.

Matthew went to the sink and poured her a glass of water. "Drink this."

Natalia gulped it down. "The report was on CNN Breaking News. Cain was watching. He sometimes watches the news channels. He hopes there'll be something about him. When he saw the report, he freaked out. Al was here with him."

"I was up in front, but I could hear the TV," Al said. "Cain always turns it up way too loud. The moment I heard the news about the kid wearing a Cain T-shirt, I figured there'd be trouble, so I started back to see if he was okay. I was afraid he'd be upset, but I didn't expect anything like what happened. He was out of control, raging around his room, screaming, 'Bastards! You bastards! You did this!' Then he stormed off the bus. When I tried to stop him, he knocked me against the sink and ran past me.

"He and I took his chopper out of the trailer today so he could monkey with it. He pretends he knows something about mechanics. Anyway, the chopper was still sitting there. I hadn't put it back yet, and he jumped on it and rode off."

"The reporters are sure to find him!" Natalia groaned. "Or if not him, his chopper. It's custom-made, black with orange flames and 'God is Dead' painted on the side. West Coast Choppers even has a picture of it on their Web site. And if the press finds him, and I'm not there, he'll say something stupid—"

Natalia hit redial on her phone. "I'm sure he blames himself. It's all very tragic, but it's not his fault!"

"The media will claim it is," Woof remarked gloomily. "Always blame rock and roll."

"Although the media will claim it is," Natalia said in an eerie echo. "All because the kid was wearing a Cain T-shirt. He's still not answering! Damn it, why doesn't he call? He must know I'm worried sick!"

"What do you suppose he meant when he said, 'Bastards, you bastards! You did this'?" Matthew asked. "Isn't that an odd thing for him to say?"

"Oh, who knows!" Natalia responded wearily. "Maybe he was talking back to the TV. He does that a lot. It's really annoying trying to watch a movie with him."

She hit redial on her phone again. "Come on," she said softly, "answer . . ."

Cain didn't. She got voice mail again.

Time passed. Al went to Cain's room to flip through the local TV channels to see if anyone had spotted the famous rock star. Natalia walked over to the band bus to let them know what was going on. Matthew glanced toward the back to make sure Al was occupied, then he sat down beside Woof, who was playing air guitar and singing a remarkably depressing song about this being "the end."

"The Doors," Woof said, strumming away on nothingness. "Jim Morrison. You know, I was hoping when I died I'd at least find out what really happened to him. His mysterious death and all that. No one's talking, though."

"So what do you think of this?" Matthew asked.

"Think of what?" Woof looked suddenly wary, as though Matthew was trying to trap him.

"That kid murdering his mother, then killing himself. Wearing a Cain T-shirt."

The girl Matthew had exorcised had been wearing a Cain T-shirt. He'd forgotten all about that until now.

"Oh, that." Woof shrugged. "Demon rock and roll. Leads

kids straight to Hell. Shoot, they were sayin' that clear back in the fifties. My mother wouldn't let me watch Elvis on TV. She termed Pat Boone 'a bad influence' and Ringo Starr was the end of civilization as we know it. All the time, the real crooks were in the White House . . ."

He went back to playing his nonexistent guitar, singing in a nasal twang, "Don't let your babies grow up to be cowboys . . ."

When Natalia came back, she grabbed a sandwich from the tray and ate it standing up. Matthew had the idea she was so preoccupied she wasn't even aware she was eating.

Her phone buzzed. She glanced at it and suddenly leaped on it. She fumbled, nearly dropped it, and then yelled, "Cain! Is that you? Thank God! Al, it's Cain!"

Al came out of the bedroom. He caught Matthew's eye and made a grimace.

"Listen to me, Cain," Natalia was saying. "Yes, I heard what happened. Yes, it's terrible, but it wasn't your fault. You can't blame yourself. Millions of kids are wearing Cain T-shirts this very moment. Kids who are doing good, like those fans of yours who are raising money to send to Darfur. . . ."

She paused, then said, "No, no. I'll handle the press. You don't say a word! Understand? I don't want you making this worse. Where are you?"

Natalia listened, then covered the phone to tell them, "He's feeling better. The chopper broke down. He said to send: 'lawyers, guns, and money.'"

"How about I send the limo instead?" Al suggested dryly. "Where is he?"

"Cain, the limo's coming to get you. We need to know where you are. Well, look around. What do you see?"

There was a pause. "Thanks for that description, but I'm not sure 'a bunch of trees' is going to help. I swear, Cain,

I'm going to microchip you like a dog. Is there someone you can ask? Good. Go ask someone where you are. I'll hold."

She glanced at Matthew. "Cain thinks I'm kidding about the microchip. I'm not." She was back on the phone. "You're where? Did you say 'Land's End'?" She looked at Al. "Someplace called 'Land's End.' Okay, Cain, Al is sending the limo. Just stay there. Don't move! Keep a low profile. Yes, we'll have the bike towed."

She listened again, then said gently, "Are you okay, Cain? Really okay? All right. I'm glad you've thought it through. Love you. Stay put! Don't go anywhere! And don't talk to anyone. Bye."

Al was on the phone with the limo service. Natalia hung up and gave Matthew a bleak smile. "Now the real work begins."

The phone buzzed. She looked at it, sighed deeply, then answered, "Yes, Crandall, I heard the news. I know, it's horrible. No," she added, shocked, "of course, it wasn't Cain's fault! . . ."

Except that Cain believed it was his fault, Matthew thought.

Why else had he run away?

Chapter 16

$\mathcal{A}$ limousine brought Cain back to the bus. He was whisked past the crowd of reporters and photographers and hustled into the bus by Natalia. Once there, he avoided meeting anyone's eye. He walked past them without saying a word, went to his room. Natalia followed him and gently shut the door after.

Natalia talked in low tones. Matthew couldn't hear what she was saying, but she sounded soothing, comforting. He heard Cain mumbling, then what sounded like him breaking down and sobbing. Then the sound of the shower running. Natalia came out of the bedroom.

"I think he's feeling better now," she said.

"Like anyone gives a damn," Woof muttered.

Matthew poured himself a bourbon and went to his bunk.

The bunks were similar to what they used to call sleeping compartments on railroad cars, only these were nicer. Each bunk was curtained off from the others. Each had a reading light and an electric outlet and was roomy enough that its occupant could sit up comfortably. Matthew propped himself against the pillows, drank bourbon, and looked over his notes for the act. An hour or so passed. Natalia was on the phone for most of it. Then there came the sound of chains jingling and heavy boots thumping on the floor.

"Excuse me. I'll call you back. I thought we agreed you were staying in tonight, Cain," Natalia said. "We're playing poker with the band."

Matthew cautiously parted the curtains of his bunk and peered out. Cain was standing nearby, dressed in a black tank top and black jeans, with a spike-studded leather belt and boots.

"Rick Rubin, the producer is in town," Cain told her. "He called me this afternoon. He's having a party. Penthouse suite. Everyone from the industry will be there."

"I don't like it." Natalia frowned. "The last thing we need is a shot of you whooping it up after the tragedy—"

"Like you said, it wasn't my fuckin' fault!" Cain yelled. He was so worked up, he was shaking.

Natalia stared at him, startled. "Don't shout at me. It *wasn't* your fault. Still, it doesn't hurt to keep a low profile."

Cain crossed his arms over his chest and stood glaring at her, a sullen expression on his face.

"Well, mother, can I go?" he asked, sneering.

Natalia sighed. "I'll talk to Rick." She made a phone call, spoke for a few moments, then hung up. "All right. Rick's sworn on a stack of *Peter Frampton Live* albums that there will not be any press. You go straight to the hotel, come straight back. No detours. And no tossing sofas out the window. I'm sending Kimo with you."

"Fine. Right. Whatever," Cain muttered as he stalked out of Matthew's line of sight. "Don't need a goddamned hulking babysitter."

"Don't get drunk or strung out. We still need to go over the exorcism performance sometime!" Natalia called after him. "Preferably before you perform it!"

Cain said something in response that made Matthew grit his teeth to avoid saying something that would have caused trouble. He crawled out of his bunk.

"Would you mind if I broke his jaw?" Matthew asked.

"Be hard for him to sing," Natalia remarked wearily. "I swear sometimes I *do* sound like a mother."

"Call me old-fashioned," Matthew told Natalia, "but no man, not even a rock star, should talk to a woman that way."

"You're old-fashioned," she said, but she smiled at him, then went back to making phone calls.

Matthew sneaked another bourbon, returned to his bunk, and thought about Cain T-shirts, roadies, suicides, and co-incidences. He must have dozed off, because he was awakened by a tapping on the panel by his head.

"You decent?" Natalia asked.

Matthew parted the curtains.

"Yeah," he said, still half-asleep.

"Are you going to stay in there all night?"

"I thought I might, yes," he answered, somewhat groggily. "I'm going over my notes—"

"Oh, forget that for the time being," Natalia said. "Come with me. We'll go out to dinner."

Matthew shook his head. "Thank you, but, really, I'd rather stay in. I'm not much for socializing. Not very good company."

"The Man with No Name," said Natalia. She perched

herself comfortably beside him on the bunk. Her hip nestled against his thigh, shoving him a little to force him to make room for her on the bed. A tingle went through him.

She'd changed her clothes. She was wearing a long silk Chinese tunic, with gold peonies embroidered on it, over black leggings and matching flat ballet shoes.

"Matthew Gallow, mysterious stranger. Come on, Matthew," she pleaded. "This has been a horrible day, and I just want to forget about it. I heard about this great little restaurant that no one knows except the locals. It's called Aperto in Portreo Hill and it has wonderful Italian food. Dinner will be my treat. Think of it as my 'Welcome to the Nuthouse' dinner. You have to eat . . . You can't live on bourbon."

She plucked the empty glass out of his hand and set it on the floor. Then she bent over him. He could see the curve of her breasts under silk and feel their softness press against his chest. Her body was warm. She was wearing an exotic perfume that smelled fresh, clean, like a Tuscan hillside in March.

"It's the boss talking," she whispered. "You can't say no."

Her lips brushed his cheek. Before he could react, she was gone. The curtains fell back in place.

"You have five minutes to get ready."

"Yes, ma'am," Matthew said. He lay still a moment, trying to catch his breath, and also trying to think how he could get out of going with Natalia. All the excuses sounded lame, and he realized they sounded lame because he didn't really want to have to use them. He crawled out of the bunk, went to the bathroom to wash his face and change his shirt.

"How are you at poker?" she called through the bathroom door.

"I'm actually pretty good," he answered.

Gambling had been a career in a previous life. Monte Carlo. High-stakes games in smoke-filled rooms. Fine cut-crystal glasses. The clink of the chips, the smooth swishing sound of cards being shuffled by an expert. The rush of risking it all with a pair of twos in your hand and thousands on the table. Night after night until the night the rush was no longer there. It was just the cards, just the chips, just the bourbon. And then, pretty soon, it was just the bourbon. . . .

"I'm good at poker," Matthew repeated.

"So am I," said Natalia.

Matthew needn't have worried about being sucked into a romantic dinner. If it had just been the two of them, he might have had something to worry about—Natalia was fun, bubbly, lively, and talkative. The wine tasted better than he remembered wine tasting. The food at Aperto was good, so good that Matthew actually found himself enjoying it. All in all, it could have been a very romantic evening, except for the fact that Woof's ghost tagged along.

Matthew found it difficult to act as though there wasn't a third person around, especially when Woof kept joining the conversation.

Natalia told Matthew stories about her life on the road with the bands, and he told her stories about his life on the road, and they both agreed that being gypsy vagabond rovers was the only way to live. She even paid him the compliment of turning off her phone, though she did check her voice mail during dessert. When she went outdoors to make a call, Woof regaled Matthew with stories about his own life on the road.

Matthew found himself liking the old hippie. He wasn't sure why. Maybe it was because they both disliked and distrusted Cain. Matthew found himself enjoying the ghost's stories. Woof had died relatively young—he'd been only fifty-nine when he'd dropped dead from sudden, massive heart failure. Listening to Woof's tales of boozing, pot-smoking, acid-dropping, following the Dead, Matthew thought that if only half of them were true, it was a miracle Woof had lived as long as he had. Apparently Natalia was responsible for helping him straighten out. When Woof had started taking care of her, in lieu of her alcoholic parents, he'd given up the drugs.

"Smoked a joint now and then is all," he'd told Matthew with a wink. "Don't worry. She'll have the same effect on you. Notice she doesn't nag about the drinking? She just looks so damn disappointed. Like you really let her down. I couldn't stand it . . ."

After dinner, a driver took them back to the bus. The trip back was a little awkward. They were in the backseat of an enormous limo, all alone. Or rather, they would have been alone, except for Woof.

"Feeling better?" he asked Natalia. He would have put his arm around her, but he could see Woof glowering at him.

"Yes, thank you," she said, and nestled close to him.

"Cary Grant," Woof intoned in a sepulchral voice. "Loretta Young . . ."

"Get lost!" Matthew snapped, forgetting himself.

"What?" Natalia pulled back, stared at him.

"I . . . was afraid . . . we might get lost," Matthew said.

Natalia laughed and nestled close. "Would it be so bad if we did?" she whispered. "I'm comfortable here."

She was warm and alluring; one of the most fascinating women Matthew had ever known. He was attracted to her. Attracted—hell! He wanted her, desired her. She wanted him; she'd made that clear. They were both adults. He could give her what they both wanted. Make love to her here and now; ghost or no ghost. God knew he'd made love to scores of other women before this. Well, not made love. Had meaningless sex was more like it. Instant pleasure that was rarely pleasurable and left him feeling more alone when it was over.

His partner would go to sleep, and he would lie awake, staring into the darkness, trying to remember not only her name but something about her. What did she look like? He couldn't distinguish her face from the faces of hundreds of others.

Natalia was different. He couldn't get rid of her face. He saw her smile when he was lying in his bunk, saw her eyes when he was dozing off, saw her face in his dreams. He wanted to touch her, smell her perfume, taste her kisses. He wanted to make love to her over and over, then fall asleep entwined in her arms.

And if I do, Matthew asked himself, *will I forget what she looks like? Will I lie awake beside her trying to remember her name?*

A cold, gut-wrenching feeling of panic seized him. He didn't want to lose her. He didn't want to go back to what he had been. Matthew Gallow, who had lived for almost two thousand years, had forgotten what it meant to be alive. Now life, love, joy danced and sang and cavorted inside him. He reveled in it, and he was terrified that he would do or say something to cause it all to go away, leave him once more with nothing but the taste of ashes in his mouth.

What terrible irony. The one woman he yearned to love was the one woman he was afraid to love.

"Why do you look at me that way, Matthew?" Natalia asked softly. She reached up, caressed his cheek. "You look . . . so sad . . ."

Soft purple lighting in the limo cast an eerie glow over her, making her eyes shine, her lips glisten.

Natalia put her arms around him and pressed her lips against his, kissing him.

He clasped her in his arms and kissed her, reveling in her, feeling his desire hot and hard. And, feeling that, with a groan of physical agony, he shoved her away.

"Matthew, what is it?" Natalia asked, confused. "What's wrong? It's nothing serious. Just sex, Matthew. We could have some fun. . . ."

"No!" He shouted the word at her, and she drew back, startled.

"No, Natalia," he repeated, more calmly. "Not with you. I couldn't . . . Not with you."

She regarded him strangely, then she said, "All right," and slid across the seat away from him.

He was worried she might be angry or insulted, but she didn't look angry. She looked . . . startled, bewildered.

Suddenly, she turned to face him. "Any other man would have been in my pants in under two seconds flat. You push me away. And I don't think it's because you find me repulsive—"

Matthew shook his head. He started to speak, but she reached out, put her fingers on his lips.

"You want me. I can see it, feel it. But you aren't telling me something, something big. And I'm not talking about all the mysterious, no name, no social security number stuff. There's something bigger than that, and it's holding you back. I want to know when you're going to trust me."

Matthew felt his heart expand until it squeezed off his breathing. He was suddenly terribly, horribly afraid he was falling in love.

"Soon," he managed to say, and he even managed, God knew how, to smile when he said it.

She smiled back. They completed the limo ride in companionable silence. Woof—for the first time since Matthew had encountered the ghost—had nothing to say.

For which Matthew was exceedingly grateful.

Once they arrived back at the theater, Matthew thanked Natalia for dinner and turned to flee. He wanted the solitude of his bunk, wanted time to think.

"Where are you going?" Natalia asked. "We've been invited to play poker with the band."

Matthew tried to escape. "I'm really tired after all the upheaval and the rehearsing. I'd like to get to bed. Big day tomorrow—"

"It's only ten o'clock," said Natalia, "and you and your friend Jim Beam took a nap this afternoon. This is a good way for you to meet the band members, get to know them, bond with them."

Matthew chose to ignore the remark about Jim Beam. "I would have thought the band would be out partying with their gropies—"

"Groupies," Natalia corrected, laughing, "though your term is appropriate. Seriously, though," she added more somberly, "they were shook up by what happened today. Playing some poker, relaxing will be good for morale."

Matthew could hear raucous laughter coming from inside the other bus. Woof was grinning hugely and cracking his knuckles in anticipation.

"I always enjoy poker night," said the ghost.

"Life on the road's a good life, but it can be lonely," said Natalia.

"Maybe that's one of its charms," Matthew remarked dryly. "I don't get lonely."

Natalia smiled at him. "You're part of the family now,

Matthew, whether you like it or not. We're a big, scary, dysfunctional family, but we're all any of us has."

She sighed a little as she said this and Matthew gave way.

"All right. I'll play poker. But I have to warn you, I'm *extremely* good."

"Put your money where your mouth is, Father," said Natalia, and she knocked on the bus door.

Chapter 17

*N*atalia hurried through the backstage area of the theater in San Francisco. This was a smaller venue and required a different stage kit than the Vegas show. She was worried about how the stage setup was going. She was worried about Cain and whether or not he would be back from the producer's in time to rehearse. She was worried about the new number. She was worried about security. All in all, she'd been gulping Tums like they were jelly beans.

The murder/suicide had been all over the news. Natalia had refused to let Cain make a statement. If he did, it would appear as though he considered he was to blame.

She had hired extra security to protect everyone: Cain, the band, the fans. The Vegas riot was *not* going to happen again if she had to glue the fans' little pink bottoms to the seats.

Her phone buzzed. It was Cain, calling to say he was having a good time. He actually sounded sober and cheerful. Natalia told him to be back in time to rehearse the act with Father Gallow. Cain muttered something at this and hung up.

Natalia shrugged. If he made it, fine, if not . . . She wasn't going to sweat it. Matthew knew what he was supposed to do, and she had confidence he could handle whatever Cain threw at him. After all, according to Matthew, he'd handled his shill running off and leaving him to confront a real-live demon. Natalia grinned as she thought of it. She wondered why he kept insisting that had all been real. He was a strange man. Dark, brooding, mysterious. Her heart did a little flip every time she thought about him, and she had to force herself to think about something else, like the fact that she couldn't find the band.

"I need Jordan, Mike, and Ryan backstage as soon as possible," she said into her headset. "If any of you see them, grab them and shove them into the green room and lock the door until I get there. Everyone copy?"

Ten voices resounded in her headset.

Natalia had told the band to meet her backstage ahead of time to go over their instructions for the first night of the exorcism act. She'd been trying to track them down all day, but they'd gone missing before she could catch them. Their driver said something about their leaving to play cable-car paintball.

Natalia hoped the band had been kidding him. Unlike her driver, Al, Jake was an easy mark, and the guys were always playing practical jokes on him, telling him the most outlandish tales. (The one about burying a body in Pittsburgh had caused them all to spend an uncomfortable night being grilled by the cops.) In truth, the guys were relatively well behaved, all things considered.

Ryan, his brother Jordan, and their friend Mike had been with Cain from the beginning. By now they'd been around the concert scene long enough to have had most of the stupid either knocked or stomach-pumped out of them. Since she hadn't received any phone calls from the San Francisco police about the guys defacing public property, Natalia was hoping that they'd just been kidding Jake and that in reality they'd gone off to shoot pool.

She opened the door to the band's green room, and there were all her guys lounging around, two hours before the show. She could have hugged every one of them.

"Thanks for meeting me here. I want to review with you the new staging for our big finale tonight. You met Matthew Gallow last night. What'd you think of him?"

"What are we supposed to think of him? He took all our money playing cards," grumbled Ryan, the bass guitarist. "And him a priest, for Christ's sake! Where does a priest learn to play poker like that?"

Ryan was buzzed, but then he was always buzzed. He hated hangovers, he said, and the best way to avoid them was to stay mildly intoxicated. He was never completely drunk, just never completely sober. Natalia had learned to live with it. He actually played better when he was half-lit.

"Trust me, Ryan, a Girl Scout could take your money at cards," Natalia told him. "And Matthew isn't a real priest. I keep telling you that."

"Are you sure?" Ryan demanded. "'Cause he acts like a priest. All serious and judgmental. And his eyes. Intense. Like he can see right through me like I was naked. Gave me the willies."

Mike laughed. Ryan's older brother Jordan, the keyboardist, spoke up. "You've got a guilty conscience, Ryan, that's all."

Jordan was in his late twenties, the stabilizing influence in the band and a damn fine keyboard player.

"Now that you've all met the good father," said Natalia, "and he's taken Ryan's money, let's discuss what his role in the show will be tonight. Here is the set list. Feel free to change it around if you like, except for the last song. You need to play 'Possession' last. That's when Father Gallow does his thing."

"So he is a priest!" said Ryan triumphantly.

"No, he is not—"

"You called him 'Father.'"

"Stage name, Ryan," said Natalia. "Try to keep up."

"So what exactly is this fake priest going to do?" Mike, the drummer, asked.

Mike had been the cliché self-destructive drummer until he'd fallen head over heels for a fan girl who'd insisted he go into rehab before she'd marry him. After he got cleaned up, she decided she didn't like him sober, and left. He had discovered that he preferred sobriety to his girlfriend and didn't seem to be bothered by her departure one bit.

"Matthew is going to *pretend*"—she emphasized the word for Ryan's sake—"to exorcise a demon from Cain. Here's how it goes. Tonight, after the song's intro, the good Father Gallow is going to go up on the stage and try to rid Cain of his demons by performing an exorcism."

"Can he exorcise Cain's ego while he's at it?" Ryan asked, and the other two guys grinned.

"Seriously, Natalia, the guy's been a total asshole lately," Jordan stated.

"Yes, I hear what you're saying," Natalia corrected, "and while I know you and Cain have some issues—"

"*I* don't have issues," Ryan protested. "He's a fuckin', conceited jerk-off, but that's his problem, not mine."

"Keep counting the dollars, Ryan," said Natalia. "When this tour is over, you'll be able to afford your very own entourage of slutty starlets. All thanks to Cain."

Ryan lurched to his feet and flung his arms around Natalia. "My own slutty starlets! It's what I've always dreamed of. Is that a promise, Nat? Can we put that in my contract?"

"Right next to your sobriety clause," Natalia said severely, shoving him away.

"Ouch!" Ryan winced and stumbled backward into a stool.

He picked himself up and wandered over to the fridge, to pop the top on another beer.

"Can we get on with this meeting, Natalia?" Mike begged. "*Northern Exposure* reruns come on in five minutes."

"I thought you already had them all on DVD?" Natalia asked. "Okay, okay, moving along. There will be lots of fire and smoke, explosions, that sort of stuff. We haven't rehearsed it—not that rehearsing the act would matter because Cain never does the same thing twice. You guys will need to be ready for anything. All you have to do is keep playing."

"Got it," said Mike, fidgeting. "Is that all?" He crossed the green room to flip on the TV.

"I am too a good poker player." Ryan pouted.

Natalia patted him on his head and left.

Her next stop was to find Matthew. She knew where to look for him, however, and, leaving the theater, she headed back to the bus.

"Hello?" she called, stepping on board. "Matthew?"

No answer. She walked back and found him lying in his bunk. The curtains were open. He had on a pair of headphones and was listening to her iPod. An empty glass stood on the floor by the bed. She could smell the bourbon. And there, beside the glass, was an old tattered Bible. The binding was almost worn away. She looked at it in astonishment. What was that for? Inspiration for the act tonight?

Matthew took off the earphones. "I was listening to Cain's music." He looked troubled. "I know you said the soul-selling business was a metaphor, but he's dealing with some pretty dangerous notions—"

Natalia put her hand on her hips. "Oh, come now, Matthew," she said, exasperated, "are we back to demons again? You can't honestly believe . . ." She paused, glanced at the Bible and flushed. "Oh, wow. You do, don't you?"

She ran her hand through her hair. "How can I explain this? The song's harmless. It speaks to every teen's inner angst, feelings of isolation, rejection—"

"Like the feelings of that kid who killed his mother?" Matthew asked gravely.

Natalia's face went livid. She caught her breath, glared at him.

"Here's a copy of the set list," she said in frozen tones, flinging a sheet of notebook paper at him. "The set may change if the band wants to mix it up, but Cain's song, 'Possession,' which is your cue, will always come on last. You need to learn the intro."

She turned on her heel and started to walk off. Matthew rolled out of the bunk. Running after her, he caught hold of her arm to detain her.

"I'm sorry, Natalia," he said remorsefully. "That was stupid. I didn't mean—"

"Yes, you did!" she cried angrily, pulling away from him. She cast another glance at the Bible. "Look, just because you *play* a priest doesn't mean you get to go all sanctimonious and self-righteous on me!"

"I'm worried, Natalia," Matthew told her. "I'm worried about Cain. About you. I don't like what's going on. It's as if I feel dark wings hovering over you, casting shadows . . ."

Natalia thought back to what Ryan had said, about the way Matthew looked at a person. Intense. Like he was seeing right through you. His eyes were dark blue, like the ocean, and like the ocean, they seemed fathoms deep. She could dive into them and swim down and down and never reach the bottom.

She was caught, held by his penetrating gaze, transfixed. The ocean seemed to roar in her ears. She couldn't hear what he was saying, didn't care. She was confused: half of her was furious with him, the other half wanted to kiss him again, as she'd kissed him last night. She could always be furious, she decided. It would be much more fun to kiss him. She leaned into him . . . and her phone buzzed.

"Damn!" she muttered. She answered it, shouting, "What do you want? Oh, Mr. Rubin"—Natalia had to pull herself together—"thanks for returning my call. Cain's on his way back? Great. No trouble was there? Excellent. Thank you for inviting him."

She hung up.

"What were we talking about?" she asked.

Matthew frowned, cleared his throat, and took a step back from her. "We were talking about Cain's music. That song, 'Possession'—"

Natalia was back to being furious. She turned around and marched off the bus. As she was leaving, she yelled over her shoulder, "Speaking of dark forces, what does that Bible of yours say about guzzling bourbon at ten in the morning?"

"I haven't been drinking," Matthew said quietly. "That glass was there from last night."

She ignored him, stormed off the bus, and fumed her way across the parking lot.

Now she had another worry. A major one. And a major disappointment. Matthew Gallow had seemed like such a wonderful guy!

He had been brave and calm during the riot. He'd saved

her life, she was convinced of that. Like her, he was an adult in a world of kids. They'd had a wonderful dinner last night. Intelligent conversation about world affairs, politics. Not like her usual conversations with the band, which generally centered on how many tequila shooters a guy could down before he threw up.

He had gotten along well with the band, despite the fact that most of his dry remarks had sailed right over their fuzzy heads. When that happened, he had looked at Natalia, and they'd shared a secret smile.

Matthew was a professional. He had his act down cold. With all her other concerns, she had thought she could at least count on him.

Now, what if it turned out he was a drunken Bible-thumping religious fanatic? What if he screwed up the act or, worse, started preaching to the kids? It would be her fault. She should have realized there was something wrong with him when she couldn't find any background information on him.

She made a phone call. "Cain . . . Yeah, I'm glad you had a good time. Listen, I was thinking that maybe we should cancel the exorcism act. You haven't rehearsed it, and I was just . . ."

Natalia paused, listened in astonishment. "Okay, okay! Calm down," she said when she could get a word in. "It's just . . . I thought you didn't want to do it. . . . Yes, you're allowed to change your mind. And don't start with me!" she told him angrily. "I have enough going on today without you giving me attitude! Meet me in the green room. If you're going through with this exorcism, you should at least know what the hell you're doing. No pun intended."

She hung up.

* * *

Natalia had not taken her usual place in the sound booth. She was so worried about the last act, she decided to wait in the wings, ready to leap into action in case something went wrong. And she had the queasy feeling something was going to go wrong.

Cain knew nothing about the act. He had no idea what he was supposed to do. She'd tried to talk to him about the exorcism in his dressing room, but he'd refused to pay attention. All he wanted to talk about was the contest winners. Were they there? When she'd said yes, he'd insisted on having them brought to his dressing room.

Natalia had agreed. She was actually relieved by this. She'd been afraid that after the tragedy with the last contest winner, he wouldn't want anything to do with them anymore. On the contrary, however, he had seemed to be trying extra hard to be nice to them. One boy's father had come along. Turns out he was some bigwig in state politics, and he was obviously uncomfortable about having his sixteen-year-old son hobnobbing with Cain.

Natalia, with some misgivings, brought the father backstage. Cain was polite and well behaved. The father was charmed and asked if he could stay to see the show along with his son.

When the kid, who was deeply embarrassed at having his father with him, made some crack about the "old man" after his father left to go to his seat, Cain lectured him, telling the kid he should be grateful he had a father who cared enough to look after him.

"Some of us weren't that lucky," Cain said, and he shared a rueful smile with Natalia.

She had known what he meant. His home life had been about as crappy as hers. At least she'd had Woof. Cain hadn't had anyone.

When the kids had all gone off to meet the members of the band, she had tried once again to talk to Cain about the act, but he'd started tuning his guitar, and at last she'd given up and left. She had the uneasy feeling that he was plotting something. He had that look about him—a smug, self-satisfied look he got sometimes. And she had the terrible feeling his scheming had to do with the final act.

So here was Matthew, who had suddenly taken it into his head to save the world from the evils of rock and roll, and here was Cain, plotting God knew what mischief. At this point, Natalia just hoped they all lived through it. She ordered security to be ready for anything.

The concert went well. Cain came in on all his cues. The band outdid themselves. He and Ryan did some stage business together, just like the old days, to the audience's delight. The fans were having fun, but no one was out of control. Yet. In Vegas, the riot hadn't broken out until the final number.

This was it. The curtain came down. Cain ran off to do a quick costume change. Natalia looked around for Matthew, but couldn't see him, and she felt a qualm of panic.

"Where's Father Gallow?" she called into the radio.

"He's here," said someone immediately. "Stage right. That's where he's supposed to be, isn't it?"

"Yes, of course. Just checking," said Natalia. She peered across the stage, saw him standing there. He was looking really good. The austere clerical garb suited him. He caught sight of her and gave her a lopsided, apologetic smile.

"I'm sorry," he mouthed.

"Me too!" she mouthed back, adding, "Break a leg!"

The audience began to clap and stomp their feet. They were chanting "Poss-es-sion," breaking it up into three syllables with a stomp in between. Natalia was so nervous, she felt sick to her stomach.

The lights dimmed. The audience went silent, catching its breath in heart-pounding anticipation.

The band took the stage. The curtain was still closed. On cue, Ryan thrummed out the first few bars of the song on the bass guitar. The audience recognized the song and went wild. In the lowered lights, Natalia could see girls in the front row, their hair ragged with sweat, weeping.

And here was Cain's cue, and he was nowhere to be seen.

"Where's Cain?" she demanded, shouting into the mike.

The band members were looking at each other. Jordan gave Ryan the high sign to keep on playing. Mike the drummer glanced at him and shook his head.

The music rose and the rear stage lights flashed brightly, blinding Natalia and the audience for a few seconds. When her eyes readjusted to the light, there was Cain. He started to sing. The audience began to cheer wildly, then they stopped, staring in astonishment as Matthew Gallow walked on to the stage.

He was wearing his priestly vestments: collar, shirt, purple sash around his neck, and carrying a Bible and a crucifix. Natalia's heart was in her throat as she watched Matthew walk slowly and purposefully toward Cain.

"You are possessed by the devil!" Matthew said into his mike, and Natalia was thrilled by how well his deep voice carried over the music.

The audience was startled, at first, but when Matthew cried out that he was going to save Cain, they began to boo and hiss.

Cain grinned at his fans, then suddenly leaped off the platform on which he performed and began defiantly singing in the "priest's" face.

The song's tempo increased. Father Gallow raised the crucifix. Cain stopped playing. He began to smash up his guitar, hitting it against the stage floor. Natalia gasped. She had no idea what he was doing. Jordan immediately stopped playing, having sense enough to realize that the band's music would sound lame without Cain's. He must have also realized that silence right now would be more dramatic.

"Find him another guitar!" Natalia was yelling into the mike and, backstage, people scrambled.

Onstage, Cain flopped over on his back onto the stage floor and began to shriek and writhe. The fans shouted in glee and flung plastic cups and water bottles at the "priest" who was the cause of this. Matthew must have been as shocked as Natalia by Cain's antics, but he was playing along. He moved and spoke with confidence and grace. He didn't once acknowledge the audience or even glance at them. He kept his focus on Cain.

Cain began screaming the lyrics into his mouthpiece. They sounded eerie without the music. Matthew walked over to Cain, who was still on the floor, and put his hand on Cain's arm, as if to try to calm him. Suddenly, Matthew gasped and snatched back his hand. He looked at Cain strangely, and completely fumbled his next lines. This wasn't how he and Natalia had rehearsed this scene, but then none of this was how they'd planned it.

Cain continued to shriek out the song. Matthew recovered himself. Lifting his crucifix, he began to chant Latin. A single white spotlight shone on Matthew. He was handsome and commanding, his voice strong and powerful. The audience was awed. They quit booing.

They're not trying to kill each other! Natalia thought. *This is fantastic.*

Cain gave a hideous cry and ran offstage. Matthew looked a little startled at this. He was now center stage all by himself. Natalia had no idea what was going on. She was about to go find out, when Cain suddenly reappeared onstage, entering from the back. He was carrying a guitar made to look like the face of a devil.

Natalia gasped. This was amazing. She'd never seen a guitar like it. He must have special-ordered it, never said a word to her.

Matthew was caught completely by surprise, but he reacted well. He frowned darkly and drew back, as if horrified.

Cain began to play, and the band joined in again. The song reached its zenith, and, at that point, it stopped. Dead silence took over for a moment, then Cain began to play his famous solo.

The music was fast and hard. Matthew continued chanting, but he was now starting to sound desperate. Cain aimed the guitar at Matthew, and the demon-guitar belched forth red-and-black smoke out of the neck. The smoke enveloped Matthew, curling around him like crazed demons. The pyrotechnics went off, sending flames dancing around the stage. Matthew began to choke. He grasped at his throat, unable to breathe. He couldn't take it anymore and, as they'd rehearsed, he ran off stage.

Cain stood triumphant. He finished his solo to the roar of the crowd, who were shouting so much they probably couldn't hear the music. When he finished, he gave a low bow. The curtain came down.

The audience leaped to their feet, but not to riot. They jumped up to cheer and applaud. They kept cheering, kept applauding even as the houselights went up, and security began trying to herd them out.

Natalia realized suddenly she'd been screaming, "That's it! That's it!" into her headpiece. She must have deafened half the crew.

And here came Matthew, walking into the wings. His face was black with soot. His eyes were streaming tears, and he was still coughing.

Natalia ran toward him, flung her arms around his neck, and kissed him.

"You were wonderful! Absolutely freakin' wonderful!"

Chapter 18

Matthew was dazed from the blasting music and the explosions (he had forgotten to put in the earplugs, as Natalia had recommended). He was half-asphyxiated from the smoke, half-blinded by the light, and shaken by the entire experience. The sight of Natalia running toward him, her eyes shining with pleasure and excitement, increased his confusion. Before he knew what was happening, she was in his arms, her lips pressing against his, and he fumbled to hold on to her and his Bible and crucifix.

"Great job!" Woof was beside Matthew, grinning, and thumping Matthew on the back.

What Matthew did feel was sudden, searing pain. He gasped and winced and looked down at his right hand, which had been clutching the Bible.

Natalia gave Matthew another swift kiss, then let loose of him to answer her phone and, at the same time, shout into the radio.

Matthew shifted the Bible to his left hand and lifted his right hand to the light.

"Jesus!" Woof exclaimed in awe.

"My God!" Natalia gasped, and hung up in the middle of a call to grab hold of his hand. "How did that happen?"

Matthew stared at his hand in astonishment. The skin of his fingers and palm was badly burned. Blisters were forming, and it hurt like hell. How *had* he done it? There had been so much twanging noise and pounding drums, confusion and smoke and flames and blinding light, that he was having difficulty remembering what had happened to him back onstage.

"I don't know . . ." Matthew said, perplexed.

"You touched him, man!" Woof said. "You put your hand on Cain's arm, then you flinched and snatched it away."

Matthew thought back to the performance. Woof was right. He'd forgotten all about that. He had put his hand on Cain's arm. He remembered now feeling a strange sensation, but the entire few minutes out there had all been so extraordinarily strange that he hadn't noticed.

"I guess I must have gotten too close to the Pyroflare 3600," Matthew told Natalia ruefully. He gently, but firmly, drew his hand out of her grasp.

"I guess you did!" Natalia exclaimed. "Come with me. First aid." She took hold of his sleeve and tugged him along. "They keep a burn kit."

Matthew could already feel the pain in his hand easing. If he looked at his palm, he would see the blisters starting to fade. And so would she. Matthew came to a halt.

"That won't be necessary," he said. He shoved his hand into the pocket of his cassock.

"But that's a serious burn," Natalia argued. "You should have it treated."

"I have some special ointment of my own. In my dressing room," Matthew said, remembering Hannah, who was always wanting to dose him with some sort of herbal remedy or other. He grabbed hold of the first name he could remember. "Echinacea."

"You take that for a cold," said Natalia.

"It's good for burns, too," Matthew said. "Look, I'm sure you've got lots to do. I'll just go clean up. Take care of this." He indicated his hand.

She regarded him skeptically. "You're not planning to soak it in bourbon, are you?"

Matthew smiled. "Alcohol kills germs, you know. I'll see you back on the bus."

"No, you won't," Natalia said severely. "I'll see *you* in the green room. You need to meet the sponsors and the contest winners. It's in your contract," she added, seeing him about to protest.

Matthew grimaced. "All right. I'll be there. Okay if I change into street clothes?"

Natalia nodded. "You were wonderful tonight, Father Gallow," she added, and she kissed him again, this time on the cheek. Then she ran off, talking into her microphone as her phone buzzed.

He walked slowly and thoughtfully to his dressing room, which was very small, almost a closet, not nearly so grand as Cain's. He walked inside, shut the door, then realized Woof was standing next to him.

"Shouldn't you be out there dropping chandeliers on people's heads?" Matthew asked rudely.

"Phantom of the Opera," Woof said approvingly. "You're learning."

He was staring fixedly at Matthew's hand.

"Deeply weird," the ghost remarked, frowning. "I saw that scaffolding come crashing down right on your back, Angel Boy, and you came out of there without so much as a scratch. But you touch Cain's arm, and suddenly your hand looks like a slab of Kansas City barbecue."

Matthew began to pack his things away, ignoring the ghost, hoping Woof would get bored and leave.

Instead, Woof sat down in a chair and made himself comfortable.

"According to Natalia, the same thing happened to you in that revival tent. I saw the video, man. Your hand was on fire. You were in some serious pain. Is Cain possessed?" Woof demanded. He bounced off his chair. "Is that it? If it is, by God, I *will* drop a chandelier on his head—"

"Calm down," Matthew snapped. "To be honest, I don't know." He looked at his hand. The burns were almost completely faded. "I didn't feel anything that time I touched Grace. It wasn't until I began to battle the demon inside her that my hand caught fire. This time . . . all I did was touch Cain's arm . . ."

Matthew had touched Cain's arm, and something frightening had nudged Matthew's soul, like a shark bumping its prey to see if it pushes back. Or like taking hold of a frayed electrical cord while it was still plugged in to the walls. He felt a shock, a jolt, then the burning.

"You've touched Cain before, right?" Woof asked.

Matthew grimaced. "I've tried to avoid it, but, yes, I've bumped into him on the bus or brushed up against him."

"And nothing caught fire," said Woof.

Matthew reached for the bourbon bottle. He didn't want to discuss this anymore.

"Shouldn't you be off somewhere smoking something and contemplating the universe?" he said to the ghost.

"I'm going, Angel Boy," said Woof. "And you know what I think? I think that was a warning."

"A warning?" Matthew repeated. "About what?"

"Damned if I know. You're the angel." Woof shrugged and wandered off.

Matthew stared at himself in the mirror. It had all been an act. He hadn't performed a real exorcism. Or did that matter?

"A warning," Matthew muttered. "Maybe the old reprobate is right. Maybe that was a warning to back off, keep my distance."

He eyed his reflection: the black cassock, the clerical collar, the golden crucifix. "But if so, that means someone knows this isn't an act. Someone knows I can exorcise demons for real. I told Natalia that it wasn't an act, but it's obvious she doesn't believe me. Still, she might have told someone . . ."

The most obvious answer was that she had told Cain. And he claimed to have sold his soul to the devil. He certainly acted like a being possessed. He was rude, obnoxious, self-centered, boorish, crude. A demon who had hold of Cain might well try to warn Matthew away from his prize.

But that didn't make sense. According to Natalia, it had been Cain's idea to put "Father Gallow onstage."

No, not Cain. The roadie. Burl. Who'd been trying to sabotage the scaffolding.

And if Burl knows I can exorcise demons, why go to all this trouble to keep me here, then turn around and warn me away?

Matthew remembered the conversation between the two roadies during rehearsal.

"I don't see why we can't go through with the original plan and get rid of him."

"Because the higher-ups think he's onto us. We need to know how much he knows and if he's told anyone. This is too important to screw up."

"Why don't we just shut down operations?"

"We can't. It's gone too far. Our job is just to keep an eye on him."

Him. He'd been assuming the "him" was Cain. What if it wasn't? What if the him was *he?* Matthew Gallow? And what if the higher-up wasn't a rock-star promoter or record-label executive. What if it was . . . an archangel.

I guess you didn't get the e-mail . . . Archangel William had said.

They permitted some of Hell's most powerful archde-mons to cross over, materialize on Earth. They are now working to throw the world into chaos. . . . You have to stop these exorcisms, Matthew. . . . You're venturing into deep, dark water, and you're going to end up over your head.

First I exorcise a girl who happens to be wearing a Cain T-shirt, and I discover she's possessed by a real demon. Then I get an invitation to join up with Cain and become part of his act. I hear roadies talking about some sort of plan. And shortly after that, a kid wearing a Cain T-shirt is involved in a murder/suicide.

It might all be coincidence, Matthew thought, but if so, these coincidences are certainly starting to pile on.

"Or I could be paranoid," Matthew commented to his reflection.

That seemed far more likely.

He took a firm and comforting grip on the bourbon bottle, sloshed some into a glass, drank that, and helped himself to another. He washed the soot off his face and changed into jeans and a button-down shirt, compliments of Natalia, who had told him he'd be meeting the public, and he had to look presentable. He remembered, at the last minute, to wrap a bandage around his hand, which had now completely healed.

He listened through the closed door. Cain and the band members and their guests were really whooping it up. He could hear Natalia's laughter. Someone knocked on his door, and yelled, "You're wanted in the green room, Father!"

On an impulse, Matthew opened his Bible and flipped through the pages. There, in the back, was a card. He thought he remembered having stashed it there. He wasn't sure why he'd kept it. Maybe a reminder of the one good thing he'd done in his many lifetimes.

He drew out his cell phone and dialed the number.

"Mrs. Swithenbank," he said. "This is Father Gallow. Yes, it's a pleasure to talk to you again, too. How is Grace? I'm very pleased to hear it. I don't want to take up your time. I just had a quick question. Has Grace ever personally met Cain Lukosi? Yes, the rock star. I noticed she was wearing a T-shirt . . . She did? . . . Was it at a concert? A private party. I see. You were there, as well . . . Cain was quite the gentleman. Yes, I'm working for him, part of the act. I'm hoping to bring them all to God," Matthew answered patiently. "Thank you. Good night.

"Maybe I'm not so paranoid, after all," Matthew remarked, hanging up. Unfortunately, that knowledge wasn't very comforting. Grace had met Cain in person and been possessed by a demon. The Rolex kid had met Cain in person, then killed his mom and himself.

Matthew didn't have the answers. All he had were lots of questions.

But he was starting to feel dark water lapping at his chin.

Chapter 19

The green room was packed with people, who were either laughing gleefully or shouting at each other at the tops of their lungs. To add to the noise, loudspeakers were blasting Cain's music at them. Wishing he'd brought ear-plugs, Matthew tried to find a quiet corner. Once there, he snagged a bottle of cold water from a waiter passing with a tray and drank it thirstily. He could still feel the smoke in his throat. He stood in the corner by himself, not knowing what to do.

Cain was the center of attention. He stood in the middle of the room, surrounded by an admiring audience of fans and press and celebrities. The guys in the band were all receiving their share of adoration. Matthew looked around for Natalia but didn't see her. He couldn't even find Woof. The noise and commotion grated on Matthew's nerves. He didn't want to be here.

Deciding that no one would miss him if he left, Matthew was starting to beat a hasty retreat when Natalia shoved her way through the crowd and seized hold of him.

"Oh, no, you don't!" she cried. "No sneaking out of here! You're one of the stars. Everyone wants to meet you."

Matthew started to say something, but the smoke caught in his throat, and he went into a fit of coughing.

"You're not supposed to inhale the stuff, you know," shouted Natalia, eyeing him in concern.

"I didn't have a choice!" Matthew gasped when he could speak. "What chemicals are in that smoke anyway?"

"I have no idea," Natalia said. "The Pyro guys just warned me that people shouldn't inhale it."

"No problem. The next time I do the act, I'll remind myself that breathing is bad," Matthew said.

"Don't be such a baby," Natalia said, grinning at him. "We all have our sacrifices to make."

Matthew wondered moodily if those sacrifices included souls.

"How's your hand?" Natalia asked.

He exhibited his hand, wrapped in a neat bandage. "Feels fine."

"The echinacea," Natalia said dubiously.

"Wonderful curative powers," said Matthew.

"Yeah, well, I'll wait to read your write-up in the *New England Journal of Medicine*. Now I want you to come meet some people." Natalia snagged a glass of champagne from a passing tray, handed it to Matthew, and hauled him over to a group of people he didn't recognize. She interrupted their conversation to introduce him.

"Kitty, Fred, Kent, I'd like you to meet Matthew Gallow," Natalia said.

Two men and a woman turned to him. The men were smiling, friendly. The woman was more than that. She regarded Matthew with open admiration.

"Kitty and Kent are from the local radio station that helped sponsor our show tonight," Natalia explained.

"You were amazing, Father," gushed Kitty. "Simply amazing."

"I'm not a priest," said Matthew.

"What?" Kitty blinked, not understanding.

"You can call me Matthew, not Father," said Matthew. "I'm not a priest."

"Then this is my lucky day," said Kitty in a throaty gurgle.

"I just spoke to the station," Kent was saying. "The phones haven't stopped ringing since the show ended. The kids are requesting Cain's song 'Possession' over and over again. Of course, most of that's because of Cain, but part of the success of that number is you, Father."

"Not Father. Just . . . Matthew," said Matthew.

He glanced at Cain out of the corner of his eye. A group of young fans were crowding eagerly around him.

"I would shake your hand," said Kitty, moving close to him. Her hip rubbed against his thigh. "But I see you've hurt it. Did you get too close to the fire?"

She smiled suggestively over her champagne glass. "Perhaps I could kiss it and make it better."

Matthew had no idea what to say in response. He'd never been very good at small talk.

"Excuse me, Kitty, dear," said Natalia, "I hate to introduce and run, but more of Matthew's fans would like to meet him."

"Congratulations, Father Gallow," Natalia added with a smothered laugh. "You have your first groupie."

"What? No!" Matthew stared at her, then looked back over his shoulder.

He had assumed Kitty was kidding, but, sure enough, she was still watching him. She winked at him and pursed her lips in an airy kiss. Matthew couldn't believe it. He'd known hookers who were more subtle.

"Feel free to ask her out," said Natalia archly.

"Maybe I will," said Matthew, teasing.

Natalia gave his arm a hard squeeze and leaned over to yell in his ear. "You do, and I'll crank the Pyro 3600 up full blast! You'll never breathe again."

Matthew laughed heartily. He couldn't help laughing when he was with her, couldn't help enjoying himself, enjoying the simple pleasure of being alive. Her laughter made the dark waters recede . . .

Natalia glanced at him from beneath her lashes. "Besides, I thought you and I might have a late dinner."

Matthew could think of nothing he'd rather do, nowhere he'd rather be than with Natalia. He could see where this was leading, and he knew he should put a stop to it right now before one or both of them got hurt.

The golden flecks began to fade from Natalia's eyes. "Of course, if you'd really rather go out with Kitty—"

Matthew cleared his throat, pretended to cough. "Sorry. The smoke got to me again. I was about to ask you out to dinner. You beat me to it."

Natalia smiled at him. The golden flecks danced. "I know just the place. I'll call, see if they have a table."

She made the call, shouting into the phone in order to be heard over the commotion in the room.

"We have a table!" she yelled at him.

"Good," he said. "Let's leave now."

Natalia shook her head. "Just a few more people you have to meet."

Matthew gave a deep sigh.

"Cheer up," Natalia added, smiling. "It will all be over soon!"

She pushed her way through the crowd around Cain,

dragging Matthew with her. Cain had his shirt hiked up, exhibiting the tattoo of a serpent on his chest to his adoring fans. And there was Woof, hanging around Cain. Catching sight of Matthew, Woof raised his eyes to heaven and mouthed the word, "Asshole."

"You need to meet the contest winners," Natalia told Matthew. "These fans won this chance to come backstage with Cain today. This is Kate, Steve, and Sawyer, and Sawyer's father, Mr. Krause, kids, this is Matthew Gallow. He performed the exorcism on Cain tonight—or tried to," she added, winking at Matthew.

The kids barely even glanced at him. They had eyes only for Cain. Mr. Krause shook Matthew's hand.

"Sorry! I can't hear a thing," the dad shouted.

"Me either!" Matthew shouted back.

He figured he'd done his duty and was about ready to leave, when to his astonishment, Cain actually deigned to speak to him.

"Bummer about your failure tonight, padre," Cain remarked to him, grinning.

"Yes, it was," Matthew agreed calmly. "But there's always next time."

Cain seemed a little startled at this remark. His smug grin froze on his face, his eyes glittered.

"This is war between us, Father," said Cain, and for a moment Matthew thought he was serious.

Then Cain laughed and nudged Matthew with his elbow. "Just kidding, padre. Jeez, can't you take a joke?"

He turned his attention back to the kids, who were loving it. "C'mon back to my dressing room. I'll show you my demon guitar!"

The kids squealed with excitement, and Cain departed in state, followed by his adoring entourage. Natalia skillfully managed to detach a couple of groupies, who were trying to tag along. She handed them off to one of the band guys. Then the dad asked how long his son would be gone and if there was any adult supervision. Natalia assured him there would be chaperones and said he could either go with the kids to see the demon guitar or she could find him a quiet room. Mr. Krause thankfully chose the quiet room and inquired if she had any aspirin.

Matthew was staring thoughtfully after Cain. Had that exchange between them been Cain's idea of witty banter, or had he meant it?

"Uh-oh," cried Natalia, clutching Matthew. "Scary groupie woman Kitty is heading this way. You've done your duty. We can leave now, if you want. I've got a car waiting for us."

"What about the contest kids?" Matthew asked. "Don't you have to stay with them?"

Natalia shook her head. "They'll be in Cain's dressing room an hour or so. He'll show off his guitar and tell them stupid stories, then the limo will pick them up and take them home."

"And Cain?" Matthew asked.

"He's going back to the bus," Natalia said firmly. "No wild parties for him tonight. Though he and the band guys might get together later. They actually seem to be speaking to one another for a change. Anyway, it's not my problem. After the show, I'm officially off duty."

They left the party. They passed the dressing rooms, and Matthew looked into Cain's. The rock star was writing his autograph on Sawyer's forearm. Kate was oohing and aahing over the demon guitar, and the others were gathered about Cain, waiting for their share of attention.

Matthew shook his head and walked on.

"Do I need to change clothes for the restaurant?" he asked, halting outside his own dressing room. "Put on a suit and tie?"

Natalia shook her head. "No. You might get wet," she said, and she laughed at Matthew's astonished look.

"You'll want to pack a toothbrush, though," she told him. "I've reserved you a room in the Fairmont Hotel. I'm staying there, too. I have my own room," she added, seeing him look uncomfortable. "My God, Father Gallow, are you sure you're *not* a priest?"

What could Matthew say? That he had sworn an oath on a well-worn Bible and an empty bourbon bottle that he'd never let himself fall in love again? That he thought her rock-star friend was very possibly in league with the devil? That her dead grandfather's ghost was standing right beside her, glaring at him!

"The driver will bring you back if you don't want to stay in the hotel," Natalia was saying. "I should warn you, though, that Cain will be too wound up and strung out to go to bed. He'll be up all night in the bus drinking tequila and smoking pot and playing video games. *Loud* video games."

Matthew relented. She had said they would have separate rooms. And this would be a good chance to find out more about Cain.

"I'll grab my things and meet you in the parking lot," Natalia said, and, waving at him, she hurried off.

Matthew walked into his dressing room. He picked up his briefcase and was about to leave, only to find Woof blocking the door.

"You better not let down my little girl, Angel Boy," said Woof, glowering.

"How many times do we have to keep having this conversation?" Matthew demanded irritably. "And stop calling me that!"

"It's just I worry you're going to be a disappointment in the sack," Woof stated. "You bein' an angel and all. Natalia really enjoys sex. So try to measure up."

Matthew's jaw dropped.

Woof grinned hugely. "See you at dinner," he said, and vanished.

Chapter 20

*T*heir reservations were for the Tonga Room. Located in the basement of the Fairmont Hotel in San Francisco, the Tonga Room was lovingly known among the natives as "Tacky Tiki."

"You'll see why," Natalia assured him. "You'll also see why it's my favorite restaurant ever!"

After they had each checked into their respective rooms, he and Natalia went to the restaurant. Here they sat under a thatched roof near a large pool of water, surrounded by plastic orchids.

The specialty of the bar was exotic drinks served in a variety of exotic glasses, adorned with small paper umbrellas and lots of fruit. Natalia was horrified when Matthew said he was going to have bourbon. She told the waitress he would have a Mai Tai.

"I hear they're amazing," she said. "Besides, I want your cherries."

She herself ordered a "Diet Coke with a side of maraschino cherries." Matthew discovered that the Coke came with an obligatory umbrella, which Natalia stuck behind her ear.

"I never heard of anyone ordering a side of cherries," he said.

"Either I order a bowl of cherries or you watch me fish them out of my drink all night with my fingers," Natalia said.

He was about to reply when suddenly lights flashed and thunder erupted and rain began to fall from the ceiling into the pool. Matthew understood now what she'd meant about getting wet. It wasn't raining on him, but he could feel the spray from the water. A small tiki hut on a barge floated out into the middle of the water. A woman riding on the barge began to sing.

"Isn't that storm the coolest thing ever?" Natalia demanded, biting into a cherry.

"In all my years, I've truly never seen anything like it," Matthew remarked. And that was saying something.

Natalia slurped another cherry. Her lips were red with the juice. "Electric tiki torches, fake orchids, thunder every thirty minutes. I love this place. I come here every time I'm in town."

Woof loved the restaurant, too, apparently.

"Want to see me walk on water?" he asked Matthew with a wink, and he floated out across the pool to join the lounge singer in a duet.

Natalia caught dripping cherry juice on her chin with her fingers. She licked her fingers. Matthew couldn't take his eyes from her. He could feel tension pressing against the seam of his pants.

"I know what you're going to ask me," said Natalia.

"You do?" Matthew was startled.

"You're going to ask me if I can tie a cherry stem in a

knot with my tongue like those girls on TV. Well, I can't. I tried once and accidentally swallowed the stem and it went down the wrong way and I damn near choked to death. So you have to live without seeing me do that."

Natalia looked out over the pool at the lounge singer and sang along softly. "'Comes the measles, you can quarantine the room. Comes a mousie, you can chase him with a broom. Comes love, nothin' can be done.' That's an old Billie Holiday song. My grandfather used to play the record all the time. I always sang the part about the mousie."

Unlike what the song lyrics said, Matthew *could* do something about love. He was going to make sure of that. Never mind that Natalia's eyes crinkled when she laughed or that watching her eat cherries sent thrills through his body.

Woof joined the lounge singer in the next song. Fortunately, neither the audience nor the lounge singer could hear how bad he sounded. Unfortunately, Matthew could. If Woof ever made it to Heaven, he would not be asked to join the heavenly choir. The ghost was certainly having a great time, however.

Woof is getting more enjoyment out of death than I am out of life, Matthew thought, and then he realized how absurd that sounded, and he began to laugh.

Natalia looked at him, startled, then she reached across the table to take hold of his hand.

"You have a great laugh," she said. "You should do it more often."

Her hand was sticky with Diet Coke and cherry juice, and her touch warmed him like rum from the Mai Tai. He drew his hand away.

"I'm sorry," said Natalia, suddenly concerned. "I forgot about your burn. Does it hurt very much?"

That wound had already healed, but her question served to remind Matthew that he'd come here for a reason—to learn more about Cain.

"Don't you find it a little strange that Cain seems to enjoy hanging out with kids? They're what—fifteen, sixteen years old? I would think he'd rather be with . . . well . . . adults. He's what—nearly thirty?"

"I think it's the adoration, the attention they give him," Natalia replied.

The waitress brought appetizers, and Natalia ate coconut shrimp along with the cherries. She held out a shrimp to Matthew. "You have to try these."

Matthew ate a shrimp and found he enjoyed it.

"We'll have another order of shrimp for my friend here," Natalia told the waitress.

"I've seen it before with rock stars," she continued. "Once the show ends, and the audience goes home, the rock star's left with no one to worship him. He feeds off the attention. I think that's why so many rock stars abuse alcohol or drugs. It fills the emptiness inside—for a little while at least. The same could be said for others. Fake priests, for example."

She stared hard at Matthew as she said this. He chose to ignore it.

"What about the guys in the band? They don't seem to like Cain very much."

"That's sad," said Natalia. "Jordan and Mike and Ryan and Cain were all friends back in the day. But their friendship ended when Cain became a superstar. Now they don't get along. Jordan and Ryan and Mike are happier doing their own thing without him around. They say he sucks the air out of the room.

"As for the contest winners, the contest was Cain's idea, and he really takes an interest in it. He reads through all the entries, picks out the winners personally. And he likes to entertain the kids. I think he gets a kick out of it."

"The contest winner, the boy who killed his mother, did he go with Cain on the bus?" Matthew asked.

He was immediately sorry he brought that up. The light went out of Natalia's eyes, leaving only smoky shadows, as if he'd extinguished the flame on a candle.

"We're not talking about that tonight," she said, subdued. "We're not talking about anything unhappy. Agreed?"

"Agreed," he said. He didn't like it when the light left her eyes. The whole world seemed a darker place.

"So how did you meet Cain anyway?" Matthew asked, changing the subject.

Natalia smiled at the memory.

"It was years ago. I was twenty years old and traveling with the Ella Music Group. I sold their CDs and T-shirts at a booth during the show, and that's where I met Cain. I guess he was kind of a groupie himself. He followed Jordan's band, went to all their shows, bought all their CDs. I got used to seeing him around. He would come chat with me if action at the booth was slow. We talked about his guitar playing and the songs he was writing and his hopes and dreams. All that stuff.

"Well, one night, I was at a punk rock concert with some friends. I was in the mosh pit, having a really good time—"

"A what kind of pit?" Matthew interrupted.

"A mosh pit. People crowd into the mosh pit to dance and bash into each other, do stage diving, that sort of stuff."

Matthew remembered bear pits from the eighteenth century, when the audience paid to see dogs fight bears or bears fight each other. It sounded similar.

"—someone knocked me down," Natalia was saying.

"It was wild! Kids were going crazy, punching, kicking. I don't remember what happened, but Cain told me I was trying to get back to my feet when some guy accidentally kicked me in the back of my head, and I dropped like a stone.

"Cain was in the mosh pit. He picked me up and hauled me out. He drove me to the hospital and sat with me for hours in the emergency room while they fixed me up. I asked what I could do to repay him for saving my life, and he said I could come see one of his shows, and if I liked it, would I help him get started in the industry.

"Long story short, I saw his band, and I was impressed. He was doing some really creative shit. I introduced him to Jordan and the guys, and they were impressed. They'd been looking for a song writer/singer, you see. The next thing you know I'm Cain's manager—which isn't as crazy as it sounds. It's how most managers get started.

"Cain was really dedicated," she added with a wistful smile. "He played his heart out—even in the crappy venues. I remember, we were in one place that was such a dump, he fell through a hole on the stage. We ended up patching it by laying a folding table across it. We laughed about that . . ." She sighed. "Now we don't laugh about anything. We just yell at each other."

"So fame has changed him," Matthew said.

Natalia gave an emphatic nod. "He's moodier now, completely unpredictable." Natalia toyed with a cherry. "In fact, I'm worried that he's starting to lose control. Like breaking up hotel rooms or smashing his TV or riding off on his bike like he did the other day. He would have never done stupid stuff like that before.

"But, then, all celebrities behave like that, don't they? We fans give them carte blanche to be jerks. That's how we justify ourselves. We glamorize their boozing and drugging by saying they're geniuses. They're not like the rest of us. That way we can still idolize them while they're doing drugs and sleeping around and behaving like spoiled-rotten children."

"*Is* Cain a genius?" Matthew asked.

Woof had returned to the table with them, the lounge singer having departed.

"He used to be, maybe," Woof grunted. "Not anymore."

"He used to be," Natalia said, eerily echoing her grandfather. "I'm not sure now. He hasn't written anything new in months. Says he can't concentrate."

"Maybe he really did sell his soul to the devil," Woof remarked, chuckling, and he began to sing, "'I went down to the crossroads, fell down on my knees . . .'"

"Maybe he did," said Matthew quietly.

Woof stopped singing to glare at Matthew. "I was joking, man!" He gave a shudder. "Jeez, don't say things like that."

"'Maybe he did what?'" Natalia asked, having heard only Matthew's end of the conversation.

Fortunately, another thunderstorm broke out at that moment, and Matthew was spared from answering.

Natalia waited until the storm had passed, then handed the menu to Matthew. "I'm tired of talking about Cain. Let's order dinner before they shut down the kitchen for the night."

They ate their meal. Matthew ordered another Mai Tai though he would have preferred bourbon. He would have drunk water if it came with cherries, just for the pleasure of watching Natalia. He tried asking her more questions about Cain over dessert, but Natalia shut him down.

"I'm bored with Cain. Let's talk about you," she said.

Matthew Gallow was the last person Matthew wanted to discuss. He answered her questions in monosyllables, and the conversation dried up. An uncomfortable silence fell between them.

"There must be angels around," said Natalia.

Matthew was so startled he sloshed rum on his pants. Woof nearly fell out of his chair laughing.

"I beg your pardon?" Matthew said.

"Angels nearby," Natalia repeated. "That's an old saying. Whenever silence falls between two people, it's because they're in awe of the angels. Haven't you ever heard that?"

Matthew had not. And despite the fact he was seated at the dinner table, he knew the uncomfortable silence wasn't because Natalia was in awe of him. The silence was due to good, old-fashioned sex. He was conscious of Natalia's body, conscious of the movement of her breasts beneath her blouse, conscious of the touch of her foot when it accidentally stepped on his, or the time their knees bumped beneath the table.

He wasn't the only one having a problem. As they were waiting for the check, Natalia stood up to go to the restroom. She bent down to whisper, "You looked really good onstage tonight. You looked sexy."

Her lips brushed his ear. Matthew's throat constricted. Desire flooded through him. He wanted to take her in his arms there and cover her with kisses. He looked at her, and before he knew what he should say, she saw what he wanted to say in his eyes.

"I'll be right back!" she said, with a catch in her voice. "Don't go anywhere!"

Matthew sat at the table. Picking up a cherry stem, he tied it in a knot.

Natalia came back to him. He stood up. She slid her hand into his.

"Are you tired? I'm not. My room?" she whispered, smiling.

He opened his mouth to say that he was going to go back to his room, alone, and instead found himself kissing her.

Chapter 21

Natalia leaned forward into his kiss, kissing him slowly, seductively. She could feel her heart pounding, her breath coming faster. He drew back, obviously with reluctance. They walked to her room in silence. Natalia tried playing out what would happen next, but she came up with nothing. Sometimes Matthew seemed like an enigma to her. Other times she felt she knew exactly what he was thinking and feeling.

She slid her key card into the slot and opened the door. Matthew followed. Natalia kicked off her slippers and padded barefoot to the minibar. She opened the door and pulled out the small bottle of bourbon. She took a glass, filled it with ice cubes from the bucket (silently thanking nighttime turn-down service), and poured the bourbon over the ice. She handed the glass to Matthew. He was sitting on the corner of the bed quietly, his brow furrowed.

"Here," she said. "Don't you want it? Your reward for choking down those Mai Tais."

He looked up at her, smiled. Taking the bourbon, he set it down, untasted, on the nightstand.

Natalia climbed catlike across the bed to sit near the headboard, brushing near him as she moved. He turned to face her. He was so handsome—the way his hair fell across his forehead, almost to his eyes. God, his eyes! They were the deepest, darkest blue she'd ever seen, and full of turmoil, like a tempest was constantly brewing in them. His gaze never wavered from hers. It unnerved her, but in a good way.

"You're not afraid of anything, are you?" she asked him suddenly.

"You mean, am I afraid of you?" He drew near her.

"Yes. Sometimes I think you are. Oh, not afraid of me punching you out," she added, laughing. "Maybe afraid of, well . . . liking me . . ."

"I'm terrified."

He leaned near. Natalia reached her hand up to caress his face, but he drew her close and kissed her hard. The next thing Natalia felt was Matthew holding the back of her neck and kissing her harder, his lips pressing against hers harder and harder as he slid his tongue against hers, then caressed her lips.

She felt a rush of warmth sear the back of her neck, almost as if his touch burned her. His kisses grew more and more passionate as he moved his mouth down to her throat. He was on top of her now, pressed against her. Natalia was exhilarated by his touch and the urgency with which he grabbed at her. He nuzzled the hollow in her throat. She could feel his breathing, his body tense against hers. Natalia pushed her hands into his hair, which was soft and smelled like rain from the thunderstorm. She returned his fierce kisses with her own, moving from his mouth to his neck.

She was swept up in his frenzy. She felt his need to possess her, his need and his loss of control. Natalia pulled his shirt off, over his head.

Matthew reached beneath her tunic. She wasn't wearing a bra. He tugged at her tunic, deftly unfastening it at the neck and pulling the silk over her head. He leaned down to pull her nipple into his mouth. Natalia felt her body react to him.

She had never imagined Matthew as being such a passionate lover. He had always seemed so serious, so controlled. She released her worries. Cain could jump off a bridge for all she cared right now. The show could be canceled, the audience could kill each other, it could all go to hell right now, and she didn't care. She cared about Matthew, about his touch, the weight of him on top of her, his smell of rain and thunder, the tempest in his eyes . . .

Matthew pulled off Natalia's satin panties, then slid out of his shorts. His skin was soft. Not at all what she expected. He ran his fingers up the outside of her leg, tracing a line from her calf to her knee to her thigh. He touched her delicately, then seemed to lose control of himself again, and he reached around her back and pulled her to him tightly.

Natalia's breath wavered for a moment. Matthew's ferocity startled her but thrilled her at the same time. So many men in the past had treated her like a fragile, timid creature. Well, she wasn't! Matthew's urgent caressing and kissing confirmed the fact that he found her desirable. He wanted her. She'd known it from the beginning.

Matthew covered her body in kisses. Natalia's breathing came harder as her body yearned for his, reacting to his attention. He moved lower, kissing her stomach, her thighs.

She could feel his breath on her, the tender part between her legs, and she arched her back in pleasure.

Matthew held her tighter. Natalia pulled Matthew to her.

"Make love to me," she whispered.

Matthew looked at her searchingly, almost as though wondering if she meant it. Then he pulled himself on top of her, held her arms, and entered her slowly. Natalia gasped and came up to meet him, sucking in her breath at the feel of him inside her. She caught hold of his arms, dug her nails into his flesh.

Looking into Matthew's eyes, she saw the tempest swirl and, for the briefest moment, seem to calm. Matthew kept his gaze on her and started rhythmically to thrust into her, meeting her hips with his own. Natalia moaned. She felt warmth, tenderness, and his eyes on her. His eyes never left hers.

Together they found release. Natalia cried out as great spasms built up in her body, only to push her beyond limit. There she found freedom, and still Matthew's eyes on her. He looked at her as if he could never take himself away from her again.

Natalia never wanted this moment to end and willed herself to remember it always. This is what it's all about. These fleeting moments.

He rested his head on her breast. She tousled his hair, ran her fingers through it. They held each other for what seemed like no time at all to Natalia. Then Matthew lay back.

Natalia moved against him, nestled her head on his chest.

He lay staring at the ceiling.

"That was wonderful!" Natalia said.

She ran her hand caressingly over his chest, felt him groan in response. "How about an encore . . ."

He suddenly slid out from under her, stood up, began putting on his pants.

Natalia sat up. "Matthew, what's wrong?"

"I can't do this," he stated.

Grabbing his shirt and shoes, he walked out of her hotel room, letting the door slam behind him.

Chapter 22

$\mathcal{N}$atalia sat in her bed and stared at the door. She was stunned, absolutely stunned. Stunned and shocked and bewildered. Bewildered and confused. One minute she and Matthew were in each other's arms, making love, and the next minute, he was gone. Poof.

"'Like dust in the wind,' as Kansas would say," she muttered.

Natalia couldn't make sense of it. She sat there and went over the evening's events in her mind, from start to finish. And at no point could she see where she had offended Matthew, at least not enough to make him leave her alone in bed!

And he hadn't seemed angry, she thought. In fact, she could have sworn he was into her as much as she was into him. His lovemaking had been passionate, tender, caring . . . experienced. She was still aroused, could still feel his lips, his hands caress her . . .

She wrapped her arms around her pillow, for want of

anything else, and hugged it close. She didn't cry, but she was close.

Damn it. She liked Matthew. He was mature. He wasn't a kid, like most in this business. He wasn't self-centered, self-absorbed. Matthew didn't feel the need to try to impress her. He was secure in himself. He was serious and grave—maybe too serious, too grave. Yet he had laughter inside him, even though she had the feeling he hadn't let it come to the surface much. She wanted to make him laugh. She wanted to make him forget about whatever unhappy things had happened to him in the past.

Because unhappy things had happened. She was sure of that. There was something mysterious about him. Natalia had to admit that was attractive. The Bible reading, the bourbon drinking. That didn't add up. And all these questions about Cain. It wasn't morbid curiosity. She had the feeling he really cared about Cain . . . and no one except her and Cain's fans cared about Cain. And his fans only cared about the carefully crafted image.

Natalia had the feeling Matthew cared about her, too. And so what does he do to show it? He gets up from the bed in the middle of the night and walks out!

"Yeah, that makes a lot of sense," Natalia muttered into the pillow.

Maybe she'd come on too strong. What was it her mother had always said in her endless lectures on how to land a husband—implying men were somehow like catfish. Play hard to get. "A man chases a woman until she catches him."

Maybe that was it. She had let it show that she had feelings for him, and he had bolted like a racehorse from the gate. Now she felt stupid.

Workplace relationships. Always bad news. This was going to make things damn awkward between them. She was his boss. He might feel so uncomfortable he'd quit! She couldn't have that. The act had been spectacular, better than she'd hoped. The kids had loved it. She had to fix this. She had to convince him that she didn't care about him in the least. That way, he wouldn't feel guilty.

"I was looking for some fun. Just foolin' around. Casual sex. Friends with benefits. I do this sort of thing all the time," she said, practicing a light and airy laugh.

Except, she didn't . . .

Natalia put her head down on the pillow and sighed deeply. Then she gave herself a mental slap. Don't be a baby. You have work to do.

She couldn't let him go to bed brooding over this. She reached for the hotel phone to call Matthew's room, juggled the receiver a moment, then put it down.

No, calling was cowardly. She had to face him, be convincing. Otherwise, he might not believe her. She went to the bathroom, did a repair job on her makeup, brushed her hair, put her clothes back on, and headed out the door.

Her phone, which she'd left on the nightstand, started buzzing. She considered leaving it, but that was like leaving her right hand behind. She grabbed the phone, looked at the number, saw it was Crandall. At two in the morning, this couldn't be anything good.

Well, it would have to wait.

She sent him to voice mail.

Matthew couldn't open the door to his hotel room. He tried four times and had almost concluded that his plastic swipe card didn't work (what had happened to old-fashioned keys?) when he realized he was holding the card backward. He turned the card around and swiped it and the door opened.

He went inside, shut it, stood in the dark a moment with his back against the door. Then he switched on the light, walked into the room, flung the plastic card on the bed, where he was certain to forget it, and went to the minibar—one modern innovation of which he highly approved.

Natalia had, of course, reserved VIP rooms. Someone had turned down his bed, switched on the radio to soft music, placed a chocolate on his pillow, and, best of all, filled his ice bucket. The bed was enormous, the room luxurious—a far cry from the Inn-B-Tween motel on County Road H. He put ice in his glass and started to pour the bourbon out of the small bottle.

"You're a real bastard, you know that!"

Woof's voice went off like a bomb behind Matthew, causing his hand to jerk. He sloshed bourbon over most of the counter, the floor, and his feet.

Matthew closed his eyes, waiting for his pounding heartbeat to return to normal. Then he opened his eyes, finished pouring the bourbon, and said flatly, "Get out."

"You hurt her!" Woof stated angrily.

"The truth is I'm trying *not* to hurt her," Matthew said. Bourbon in hand, he picked up his briefcase, flung it on the bed. "So just clear out."

He had only unpacked a few things—his shaving gear, Bible, the bourbon, clean underwear. It didn't take too long to toss those back into his case.

"You're leaving," Woof said.

"Nothing gets past you," Matthew returned.

"You goin' back to the bus?" Woof asked.

"I'm going," said Matthew. "Just . . . going."

He shut the case, glanced around the room to see if he'd forgotten anything. The bourbon bottle was still on the table. He couldn't very well take that with him. He decided he might as well finish it. He poured out another glass.

"Poor Natalia is crying her eyes out!" Woof yelled.

Matthew smiled wryly. "I don't think Natalia's the type to cry over a man. More likely she's throwing things."

"You're right," Woof returned. "She's got more sense than to cry over a bastard like you. Isn't she good enough for you? You bein' a high-and-mighty angel and all—"

"Damn it!" Matthew swore. "I like Natalia! I could do more than like her. What man wouldn't? She's interesting, intelligent. Beautiful. Desirable, sexy . . . How many other adjectives do you want to hear?"

Matthew tossed down his drink, then said quietly, "I'm trying not to hurt her. I'm trying to spare her—and myself— a whole world of hurt later."

"You can't quit! You signed a contract!" Woof stated.

"I used ink, not blood," Matthew returned.

He walked toward the door, and was reaching out his hand for the handle when the empty bourbon bottle lifted up off the nightstand, whizzed through the air, and smashed against the door, spattering Matthew with shards of broken glass.

Natalia exited the elevator, walked down the hall, came to Matthew's door. She was about to knock, when she heard his voice. He was talking to someone. At first, she thought he was talking on the phone, but the more she listened, the more it sounded to her as though someone else was in the room with him.

Then there was a crash and the sound of breaking glass. Natalia stared, startled.

Her first thought was a girlfriend. They were having a row. Maybe it was that Hannah! That's why he left me! Why, that bastard . . .

Natalia was angry now. She knew she should leave. This was none of her business.

Except he's now part of the act, she rationalized. *I need to know what's going on, clear the air.*

Natalia drew closer to the door. It was hard to make out what they were saying. Matthew tended to be soft-spoken, and now his voice was muffled by the door. She couldn't hear the other person at all. . . .

"You're a coward!" Woof cried, glowering at Matthew. "You know something bad is goin' on, and you're goin' to run away and leave my little girl to face it all alone!"

"She'll be safer if I'm gone," said Matthew. He brushed bits of glass off his jacket. "The night of the riot, I ran under the scaffolding, and I saw those two roadies, Burl and John, sabotaging it. They knew Natalia was up there, and they were deliberately trying to bring it down—"

Woof glared at him. "Don't change the subject."

"Listen to me, damn it! What I saw under the scaffolding wasn't human. They were demons."

"Yeah, right." Woof snorted in disgust. "As I remember, you'd been hittin' the bourbon that night—"

"I saw demons, not pink elephants," Matthew retorted. "You remember that Cain was adamantly opposed to hiring me—for no very good reason. Natalia was the one who was insisting on it. So—they get rid of her, and that's the end of it."

"Doesn't jibe, man." Woof shook his head. "Burl was the one who told Cain to keep you."

"After the scaffolding incident. I believe I know why," Matthew said slowly. "I saw them. And I'm starting to think they must have seen me."

"Then Burl wanting Cain to keep you makes even less sense—if that's possible," Woof stated.

"Not if they saw the *real* me," Matthew said somberly. "Then they'd be afraid I was onto them. They'd need to keep me around to find out what I knew . . ."

"And what do you know?" Woof asked.

"Nothing," said Matthew bitterly. "Absolutely nothing."

The ghost fell into a troubled silence for a moment, eyeing Matthew thoughtfully. Then he said in a low voice, "You honestly think Cain sold his soul to the devil? For real?"

"I think it's possible," said Matthew. "A . . . um . . . person I met with certain high-level connections told me that traitors in Purgatory allowed the demons to break through the battle lines, and now demons are here on Earth, trying to bring about the downfall of mankind."

Woof flung his hands. "If Satan is trying to bring about the downfall of mankind, why choose an asshole rock star? Why not someone with influence like the president or Oprah . . ."

Matthew dropped his briefcase and began to pick up pieces of the broken bottle. Otherwise, when the maid came in, she might step on it, get hurt. Too many people were getting hurt tonight.

"I can see why Satan would choose Cain," Matthew said, tossing the pieces in the wastebasket.

Woof snorted. "Why? Sure, Cain's an asshole, but he's a harmless asshole."

"Is he? There's that boy who killed his mother and himself—"

"Bah! So the kid was wearing a Cain T-shirt. Big deal. What if he'd been wearing a Yankees T-shirt? Would they say Roger Clemens made him kill his mom? It was a coincidence—"

"I'm not so sure. And you saw what happened to my hand when I touched him!" Matthew sat up, faced Woof. "According to Natalia, Cain became an overnight sensation. *Overnight*. One day no one's heard of him and the next day the whole world is in love with him."

"He found his fifteen minutes of fame," said Woof. "The same way you found yours. One minute you're in a revival tent, and the next you're fighting off groupies."

"Don't think I haven't wondered about that," Matthew said quietly. "Buddhists believe there is no such thing as coincidence. Everything you do is cause and effect. I exorcise a demon who's possessed a girl who has met Cain in person and, lo and behold, that very night Cain's manager is in the audience, and she sees me and wants to hire me."

Woof frowned and scratched his grizzled chin. "You're saying the Buddhists are behind this? I don't know, man . . ."

"Forget the Buddhists!" Matthew said, exasperated. "I'm sorry I brought them up."

Matthew picked up his briefcase again.

"When I was alive," said Woof, subdued, "I didn't believe in God or Heaven or any of that shit. Came as quite a surprise when I found out different. Shocked the hell out of me, you might say."

"One reason you never made it as far as Heaven?" Matthew asked.

Woof flushed. "Maybe. Hey, it takes a little getting used to the idea! If you must know the truth, I wasn't all that sure of my welcome. I broke a few of the rules in my time. Nothin' really bad, mind you. . . . Well, how was I supposed to know God was real?" Woof demanded defensively. "I didn't think anyone gave a damn!"

"If there's one thing Heaven's good at," Matthew said, "it's forgiveness."

"Something you're *not* good at, huh, Angel Boy," Woof remarked. "Spend your time going around performing fake exorcisms. Seems to me you must enjoy poking God with a sharp stick. So if you're such a badass, why aren't you in Hell?"

"What makes you think I'm not?" Matthew retorted. "Take care of Natalia."

He had his hand on the handle and was starting to turn it when he heard the familiar sound of a buzzing cell phone . . .

"Damn!" Natalia exclaimed and answered it just to shut it up.

"Crandall! This is not a good time," she said in a loud whisper, hurrying down the hall in case Matthew came to the door. "What the hell do you want?"

She listened. A sick feeling came over her.

"What?" she said with only half a voice. "Are you sure. The police . . . Oh, my God."

She went hot all over. The hallway started to tilt, the floor heading up into the ceiling. The hall lights were behaving oddly. The phone slipped from her hand and landed on the floor, then she was on the floor with her phone, and the next thing she knew Matthew was kneeling beside her.

"Natalia! Are you all right? What happened?"

She tried to sit up.

"I'm okay," she said thickly, only she wasn't.

"You don't look it," he said. He lifted her in his arms and carried her back to his room.

He was strong and warm and safe and secure—even if he was crazy. Natalia rested her head against his chest and closed her eyes. Maybe this would go away. Maybe it would all go away.

Matthew laid her down on his bed. "What happened?" he demanded. He looked really worried. "Did someone attack you in the hall? I heard your phone buzz—"

"My phone!" Natalia sat up dizzily. "I have to make a call . . ."

"No, you don't," Matthew said firmly. "You should rest. I'll call security—"

"I wasn't attacked!" Natalia tried to stand. "I heard some . . . bad news. You don't understand. I need my phone . . ."

"Wait here," said Matthew. "I'll get it."

He went back out in the hall. When he returned, he handed her the phone. Natalia looked at it and remembered what Crandall had just told her.

"Oh, God!" she groaned, and sank back down onto the pillows. She felt sick to her stomach.

Matthew poured her some water. The phone was buzzing again.

Matthew picked it up, answered it brusquely. "Natalia Ashley's phone. No, Crandall, she can't talk right now. She's not feeling well. She'll call you in the morning. Look, you ass, I don't care what happened—"

Crandall was shouting, and Natalia could hear him almost as clearly as if she were holding the phone. Matthew fell silent, listening in shock.

Natalia watched Matthew's face. She saw it go tense, rigid. "I see," he said. "Okay, well, give her a few moments. This has been a shock."

He hung up and silently handed her the phone.

"I have to go to Cain," Natalia said, and she tried again to sit up and this time had more luck. "He'll be terribly upset."

"Will he?" Matthew asked coldly.

"Of course he will!" Natalia said. "A kid kills himself and writes in his suicide note that Cain told him to do it! Cain will take this really hard. I have to be the one who tells him."

"This kid was one of the contest winners tonight, wasn't he?" Matthew asked, still in that same horrible, cold voice.

"Yes," said Natalia shakily. "That's why I have to call Crandall back. The press doesn't have that news yet, but when they do . . ." She stopped, stared at him. "How did you know? Like I said, Crandall doesn't even know. I recognized the name, but you—"

"Just a guess," Matthew said. He looked grim.

She remembered the snatches of conversation, the things he'd been saying to whoever it was he'd been saying it to. She looked around the room. Who had he been saying them to? No one else was here. Of course, whoever it was could have left when Matthew came out to see what had happened to her.

No, the person would have had to walk past me to reach the elevator, and even though I was lying on the floor, I'm positive I would have seen someone walking past. But the only person I saw was Matthew.

So he was here alone, talking to himself, saying things like: *And you saw what happened to my hand when I touched him . . . Cain became an overnight sensation. . . . Buddhists believe there is no such thing as coincidence. . . . I exorcise a demon who's possessed a girl who has met Cain in person and, lo and behold, that very night Cain's manager is in the audience and she sees me and wants to hire me. . . .*

A thousand questions tumbled around Natalia's mind. And she couldn't ask any of them because then he would know she'd been spying on him. There was one thing she could ask him, though. Her gaze went to the briefcase, packed and closed, on the floor by the door.

"You were leaving, weren't you," she said. "You were gonna bail on me!"

"I'll call you a cab," said Matthew. He reached for the hotel phone. "I'm coming with you. You shouldn't be by yourself."

"I can manage on my own," Natalia said angrily. "I've been doing it since I was sixteen. So just . . . go catch your plane. Don't worry about your contract. I'll tear it up. I hope you have a nice life . . ."

She stood, swayed on her feet, and Matthew was there by her side. He put his arm around her, supporting her. His eyes were soft with concern.

"I'm coming with you," he said in a tone that meant there would be no argument. "I won't interfere with your work. I'll spend the night on the band bus if you want me to, or I'll go catch that plane, if you want me to. I just need to make sure you reach the bus safely."

She wanted to tell him to go to hell and walk out, but her knees felt wobbly, and her dignified exit stage left wouldn't look so hot if she collapsed in front of the elevator.

Matthew grabbed his briefcase and helped her back to her room. Moving numbly, mechanically, she packed up her things, while he waited for her. By the time she had finished packing, she was feeling a little better. She went to the bathroom, carefully arranged her face so that it would show no emotion.

"Look, about tonight . . ."

"I'm sorry about tonight," Matthew said. "You're right. I *was* planning to leave."

Natalia's lips trembled. Her carefully arranged face was starting to slide.

"I was going to leave," Matthew continued, "for the simple reason that I wanted to be the first one out the door."

Natalia blinked, confused. "I don't understand . . ."

"I wanted to leave you," Matthew said quietly, "before you left me."

Natalia's face slid into ruins. She broke down and began to sob uncontrollably, painful sobs that went clear down into her chest. He put his arms around, held her tight. Just held her.

"I'm going to put a stop to this," Matthew said. "This has to end."

Natalia looked up at him through her tears. She had the strangest feeling he was talking to someone else.

Chapter 23

For Natalia, the cab ride at two in the morning through the city was surreal, eerie. The streets were deserted except for, here and there, a solitary person either hurrying along, glancing nervously over his shoulder, or a homeless person huddled in a doorway. The streetlamps shed pools of radiance that illuminated only small patches of sidewalk and only served to make the surrounding darkness seem that much blacker.

The cabdriver was the silent type, thank goodness. Natalia leaned her head against the window, watched the lights flash by. She tried to go over everything she had to do. First, she had to break the news to Cain. She had no idea how he would take this. She knew how he would have taken it a year ago. He would have been devastated, appalled, heartsick. But now . . . He'd become so irrational, unpredictable. She would have to make sure Al or Kimo was with her, keep Cain from doing something stupid, like riding off on his bike again.

She'd have to break the news to the band, as well. They'll be upset. Maybe she should send them all home for a week, give them time to work things out. No. Bad idea. The press would track them down, plus they still had tour dates, commitments.

We're a family, she told herself. *We have to stick together, work through this.*

She had told Matthew the rest of the concerts might be canceled. If it were up to her, they would be. She had the feeling the attorneys wouldn't stand for it. Canceling the concerts would be tantamount to an admission of guilt. She would have to talk to the lawyer, work with him on a press release, decide whether or not to do a press conference with Cain. If yes, Cain's attorney would have to be there, to keep him from admitting to anything.

Not that there was anything to admit to, Natalia hastily reminded herself. It's all a horrible tragedy.

She wondered what had happened, what made this kid snap. She wished desperately she'd stayed with Cain and the contest winners. She was certain Cain would not have said anything. The first thing she would do, after she talked to Cain and the band, was talk to Kimo. He'd been there, along with the other members of the security team.

Natalia remembered the contest winner clearly. She remembered the father, who had come with the boy. Natalia kept replaying her interaction with the two over and over in her head. The kid had seemed normal, well-adjusted, happy. The father had seem a bit dazed, but good-natured, relaxed. Perhaps if she'd paid more attention, she might have noticed something. But she'd been preoccupied with keeping tabs on Cain and—admittedly—by her feelings for Matthew.

Thinking of Matthew, she glanced sidelong at him. He was sitting about as far from her as he could manage, not talking, absorbed in his own thoughts, which were pretty grim, to judge by his expression. Natalia sighed. Back in the hotel, he had held her until her sobs had quieted, then he'd very gently let go of her. He'd carried her overnight bag, as well as his briefcase, and helped her into the cab, and given the cabbie directions on where to take them.

Sensing her watching him, Matthew looked over at her. He gave her a smile, but it was a grave, serious smile. His eyes were dark, unreadable.

He sat to her left. His right hand rested on his knee.

Natalia reached out, took hold of his bandaged right hand and squeezed it.

"Who are you, Matthew Gallow?" Natalia asked suddenly.

Matthew gazed down at her hand in his for long moments, then he slowly closed his fingers over hers.

"I've never lied to you, Natalia," he said. He didn't look at her. He stared straight ahead. "I've told you the truth all along."

"But not the whole truth," she said tremulously.

"No," he said, after a pause. "Not the whole truth."

She waited.

At last he said, "No one ever tells the whole truth, Natalia, because we don't know it." He paused, then added, "We think we do. But we don't."

"You know something about why these terrible things are happening," Natalia cried. "What do you know? You have to tell me!" She grabbed his arm in her desperation, dug her nails into him. "Tell me!"

He reached down, closed his hand over her hand. He turned to face her.

"Cancel the rest of the tour," he said. "Now. Tonight."

"I don't think they'll let me," Natalia said, startled by his vehemence.

"*Who* won't let you?" he asked sharply.

"The attorneys. I'll ask, but I'm sure they'll say it would be seen as an admission of guilt. The Bill O'Reillys out there will see it as weakness and go after Cain."

Matthew removed his hand. He faced forward again, resting his hands on his knees.

"Matthew," said Natalia, "you're frightening me. If you know something about Cain or . . . or anyone that has to do with this, you *have* to tell me!"

"I don't know anything," he said quietly.

"But tonight you said—" She stopped.

"Said what?" Matthew asked tersely. He was smiling, but only with his lips. His eyes weren't smiling, and they were fixed on her, skinning her, tearing her apart, sinking deep, deep into her. His dark brows drew together. "What did you hear me say?"

Natalia wanted to ask about all those things she heard him say to whoever was in his room, but she couldn't admit she'd been spying on him.

"At dinner," she said lamely. "You were asking all those questions about Cain . . ."

Matthew relaxed. He shifted his gaze away from her, folded his arms, withdrew into himself.

"You want my advice. Cancel the rest of the tour," he said flatly.

Natalia felt drained. She moved over to her corner of the cab, pressing against the door, and closed her eyes.

They continued the ride in silence.

When they arrived at the venue, Natalia asked the cabdriver to take them around to the back of the parking lot. Even at this hour, the press were sure to be circling. According to Crandall, the news hadn't broken yet, but reporters were like sharks. They could smell blood in the water. She paid the driver, and she and Matthew walked silently across the empty parking lot toward the buses. Even though Matthew was with her, she felt vulnerable and alone. Or maybe because Matthew was with her. She was confused, conflicted. Part of her wanted to be held again, safe in his arms. Part of her wanted to bust his jaw.

And then she had to quit thinking about Matthew. Lights were on in Cain's bedroom, and even from here, she could hear the music blaring out into the night.

"Is someone in there with him?" Matthew asked grimly.

"Al went to Wisconsin to see his family," Natalia said. "Kimo's there. Or he should be."

"I'll wait with you to make sure," said Matthew.

Natalia nodded. She knocked on the bus door.

"Kimo was with Cain tonight when he was entertaining the contest winners, wasn't he?" Matthew said. "Ask him what happened."

"I plan to," Natalia said.

Kimo's broad face appeared in the window, looking out to see who was knocking. Seeing Natalia here at this time of night, he must have guessed something was wrong. He opened the door. The reek of pot hit Natalia as she walked on board. She wondered that Kimo wasn't high just from the residual smoke. Her heart sank. This was going to be difficult enough without Cain's being stoned.

She boarded the bus, acutely aware of Matthew following right behind her.

"Did the contest kids leave when they were supposed to?" she asked Kimo.

"Yes, ma'am. The limo picked them up at midnight."

Natalia swallowed. "Did they . . . did they seem okay when they left?"

Kimo looked surprised at the question. "Yes, ma'am. I guess so. I'm not sure what you—"

"They hadn't been drinking or smoking pot or anything?"

"No, ma'am," Kimo said firmly. "I was with them the entire time. They talked to Cain—or rather, he talked to them. Mostly about himself. They drank Coke and ate pizza, then they left."

"Cain wasn't smoking pot while they were with him, was he?" Natalia asked nervously.

"No, ma'am," Kimo said gravely. "I wouldn't have allowed that. Not with the kids around."

"Good," said Natalia. "That's good. Something bad has happened, Kimo, really bad. I'll tell you later. Right now, I have to talk to Cain. Would you wait outside the door, Kimo? Just in case I need you?"

"Yes, ma'am," said Kimo gently. He exited the bus, took up his position.

Natalia turned to Matthew. "Thanks for coming with me. I need to handle this alone now. Would you do me a favor? Would you go wake up the guys in the band if they're asleep, tell them I need to talk to them? I'll be there in a few moments. This can't wait until morning. When the press gets hold of it—they listen to the police scanners y'know." She shook her head.

Matthew glanced back toward Cain's end of the bus. The music was so loud the bass beat was actually shaking the bus. Cain was singing along with it. Or rather, screeching along with it.

"I think I should stay," Matthew said.

"I'll be all right," Natalia assured him. "I should talk to Cain alone. And Kimo's right outside . . ." She didn't finish that thought. "Thank you for coming with me," she said again.

Matthew nodded. He deposited his briefcase on the floor, then walked toward the bus door.

Natalia drew in a shaky breath and walked to Cain's bedroom. She hammered on the door.

"Cain! Open up! I need to talk to you!"

Natalia pounded on the door for several minutes before he finally opened it.

Cain was half-naked, dressed only in his underwear. He was a mess. His hair was disheveled, hanging over his face. He smelled of booze and pot. He swayed on his feet, grinned at her drunkenly.

"Natalia, baby, you decided to come party with me!" Cain staggered past her, heading for the liquor cabinet. "Whatcha drinkin'?"

"Cain, I need to talk to you."

She grabbed hold of his arm, spinning him around.

"Whoa, Nat, sweetie! Takin' me to bed?" He tried to put his arms around her, kiss her.

Natalia gave his arm an expert twist. He grimaced and yelped. "Hey, that hurts. That's not funny."

"I'm in no mood to be funny, Cain," she said. She was afraid she might start crying, and that would be bad. Never show weakness. "Back to your room." Once there, she switched off his music.

"That was Nine Inch Nails!" Cain wailed.

"Cain, you need to listen to me," Natalia said desperately. "Sit down on the bed. Something horrible has happened. One of the contest winners committed suicide tonight. And he left a note. The note claims you told him to kill himself."

For a moment Cain was silent. He stared at her, trying to focus, then he asked, in a kind of awed voice, "He mentioned me by name?"

"Yes. That's what the police told Crandall. I know this is a terrible shock for you, but you have to remember—"

"Terrible. Yeah." Cain gave a drunken laugh. He shook his head, mumbled something.

"What did you say?" Natalia demanded.

"I said think of the publicity, Nat!" Cain repeated, his voice slurred. He stood up, began staggering about the room. "Where're my shoes? Talk to . . . press. My name. Cain Lukosi. All over news . . . . I'll wear my . . . my . . . Ouch, damn it!"

He had fallen over his shoes, stubbing his toe. He began to swear.

"Cain, what is wrong with you?" Natalia cried. "A kid, a fan of yours, is dead. He has parents, a little sister . . ."

"Fuckin' shoe." Cain slumped down on the bed. "Where's my foot? Oh, there it is. You're right, Nat. Horrible, horrible. Note had my name in it . . . That's good. That's very good. I hope . . . kid spelled it right . . ."

He began to laugh again. Natalia slapped him, hard, on the cheek. His laughter ceased.

Cain looked at her. His jaw sagged, his mouth hung open.

"You hit me," he said. "You're always hitting me!"

"I didn't hurt you, you baby. I'm trying to knock some sense into you," Natalia said, incensed. She leaned over, pinned his arms to his sides. "And I'll hit you again if you don't shut up and listen to me. I told Crandall to keep in touch with the police and to notify everyone that you don't have a statement yet. I'll have one ready for you tomorrow. There may be a press conference."

"I know. Press conference. I'm trying to get dressed for it, if you'd let go of me," Cain said soddenly. "Can't find . . . other shoe . . ."

"It's three in the morning," Natalia cut him off. "And you're *not* going to the press conference. Not if we can get out of it. Your lawyer will hold it. You're in no condition to be dealing with this. Put down the damn shoe!"

"First you hit me . . . now you yell at me . . ." Cain whined.

"No more pot." Natalia began cleaning up, picking up his pipe and his bottle and the half-empty glass. "No more booze. Get to bed. Sober up."

"Funeral. When's funeral?" Cain asked, standing up again and lurching into the closet. "I'll wear my black leather pants . . . Photo op . . ."

Between Cain's behavior and the stink of pot and booze, Natalia felt sick to her stomach. She came close to throwing up. She flung open a window, drew in a breath of fresh air, and waited for the dizziness and nausea to pass. Then she turned around, asked the question she had hoped she wouldn't have to ask.

"Cain," said Natalia, trying to keep her voice level, "you *didn't* tell that boy to . . . to hurt himself, did you?"

Cain shook his head. He was fumbling around inside the bottom of his closet. "Me? No! Why'd I do . . . stupid thing like that? Fans keep killing themselves . . . cuts down on . . . sales . . ." Cain laughed.

"Cain, stop it!" Natalia cried. "Why are you acting like this?"

Cain stood upright.

"Because I can, Nat," he said. "I'm a star." He lurched toward her, his hand extended. "It's good. It's all good . . ."

"That does it," said Natalia. "I have no choice. I'm canceling the rest of the tour. You've lost your mind."

Cain went white. Natalia had always read about the blood draining out of a person's face, but this was the first time she'd ever seen it. The sight was terrifying. Cain's skin was so pale, she could see the blue veins stand out in his jaw. He seemed to quit breathing. His bloodshot eyes were wide and white-rimmed.

His lips moved. No sound came out, but she understood him. "You can't do this to me . . ."

"Cain, I'm sorry," Natalia faltered, alarmed at the way he

looked. "I don't want to, but I think it would be best. The way you're acting—"

"You don't understand! They'll kill me, Nat!" Cain cried wildly. "They'll kill me—"

He doubled over and screamed—a terrible scream, as though his insides were being ripped out. Then he slumped down onto his knees and began to weep. Sodden weeping, like a little child. Skinny and naked and shivering, he curled into a ball on the floor.

"Cain . . ." Natalia said, kneeling down beside him.

"Go away!" He started to roll back and forth in agony.

"Cain . . . your fans won't kill you," Natalia said, trying to soothe him. She was baffled. She'd seen him in all sorts of moods, but never anything like this. "They'll understand . . ."

"What? That I'm a monster?" Cain's head jerked up. His eyes were bloodshot, and the veins in his neck were standing out. He surged to his feet. Fists clenched, he came at her.

"Get out!" he screamed savagely.

Natalia backed up precipitously. Cain glared at her with such rage that she feared he was going to strike her. Instead, he whirled around, reached up to a shelf that held his CD collection, and pulled them all down. They smashed onto the floor and he flung himself face-first onto the bed.

"Jus . . . get out . . ." he mumbled into the pillow.

Natalia decided that getting out would be the best idea. She was stunned, confused. What had gotten into him? Wanting to turn this tragedy into some kind of sick publicity stunt? Not even Johnny Rotten would have been that cruel, callous.

Natalia left, but she remained standing outside the bedroom door, leaving it partially ajar, listening to make sure

Cain was all right. As she stood there, she caught sight of Matthew standing by the window.

He'd been eavesdropping.

Seeing her looking at him, he shook his head and walked off.

Concerned for Natalia, Matthew had taken up a position outside the window. He wasn't alone. Woof was with him. They both listened to Cain's deranged reaction.

"Asshole's lucky I'm a ghost," Woof had growled. "Go to the funeral! I'd like to grab him by his scrawny neck, pull him inside out, and make him swallow himself!"

Matthew had also been appalled and disgusted. He had been about to walk off, thinking he couldn't stomach much more of this himself without resorting to violence, when Cain said something that brought Matthew up short.

You don't understand . . . They'll kill me . . .

And the next moment he'd screamed in pain and collapsed into a sodden heap.

Natalia assumed Cain was talking about his fans. *Your fans won't kill you*, she had said to him. *They'll understand.*

But Cain wasn't talking about his fans. He was terrified, scared out of what wits he had left after soaking them in booze and pot.

Matthew went cold. He had spoken glibly enough to Woof about the Buddhists and coincidences and that Cain had sold his soul to the devil, but, Matthew had to admit, the logical part of him hadn't really believed it.

Now he had to consider that it might be a fact. What would selling one's soul to Satan entail? Presumably you exchanged your soul for fame and fortune or whatever it was you wanted; then instead of going to Heaven after death, you went to Hell.

Okay, maybe that's what had happened to Doctor Faustus

back in the old days. But now things were different. Satan's minions had escaped from Hell and were walking about freely on Earth, trying to bring about the downfall of man. Which meant that Satan might not have to wait until after death to collect on his bargain. Satan could use Cain's soul while it was *still inside his body*! Force Cain to do his bidding.

Suddenly, pieces that didn't even appear to be from the same puzzle were all fitting together neatly.

What Cain had said when he'd found about the boy who'd killed his mother: *Bastards! You bastards! You did this!*

Cain agreeing to hire Matthew because a roadie had ordered him to do it. A roadie who was, literally, a roadie from Hell.

And now: *If you cancel the concert tour, they'll kill me . . .*

Cain had claimed he hadn't told that kid to kill himself. Matthew believed him. The wretched young man hadn't seen this coming. Cain had sold his soul, reaped his reward, and he'd naively thought that was the end of it.

"You're onto something, aren't you, Angel Boy," Woof said, eyeing Matthew. "What is it?"

"That there's going to be hell to pay," said Matthew.

Natalia waited outside Cain's room until he grew quiet. She peeped inside. Cain lay sprawled on his stomach on his bed, his mouth wide open, his breathing raspy. His eyes were closed. She shut the door softly and walked back to the front of the bus.

"Cain's asleep," she said to Kimo. "Would you keep an eye on him?"

Kimo nodded and went back inside.

Matthew was standing by the band bus. He'd been eavesdropping on her. She didn't like it, but she supposed she had it coming. She was too tired to care. And the night was not yet over. She still had to break the news to the band members and figure out what to do about the rest of the concerts.

She wanted to call the tour off. Face it, the concerts hadn't been going that well anyway. It was like they were cursed. First the riot, then the murder/suicide, now this. She could postpone the tour for a year. Cain could sober up, maybe go into rehab. That was the "in" thing for celebrities to do these days anyway. She could try to repair relations between Cain and the guys in the band. After that, they could start work on a new album. Put this nightmare behind them.

Natalia heaved a sigh. It would be the best idea, but she knew it wasn't going to happen. Cain had made it clear he wouldn't let her cancel the tour, and she guessed that his attorney would back him up.

Matthew was still standing outside the band bus. No lights in there. The guys had gone to bed. She'd have to wake them up.

Time enough for that. What she wanted now was Matthew's arms around her, Matthew holding her, telling her everything was going to be all right. He would be telling her a lie, but right now it was a lie she needed to hear.

She gave him a wave, but he wasn't looking her direction. He hadn't seen her. She starting walking toward him, when he turned around and she saw that he was on his cell phone.

Who on earth was he calling at three in the morning?

Matthew caught sight of her, snapped the phone shut.

"Who were you calling at this time of night?" Natalia demanded.

"Just checking my voice mail," he said.

Natalia stared at him. "What voice mail? No one ever calls you."

Matthew slid the phone in his pocket. "Why don't you get some sleep," he said to her with concern. "Let the guys sleep. Leave it until morning."

Natalia felt sick to her stomach. This was just all she needed.

"I can't," she said. "A reporter might call them or their families. They have to know what to say."

He started to reach for her. She sidestepped past him.

"No reason for all of us to lose sleep," she said coldly. "And that burn on your hand must be hurting you. Go on back to your own bunk. Cain's out. He won't be a bother."

She turned her back on him, reached up her hand as if she was going to knock on the bus door.

She could see, out of the corner of her eye, Matthew looking at her strangely. She hoped he would say something, offer some plausible explanation.

In the end, all he said was, "Try to get some sleep." Then he walked off, shoving his bandaged hand in his pocket.

Closing her eyes, Natalia leaned her head on the bus door and beat softly on it with her closed fist.

Damn, damn, damn!

There could be only one reason for Matthew Gallow to be talking to anyone on the phone tonight, then lie about it.

He was going to sell Cain out to the press.

Chapter 24

The guys in the band were badly shaken when Natalia told them about the tragedy. Jordan said he thought they should cancel the rest of tour, or at the least the radio contests.

Natalia shook her head. "I haven't talked to the lawyer, but I know what he'll say. If we do that, it will practically be admitting that Cain was responsible for this. And he wasn't. Everyone has to understand that."

She fixed Ryan with her gaze as she spoke. She'd had a difficult time waking him and though his eyes were open, he still appeared to be half-asleep. He scratched his head and gazed blearily at her.

"So you're saying Cain didn't tell this kid to kill himself."

"I'm not only saying it, it's the truth," returned Natalia sternly.

"Even though the kid said he did," Ryan argued.

"The poor kid was troubled," Natalia said, sighing. "He

didn't know what he was saying. He might just as easily have claimed Paul McCartney told him to kill himself."

"Paul would never do anything like that," Ryan said solemnly.

"And you're saying Cain would?" Natalia demanded.

The three guys glanced at each other. Jordan looked away. Ryan bit into a cold Pop Tart and washed it down with beer.

"Cain's gotten really weird, Natalia," Mike explained.

"We know, Mike," Jordan said. He put his arm around Natalia. "Whatever decision you make, Nat, we'll be fine with it. Now go get some sleep. I'll see to it none of us talks to the press."

Natalia made her way back to the bus. She had set her phone to vibrate and it had been buzzing like a rattlesnake in her pocket for over an hour now. Seeing the astounding number of voice mail messages—astounding because it was four in the morning—she shut the phone off.

She checked on Cain. He was sleeping soundly. Matthew was asleep, as well. She could hear his breathing, even and regular. She wanted to wake him, demand to know if he'd betrayed her. She even put her hand on the curtain to his bunk, ready to pull it aside. She stopped, drew her hand back. She would give him the benefit of the doubt. See what happened tomorrow. Natalia yawned her way through a hot shower, put on her penguin jammies, and crawled into her bunk.

She was jolted awake by an odd sound. She sat up, pulled aside the curtain, and was half-blinded by the bright sunlight streaming inside the front of the bus. Natalia grabbed her cell phone and looked at the time—9:00 A.M. Damn! She hadn't meant to sleep so late! She was starting to climb out of her bunk when she heard the sound again. She parted the curtain slightly, peered out.

Matthew was getting dressed. He was trying to do so quietly, so as not to wake her. This could have been consideration on his part, but she didn't think so. He looked sneaky, and her suspicions from last night came flooding back to her. She noticed he kept glancing in the direction of her bunk as if to make certain she was still asleep.

Of course, Matthew could just be going out to eat, except in all the time he'd been traveling with them, he had never once gone out for breakfast. He ate whatever she had on hand: Pop Tarts or cornflakes or bagels. It didn't seem to matter.

There was only one explanation. He was going somewhere to meet with a reporter. Damn him anyway!

He's going to sell us out to some tabloid weasel for a lot of money, then leave us high and dry, and it'll just be Cain and me drowning, Natalia thought angrily.

Which was a mixed metaphor, but she didn't care.

I'll have to fire him, she thought. *He's breaking his contract.*

She didn't want to fire Matthew. Aside from the fact that she was crazy, head-over-heels-in-like and maybe more with him, she needed Father Gallow. If the lawyers insisted on Cain's finishing the tour, she was considering changing the act. Father Gallow would "win" the battle, "redeem" Cain. Maybe he'd "banish" the demon guitar. Cain would throw a fit, of course, but he wouldn't have much choice but to go along with it.

Matthew stealthily sneaked off the bus. Natalia leaped out of her bunk. Flinging on clothes, she kept a watch on him through the bus windows. He avoided the press by heading across the parking lot the same way they'd come last night. He must be selling his story as an exclusive. He headed for the street, either planning to hail a cab or, more likely, he'd called one to come pick him up.

Natalia ran out the bus door, hoping she would be lucky enough to find a cab, when she met Al coming in. His plane must have landed early this morning, and that meant he'd taken a car from the airport.

"Thank goodness!" she cried, grabbing him. "Where's the car?"

"Just leaving—"

"Call the driver! I need it!" she ordered.

Al put in a call and told the car to wait.

"Did you hear the news?" Natalia asked bleakly.

"It's the lead story on every network," Al replied, and he shook his head.

"Keep an eye on Cain. Don't let him off this bus. Handcuff him to the toilet if you have to. I've got to go!"

Natalia dashed past Al and ran for the waiting car, keeping an eye on Matthew as she did so. She jumped inside.

"Sit tight," she told the driver.

Matthew walked swiftly across the parking lot. He seemed absorbed in thought, his head down, hands jammed into his pockets. When he reached the street, he stood there waiting.

In a few moments, a cab rolled up to the curb and stopped in front of Matthew. He got in, and the cab pulled away.

"Follow that cab," said Natalia. "And don't let him see us."

"We're in a black Cadillac, ma'am," said the driver. "It reeks of being a tail."

"Yes, well, do the best you can," she said.

She slumped back into the leather seat. Switching on the car's TV, she saw Cain plastered all over the screen. They'd used the footage from the night he'd been arrested. He looked demonic, completely out of control. Natalia heaved a deep sigh. She turned off the TV. She picked up her phone, sighed even more deeply, and switched it on.

Almost immediately, it began to buzz.

"The cab's stopped, ma'am," said the driver.

"Pull up here," she said. Telling Cain's attorney she'd call him back, she hung up to watch Matthew climb out of the cab. He spoke to the driver, apparently telling him to wait, for the cab remained parked at the curb. Matthew walked across the street and entered a building.

"Is that a church?" Natalia asked, astonished.

"Yes, ma'am," said the driver, and he gave her an odd look in the rearview mirror.

Natalia felt like an idiot. Of course, it was a church! It's not like the beautiful, ornately designed cathedral could be anything else!

"I meant to say, what church is this?" she asked.

"Mission Dolores, ma'am. The small white building to the left of the basilica is the mission. One of the oldest buildings in San Francisco."

A church wasn't the place she would have picked to betray someone, but then perhaps Matthew was channeling Judas.

He walked into the mission, not the cathedral. A tour group was coming out. He held the door for them, then entered.

Once he was inside, Natalia jumped out of the car and ran across the street, heading for the mission. Her plan was to storm inside, see this reporter Matthew was meeting, throw him out on his ear, then have it out with Matthew. She had decided not to fire him. But she would make his life pretty damn unpleasant.

Arriving at the door to the mission, she looked around. Everything was so calm, so peaceful, so quiet. This was not the place for a confrontation. There might be an unpleasant scene, and she didn't want to cause an uproar in the middle of a church. Natalia prowled around outside for a few moments, hoping Matthew would have second thoughts. When he didn't come out, she decided to go back to sit in the car to wait for him.

Chapter 25

*M*atthew stepped from the cab and pulled his jacket tighter around him. He was always cold in San Francisco. Must be the damp. He looked up at the mission, beautiful in its white simplicity. More beautiful, he always thought, than the grandly ornate, attention-grabbing basilica. He walked to the front door.

A group of tourists was coming out. He held the door for them and entered. The interior was shadowy, and it took a moment for his eyes to adjust after the sunlight. He paused a moment, enjoying the silence. He didn't know why, but there was something about the silence of a church that was unique, like no other silence in any other place. It wasn't an expectant silence, as in a theater, or a tense silence, as with fear. It was an easeful silence, soothing, gentle.

He took a moment to admire the mission's interior, which was breathtaking, with its amazing ceiling beams, brightly painted in native designs. And there was William—seated in a pew near the front.

He was easy to spot because he was wearing a bright red jacket and carrying a shabby hat in his hands.

Matthew slid into the pew next to William, who beamed at him.

"Like my jacket?" William asked. "I'm quite fond of it, myself."

Puzzled, Matthew glanced at it, not understanding.

"LA Angels," said William proudly, pointing to the letter "A" on the breast. "Angels. Get it?" He chuckled.

Matthew didn't smile.

"We've got a problem," he said.

"We?" William raised an eyebrow. He looked pleased. "Meaning 'we' as in 'we—you and me and God'?"

"No, I don't mean 'we,'" Matthew said grimly. "That was just a figure of speech. I'll rephrase it. *You* have a problem. Heaven has a problem."

He told William everything. Well, almost everything. Matthew left out Woof. No sense in getting the old hippie ghost into trouble. And Matthew didn't go into his feelings for Natalia. That was none of Heaven's business. He told William everything about Cain, however, from the conversation he'd overheard between the two roadies to his burned hand when he'd touched Cain's arm during the concert to the tragedies involving the contest winners and Cain's bizarre reactions.

William listened in silence, his expression growing increasingly grave.

"After touching Cain damn near gave me third-degree burns, I started thinking about things. You remember that young girl I exorcised," Matthew said. "I got to thinking about her involvement with Cain, and I spoke to her mother. Grace hadn't been a contest winner, but she'd met Cain at a party."

Matthew frowned. "Her mother was there with her,

though, and she said that Cain had been a relatively nice guy. He hadn't done or said anything that gave her cause for alarm. But it was after she met Cain that her daughter had started to act like she was possessed.

"And then there was the kid who met Cain who killed his mom and himself, and now another kid who met Cain kills himself and says Cain told him to do it."

"So what do you think is going on?" William asked.

"At first I thought it was all coincidence," Matthew said. "But now too many pieces are fitting together, and they're forming a picture I don't like." He was quiet a moment, then said, "Cain claims he sold his soul to the devil. All for publicity purposes, of course, but I'm wondering if he really did it—signed a contract in blood at the crossroads or however it's done these days."

"And what do want me to do about it?" William asked mildly.

"Take over," said Matthew. "Send in the heavenly SWAT team. Saving souls is your specialty, Archangel, not mine. God can get off his butt and do something for a change."

"God is doing something," William said. "God sent you."

Matthew stood up. Leaning over the pew, he raised a finger, spoke directly into William's face.

"I am not like you. I'm not God's toady! God did not send me!" Matthew said, his voice rising angrily.

"Tsk, tsk. You're in church. Keep your voice down," William said. "As for God sending you, it's a distinct possibility. 'God works in mysterious ways his wonders to conceal.' Or is it 'reveal'? I can never remember. Anyway it seems to me there's more than one soul at stake here, Matthew Gallow. You stand at your own crossroads."

William pointed to Matthew's injured hand, and added, "You have the 'X' to prove it."

Matthew stared down at his bandaged palm. "So that's what—" He paused a moment, seething, then said, "Fine. I'm at a crossroads. *I* choose the direction *I* take."

"Of course, son. All mortals have free will. But you're not mortal. . . ."

"What do you mean?" Matthew demanded.

"If you care about these mortals—and I think you do— you're going to have to get into the game whether you like it or not, I'm afraid," said William. "No more watching from the sidelines. That's a sports analogy. Goes with the jacket."

Matthew eyed the archangel suspiciously. "Why are you trying to drag me into this?"

"*I* didn't drag you into anything," William protested. "If you'll remember, I tried to warn you—"

"All right, I've been a bad boy," Matthew said, exasperated. "I've been bilking people out of money by pretending to save their souls, except maybe I have saved a few souls now and then. I still don't see why I have to be involved in this—"

"If you'll sit down and stop shouting, I'll explain."

"I'm not shouting," Matthew shouted. He wavered, then sat down. "You have five minutes."

"You can't figure out why the roadies-slash-demons would first try to get rid of you, then want to keep you around. I have the answer."

"Yeah, what is it?"

"Think back to what happened under the scaffold. You saw them for what they were—demons from Hell. And you said they saw you and—" William interrupted himself to ask, "How did they look when they saw you?"

Matthew thought back. He shrugged. "Astonished. Amazed. But that makes sense. I'd just caught them trying to tear down the scaffolding."

"Then wouldn't it make more sense if they'd looked guilty or frightened? Instead, they were astonished to see you. To see *you*." William emphasized the word.

Matthew didn't say anything.

"But, then, you've already thought of this, haven't you?" William said.

"Maybe. I didn't get much sleep last night," Matthew said. "Spell it out."

"You looked at them and saw demons," said William. "They looked at you and saw an angel."

"Goddamn it!" Matthew muttered.

William winced. "You are in the Lord's house, you know, Matthew. Show a little more respect."

"But how could that happen? How were they able to see me? Come to think of it, how was I able to see them?"

"My guess is that you are able to see the demons because you crossed over into the spiritual plane when you exorcised Grace. You saw the demon then, you heard it, you touched it."

"But when I see the two guys now, they look human. Why don't I see them as demons?"

"At the time you were in the throes of a strong emotion— you were afraid for Natalia's life. Perhaps I think that gave you the impetus to cross over to the spiritual plane—if only for a few seconds. Or perhaps the demons were having to use their demonic powers to bring down the scaffolding, and because they were using their powers, they were visible to you."

William shook his head. "I don't have all the answers. But whatever the reason, the demons suddenly realized they had an angel to contend with. They had to find out why you were there, how much you knew. So they decided to keep you around."

"But if they know I'm an angel, why wouldn't the demons just leave? Wouldn't the sight of an angel strike the fear of God into them?"

"Have you looked at yourself in a mirror lately, Matthew?" William asked gently.

Matthew brushed this aside. "So I'm not wearing white robes and playing a harp—"

William looked very grave. "Shall I tell you what the demons see? What I see when I look at you?"

Matthew's lips tightened. He didn't answer.

William drew in a deep breath, let it out slowly. "I see an angel without wings to soar. An angel without light to shine. An angel whose white raiment has been dragged through the mud and muck. An angel who long ago tossed his sword of righteousness and truth into the gutter.

"In fact," added William, "you're just their type. I think they might try to recruit you."

Matthew stared at him. Then he gave a brief and bitter laugh. "Some recruitment drive! They try to burn off my hand!"

"Oh, that's the old protection racket," said William cheerfully. "One day they throw a brick through your shop window. The next day they offer to sell you protection against people throwing bricks through your window."

"I still don't see why God just can't send in someone big and powerful like the Archangel Gabriel—"

"Because that would scare them away," said William patiently. "And we'd never find out what Satan is plotting. He'd bide his time, lie low, then, when he thinks we're not looking, he'll go ahead with it. Whereas you have a chance to discover the plot and stop it."

Matthew eyed William. "If you think I'm such a badass, how do you know I won't ask to be traded to the other team?"

"Sports analogy. Very good." William smiled, though his smile was a bit sad. "As a matter of fact, I don't know for sure, Matthew. You are very close to the edge. I will tell you this. If Cain *has* sold his soul to the devil, everyone around him could be in terrible danger. Everyone you've come to care about—Natalia, Al, Kimo, the guys in the band . . . Not to mention Cain himself."

Matthew snorted. "That asshole! It's all his fault. He deserves whatever he gets."

"Probably so," William conceded with a sigh. "But if we all got what we deserved, Hell would be filled to the rafters, and Satan would be the big winner."

"So, if I decide to stick around, what do I do?" Matthew asked grudgingly.

"I can't tell you that, son," William answered.

Matthew bounded up, glaring at the archangel irately. "Then why did I come here? What good was any of this? I need help—"

"You need help? Then why didn't you say so in the first place?" William said, pleased. He held out the shabby hat. "Now, take this dormouse . . ."

Matthew stared at the hat. "What are you talking about?"

"No, I mean, you take this dormouse. The one in the hat."

Matthew backed up a pace. "You know what I think? I think Heaven's lost it. I'm not surprised. What with people like you running the show. What in the name of holy hell would I want with a dormouse in a hat?"

William winced again. "Matthew, swearing, please . . . . As for this dormouse . . ."

He opened the hat. A small, furry creature, about three inches long, lay curled up in the bottom. The dormouse blinked at Matthew sleepily. "All God's creatures are blessed, but this little fellow is specially blessed. If he likes you and if you take good care of him, Arthur—his name is Arthur—will help you."

Matthew snorted. "Help me how?"

"Take a guess," said William eagerly.

"I'm not guessing—"

"Arthur opens doors!" William laughed heartily. "Get it? *Dor*mouse. Opens doors—"

"I get that," Matthew said impatiently. "What I don't get is why I need a furry rodent which, by the way, we used to eat back in the day. They're quite good, dipped in honey and coated in poppy seeds—"

William quickly closed the hat. "Don't say that! Arthur's sensitive. You'll frighten him. And he doesn't open just any old door. He can open the gates to the spiritual plane. Anytime, anyplace, anywhere."

Matthew rolled his eyes. "I'm sorry I came. Be seeing you around. Oh, wait. No, I won't. Because *I'm* leaving, and you're staying."

Turning around to march down the aisle, Matthew walked smack into Natalia, nearly knocking her over. He gasped, reached out his hands to steady her.

"Natalia! What are you doing here?"

She stood in the aisle, her hands on her hips, and she looked angry clear through.

"The question is—what are you doing here?" Natalia demanded, jabbing him in the breastbone. "And who's your slimy friend?"

She glared at William, who smiled at her benignly.

"Hello, my dear," he said.

"Who do you work for?" she demanded, pouncing on William. "The *Examiner*? *Chicago Sun-Times*?"

She turned back to Matthew. "How much did this weasel pay you for your story?"

"That would be Father Weasel, my dear," said William mildly, and he unzipped the red jacket to reveal his clerical collar.

Natalia stared at him in bewilderment, then she gulped. She looked at William, then at Matthew, then back at William. Then she looked at her surroundings—the beautiful altar, the bright candles, the font of holy water . . .

"Actually it's Father William, not Father Weasel," William added.

Natalia's face flushed bright red. "So you're a . . . um . . . a father. Not a reporter for tabloids . . . and you . . ." Natalia glanced sidelong at Matthew. "You're not selling Cain out . . ."

"Quite the contrary, my dear," said William. "Matthew came to me because he's deeply concerned about Cain."

"Oh, my God!" Natalia groaned and sank into a pew.

"Lord's house," said William as a reminder.

"I'm sorry. Bad habit. I feel such a fool!" Natalia lowered her head in her hands. "I followed you, Matthew. Spied on you! Again! I'm so sorry! I can't seem to do anything right these days!"

She sat huddled in the pew, her head in her hands. She was not crying. For Matthew, her silent misery was worse. He stood watching her, uncomfortable, not knowing what to do. He glanced at William, saw the archangel regarding Natalia with a worried expression.

"There's a problem," said William, drawing Matthew a slight distance away.

"What now?" Matthew demanded.

"Your friend has no guardian angel," said William.

"What?" Matthew stared back at Natalia. "Are you sure—"

"Oh, uh, I can explain that," said a voice.

Matthew sighed. He had no need to turn around to see who was talking.

"William," he said. "Meet Woof. Natalia's dead grandfather. Woof, this is William. An archangel."

"How's it hangin', dude?" Woof said by way of greeting.

"Uh, fine, thank you," said William. "About the guardian angel—"

"Oh, yeah, that. Well, you see, Natalia's guardian angel was her grandmother on her father's side. She was one of those real religious types—no offense, sir." Woof looked embarrassed.

"None taken," said William.

"Anyway, she didn't hold with any sort of fun. Life is earnest, life is real—all that crap. She was always lecturing my girl. Trying to get her to get married, settle down, start a family. I got fed up and told her to take a long walk off a short pier." Woof shrugged. "I guess she did, 'cause I haven't seen hide nor hair of the old biddy in quite a while. That's all right, though. Natalia's got me to look after her."

"Oh, dear God!" William murmured.

"Lord's house," said Matthew.

"Yes, right. Sorry." William glanced heavenward in apology.

Matthew stood gazing down at Natalia. He sighed deeply. She was alone. No guardian angel. Only an old hippie ghost to watch out for her. A hippie ghost and a fallen angel . . . Poor kid.

Natalia stood up, gathered herself together. She held out her hand to William.

"It was nice meeting you, Father."

"A pleasure, my dear," said William.

Natalia cast a sidelong glance at Matthew. "Are you coming back with me?"

Before Matthew could answer, William said, "Don't forget your hat." He held out the hat with the dormouse inside.

"Can I speak to you a moment in private, *Father*?" Matthew grabbed William's arm and steered the angel none too gently down toward the altar.

"I don't want the damn dormouse," Matthew said in a low voice. "And even if you are an archangel, do you think it's right to go passing yourself off as a priest?"

"Isn't that the pot calling the kettle black?" William asked mildly. "I really was a priest, you know. Back in the day. As for Arthur, you're going to need him if you want to find out what is going on. You need to open the door to the other side. Arthur can do that for you."

"God could grant *me* that power if He wanted me to have it. The dormouse is His way of having a little laugh at my expense, right? Or, teaching me a lesson? That's it. Heaven's big on teaching people lessons. What's this one—caring for the smallest of God's creatures—"

"It's not a joke, Matthew," said William patiently. "It's not a lesson. It's just a dormouse. Do you want Arthur or not?"

Matthew stared at the hat. He was committed to staying . . . *Committed*. That was the operative word.

"And what am I going to do with the smelly little rodent while I'm on the tour?" Matthew demanded, relenting.

"He's not smelly, and he doesn't like being called 'rodent,'" William said indignantly. "His name is Arthur. He's quite happy in his hat, and no one has to know he's there."

"So people see me carrying around a hat, but never wearing it. How am I going to explain that?"

"Well, you could either wear the hat with the mouse, or carry the mouse in the hat, or wear the mouse and carry the hat. Your decision," William said. "People might question a mouse on your head more than they would the hat, but that's just my observation."

William held out the hat.

"Arthur's particularly fond of hazelnuts."

Matthew hesitated, then snatched the hat out of the archangel's hand. He thrust it—carefully—into his pocket.

"Good luck, Matthew," said William. "If you need anything, just ask."

"Yeah, right!" Matthew returned bitterly.

He walked swiftly from the church, not looking to see if Natalia was coming with him. He hoped she wasn't. He hoped she would just go back to the bus, leave him in peace. He couldn't think when she was around, and he desperately needed to think.

Natalia didn't go back to the bus. She followed him to the sidewalk, apparently misconstruing his hasty departure.

"Matthew, I know you're offended," she said, catching up with him. "I am truly, truly sorry. I hope you're not *too* mad at me."

She sounded wistful. She stood in front of him, her hands jammed into the pockets of her jeans. She was a mess. She hadn't combed her hair. She'd tossed on clothes haphazardly, apparently, because her shirt was on inside out. She had smudgy circles under her eyes, and her face was pale and drawn.

"I'm not mad at you. I understand," Matthew said at last. "It's just . . . I needed to talk to someone . . ."

"To a priest," said Natalia. "About Cain."

"Yes," he said. "That's right."

She shook the straggling hair out of her face. "Do you mind telling me why? I mean, if it's not under the seal of the confessional or whatever that's called. I'm not being nosy. I have Cain and his reputation to consider."

Matthew didn't answer. He was trying to decide what to say or if he should say anything.

"You're part of the act," said Natalia. "An important part.

We're going to have to continue this tour. I hate it, but I spoke with Cain's attorney and he says we have to. I need you as part of the act, and therefore I need to know what's going on with you! What's inside your head?"

How can I explain? Matthew wondered, frustrated. I don't understand what's going on myself.

"Cain claims he sold his soul to the devil . . ." Matthew began, but she wouldn't let him finish.

"Oh, for heaven's sake!" Natalia interrupted. "Is that what this is all about? I told you, that's a publicity stunt."

Matthew shook his head. "In that song, Cain talks about giving himself to the powers of darkness. It's dangerous, Natalia. He's dealing with powerful forces he doesn't understand—"

"Stop right there!" Natalia said grimly. "I've heard it all. My grandmother went on and on about 'demon' rock for years. 'It'll take you straight to hell,' she used to say. The song lyrics are just *lyrics*! Cain's guitar is painted to *look* like a demon!"

Matthew shook his head. He couldn't argue with her. He had no proof.

"Yes, you do," said Woof, drifting up to float protectively near Natalia. "Show her your hand."

"No," said Matthew flatly.

"No, what?" Natalia asked, confused.

"She needs to be prepared," Woof argued. "She has to be ready to face whatever it is she may have to face whenever she might have to face it."

"That doesn't even make sense," Matthew retorted.

"Who are you talking to?" Natalia demanded. "Do you have an imaginary friend? My God, the whole world's gone crazy!"

"I'll meet you back at the bus."

Matthew started to cross the street, returning to where

the taxi was waiting for him. He had taken only a step when the bandage around his hand suddenly unwound all by itself, fell off, and dropped to the pavement.

"Thanks, Woof, thanks a whole hell of a lot!" Matthew tried to shove his hand in his pocket. Before he could, Natalia grabbed hold of his hand. She turned his palm to the sunlight.

She gasped. "What the . . ."

Caught, Matthew stood his ground.

"But your skin was burned . . ." Natalia breathed. She gingerly touched his palm that was smooth, except for the strange white scar. "I saw for myself . . ."

She dropped his hand, stared at him. "I don't understand. What's going on?"

"I lied to you, Natalia," Matthew told her. "Not about Grace or the demon or my hands catching fire. All that was true. I lied when I told you how I burned my hand last night. It wasn't from the special effects. I burned my hand when I touched Cain. When I touched his arm."

"That's crazy!" Natalia gasped. "*You're* crazy! You're fired!"

"You can't fire me," said Matthew flatly. "I have a contract. I'll see you back at the bus." He dashed across the street and jumped into the taxi.

Natalia, looking dazed, remained standing on the sidewalk.

"Where to?" the driver asked.

Matthew could feel Arthur squirming around inside his hat, which, he noticed, was starting give off the distinct odor of dormouse.

"Some place that sells hazelnuts," Matthew said with a sigh.

Chapter 26

Matthew stopped at a superstore, bought hazelnuts for Arthur and a little plastic cage in which to house him, plus other necessities for the small rodent owner. Or at least, the sales lady in Pet Supply had assured him they were necessities. Matthew was dubious himself. Arthur didn't seem the type to take a spin on an exercise wheel. After that, he ordered the driver to take him back to the theater, where, he presumed, the buses were about ready to depart.

Matthew spent his time in the taxi going over in his mind what he was going to say to Natalia. He didn't get very far. The truth sounded crazy—even to him. Yet he was more and more convinced he was right. And, he had to admit, he came to the grudging conclusion that William was right. Matthew was in a unique position to find out what was going on and, hopefully, put a stop to it.

The devil is going to a lot of trouble, Matthew thought. *Something big is in the works. But why a rock star? Like Woof said, why not the president . . .*

It all hinged, he believed, on the contest winners. He'd always thought it was strange that Cain enjoyed hanging out with kids.

But how to explain all this to Natalia? Especially when Cain was around?

As it turned out, Matthew didn't have to.

When he arrived at the bus, he found that he and Al were the only ones on board.

"Natalia and Cain are taking a private jet," said Al. "Kimo went with them. To avoid the press."

"Good idea," said Matthew, who privately thought it a very bad idea.

"You, me, and the guys in the band go by bus. Guess she's not worried about us talking to the press," Al commented, eyeing him.

"Guess she's not," Matthew agreed. "What about the two roadies?"

"What two roadies?" Al asked, shutting the bus door.

"The two guys who travel with the band. Burl and what's his name. John."

"Oh, them." Al shrugged. "They're on the band bus. Jake'll keep an eye on them. What the hell is that thing?"

"A dormouse," said Matthew.

"It's riding with us?" Al was disapproving.

"Looks that way, doesn't it?" said Matthew.

"You clear this with Natalia?"

"Of course, it's for the act," Matthew lied.

Al shook his head and climbed in the driver's seat.

Matthew settled Arthur in his new home. The dormouse took a brief tour of his cage, then settled down inside the exercise wheel and fell asleep. Matthew poured himself a bourbon and retired to his bunk.

He told himself he was relieved. He hadn't been able to

figure out what to say to Natalia, and now he didn't have to say it. And he was especially glad he didn't have to travel with Cain.

The miles went by, and Matthew couldn't take lying in his bunk anymore. He rolled out, went to sit at the table, flipped through some magazines. He even resorted to trying to play with Arthur—tapping the cage to try to wake up the dormouse. The creature curled up into a tight ball and put his paws over his eyes.

Matthew roamed around the bus, sat down, stood up, and roamed some more. He poured himself another drink (conscious of Al's disapproving eye on him), but the bourbon didn't taste as good as usual, and he dumped it down the sink. It wasn't the bourbon. Natalia bought the best. It was the bus. It was too damn quiet. It was Natalia—traveling alone with Cain. It was no buzzing phone. No yelling at Crandall. No bubbling laughter. No golden flecks in hazel eyes.

"I *don't* miss her!" Matthew said firmly to himself. "Damn it, I don't!"

As if Natalia didn't have trouble enough, Cain was more than unusually obnoxious on the plane. After three glasses of champagne, he tried to persuade the stewardess on board the private jet to join the Mile-High club. The stewardess politely turned him down, at which Cain tried to grab her, knocking a tray of food out of her hands. At this, Natalia intervened. She apologized to the stewardess, told her to cork up the champagne bottle, and told Cain to quit acting like a drunken frat boy.

Cain went sullen and sulky on her. He threw himself in his luxurious leather chair and began to play his Nintendo DS.

Natalia curled up in her luxurious leather chair and thought about Matthew Gallow, the most intriguing, most mysterious, most exasperating man on the planet. A man festooned with question marks.

How *had* his hand healed overnight, leaving a scar in the shape of an X?

Why had he—a self-confessed con artist—gone to a *priest* for advice?

And what right did he—who had admitted bilking innocent churchgoers out of money—have lecturing *her* about the evils of rock music?

Natalia tried to put him out of her mind. She didn't want to think about Matthew. She had lots more important problems. She tried to write a press release, and he kept popping into her head. She tried to talk to Crandall and heard Matthew's voice. (Which made for a confused phone conversation.) Matthew occupied her thoughts fully, and, finally, she gave up trying to think about anything else. She attempted to find some sort of explanation for everything that had happened—an explanation that was logical and did *not* involve Satan. Her mind jumped to Dana Carvey on *Saturday Night Live*. When he was dressed as the church lady and would say "Saaaa-taan" in a funny voice. Unfortunately, there weren't any explanations that didn't bring the devil to mind.

Natalia even toyed with the idea of asking Cain outright, but she couldn't figure out how to phrase it so that she didn't sound completely loony.

Excuse me, Cain, dear, did you really sell your soul to the devil? What's he like? Horns, tail, Armani?

Face it, Natalia thought somberly. *You should fire Matthew. Cut him loose. He's crazy! A religious fanatic. No sane person these days actually believes in angels and demons and Satan and God.*

Natalia didn't. She'd had long talks with her grandfather, Woof, about such things. They'd agreed it was all myth, superstition. When you died, you were dead. End of story.

Then she thought of another possibility. Matthew was a con man. He could be conning her with this story about Cain and the devil. She didn't know exactly how or why he would, what he hoped to gain. Nor could she say how he'd managed to heal his hand.

I have grounds to fire him, she thought. *He broke his contract by telling secrets about Cain to . . . to a priest. Oh, yeah, that would stand up in court!*

Natalia sighed. She leaned back in her chair and gazed out at the blue sky and puffy white clouds. She liked imagining she could walk on those clouds. They looked firm, substantial. Which just went to show that not everything was what it appeared.

Which is why I can't fire Matthew. And it's not because I'm falling in love with him. (Okay, there! You admitted it!) It's because he's not what he wants everyone to think. He wants people to think he's a badass. He wants people to think he's callous, doesn't give a damn. He does, though. He truly cares. That's why he went to the priest.

Natalia kept seeing Matthew on the video during that exorcism. She'd watched it again and again. He had cared about Grace. Natalia could see caring in his face as he tried to save her. Of course, that could all be good acting. At first, Natalia had assumed that's what it was, but the more she watched it, the more she came to believe he wasn't putting on an act. You can't fake feelings like that. You can't fake the fire in the eyes.

Matthew had claimed he'd always told her the truth. He had admitted conning people, but he had said he wasn't conning then. With Grace, it had been real. He'd truly freed her from a demon.

He'd burned his hand touching Cain . . .

Natalia thought reluctantly of everything that had gone wrong on the tour. Cain's arrest, the murder/suicide, now the suicide . . . What if it was all connected . . . . What if . . .

Now you're just being silly! Natalia scolded herself. *You can't explain David Copperfield's magic tricks, can you? They look real. But they're not. Everyone knows they're not. It's all smoke and mirrors. You're going to put Matthew Gallow and his beautiful eyes and his crazy claims out of your mind and go back to work!*

The band bus broke down on the highway somewhere outside of Phoenix.

Al brought their bus to a halt, went back to consult with the driver of the band bus. It was odd that this should happen, Al remarked, for this was a brand-new bus. He got on the phone to the leasing company, gave them hell. They promised to come fix it immediately.

Matthew didn't give it much thought, except that it gave him an excuse to get out of the bus, stretch his legs. He'd spent only a few moments in the broiling desert sun before he decided that coming out had been a mistake. He was about to head back to the comforts of air-conditioning, when he heard someone call out.

Matthew turned to see Burl and John, the roadies, come walking around the side of the bus.

The air temperature seemed suddenly a lot colder.

"If you're looking for Al," Matthew said, "he's inside, talking to the bus company . . ."

"It's you I wanted to talk to, Father," said Burl with a friendly smile.

"I'm not a real priest," Matthew said.

"Yeah," said John. "We know."

"We know a lot about you," Burl added. "We did some checking."

"Hell's equivalent of Google?" Matthew asked.

Burl grinned and chuckled. "We like you, Matthew Gallow. The boss likes you. He thinks you got a rotten deal—getting kicked out of Heaven like that."

"He should know," said Matthew dryly.

Burl frowned, John's expression darkened, and Matthew realized he'd gone too far.

"Sorry, fellas," he added. "I'm just in a bad mood, that's all."

"For a guy who lives forever, you don't seem to be enjoying yourself much," said Burl.

"Yeah, well, it gets old after a while." Matthew didn't have to fake the bitterness in his voice.

Burl and John exchanged glances. Burl nodded.

"The boss was thinking you might be ready for a change," said John.

"Start enjoying life again," said Burl.

"Actually," said Matthew, "I'm liking it where I am just now. Traveling with a band. Always been one of my dreams. Well, since the fifties at any rate."

John was skeptical. Burl looked puzzled.

"But I'm open to an offer," said Matthew. "One question, though. What's up with Cain? I know he's working for your boss in some capacity. He made that painfully clear." Matthew flourished his hand.

"Sorry, that's privileged information," Burl replied.

"Besides, what do you care?" said John. "You're going to be leaving the tour shortly anyhow."

"Moving on to bigger and better things," added Burl.

"I see," said Matthew. "I'd like some time to think about this. Like I said, traveling with the band. Always been my dream . . ."

Burl was no longer smiling.

"Take your time. But one way or the other, Matthew

Gallow, you're moving on. The boss can make it pleasant. Or not. Up to you."

The two departed. Matthew went back on the bus.

"It's the craziest thing," said Al a moment later, "but it seems the bus is running again. All of a sudden, it started up just fine."

Matthew poured himself a bourbon.

The craziest thing . . .

Chapter 27

Cain performed in Phoenix to a sold-out crowd, much to Natalia's astonishment. There were protesters, of course, but the negative publicity only seemed to raise the price on eBay for tickets to the concert.

Natalia was torn between being pleased that the concert was a success and upset at the vagaries of human nature. Matthew wasn't surprised. He remembered the old days in London, when a family outing consisted of packing a lunch and taking the kiddies to watch the public hangings. Humans only thought they were becoming more civilized.

He didn't say anything to Natalia, however. He didn't even see her until the day of the performance, for she was busy handling the press, as well as all her myriad responsibilities for the show. Matthew wandered around backstage, waiting to talk to her. She appeared to be avoiding him, however, and finally he had to confront her.

"Yes, Matthew, what is it?" she asked.

"You were considering changing the act to let Father

Gallow succeed. I was wondering if that was happening?" Matthew asked.

Natalia shook her head. She was pale and drawn and looked exhausted. There were dark smudges beneath her eyes, and the golden flecks were nowhere in sight.

"No, we'll leave it the way it is. There's no time to rehearse it, for one thing. I know you don't like it, but changing the act will upset Cain, and I don't need that right now. I *will* see to it that the smoke blows away from you. And try to keep from setting yourself on fire."

She turned from him, started to walk off.

"I'll keep from touching Cain if that's what you mean," Matthew said to her back. "Will he be entertaining contest winners tonight?"

Natalia flinched, kept walking. "Yes," she called over her shoulder, not looking at him. "Don't worry. The meeting will be at the hotel, and it will be well supervised."

Matthew hurried to catch up with her.

"I'm sorry, Natalia. That was a cheap shot. But we need to talk about this—"

"No, we don't," cried Natalia, turning to face him. "I don't want to think you're crazy, Matthew!" Her gaze was pleading. "Can't you just drop it? You're spoiling everything! It's all rock and roll, Matthew. It's all fun."

And as she said this, her eyes filled with tears.

Matthew wanted to be angry at her. He wanted to shake some sense into her. Instead, he reached out his hand to gently stroke back the lock of hair that kept falling in her face.

"Yeah. Fun," he said gently.

He put his arms around her, and for a moment it seemed Natalia would melt into his embrace. But then she stiffened. She shoved away from him and, wiping her tears away on the sleeve of her T-shirt, said huskily, "Makeup at 5:00 P.M.

Don't be late. Oh, and by the way, Cain says you have to get that rat of yours off his bus, or he'll flush it down the toilet."

"I'll just get myself off *his* bus," said Matthew coolly. "That will solve everything."

"Matthew, I didn't mean *you* had to leave," said Natalia unhappily. "It's just that Cain is freaked out by rats. I'm really sorry . . ."

"It's not a rat. It's a dormouse. And I'm the one who's sorry," Matthew returned angrily. "Sorry I ever got mixed up with you *and* Cain!"

"Please, don't be mad. I'll make you a reservation at the hotel," said Natalia. "We're all staying there tonight anyway—"

"Fine," said Matthew, walking off. "I'll go pack."

"Fine!" Natalia called after him.

He pretended not to hear. He kept walking. But he was slamming his way out the door, he paused, glanced back. Natalia remained standing in the wings. Her shoulders sagged, her head drooped. She looked forlorn and alone, and she was alone, Matthew thought. No one watching over her except for the old hippie ghost, who was patting her shoulder. She could have no idea he was there and, yet, she seemed to be comforted. Then someone yelled out her name, and, at the same time, her phone began buzzing. She straightened her shoulders, answered her phone, and hurried off to deal with the latest crisis.

Matthew fumed his way back to the bus. He packed his things and picked up Arthur, who was still slumbering in the exercise wheel.

"You better wake up, you little furbag," Matthew said, reaching into the cage and giving the indignant dormouse a poke with his finger. "You and I have work to do."

* * *

That night, the performance went off without a hitch. Cain was brilliant. The fans went wild for him, clapping and applauding and yelling for more long after the houselights had come up. It was only when security started yelling for them to move that they groaned and started to file out.

Father Gallow's act went well. Matthew tried to avoid inhaling the smoke, and he was careful to avoid touching Cain, who seemed more than usually smug, smirking at Matthew in triumph and making cutting comments about the padre's "failure" as the two walked to the dressing rooms. Matthew wiped off the smoke and the makeup and changed his clothes. He managed to dodge Natalia, who was trying to snag him for the backstage party, and left the theater immediately after the performance, catching a taxi back to the hotel—the posh Pointe Hilton Tapatio Cliffs resort.

Natalia had rented an entire floor. Matthew couldn't imagine how much that cost, but obviously Cain could afford it. Or rather, Satan could afford it. As Matthew was going over his plans in his head, he wondered suddenly if Cain knew the truth about Matthew, knew that he was an angel. Had the demons told him? Did Cain know the truth about the roadies? Did he know they were demons?

Cain had made Natalia hire them full-time and he had insisted—undoubtedly at their instigation—that they ride on the bus with the band members. Having his "handlers" tagging along to make sure the job was done properly was probably one of the conditions of his contract. He was doing their bidding. Was he doing so because he was afraid of them? Matthew guessed that this was the case. Cain had obviously not read the fine print on his contract.

The murder/suicide had come as a shock to him, that much was clear by the way he'd reacted. The second suicide, claiming Cain had been involved, had also seemed to take him by surprise. He didn't like what was happening, but he had made a deal with the devil, and now he couldn't get out of it.

Cain could if he wanted to, Matthew thought grimly. *He's too weak. He likes the fame, the adulation too much.*

What truly worried Matthew was that the suicides and the murder were dress rehearsals for the big finale. According to Archangel William, Satan wanted to bring about the fall of mankind. That meant world upheaval, economic collapse, starvation, plagues, wars. The devil wasn't going to cause worldwide chaos by inflicting tragedies on a handful of families. Satan had something bigger in mind. He'd chosen a rock star for a reason. Matthew had to find out what that reason was.

Guards were posted at the elevators to make certain only those with security passes could enter the floor where Cain and his entourage had their suites. They passed Matthew with a nod and a friendly smile. Arriving on the floor, Matthew came upon the hotel staff setting up for the party for the contest winners, which would be in Cain's suite. He was startled to discover there were a large number of winners tonight, almost thirty.

And there was something else disturbing. Matthew thought back to a conversation he'd overheard between Natalia and Cain.

"I've been investigating these contest winners. Did you know they all come from wealthy families?" Natalia had asked Cain. "These kids could afford to buy their own tickets—even at the exorbitant prices the scalpers are charging. The contest winners should be a cross section of your fans."

Matthew hadn't heard Cain's reply. He didn't care. He suddenly started to put the various puzzle pieces together, and he didn't like the looks of the picture they were creating.

Matthew secreted Arthur in his hat, which he shoved into

the pocket of his sport coat. He removed a hip flask filled with bourbon from his jeans pocket, swished some bourbon around in his mouth, spit it out in the sink, then sauntered over to watch the preparations for the party. The hotel staff had soft drinks on ice, bowls filled with snacks, plates and silverware set out for the pizza. Matthew gave everyone a friendly wave, saying he was just here to see that everything was under control.

He lounged a bit, pretending to drink from his flask now and then, and finally muttered something about having to use the facilities. No one paid any attention to him. He went into the master bedroom, slipped into a clothes closet, shut the door behind him, and settled down to wait. Matthew was fairly certain he would be safely concealed in the closet since Cain never bothered to use one. He always left his clothes strewn over the floor or piled up on the bed or wadded up in the suitcases.

Matthew sat in the darkness of the closet and thought about Natalia. He didn't want to, but even when he tried to slam the door in her face, she had a way of bursting through it, with her engaging smile and her golden-flecked eyes and her laughter that made him forget he was almost two thousand years old, made him remember what it was to be young and hopeful, made him remember what it was to enjoy life, to live life, not merely to endure it.

And depending on what I find out tonight, Matthew thought grimly, *I may end up ruining her life.* He pulled out the flask, started to open it and take a drink for real, hesitated, then thrust it back in his pocket. He remembered what Woof had said to him, how Natalia didn't nag him about smoking pot. She didn't nag Matthew about drinking. She just looked so damned disappointed.

The wait seemed interminable. He was just starting to wonder if the plans had changed, and Cain had moved the party, when he heard sounds of laughter outside in the hall. The door to the hotel room opened, and the laughter grew louder. He could hear people entering the room. Cain's voice rose above the rest, inviting people to help themselves and ordering Natalia to find out where the pizza was.

Someone walked into the bedroom, and Matthew froze.

"I'll be there in a second!" Cain yelled out to someone. "Gotta take a piss."

Matthew heard Cain's heavy boots clomp across the floor to the bathroom. He was gone for quite a while. Matthew smelled pot smoke and guessed Cain was having a little refresher after the rigors of the concert.

"Hey, Cain," a voice called out, "where the hell are you? Your fans are starting to get restless."

"I'll be there in a minute!" he yelled.

The toilet flushed, and Cain came clomping back out. He was apparently changing clothes because Matthew could hear him tossing things out of the suitcase and swearing as he tried to find a particular shirt. Unable to find it, he walked over toward the closet, muttering something about it being in there. Matthew held his breath. Cain stopped about halfway, however, and turned around. Either he found the shirt, or he decided to wear something else because he left a few moments later.

"Okay, kids, I'm all yours!" he bawled as he left the bedroom and entered the living area.

The kids cheered.

Matthew breathed again.

Reaching into his pocket, he took out the hat and opened it up. He picked up the dormouse, held him in his palm. Matthew had brought a small penlight with him, and he shined it on the dormouse.

Arthur didn't like the light. He curled up in a tighter ball and put his little paws over his eyes.

"Come on, Arthur, old pal," Matthew said persuasively. "Do your thing."

Arthur remained asleep. Matthew poked at the dormouse with the penlight. Arthur curled up tighter.

Matthew heaved an exasperated sigh. Perhaps Arthur was waiting for instructions.

"All right, God," Matthew said, relenting. "I'm fighting your fight. I could use a little help—if it's not too much to ask."

That was the first prayer he'd prayed in centuries. Not very gracious, nor very contrite, but he wasn't feeling either. He was tense, nervous. The air had a bad feel to it, and it wasn't just because it reeked of pot smoke.

He poked Arthur again with the penlight, and this time the dormouse opened his eyes. He blinked at the light. He blinked at Matthew. Then he rolled over in Matthew's hand and bit him on the thumb.

Matthew stifled a yelp and threw the dormouse on the floor. Not the least perturbed, Arthur curled up and went back to sleep again. He'd bitten Matthew deeply. Blood welled out of the small tooth marks. Matthew sucked on his thumb, which hurt like hell. He wondered if the bite was Arthur's way of performing his task and granting Matthew the power to see what was happening on the spiritual plane or if the dormouse had just gotten fed up and decided to let Matthew have it.

Only one way to find out.

Matthew gathered up the dormouse, put him back in the hat, then silently opened the closet door and peered out into the darkened room. Padding across the floor that was covered with Cain's clothes, Matthew crept over to the door. He opened it a crack to see out into the living area and found his view blocked by Kimo's broad back. The big man had been posted there to stand guard, make certain none of the kids went into Cain's room on a souvenir hunt.

Matthew was thinking it would be great if Kimo moved.

Suddenly, almost as if reading Matthew's mind, Kimo shifted position a few feet, providing Matthew with a clear view.

"Thanks," Matthew muttered, with a grudging glance heavenward.

He could see clearly now, and, at first, everything seemed normal. The kids were either sitting on the floor or standing by the food, eating pizza, drinking pop, and listening enthralled to Cain, who was telling his alligator-wrestling story again. The guys in the band were not here. They disliked these parties, which were all about Cain. The two roadies were in attendance, though, standing in a corner, wearing their Cain T-shirts.

Matthew wondered that no one thought this odd. He stared hard at the roadies, and suddenly they swam in his vision, as though he were looking at them through watery eyes. He blinked a couple of times, wiped his hand over his eyes, and when he looked again, their human disguises were gone. He was staring at two demons with wizened, twisted bodies, red fiery eyes, slavering jaws, leathery wings—the same two demons he had seen trying to dismantle the scaffolding.

Matthew shifted his gaze to Cain, who was wearing his famous black T-shirt decorated with flames, black leather pants, heavy black boots. Nothing out of the ordinary. Arthur stirred in his sleep and Cain began to change. The flames on the T-shirt came to life and began to spread down his arms and across his chest. The flames twined about Cain's arms and spread to the rest of his body.

Matthew watched in horror. He was no longer in a hotel suite. He was back in the gardens of Nero's palace, watching the flames consume people tied to stakes, waiting in a frenzy of fear and terror for the fire to come to him. . . .

The room shifted. Chill sweat rolled down Matthew's neck and chest. His stomach clenched. He was afraid he was going to be sick. Why wasn't someone doing something? Why wasn't someone jumping on Cain, putting out the flames? Matthew was within a heart's beat of rushing out the door when he realized that Cain was still telling the alligator story. He was laughing and showing how he wrestled with the beast and pointing to the scars on his arms, which he claimed were from the gator's teeth . . . arms that were now covered in flames that danced and twined and writhed over his skin. Flames that apparently he didn't feel—not yet.

Shuddering, Matthew leaned back against the wall. He mopped his face with his sleeve, took a moment to recover, catch his breath, wait for the panic and nausea to subside.

Cain finished with the alligator story. He picked up the demon guitar. The kids went crazy, yelling and cheering and crying out for Cain to play his famous song, "Possession." Cain strummed a few chords and sang the opening. The room darkened in Matthew's vision, though the lights remained as bright as ever. The darkness flowed out of the guitar, sinking to the floor like the smoke from the dry-ice machine, spreading throughout the room.

Cain idly strummed the guitar, and the darkness took shape and form, gaining wispy hands and arms and trailing legs merged into smoke. The fiends drifted up from the floor and flowed effortlessly into the gaping mouths of the cheering fans.

Cain appeared oblivious to what was happening, yet Matthew had the distinct impression that Cain knew what was going on. He was pretending he didn't. He kept his gaze lowered, fixed on the guitar. He concentrated on the music.

Cain began playing and singing softly, almost to himself. The two demons glanced at each other. One of them left his post and walked over to Cain. He rested a clawed hand on Cain's arm and said in a horrible voice that sounded like someone crunching on bones, "It's time. They're prepared. Give them their instructions."

Cain shrank from the demon's touch. He shook his head and whined, "No. I don't wanna. Don't make me."

Even as he was talking, he was still singing. The kids didn't notice anything except one of the roadies talking to Cain; the two of them joking around.

"Good boys get their reward," said the demon. "Bad boys are punished."

Cain gave a pain-filled gasp and, looking frightened, he began to talk. He still didn't look at the kids as he was talking. He kept his gaze lowered. His voice sounded pinched and squeezed and he spoke in a stilted monotone, as though reading from a script.

"Your parents are evil slave masters. They are cruel dictators who are keeping you from realizing your true potential. Your parents must be stopped, or you will end up enslaved for the rest of your life!"

The kids cheered. Matthew was appalled. He looked at Kimo and the other security guards, shocked that they would allow Cain to say things like this. The guards stood there calmly, some of them even smiling. They all seemed completely oblivious to what Cain was saying. Matthew began to wonder if the guards had all gone deaf. Couldn't they hear what he was hearing?

Matthew shifted to the physical plane. He looked at Cain and saw him playing and singing. Matthew blinked his eyes and he was on the spiritual plane. Cain was speaking to the kids. The demon guitar was playing and singing the music.

"You all know about the big Washington, D.C., concert next week," Cain continued. "It's going to be televised worldwide. I want you all to be watching and listening.

When I play the final chord on this song, 'Possession,' you will rise up and destroy the slave masters."

The kids yelled and applauded.

"You won't be alone," Cain continued. His voice had lost the pinched quality. He was getting into it, enjoying the power. He lifted his head, actually looked into the young faces. "My fans all over the world will strike down their evil oppressors. You are heroes who will bring about the end of the old world and the dawn of the new one."

Matthew recalled the research he'd done on Cain just after he joined up. Cain had been invited to the White House. The president's kids were big fans. He'd been to Buckingham Palace, the Kremlin, the Great Wall of China. He'd met the kids of government and corporate leaders all over the world.

And everywhere he went, Cain turned these kids into the perfect assassins. The one person who could slip through the tightest security, the one person no bodyguard would ever suspect: the parent's own child . . .

The murder of the judge. Perhaps that had been a test run. To see if the kid would actually go through with it. Same with the suicide. Demonstrating their control. Satisfied that this was working, Satan was now gearing up for the final act. The big finish.

Matthew could imagine the state of chaos into which the world would be plunged if government and corporate and military officials throughout the world were all slain by their own children on a single terrible night.

Cain had to be stopped. Matthew was thinking how he might go about it, wondering if he was strong enough to take on the demons when he realized with a start that Natalia had entered the room. He had been so preoccupied with his own thoughts, he hadn't noticed her. She had come to check on the contest winners, make certain all was well.

She stood near the door, smiling and relaxed, pleased to see the kids having a good time. She had no way of knowing the horror in store for her.

This will destroy her, Matthew thought. *She'll never recover.*

Time to call in backup, Matthew decided. He took out the cell phone, dialed the number for the Archangel. He withdrew silently back into the room to make the call.

"Did you hear that asshole?" Woof demanded, materializing out of the darkness.

"Don't do that!" Matthew snapped. He had to wait for his thudding heart to quiet before he could make the call. "Whistle or stomp your feet or something to let me know you're coming."

"You've got to stop him!" said Woof.

"So you didn't know Cain was ordering these kids to commit murder?" Matthew asked grimly.

"Hell, no!" Woof shouted. "I never listened to the asshole before now! I—"

Woof stopped, shifted his gaze. "Oh, my God! Natalia!"

"What's wrong?" Matthew switched off the phone, just as William was answering, and looked back into the room.

Dark smokelike forms were rising up off the floor, swirling around her. She had no guardian angel to protect her, only Woof, who was beating at the fiends with his hands. The forms swirled away from the ghost, but then swooped back to wrap more tightly around Natalia.

Matthew was not the only one to see what was happening to her. Cain, looking stricken, dropped the guitar and started to go to her. The demon beside Cain dug his claws into Cain's arm and whispered into his ear. Cain hesitated. The demon kept whispering and, at last, Cain picked up the guitar and asked, in a strained voice, if the kids had any requests.

Matthew reached into his hip pocket. Flask in hand, he lurched out the door of the bedroom, went stumbling out into the middle of the room.

"Hey, there, boys and girls," Matthew slurred, swaying on his feet and giving a drunken wave. "It's Father Gallow." He took a swig from the flask. "I'm not a real priest, you know," he added, laughing, and began to weave his way across the room.

He kept walking, tripping over the feet of the kids on the floor, all the time heading for Natalia. He glanced sidelong at Cain and his demonic friends. Cain looked annoyed at being upstaged. The demons were unsure of themselves, confused. They watched Matthew narrowly, wondering if they needed to be concerned. He guessed that so long as he left Cain alone, they would leave him alone.

The fiends clung to Natalia as he drew closer. They paid no attention to Matthew, and he remembered what William had said about him: *an angel without wings to soar, an angel without light to shine.*

But still an angel, Matthew said to himself, and he added, beneath his breath, "Grant me, Lord, the power to drive back the darkness."

A gust of wind blasted through the room, tore the fiendish forms to rags, and blew them away. Matthew lurched into Natalia, who was staring at him in openmouthed astonishment. He grabbed her around the waist and kissed her and, at the same time, maneuvered her out the door and into the hall.

Matthew glanced back at Cain, saw his face twisted in a scowl. Then Woof slammed shut the door.

Chapter 28

Outside in the hall, Matthew's feet got tangled up with Natalia's as he was trying to push her out the door. He tripped her, and they both went down onto the floor.

"Are you crazy?" Natalia shoved him away and jumped to her feet. "That was quite a spectacle you put on!" She glared at Matthew. "What on earth is the matter with you? Here you go on about Cain being sober and well behaved, then you come out stinking of bourbon and make damn fools of both of us—"

Matthew took hold of her arm and began to steer her firmly down the hall. A pale and shaken Woof hurried along beside them.

"I'm not drunk," Matthew said.

Natalia snorted. "Let go of me." She tried to pull away, but he kept a firm grip on her.

"First you're going to listen to what I have to say."

Matthew escorted her to his room. She grew calmer as they walked, regarded him dubiously.

"You don't look drunk *now*," she said, watching as he unlocked the door. "But if not, why the hell the act?"

"I had to get you out of there. Come in," he added, opening the door. "We need to talk. In private."

Natalia walked inside. Looking more puzzled than angry, she sat down on the bed. He remained standing.

"So what's this all about?" she demanded.

Matthew hesitated. Now that it came down to it, he didn't know what to say.

"Tell her," Woof urged him.

"It's not that easy," he snapped.

"Don't yell at me!" Natalia said angrily, jumping off the bed. "*You* were the one who said you wanted to talk . . ."

"I'm sorry," Matthew said. "It's just . . . you're going to find all this very hard to believe."

He paused, drew in a breath, then said, "You have to cancel Cain's televised concert next week."

"I can't do that even if I wanted to!" Natalia exclaimed. "MTV would sue us! The sponsors would sue us—Coke, Nintendo. They've spent thousands on advertising. It's just not possible—"

"Cain sold his soul to the devil," said Matthew flatly. "For real."

Natalia shook her head. "Oh, for God's sake—"

"Look, I know this sounds crazy—"

"You're damn right it does. Come talk to me when you're sober," Natalia said in disgust, heading for the door.

She reached out, took hold of the handle and tried to open the door. The handle flew out of her hand. The door slammed shut. Woof stood with his back against it.

"What the—" Natalia stared at the door. She turned around to face Matthew. "How did you do that?"

"I didn't," Matthew said, sighing. "And I haven't been drinking. Please, just listen to me. Cain's meteoric rise, the

subsequent suicides, the murder, even the riot. It's all because Cain is in league with the Powers of Darkness. You
said yourself he's changed. I don't think he wanted this, but
now he's in over his head. He doesn't want to do this, but
he's being used, manipulated. Demons are going through
him to possess kids like Grace and forcing them to do these
terrible acts. On the night of the televised concert, Cain's
going to send a message out to kids all over the world telling
them to kill their parents. Kids of world leaders, military
officers, corporate officials. He's going to turn his fans into
assassins."

Matthew stopped talking. Natalia had been listening to
him in silence, her arms folded across her chest, her face
unreadable. He didn't know if she believed him or if she
was just letting himself talk himself out.

He soon had his answer.

"I suppose if I fire you, you'll go to the press with this,"
Natalia said coldly.

Matthew wasn't sure what he'd do. Somehow he had to
stop that concert, and if that meant going to the press . . .

He tried again. "Natalia, I'm not some sort of religious
fanatic. Sit down. Just hear me out."

"I can't. Not tonight. I'm too tired," she said wearily. "I'll
decide what to do about you in the morning."

She put her hand on the door handle. Woof refused to
budge, and the door wouldn't open.

"You need to let me out, Matthew," Natalia said, her
voice grating.

Matthew sighed. He looked at Woof, who shook his head
and moved away from the door.

Natalia opened the door. She paused, glanced back at
Matthew. Her eyes were dark, filled with sorrow, disappointment, hurt. She started to say something, then bit her
lip and hurried away. Matthew heard her enter her room,

which was next door. He heard her door slam shut, heard the television switch on.

Matthew pulled out his flask. He started to open it. Woof knocked it out of his hand.

"What the hell do you think you're doing?" the ghost demanded.

"Pouring myself a drink," said Matthew, bending down to pick up the flask.

"And how's that going to help?" Woof asked sarcastically.

"Cheer me up," Matthew suggested. "Make me forget I ever met her."

"You have to do something!" Woof said, flinging his arms about wildly.

"I tried," said Matthew, pouring the bourbon. "You saw how far I got. She thinks now I'm some sort of religious nut who's gone psycho on her."

"Call that friend of yours. That angel dude. Let him talk to her."

"I don't know why she'd listen to him any more than she's listening to me. You were the one who told her God was a myth and angels and demons were figments of our imagination and faith was a crutch for the weak."

"Yeah, well, I was wrong," Woof said, looking uncomfortable. "I admit it. But, damn it, man, how was I supposed to know? God could give a fellow a sign, you know. A burning bush would have done the trick. Or, maybe not." The ghost sighed and scratched his grizzled chin. "I would've probably thought I'd just dropped some bad acid . . . I better go make sure that she's okay . . ."

"It's hard to have faith, Woof," said Matthew, as the ghost slipped through the wall. Matthew tossed down his bourbon. "No one knows that better than I."

* * *

Natalia told herself she wasn't going to go all soggy and weepy. Her emotions were raw, ragged. The last few days tearing up over every little thing. Not that Matthew turning into a raving lunatic was a little thing. No, it was a horribly big, gigantic thing, and she was going to have to sort it out, and she had the feeling it was going to get ugly.

If only she didn't care about him so damn much!

Natalia had always thought she was a good judge of people. She had thought she knew Matthew, even in the short time they'd been together. She had known he was a bit mysterious, but she'd found that attractive. Now she'd learned that he wasn't mysterious. He was just plain loony. Out of his mind. Off his rocker. Elevator didn't go to the top floor and all of that. How could she have been so wrong about him? How could she *not* have seen this coming?

She needed to get rid of him, fire him. But she was afraid that if she did, he would go to the press, and they would eat this up.

Maybe that could work to my advantage, Natalia mused. *Maybe I could make it look like this was part of the act. Play it up big. Hint that Father Gallow is really onto something and that was why we got rid of him. Yes, that could work.*

She wondered if she should fire him tonight, decided against it. She really was exhausted. She needed a good night's sleep, the first in many nights. She would need to think clearly tomorrow.

She took a shower and stood in the hot water a long time, letting it relax her aching muscles and soothe her spirit. Then she put on her penguin jammies and crawled into bed. She thought she'd go to sleep instantly, but she didn't. She kept thinking about Matthew, kept hearing his voice, seeing his face.

He was in earnest, sincere. He was grave and concerned.

Deeply concerned. He obviously believed in what he was saying.

I guess that's what makes him a lunatic, Natalia thought sadly.

Natalia woke suddenly with the terrifying feeling someone was in the room. She lay still a moment to make sure she'd heard the noise and not dreamed it. She heard the noise again, someone moving about, then she felt the person bump against the bed and heard a muttered, "Ouch, damn it."

Her heart in her throat, Natalia sat up in bed and fumbled for the light switch.

"Who's there?" she said sharply. "What are you doing in here?"

The light flared. Cain was standing at the foot of her bed. He was bare-chested, bare-legged. He was wearing only his underwear, nothing else. His hair was disheveled. He staggered when he walked. His eyes were glazed and red-rimmed. She could see plainly the fresh needle mark on his arm.

"Jeez, Nat!" he said, flinging his hand in front of his eyes. "Whatcha trying to do? Blind me? Turn the fuckin' light off."

Natalia saw the bulge in his underwear, and she was suddenly frightened. She couldn't show fear, however. Cain was strung out. He didn't know what he was doing. She wondered how he had managed to get into her room. He didn't have a key.

"Cain," said Natalia firmly, climbing out of bed, "you're in the wrong room. You have to leave. Now."

She headed for the door, planning to open it and steer him gently but firmly out, then march him down the hall. His suite was close by. Hopefully, they'd reach it before anyone saw them.

Cain grabbed her from behind, pulled her up against him. He rubbed the bulge in his crotch against her thigh.

"Oh, no, Nat," he grunted, "I'm in the right room."

He tried to kiss her neck.

Natalia shoved him back, sent him staggering. He hit the bed and fell onto it.

"Get out!" she said, so angry she could barely speak.

Cain grinned at her. "You don't mean that, baby. Here. Look where I landed. Come join me." He lurched at her, caught hold of her wrist, and yanked her down so that she fell on top of him.

The lamp on the nightstand tilted and wobbled. A glass of water slid off the table and crashed onto the floor.

"You know you want it," Cain said, thrusting his crotch into her groin. "You've always wanted it."

Natalia felt sick with terror. She tried to free herself from his grasp, but his grip was strong, painful. He held her with one hand and, grasping hold of her pajama top, ripped it open. His hand fumbled at her breast.

"Cain, stop!" Natalia cried. She struggled to get away from him. "Let me go! I don't want to hurt you . . ."

"Hurt me?" Cain laughed, and his laughter was horrible to hear. "You can't hurt me, sweetheart. I'm invincible. You're my reward, see . . ."

Natalia pulled loose and started to run for the door. Cain leaped after her. He caught hold of her in a bone-crushing grip and flung her back on the bed. He pinned her arms and lowered himself on top of her.

"Cain, don't," Natalia begged, writhing beneath him, "I won't let you do this! I'll scream, and if I do, security will come and take you to jail. And this time you'll stay there."

"Scream all you want, darling," said Cain, his breath hot on her neck. He had taken off his underwear. She could feel him rubbing against her. "No one will hear you. My friends will see to that. You've been promised to me. You're my reward . . ."

He was strong, incredibly strong. *It must be the drugs,* Natalia thought wildly. He wasn't making sense. She tried to move out from beneath him, tried to free herself, but he had pressed his arm across her chest. His other hand was yanking at her pajama bottoms, trying to pull them off. He was half-smothering her.

"What are you talking about, Cain?" Natalia gasped, struggling against him. "What reward? I don't understand."

"You don't? I thought the good Father Gallow must have told you."

Cain chuckled and thrust his fingers into her. He grunted in pleasure. She moaned and twisted, trying to get away from him.

"I sold my soul, Natalia," Cain continued. "I belong to the devil. He gave me everything I asked for—fame, fortune. And now you. All for being a good boy and doing exactly what I'm told . . . My name will go down in history, Nat!" Cain's voice had a dreamy quality to it. "All the kids, all the killing, all the blood, in my name . . ."

"Oh, God!" Natalia fought to breathe. What Matthew had told her was true! "I'll cancel the rest of the tour, Cain. I won't let you—"

"No, you won't," he said, and he lifted himself up off her, stared down at her. His eyes shone with an eerie reddish glow. "If you do that, there'll be a bus accident. Jordan, Ryan, Mike will all be killed. They'll die, and it will be for nothing because I'll still do that concert. To honor their memories, of course."

Natalia screamed. "Help!" she cried. "Help me!"

But her voice was swallowed up in darkness. She could barely hear herself. Fear twisted inside her. The lamp on the nightstand was rocking back and forth in the strangest manner. She had the strangest impression there were beings in the room; dark beings with dark wings. The dark wings folded around her, dark hands held her down . . .

Natalia moaned and closed her eyes to blot out Cain's face. Tears squeezed from beneath her eyelids.

"C'mon, Nat," Cain whispered. "Just relax and enjoy it. You know you've always wanted it."

He started to thrust himself into her when the lamp from the nightstand suddenly leaped into the air, flew over the bed, and struck Cain in the head, knocking him sideways. He collapsed with a groan. Natalia half crawled, half tumbled out of the bed. She crouched on the floor, too terrified to move for fear of being hit by flying debris.

The lamp had disconnected itself when it jumped off the table. In the semidarkness, Natalia watched in disbelief as glasses flung themselves out of the bathroom and shattered against the ceiling. A chair crashed into the television. Her overnight bag sailed past her and smashed into the wall.

Cain stood up dizzily. One side of his face was bloody, but he was still conscious. Bleary-eyed, he groped around the room, searching for her.

"Nat, quit throwing stuff . . . Stop playing games . . ."

"Cain, just leave!" Natalia begged. She tensed, ready to make a run for it, though he was now between her and the door.

"Cain, please . . ."

Chapter 29

*M*atthew hadn't been able to sleep. He lay on his bed, a glass of bourbon untouched beside him. The ice had long ago melted, and it was mostly water now. He held the cell phone in his hand, but he didn't call William. He knew perfectly well what the archangel would say.

God sent you, Matthew.

Fine, Matthew thought bitterly, *but what does God want me to do?* He laughed to himself, and thought, *The second oldest question in the world, the first being, why am I here?*

The crash, coming from the room next door, startled him. He sat up straight, staring intently at the wall as though he could see through it. He heard another crash and a thump, then something heavy thudded into the wall.

Woof appeared, materializing out of the air. "Call security! Cain's in there with Natalia! He's . . ."

Matthew didn't need to hear more. He dashed for the door.

"Can you let me into her room?" he yelled at Woof.

"I'm a ghost. I can fling lamps!" Woof yelled. "I can't unlock doors. You're the fuckin' angel! Do a miracle or something!"

Woof disappeared. By the sounds of the thudding and thumps, he'd returned to the attack.

"Damn!" Matthew swore. He reached for the phone to call security and his gaze fell on Arthur, sleeping soundly in William's hat.

Dormouse, William had said, chuckling. *Opens doors . . . Get it?*

"Got it!" Matthew said. He grabbed up Arthur—hat and all—and ran into the hall. "Okay, God or Arthur or angels or whatever—open the damn door!"

Arthur woke up, yawned and blinked his beady eyes.

Matthew set Arthur and the hat down on the floor (where the dormouse promptly went back to sleep), and put his hand on the door handle. Electricity sparked, jolting him, and the light flashed green. Matthew kicked the door open and ran inside. He ducked the ice bucket that went whizzing past him, caught hold of Cain's shoulder, spun him around, and slammed his fist into Cain's jaw.

Cain fell back onto the bed and lay there, unmoving.

"Natalia!" Matthew called, searching for her.

"Here!" she cried. Rising off the floor, she ran to him and flung herself into his arms.

"It's all right now," he said. He could feel her shaking.

"Cain told me he sold his soul!" Natalia babbled, hardly knowing what she was saying. "You were right, Matthew. He's evil. We have to stop him. I'd cancel the tour, but he said if I did, he'd kill Jordan and Ryan and Mike! There would be a bus crash and they'd all die and he'd still do the tour and I was his reward. Oh, God! What do I do, Matthew?"

"There's a balcony," Woof growled. "Pretend he's a mattress and fling him off it."

"Hush," Matthew said, talking to Natalia, but including Woof. "Tell me exactly what Cain said . . . Shhh . . . Someone's coming!"

Matthew had neglected to close the door, and he could hear heavy footfalls in the hall.

"I could have him arrested, send him to jail . . ." Natalia said urgently.

"He'd only get out again. His demon friends would see to that. We need time to think," said Matthew. "Play along with me." He smoothed her hair. "Pretend you just woke up. Oh, and you better fix your top."

Natalia looked down at herself. She was half-naked, her cheeks wet with tears. She flushed and tried to obey, but her fingers were stiff and cold and she fumbled helplessly with her top. Matthew pinned the penguin pajamas for her. She wiped her face with her sleeve.

Cain was coming around. He was mumbling, trying to sit up. He had a swollen jaw. Blood dribbled from his lip.

He was dazed from the blow and strung out from the drugs, but he still managed to glare at Matthew.

"I want you gone," Cain said softly, malevolently.

"Yeah, well, you can't always get what you want," said Matthew.

"But like the song says, 'sometimes you get what you need,' asshole," Woof snarled, brandishing his fists.

Matthew hauled Cain off the bed, hustled him into his underwear. Putting his arm around Cain, Matthew steered him toward the door. Woof ranged alongside. Cain could barely walk; he was deadweight in Matthew's arms. Matthew noted as a point of interest that Cain's flesh wasn't burning him to a crisp. The reason was soon apparent.

"How about we make a deal?" Cain said softly. "You hand in your resignation, Father Gallow . . . or Natalia dies."

Matthew might have supposed this threat was just the drugs talking, but Cain was suddenly, frighteningly sober. His eyes might have been red-rimmed, but they were focused and lucid, and they were now fixed on Matthew with hatred.

"You wouldn't kill her," Matthew said trying to speak calmly, though he felt chilled to his very soul. "Somewhere inside the dark, twisted being you've become, you still love her."

"I used to . . . once," Cain mumbled. "Not anymore. I forgot how."

Matthew heard an odd note in his voice. He looked at Cain and saw a plea in the red eyes, a cry for help. For a moment, Matthew could almost hear that cry, as he'd heard Grace's spirit cry out to him during the exorcism.

"Cain . . ." Matthew began, but they were interrupted by two men who confronted them as they came out of the room. They weren't security. They were Burl and John, the roadies from hell.

"Let go of me!" Cain snarled, and jerked free of Matthew's grasp. He stumbled and nearly fell down, but saved himself by staggering into the wall.

Matthew cast an oblique glance back into the room. Natalia was standing beside the bed, wrapped up in a blanket, staring in perplexity at the roadies.

"Odd to find you two here," Matthew remarked.

"We could say the same about you," said Burl.

"We've been waiting, but you didn't get back to us about our offer," added John.

"*And* you're still around," said Burl.

"*And* you told Ms. Ashley about Cain," said John.

"The boss is annoyed," said Burl.

"Bad things happen when the boss gets annoyed," said John. He cast a glance at Cain, who was slouched against the wall, singing to himself in a slurred undertone.

Matthew looked at Cain—a miserable spectacle, drugged-up, naked except for his underwear, his eyes unfocused, hair in his face. Matthew glanced back into the room at Natalia and his blood chilled, his gut twisted.

"You did this," he said harshly.

"We didn't do anything," said Burl, grinning. "Cain here got a little out of control, that's all."

Matthew was so angry he wanted to reach into their leering mouths and shred their black hearts, but he had to hang on to what shreds of control he still held over this horrible situation.

Matthew glowered. "Yeah, you boys didn't do anything except supply Cain with the drugs and see to it that he got into Natalia's locked room. I'll bet you even put the idea into his head that she wanted to have sex with him."

"Here's the deal," said Burl. "Father Gallow disappears and Ms. Ashley enjoys nights of undisturbed rest."

"Until after what your boss has planned. Then she won't be getting much rest," Matthew remarked.

"I'll be . . . legendary," Cain mumbled. He started to slide down the wall.

"But that won't be your problem, will it, Father Gallow?" said Burl pleasantly.

Matthew gritted his teeth. He made himself answer calmly. "No, I guess it won't. I'll need some time to make my sudden departure look good."

"Take all the time you want," said John, waving his hand.

"Just be gone by morning," Burl added. "Oh, and the same goes for the old hippie."

"How am I supposed to get rid of a ghost?" Matthew demanded.

"Beats me. You're the exorcist," said Burl with a wink.

He took hold of Cain and jerked him to his feet. Cain yelped and snarled and tried to free himself. The roadie had a good grip on him, however.

Matthew remained in the hall, watching the two demons drag Cain, stumbling and staggering, down the hall to his suite.

"I wish I'd killed the asshole with that lamp," said Woof, still seething. "I tried, but I'm not real good at flinging things yet. Takes a lot of mental concentration . . ."

"And yours is a little fuzzy," Matthew remarked.

"No need to get insulting," Woof muttered, but he grinned shamefacedly as he said it.

"You couldn't have killed him anyway," Matthew added grimly. "His boss will see to that. Not until after the big performance. Then they won't have any use for him anymore. He'll be found dead of a drug overdose. They're setting him up for it already."

He didn't add what he was thinking—that Natalia would be found dead, too. Murder/suicide.

"Asshole deserves whatever he gets!" Woof said viciously.

If we all got what we deserved, Hell would be filled to the rafters . . .

Matthew walked back into Natalia's room. She was picking up shards of broken glass.

"Watch where you walk. I'd throw this away," Natalia said, trying to sound normal, though her voice shook, "but I can't find the wastebasket. And were those the two roadies I saw in the hall? What are they doing here? They should be back on the bus."

"They're not human. They're demons, Cain's handlers," said Matthew. "They're supposed to be keeping a watch on him. But I guess even the devil's finding it hard to get good help these days."

Natalia stared at him, then sank down weakly on the bed.

"Then it wasn't a horrible dream. What you said about Cain was true. What Cain said was true. Oh, God!"

She blinked her eyes rapidly and brushed her hand across them.

"I'm *not* going to fall apart," she said bleakly.

"Might help if you did," Matthew suggested.

Natalia shook her head. "No, it wouldn't. I'd just be a sodden mess. I feel so . . . lost and alone. Everything I thought I knew has blown up in my face. I never believed in Hell and Satan and demons. But I saw them, Matthew! Terrible beings with dark wings, holding me, smothering me!"

She gave a ragged sob. Matthew sat down on the bed beside her and put his arm around her. He could feel her trembling.

"Natalia," he said quietly, "there is a Hell. There is darkness. And there are weak people like Cain who believe the devil's lies and get tangled up in his deadly web. But think of this. If the darkness is true, then the opposite is also true. Faith is true. Goodness is true. Love and forgiveness . . ."

He stood up, suddenly realizing what he'd been saying. "You need to get some sleep. I'll be right next door—"

Natalia clutched at him in alarm. "Don't go, Matthew! Please!"

She shivered. "It was awful, Matthew. Cain tried to . . . to rape me. And he would have, but things started flying around the room like a B horror movie."

She gave a hysterical laugh. "The lamp jumped up and hit him on the head. That sounds crazy, doesn't it? But then I thought what you said about Cain selling his soul was crazy. Only now . . . he told me himself it was true . . . He's going to kill all those people, and he's proud of it! I can't stay here!" she cried wildly. "I can't stay in this room!"

"We'll go to my room," said Matthew. "Okay."

"Okay." Natalia crowded close to him, holding him tightly. They walked together to his room. He opened the door, led her inside.

"Is it all right if I take a shower?" she asked wistfully. "A long, long shower?"

"Sure," said Matthew. What he would have liked to do to Cain in that moment would have got him sent to Hell a hundred times over. What he did was go back into the hall and retrieve Arthur and the hat. He carried the dormouse back into room and tucked him and the hat into his briefcase.

Woof prowled about, furious and frustrated.

"What are we going to do?" he demanded, rounding on Matthew.

"You're going to make yourself scarce," said Matthew, under the cover of the running shower water.

"I won't leave her!" said Woof defiantly.

"You don't have to. Keep out of their sight. And no more lamp throwing," Matthew added.

"Just as I was getting good at it." Woof glared at Matthew. "You're going to walk out on her, aren't you?"

"I have no choice," said Matthew bitterly. "Besides, what good am I? I have no power to stop Cain."

Woof rubbed his grizzled chin and eyed Matthew speculatively. "Those were some pretty words you said to my girl, Angel Boy. About love and forgiveness. I was wondering if you meant them or if it was just talk?"

Matthew didn't answer. Truth was, he didn't know.

"I think you've got the power to stop this," said Woof. He shoved his hands in the pockets of his ragged jeans and started to fade away. "The strongest power on Earth."

"What's that?" Matthew asked.

"If you don't know, Angel Boy, then it's not up to an old hippie ghost to tell you," Woof replied, and he disappeared.

Natalia stood in the hot water for a long time, letting it wash off Cain's touch. She kept thinking about what he'd said and about what Matthew had told her, and she thought she shouldn't be believing any of it. It wasn't logical. It wasn't scientific.

But then lamps jumping off tables and flying around her room wasn't very logical either. And she'd seen that with her own eyes. She'd hear Cain admit what he'd done. She had to believe it.

But that opened up even more questions, especially about Matthew. How had he known?

Natalia shut off the shower. She dried off, wrapped herself in a towel, and went into the bedroom. Her hair was wet and straggled over her bare shoulders.

"Matthew," she said softly.

He turned to Natalia and held out his arms. She walked into his embrace.

"Matthew," she said, drawing back to look into his eyes. "Who are you?"

He shrugged and said gently, "Does it matter?"

Natalia hesitated. "No, I guess not. Just tell me this much. You're not one of them, are you? I mean, Burl *did* tell Cain to keep you—"

"Damn it, Natalia," Matthew swore, suddenly angry. "When will you ever trust me? Here I risked losing you by trying to warn you about Cain—"

He stopped.

Natalia smiled at him. "You risked losing me . . . Do you have me to lose?"

Matthew didn't immediately answer. He seemed to be

waging some internal argument with himself. At last he said, "Of course, you mean something to me." Then he added, with an exasperated sigh, "God knows why. You've landed me in more trouble than any other woman I've ever known in my life!"

He kissed her cheek. "But you've also made me happier than any other woman—"

That was as far as he got. Natalia stopped the rest of his sentence with her lips. She unwrapped her towel and let it drop to the floor.

Matthew scooped her up off her feet and carried her to the bed. This time his kisses were intense, slow and deliberate. Natalia knew now that Matthew cared for her and that he would be there to protect her. She felt safe. He didn't want to change her. He didn't want her to settle down, and she hoped he didn't want to leave her.

They made love slowly. Matthew moved his hands over her skin, his touch gentle. He seemed to marvel at the sight of her, running his hands over her legs, stomach, arms, and breasts. His kisses were deep, penetrating kisses that swelled and rose to climax, then ebbed again.

Natalia felt her tense muscles relaxing, and she sighed. Matthew's touch grew more intimate, and Natalia reacted to him. He kissed her cheek, forehead, neck, shoulders over and over again. Natalia reached out for him. She wanted to feel him on her, in her. Matthew followed her direction and moved over her.

She could feel his hardness in her. She gave a moan of delight, and Matthew's breathing grew faster. He held her tightly as they moved together. She found his rhythm and matched it with her own. Her breathing increased, and, as she closed her eyes, she could see flashes of starlight as the electricity of pleasure rose from between her thighs, moved up her spine, and exploded in her vision of the stars.

Matthew groaned and tensed. His body spasmed over and over again. He smiled down at Natalia and pushed her hair away from her face.

"Yes, I had you to lose."

"Damn right you did." Natalia nestled close to him. "Are you going to leave me now? Because, if you are, I'll just have to come after you."

"I'm not leaving," he said, and he added with a mischievous smile. "It's my room. You're the one who has to leave."

She struck him with her pillow, and he hit her with his pillow. The fight ended in another passionate encounter that left them both pleasantly exhausted.

Natalia curled up beside Matthew and drifted into sleep. He held her in his arms, and that's where she was the next morning when she woke up.

Chapter 30

The next morning, Matthew waited for the limo with Natalia in the lobby of the hotel. He was silent and withdrawn, though he kept close to her, his hand on her shoulder. She crowded near him, her arms crossed tightly over her chest, holding herself together.

Last night had been the most horrible and the most wonderful of her life. She concentrated on the wonderful, keeping Matthew's face before her eyes, letting it blot out the horror of Cain's assault. But that wouldn't last long. She would have to see Cain, talk to him, work with him. She didn't know how she could.

"I want to quit," she said. "But I can't, can I?"

"No," said Matthew, "you can't. Not if you want to protect Jordan and the others." He was silent a minute, then he said, "Not if you want to protect Cain."

"Protect Cain?" Natalia repeated, shocked and angry. "Why would I want to protect him? After what he did to me!"

"Don't think of him the way he is now," said Matthew. "Think of him as the guy who saved your life in the mosh pit. You have to talk to him, Natalia. Find out if . . ." He hesitated, not certain how to put it.

"Find out if there's anything of the old Cain left," Natalia said in a low voice. She sighed deeply. "That's why they let him tell me the truth, wasn't it? To force me to go along with the plan."

Matthew gave her a wry smile. "If it's any comfort, it's because you're good at your job."

"And after it's all over?" she asked.

Matthew wouldn't meet her eyes. He looked away, out the lobby window, into the bright sunlight. It seemed so strange to her that the sun should be shining. Everything around her was dark and cold.

"I see," she said. "The headline will read: 'Rock Star Kills Manager, Turns Gun on Self.'"

"That won't happen," said Matthew. "We'll find some way out of this. Here's the car."

Matthew walked her out to the limo, opened the door for her, and helped her inside. He started to close the door.

"Aren't you coming with me?" she asked, alarmed.

"I have something I have to do," he said evasively.

"What?" she demanded.

"I thought you were going to trust me."

"I do. It's just—"

He smiled. "If you must know, I have to see a man about a dormouse."

Shutting the door, he gave the driver the signal to go and stood on the sidewalk, keeping her in sight as they drove off. Natalia watched him until they turned a corner, and he was gone. Bewildered, she sank back into the seat.

She wanted to trust Matthew. She truly did, but there were so many questions about him. So many questions about everything.

Exhausted, she shut her eyes and stretched out in the back of the limo, pressing her cheek into the cool leather. Matthew was gone, perhaps never coming back. This terrible thing was going to happen. She couldn't stop it. The forces of darkness were far more powerful than any mere mortal. Natalia was overwhelmed by loneliness and terror. Sobs tore at her chest, tears filled her eyes. She curled into a tight ball of misery and let it all come flooding out of her.

And then the strangest thing in days of strange things happened. She felt a rough hand stroke her hair and heard a familiar voice singing softly, gruffly, the song he'd sung to her when she was a little child.

The one and only lullaby Woof knew.

"'Hush, my darling, don't fear, my darling, the lion sleeps tonight. A-weemoweh, a-weemoweh . . .'"

She could hear Woof's off-key voice braying the A-weemoweh's, the silly words that had always defeated the purpose of the lullaby by making her giggle and waking her up. She began to giggle now at the memory, though with a catch in her throat.

"A-weemoweh, a-weemoweh . . ."

She leaned back in the seat and began to sing along.

"Thanks for meeting me at such short notice," Matthew said stiffly.

"Never a problem," William replied, smiling expansively from where he was seated on a park bench. He was wearing his Angels baseball jacket. "Always glad to get out of the house. How's Arthur?"

"Fine. I bought him this plastic cage. It has an exercise wheel. He likes it. Spends most of his time on it."

"He does?" William regarded the dormouse, who was slumbering soundly, in amazement.

Matthew sat down beside him and leaned forward, his elbows resting on his knees.

"Bad news, I gather," said William, placing the hat with the sleepy dormouse on the bench beside him.

"The worst," said Matthew grimly.

He told William about how Cain traveled throughout the world, meeting the children of powerful, influential people; how the demons had taken hold of them.

"When he plays that song of his, 'Possession,' that will be the trigger that drives them to strike," Matthew concluded. "Hundreds, maybe thousands of kids the world over, will slaughter their parents."

William listened in silence, his expression growing increasingly grave.

"An ingenious plan," he said somberly, when Matthew was finished. "Truly ingenious. Throw governments and businesses into turmoil."

"That's all you've got to say?" Matthew demanded. "Look, I've done my part." Putting his hands on his knees, he levered himself upright. "Now Heaven will *have* to send in an archangel powerful enough to stop Cain."

"We could find someone, I suppose," said William thoughtfully, "though the best person for the job is right here."

He looked directly at Matthew.

"Me?" Matthew exclaimed, glowering. He tapped himself on the chest. "This is me, William! Loose cannon. Fake priest. No superpowers! Hell, I can't even break down a door without asking a narcoleptic rat to help me!"

"Dormouse," William corrected automatically. "Your friend, Woof, is right, Matthew. You have the greatest power in Heaven and on Earth at your command. You have only to call on it."

"And what's that power supposed to be?" Matthew demanded, sneering. "'All you need is love' or some crap like that?"

"Yes, Matthew," said William gently, "some crap like that."

Matthew glared at him, then he turned on his heel and walked off.

"Matthew," William said quietly, "have you been having those nightmares anymore?"

Matthew halted. As a matter of fact, he hadn't. He hadn't had one of the terrible nightmares since he'd left the Inn-B-Tween motel.

Since he'd met Natalia.

Matthew hunched his shoulders and kept on walking.

"Do you want to take Arthur with you?" William called out.

Matthew shot back an answer.

"Oh, dear," murmured William, covering the dormouse (still asleep) protectively with a fold of the hat. "Pretend you didn't hear that."

Natalia woke to find the limo driver respectfully tapping her on the shoulder. She sat up, at first confused about where she was and why she was here, then memory came flooding back. She sighed deeply and rubbed her eyes, then looked out the window. The limo was parked in front of the two buses. It was early in the morning. No one would be awake yet. One reason she'd chosen this time to arrive.

As usual, she felt better after her brief nap—a power nap, she termed it. She took time to comb her hair and touch up her makeup and smooth her clothing. Her eyes were still puffy from crying, but there was nothing to be done for that. She was going to be calm, in control. She thought about what Matthew had said. Think about the old Cain, the Cain who had worked hard, sacrificed so much . . .

Including his very soul.

Natalia knocked on the door of the bus. After a moment, Al peered out, then opened the door to let her in.

"You look like hell," he remarked, regarding her worriedly.

Natalia winced at the statement. "Thanks, Al. I love you, too. Is . . . um . . . Cain here? He wasn't at the hotel."

"Yeah, he came stumbling in here about four in the morning, higher than a kite." Al looked at her oddly. "You didn't know? Those two roadies, Burl and John, had Cain in tow. They said you told them to bring him back to the bus."

"Oh, uh, yeah. I guess I forgot. It was a difficult night," Natalia added with a wan smile.

"They said Cain busted up another hotel room."

"Yeah, fortunately this time we were able to keep it quiet. I'm going to go have a talk with him. Al, I hate to ask this, but would you mind taking a walk? This needs to be private."

He regarded her with a frown. "Are you sure, Natalia? I don't like the thought of you being alone with him in his state . . ."

"I'll be fine," said Natalia.

Al shrugged. "I'll be right outside the door."

Natalia thanked him and, gathering her courage and resolve, went to Cain's door. She banged on it and yelled his name. No answer. She hadn't expected one, so she flung open the door and walked inside.

The room was hot and stuffy and smelled of sweat and dirty clothes. Natalia flipped on a light.

Cain lay on his stomach, sprawled across the bed. He was

still dressed, even to his leather jacket and boots. His face was turned sideways, breathing through his mouth. His skin was pale, except for the purple-and-blue bruise on the side of his head and another on his jaw. His eyes were sunken, his hair tangled.

He didn't look the part of a monster this morning. He looked like a dumb, stupid kid.

"Cain, wake up," she commanded.

Startled, Cain grunted and twitched. "Huh, what?" he muttered. "Whasa matter?" He sat up, shielding his eyes with his hand, trying to see. "Whos'at?"

"It's Natalia," she said. She wasn't surprised he didn't recognize her voice. It sounded strange even to her, harsh and hard.

Cain blinked his red-rimmed eyes and brought her into focus. At the sight of her, his facial muscles contracted. His jaw quivered. He licked his lips. He quickly looked away, his eyes roving nervously around the room.

She had wondered if he would remember what he'd done last night. Obviously, he did.

"Oh, uh, hey, Nat," he said. He flicked a glance at her and looked swiftly away. His gaze fell on the clock. He glared at it, frowned, and swore.

"It's only fuckin' nine o'clock. What do you mean waking me up so goddamn early!"

"Because we need to have a talk," she said.

"Go to hell!" he muttered, and flung himself back down on the bed. He pulled a pillow over his head.

"Just because that's where you're headed, doesn't mean you're taking me with you," Natalia said coldly.

He lay still a moment, then he moved the pillow. Slowly, he sat up, faced her—or tried to. He kept having trouble looking at her directly.

"You know," he said. "How'd you find out?"

"You told me," she said, barely able to contain her anger. "Last night. When you tried to rape me."

Cain flinched. He swallowed a couple of times, then shrugged and gave a ghastly grin. "Did I? Man, I was stoned. I don't remember a thing. Sorry about that, Nat. I . . . I didn't hurt you, did I?"

"Yes, you hurt me, Cain," Natalia said. "I thought we were friends. We used to be friends. Don't you remember? All the hard times we shared—living on ramen noodles and ketchup packs we stole from McDonald's. Playing those dives where there was only one guy in the audience and he was dead drunk and passed out on the floor."

Cain stared at her dumbly. His eyes filled with tears.

Natalia wasn't afraid of him anymore. She wasn't angry at him. She was sorry for him. She sat down on the side of the bed and rested her hand on his.

"Why, Cain?" she asked softly. "Why did you do it? You didn't need to. You would have been a success. And it would have been *your* success."

He brushed his hand across his eyes. "Would I, Nat?" he asked, his voice choked.

"Of course," she said gently.

Cain shook his head. "I waited so long. And nothing was happening for me. And I wanted it so bad!"

He looked at her defiantly. "I'm better than all those bastards out there! And they all had million-dollar contracts and I . . . I had fuckin' ramen noodles. It wasn't fair."

He sniveled, wiped his nose with his sleeve.

"How . . . how did it happen?" she asked, not sure she really wanted to know.

"You mean, did I go to the crossroads at midnight?" Cain shook his head and gave a bleak sigh. "Nothing that dramatic. It was at one of those dives you were talking about. I saw this guy sitting at table while I was playing. He was listening, Nat. He was listening to the music! When I finished the set, he motioned me to come join him at his table. He said I was a genius, and I deserved to be big. He could make it happen. Make it happen overnight. I just had to promise him one thing in return. My fuckin' soul.

"It didn't seem such a bad bargain," Cain went on.

"Did this man tell you what you were going to have to do?" Natalia demanded. "How you would drive kids to kill themselves and their parents?"

"Yes, no," said Cain, confused. "I guess he did, but none of it really registered. I kept seeing the audience and hearing their applause. And . . . I don't know, Nat. I guess I thought maybe he wouldn't make me go through with it."

Cain lowered his head into his hands. He sat on the bed, hunched in misery.

"When that first suicide and murder happened in San Francisco, I knew then that he'd meant it. I tried to get out of the deal, but he wouldn't let me."

"I don't think you tried very hard," Natalia said harshly.

Cain lifted his head. He didn't look at her. His eyes grew unfocused. He stared off into the distance.

"Maybe not," he said softly. "But how could I give it up? It's about the music, you see. It's all about the music. The rest of it doesn't matter."

"Lives don't matter!" Natalia said, shocked. "The heartbreak and misery you've brought to these families doesn't matter? What about the terrible crimes you're going to force these innocent kids to commit? Doesn't any of that matter to you?"

"You don't know what it's like," Cain said, talking in a faraway, dreamy voice. "To stand there onstage with the lights shining down on you and the music pouring out of you into the fans and their love and adoration flowing back into you. I swear sometimes it's not the drumbeat I hear.

It's their hearts beating. Thousands of hearts. In time to my music. Because of my music. It's the most wonderful feeling in the world."

He looked at her, eyes focused. His tone was pleading. "I can't give that up. I can't go back to being ordinary, Nat. Can't you understand?"

"No," she said, her voice quivering. "No, I can't. You did a terrible thing to me last night. You tried to rape me. The Cain I knew would have never done anything so horrible! You're a monster."

He gazed at her. His face hardened. An ugly glint glittered in his eyes.

"I'll have you and any other woman I want! I'll be the most famous rock star to have ever lived. Elvis, the Beatles, no one will remember them. I'll live in a palace. I'll have more money than God. I'll do whatever I fuckin' please because I'll be the most famous—"

"No, you won't!" Natalia shouted at him. She stood up, caught hold of him by the shoulders, and shook him. "You'll be dead! It's lies, Cain! All lies!"

Cain hit her, knocked her backward into the wall. She stared at him, her head ringing, tasting blood in her mouth.

"Groupie whore," he said to her. "Just a trashy little groupie whore. That's all you are. That's all you ever were."

He stood up and walked over to the mirror. "I'm going to go take a shower and get cleaned up. And you're going to pack. You and I are going to take a little trip."

"No, Cain," said Natalia, picking herself up. "I'm not going anywhere with you."

"Yes, you are," he said. He gazed at her from out of the mirror, and he smiled. "Because you know what will happen if you don't."

*   *   *

Matthew walked the park for hours. He saw none of it. He paid no attention to his surroundings, barely watched where he was going. His phone rang, but he saw it was Natalia, and he switched it off. He walked and he fumed.

Incompetence. Mismanagement. Same as always. All you need is love, my ass! Heaven too damn soft, lenient. I'll fix them. I'll go away. Leave them in the lurch. Serve them right. Then they'd have to take action! Try to shove this off on me. Trying to teach me some goddam lesson. It won't work.

And so on and so forth.

Finally, he realized he was exhausted. He sat down on a bench and reached for his flask, only to find it wasn't in his pocket. He'd left it back in his hotel room. Damn it. Nothing was going right! This was going to end.

Making up his mind, he took out his cell phone, turned it on, and hit Natalia's number. He was going to quit, resign. It had been fun, but it was over. Just one of those things. A trip to the moon on gossamer wings. I'll call you soon. We'll do lunch.

He wondered if he could manage to locate Hannah . . .

He was waiting for Natalia to answer, when the cell phone suddenly flew out his hand, sailed through the air, and landed about thirty feet away.

"Damn it, Woof—" Matthew began.

The ghost burst out of thin air and landed in front of him. The hippie's eyes were wide, his hair standing on end.

"What are you doing, Angel Boy? Where the hell have you been?"

"I'm not going back. I made up my mind. I'm quitting. I was trying to call Natalia—"

"Quit!" Woof howled. "You can't quit! You've been fired! We all have! Cain fired everyone: the band, Jordan, Ryan, Al, Kimo. Cain took Natalia by force and left with her.

And that's not the worst!" Woof waved his arms, gesturing wildly. "She's going to kill him!"

"Wait a minute. Slow down," Matthew ordered. "Who's going to kill who?"

"The asshole! Natalia's going to kill the asshole! She thinks it's the only way to stop Cain."

"Kill him!" Matthew repeated, shocked.

"She's desperate. Look, man, she's not going to shoot him or poison him or anything like that, but she's been secretly searching the Internet on how an accident with the pyrotechnics could kill someone. Remember Michael Jackson setting himself on fire? Like that, only worse."

Woof jabbed a finger at Matthew. "You have to do something, Angel Boy! She's in serious trouble!"

"But where is Natalia? How can I reach her? If Cain's fired me, I can't get past security—"

"Like I keep saying, you're the angel! I can't talk now. I've got to get back to my girl!" Woof's face was drawn, haggard. "She's in trouble, man. You've got to help her!"

"Woof, wait!" Matthew tried to catch the old hippie, but the ghost evaporated in his grasp and disappeared.

Matthew stood there thinking, *This is my chance. I can walk away and leave them all and that would be that.* He knew he wouldn't, and he wondered why he wouldn't. The old Matthew would have. The old Matthew would have remembered to bring along the bourbon. The old Matthew would remind himself that there would always be more women in his life. The old Matthew would have walked off and left God to sort out the mess.

What had happened to the old Matthew?

Matthew looked down at his hands. *He went up in flames.*

Not the flames of the fires of martyrdom. Matthew had changed the moment he heard Grace's cry for help. Satan had tried to kill him, tried to scare him off. But the devil had misjudged him. Matthew might be a rebellious angel, an angel who kept tripping over his tattered wings, an angel who had thrown his halo in the mud and dragged his white robes through the muck. But he was an angel, nonetheless. He supposed that after a couple of thousand years, it was about time he started to act like one.

Even if it meant going over to the other side.

Matthew searched the park until he found William, sitting on a bench, tossing peanuts to the squirrels in direct violation of a sign that told him not to.

Matthew walked up to him.

"I know what you're planning," William said, regarding Matthew gravely. "And I'm not certain this is the best way to handle the situation."

"Can you think of something better?" Matthew demanded.

William shook his head. "Not at the moment."

"Well, if you do, let me know. In the meantime, look at it this way—you finally get rid of me."

"Not the way we had in mind, Matthew," said William sadly.

"Yeah, well, I don't have time for a sermon. Just give me the damn rat, will you?" Matthew said impatiently.

William picked up the hat with Arthur inside and handed it to Matthew.

"Dormouse," he corrected.

Chapter 31

$\mathcal{T}$onight was the night of the big concert.

Natalia sat in the living area of the luxurious hotel suite watching television. The guys in the band—Jordan, Ryan, Mike—were being interviewed on the *Today* show. The news that Cain had fired his band had made headlines around the world. The guys were going on all of the talk shows, talking about Cain and how he had changed from nice guy to egocentric maniac. The more they talked, the more outrageous stories they told, the more Cain's fans adored him. The big Halloween concert had been sold out for weeks. Tickets on eBay were going as high as $5,000.

"So you guys from the band are telling us stories about Cain," said Matt Lauer. "We know he's in an undisclosed location, keeping away from the media. But what I want to know is where is the mysterious 'Father Gallow'?"

Natalia sighed deeply. That's what *she* wanted to know, as well. She looked bleakly at her cell phone. She'd been waiting days for him to call. Not that she would have been allowed to answer it. She glanced at Burl, the roadie from hell, who was sitting comfortably in a chair right beside her, watching the show and chuckling.

Matt Lauer was continuing, "'Father Gallow' has been credited in large part with the turnaround in Cain's fortunes. Before the priest came along with his exorcism act, Cain was floundering—"

"Turn that damn thing off!" Cain ordered, coming in from his bedroom.

"Naw, I want to watch it," Burl told him. "See what they have to say—"

Cain grabbed the remote from Burl's hand and threw it at the television set. Since he'd been drinking his breakfast, his throw was wild. The remote hit the wall and bounced off. Scowling, he walked over to the TV, apparently with the intention of kicking his booted foot through the screen.

John recovered the remote and switched off the television.

"There. You happy?"

Cain stood staring at the blank screen. "Yeah, I'm happy. Who wouldn't be happy? I've got everything I ever wanted and then some."

He turned on his heel, walked up to Natalia and stood over her, glaring down at her.

"Where is he?" he demanded.

"I don't know," she said, refusing to look at him.

"Yes, you do!" Cain yelled. "He's your lover! You two are plotting something—"

He raised his hand to strike her. Natalia sat in the chair, her jaw clenched. She wasn't going to give him the satisfaction of flinching or ducking. Burl intervened.

"She's telling the truth, kid. She doesn't know where he is. She hasn't been outside this room for a week. I've monitored all her phone calls. He hasn't tried to get in touch with her."

"He's dumped me, all right?" Natalia flared. "So just drop it."

But even as she said the words, even as she told herself she meant them, she heard his words in her heart. *Of course, you mean something to me . . .* He wouldn't abandon her. He wouldn't abandon all those kids who were going to be driven to murder this very night. She had to keep faith.

Her phone rang. She looked at the caller ID—the stage manager with questions about tonight.

"I have to take that," she said.

Burl picked up the phone, looked at the ID, then handed it to her. "Make it brief," he told her.

Natalia took the call, answered the questions, then hung up.

"I need to go over to the theater," she said.

"No, you don't," Burl told her. "Everything's under control. Our people are making all the arrangements. Trust me, Ms. Ashley, the concert tonight will go off without a hitch."

"You don't even have to worry about the pyrotechnics," said John with a grin. "No accidents for our boy here."

"What does that mean?" Cain demanded, eyeing them suspiciously.

"Only that your manager, Ms. Ashley, was thinking of trying to kill you," Burl remarked with a chuckle.

Cain looked at her, shocked. "Is that true, Natalia?" He wasn't angry. He sounded bewildered. "You were going to *kill* me?"

"At this point, who wouldn't? I can't let you go through with what you're planning."

"You thought about killing me," Cain repeated bleakly.

Natalia looked at him. The mask had slipped, the façade

cracked. She'd hurt him as much as if she'd driven a knife into him. She could see inside him. He was stumbling about in the darkness, lost and alone and afraid, desperately afraid. He done this to himself, brought this fate on himself. But he was a kid. He'd made a mistake. She should hate him for what he'd done to her and to those poor kids who had fallen victim to him, but she couldn't find hatred in her heart. Only pity.

Natalia walked up to Cain. She took hold of his hands and she shuddered to feel how cold they were. Burl and John were both saying something, but she ignored them. It was just the two of them in the room: her and Cain.

"I would never have been able to do it. I love you, Cain. You're my friend. And as your friend, I'm begging you, don't play 'Possession' tonight," she told him.

Cain was startled. He cast an uneasy glance at the roadies.

"Don't look at them!" Natalia commanded. She dug her nails into his flesh. "Look at me. Don't play 'Possession' tonight, Cain. No matter what they threaten to do to you. They can't hurt you. They need you—"

"We don't need *you*, Ms. Ashley," Burl told her in grating tones.

"Don't play that song tonight, Cain," Natalia went on, gripping Cain's hands hard. "No matter what they say or even what they do. Hundreds of innocent kids will be driven to commit murder. And you'll be lost. I don't know what Hell is. Maybe it's flames and demons jabbing you with pitchforks, or maybe it's playing guitar forever in some filthy roadhouse. I do know this—whatever Hell is, that's where you're going if you let them do this."

She saw the doubt, the fear in his eyes. He was starting to waver, then his eyes left her. He seemed to be listening to some inner voice. He smiled and shrugged.

"I can't disappoint my fans, Nat," he said. "They expect me to play that song. *Everyone* expects me to play that song."

He glanced at Burl, who nodded approval. Cain smiled at Natalia, patted her hand. "Now why don't you go lie down, take a nap, Nat. It's going to be a long night."

"For you, eternal!" Natalia cried.

Burl grabbed her by the arm and dragged her off to her room. He threw her inside and locked the door.

Cain just laughed.

Chapter 32

The concert was scheduled to start at seven. Matthew looked at his watch. Five o'clock. Not long to go. He'd seen Natalia enter the theater earlier in the day. She'd gone in one of the back entrances, escorted by Burl, who had hold of her by the arm. As she climbed out of the limo, she lagged behind a little, casting a swift, hopeful, searching glance up and down the street.

She was looking for Matthew, and his heart ached for her. She looked pale and wan. Her hair was uncombed. She hadn't bothered to put on any makeup, and her dress looked as though she'd slept in it. He longed to return her hope-filled glance, give her a sign, let her know he was nearby. He couldn't take the risk, however. Not with a demon at her elbow.

"It will be all right," he promised Natalia silently. "Keep the faith."

Burl said something to her, gave her arm a sharp tug. She jerked away from him and glared at him when he started toward her.

"Don't touch me! You don't have to worry," she added coldly, "I'm not going to run off. I'm not leaving Cain. Not while there's still a chance to save him."

"Forget it, Ms. Ashley. Cain's ours. Just do your job and keep your mouth shut and no one will get hurt."

"Yeah, right!" she said bitterly.

Her head held high, she ran up the stairs that led to the stage door.

Matthew looked around for Woof but couldn't find him. That was worrisome. Of course, Matthew had told Woof to lie low, keep out of sight, and perhaps that's what the ghost was doing. Still, Matthew would have felt better knowing Woof was with Natalia.

He watched from his vantage point as Natalia and Burl entered the theater. She pressed a button on the panel. There was a buzzing sound and, after a moment, a guard opened the door. Natalia showed him her security pass. Burl showed his. The guard checked a list, then allowed them both inside. The door shut and locked behind them.

Matthew grimaced. He guessed he couldn't get in that way, and this proved it. He still had his security pass from the Phoenix concert, but that wouldn't do him much good. The passes were different for each subsequent concert venue. He had toyed with the idea of trying to bluff his way past the guard but had decided that wouldn't work.

Cain's notoriety had resulted in heightened security measures. Fans who had tickets were carefully screened as they entered. Those who didn't have tickets swarmed about in front of the theater, hoping to catch a glimpse of the rock star as he arrived. Helicopters circled overhead. Cops patrolled the streets on foot and on horseback. With all the excitement, the security guards at the theater would be extra cautious.

Matthew fidgeted, looking down the street, then he

smiled to see the huge figure rounding the corner. Matthew stepped out of the shadows to meet his friend.

"Kimo," said Matthew, reaching out to shake hands. "Good to see you."

"Father Gallow," said Kimo. "It's really good to see you! Al and me were worried something might have happened to you. We knew you wouldn't have walked out on Natalia."

Kimo's pleasure was evident in the big man's hearty handshake. Matthew winced slightly.

"Oh, uh, sorry, Father," Kimo said, releasing him.

"I'm not really a priest, you know," said Matthew.

"Yes, sir, I understand that," said Kimo. He flushed slightly, and added gravely, "But I don't know how to address an angel."

Matthew was stunned momentarily speechless. He wondered if he'd heard right.

"What did you call me?" he managed to ask.

Kimo smiled at his confusion.

"My people are sensitive to the spiritual world. I saw the truth about you when you were underneath the scaffolding. I saw the truth about the two demons, as well," he added, his expression darkening.

"You never said anything . . ." Matthew couldn't believe he was having this conversation.

"The grandfather told me you did not want anyone to know," Kimo replied. "I honor your wishes."

"The *grandfather* . . ." Matthew was puzzled at first. "Oh, you mean Woof! You can . . . er . . . see him, as well?"

"We have spoken often," said Kimo. "His love for his granddaughter is great. He finds it difficult to let go."

Matthew didn't know what to say to any of this, and eventually he decided it would simply be best to get down to business.

"All right, then, Kimo. You know what you have to do."

"Yes, sir. I find Natalia and keep her safe until I can take her out of the theater. Al is waiting for us in the car."

"I don't know where she'll be. I'm thinking she won't be in the sound booth. They won't let her out of their sight. My guess is that she'll be in the wings." Matthew added with a slight smile. "She'll put up a fight. You have to get her away from them even if you have to knock her out cold. Her life depends on it."

"Yes, sir," said Kimo.

"Hopefully, I'll be keeping them fully occupied. But if they try to stop you—"

"I can take care of it," said Kimo.

He was serenely confident, and Matthew believed him. If any human on Earth could handle a couple of demons from Hell, it would be this one.

"All right," said Matthew. He drew in a deep breath, then let it out slowly. "Here we go."

They left the stage door and walked around the back of the theater to the freight entrance. There were an enormous garagelike door on the loading dock and a smaller door to the side. Matthew had done some checking and discovered that this door, though always locked, was not guarded. Arriving truckers pressed a button, and someone came to the door to meet them.

Matthew brought out the battered, smelly hat from his pocket and opened it up.

"This is a dormouse," he said, adding, in some embarrassment, "He opens doors."

Kimo peered down at Arthur.

"My people eat them," he said.

Arthur performed as hoped. The door opened easily, and Matthew and Kimo entered the loading dock. The area was lit by security lights, which made things easy. Too easy. Anyone coming back here would spot them in an instant.

Matthew had brought his briefcase with him. He opened it, brought out his old security badges. He changed clothes swiftly, putting on the black cassock, becoming Father Gallow. He kept one of the security badges for himself, handed the other to Kimo, who was wearing the same type of uniform worn by theater security.

"Put it on backward," Matthew told him.

If a guard or stagehand saw them, they would think the badge had either been put on backward or simply rotated on the lanyard. Hopefully they wouldn't investigate further.

He and Kimo proceeded cautiously, not sure where they were going. It wouldn't do to blunder into Cain's dressing room or suddenly find themselves entering stage right. After only a couple of wrong turns, they entered the backstage area. It was brightly lit, with people hurrying about. Several glanced at them curiously and one stopped to stare.

"Father Gallow!" he exclaimed.

"That's right, my son," Matthew answered in character. "Do you know where Ms. Ashley is?"

"She's with Cain. In his dressing room."

"Thank you." Matthew turned to Kimo. "I'm in good hands now, sir. You can return to your duties."

Kimo gave a solemn nod and walked off. Matthew hoped Kimo wouldn't go barging into Cain's dressing room on some heroic mission to save Natalia. Matthew watched the big man depart, walking as confidently as if he'd been born in this theater, and he knew he didn't have to worry. Kimo would know what to do and when to do it. Matthew had his own concerns to think about right now.

The man had paid no attention to Kimo, but he was now regarding Matthew with a frown.

"What's wrong, my son?" Matthew asked mildly. "Is my collar crooked?"

"It's odd, that's all. I'm the stage manager's assistant, and we were told you weren't performing tonight."

"Ms. Ashley is a genius," Matthew gushed enthusiastically.

The man's frown deepened. "Huh?"

"Ms. Ashley had me come in the back way to avoid the press. No one has any idea I'm here," Matthew explained. "And she wants to keep it that way. She wants my appearance tonight to come as a shock to everyone—including Cain."

The man stared at him. "So what does Ms. Ashley plan to do with you, Father? Shoot you out of a cannon?"

Matthew ignored the sarcasm.

"Nothing that dramatic, I'm glad to say. If you could escort me to a place in the wings where I can watch Cain's performance without him or anyone else seeing me, that would be ideal. I'll just walk on when I hear my cue."

The assistant manager rolled his eyes and muttered something about "crazy-ass singers," but he did as Matthew asked.

Standing in the wings, hidden in the folds of a curtain, Matthew had a clear view of the stage. He could not see the audience, but he could hear them out there, laughing, talking, yelling at each other, shouting for Cain. Onstage, the two demon roadies were checking the pyrotechnic equipment; others were adjusting the microphones. Matthew glanced at his watch. Almost showtime.

Matthew was nervous, palms wet, sweat trickling down the back of his cassock. He opened his bag and groped about in the dark. He had plenty of time before he went on. Cain would play several numbers and take a break before returning to do his big finish.

Which might be a really big finish, if I fail.

Matthew found the bourbon flask. His fingers lingered on it. He wouldn't drink much, just enough to take off the edge. He toyed with it, then let it drop. He rummaged about and drew out the golden crucifix. He didn't put it on. He held it tightly.

"Look, God," Matthew said quietly, "I know I've been a pain in the ass over the last couple of thousand years . . ."

He paused, then said grudgingly, "Or maybe not. Maybe You understood me more than I ever gave You credit for. Maybe that's why You've put up with me for so long. Maybe that's why You sent me Natalia. I just want you to know, I appreciate it."

Matthew drew in a breath. This was it. He was committing himself. "I'm here tonight to ask for Your help. Not for me. I'm still angry. I still think I got a raw deal. I just want to make that clear.

"I'm asking for Cain. I know he's done a horrible thing. Still, he's not a bad kid. He's just young and stupid. And we've all been young and stupid. That's how we learn, how we grow. I think Cain realizes his mistake, and he's desperate to escape. But he can't. He's trapped. He needs help.

"And so, God, I'm here to make a deal . . ."

Natalia sat in Cain's dressing room. Burl and John hadn't wanted her here because they couldn't be around to keep an eye on her. They had their work to do onstage. Natalia had made it clear that the only way she was leaving was in a body bag, something that was undoubtedly in store for her in the immediate future, but she didn't let herself think about that. She intended to stick by Cain until the final moment, hoping to make him change his mind. Eventually, Burl and John had decided to let her stay. Probably they figured it was too late for her to do anything.

Cain didn't want her here, either. She made him uncomfortable. She was a reproach to him, a constant reminder of the terrible things he'd done, the even-more-terrible things he was about to do. He didn't want to think about *that*. He just wanted to go out onstage and play his music, bask in the adoration of his fans, have a good time. And he couldn't do that with Natalia hanging around, spoiling his fun by making him feel guilty.

He tried to get rid of her. He swore at her, called her foul names, asking her how long she'd been fucking Matthew, and so on. Natalia didn't say a word in response. She sat there, looking at him, pitying him.

Eventually, he abandoned that tactic and tried to pretend she wasn't there. He invited people into his dressing room while he put on his makeup—something he never did. He laughed and joked and goofed off. Natalia found herself edged into a corner. She stood her ground, making certain that whenever Cain looked into the mirror, he saw her reflected back at him.

Someone came in to report that the theater was packed and that crowds of fans who hadn't been able to get tickets had filled the streets outside. Cain was elated. The adrenaline was pumping, and he was getting high on it. He was ecstatic, almost crazed. And yet, every time his gaze fell on Natalia's reflection, his smile froze.

But it wasn't her he was seeing in the mirror.

It wasn't her he was glaring at with hatred and loathing.

It was himself.

"Places!" came the call, and Cain rose to his feet.

His dressing room emptied, and soon Natalia was the only other person in the room.

Cain was decked out in his leather with the red flames twining over his body. He blurred in her vision, and, for a horrible moment, Natalia saw the flames actually writhing around him. She rubbed her eyes. She hadn't slept in days. She couldn't remember the last time she'd eaten anything. When she looked again, Cain was back to what passed for normal.

He was almost ready to walk out the door.

Natalia walked over to him. "I'm going to be watching from the wings," she said.

"Then you're going to see me put on a hell of a show." He grinned at her—a rictus grin, like that of a corpse.

She regarded him with sorrow. "I had faith in you, Cain," she said. "I wish you'd had faith in yourself."

She glanced around the dressing room, paused a moment to listen to the muffled roar of the crowd, who were stomping their feet and yelling for Cain.

"You could have done this without help. You were that good."

He gave a forced laugh. "You talk about me like I'm dead, Nat!"

"You are, Cain," she told him. "You're dead inside. And that's why your music sucks!"

Cain seized hold of her arm, squeezing it painfully.

"That's a lie!" he cried angrily. "My music's the best it's ever been!"

Natalia didn't try to free herself. She didn't flinch.

"How could it be, Cain?" she asked softly. "You sold your soul, the very part of you that made it."

Beneath the makeup, Cain's face went sallow. His lips trembled. His hand on her arm shook, then it fell, as though it had gone numb. His mouth worked, his jaw shivered. He put his hand to his stomach and doubled over, as though he was going to be sick.

Burl appeared, stomping down the hall. "C'mon, kid," he yelled. "Your fans are getting impatient. We don't want a riot." He leered at Natalia. "At least, not yet."

Cain gave Natalia one last look, a look that pleaded for her to take back what she'd said. A look that begged her to tell him he was great, a superstar.

"You were that good . . ." she said.

Cain's lips tightened, then twisted. He gave her a final, cold glance, turned on his heel, and swaggered off, heading for the stage. Natalia started after him, but Burl stopped her.

"Sorry, Ms. Ashley," said Burl. "You're going to miss this performance."

He gave her a shove that sent her staggering back into Cain's dressing room, then he locked the door.

Natalia flung herself against it, pounding on it, shouting for someone to let her out. But at that moment, the crowd gave a huge roar, and Cain struck a note on the guitar. The music swelled, and Natalia knew no one was going to come.

Her legs went shaky. She began shivering. She felt weak, drained. She clasped her arms around her chest and leaned her head against the door and shut her eyes. She gave up. It wouldn't make any difference anyway. Cain was lost. They were all lost.

Matthew hadn't called her. He hadn't come to her. Perhaps he'd tried. If so, he hadn't tried very hard. Probably crawled back into his bourbon bottle. She wasn't going to cry. She'd be damned if she was going to cry . . .

"Hey, girl," said a gravel voice, "you've got to get out there. You don't want to miss the concert! In all our time together, did we ever let anything cause us to miss a concert?"

Natalia couldn't believe what she was hearing. Her eyes flared open, and she gasped. "Woof!"

Her grandfather was standing there, smiling at her, looking slightly embarrassed.

"Good morning, Starshine," he said.

Natalia closed her eyes, rubbed them, and opened them again. Her grandfather remained in front of her. He was the same as she remembered him: long, gray braids, grizzled beard, faded jeans and sandals, and his favorite tie-dyed, peace symbol T-shirt.

He was the same except for one small hitch.

"You're dead," she said, or tried to say. The muscles of her mouth wouldn't work all that well.

"Yeah, I know," Woof admitted. "I'm real sorry about that. I didn't want to leave you, but there wasn't much I could do. And I didn't really leave you either. I've been with you all this time. You didn't know it, of course. Against the rules."

He scratched his chin.

"It's against the rules for me to be talking to you like this. But then you know I've always hated rules. A friend of mine helped me cross over to this physical plane. You remember that priest we met in church in Frisco? Father Weasel? He's a really good guy. Copacetic."

Natalia could only stare. She was too dazed, too stunned to do anything else.

"The point is, you can't quit, Starshine. Not now. You have to be out there during the performance. He's going to need you."

"Cain's going to need me?" Natalia repeated, hope rising.

"The asshole?" Woof snorted and made a face. "He's on his own. Up to him what happens now. It wasn't Cain I was talking about."

"Matthew!" Natalia cried suddenly. "It's Matthew!"

She threw herself at the door again, kicking at it and beating on it with her fists.

A deep voice reverberated from outside.

"If you would stand back, Ms. Ashley . . ."

There was a smash, a thud, and the door splintered.

Kimo stood smiling at her from amidst the wreckage. "Ma'am," he said, inclining his head.

"I have to go to Matthew!" Natalia said urgently.

"Not yet, ma'am," said Kimo, still respectful, but firm.

"Why not?" She looked from him to the ghost of her dead grandfather. "Why are you stopping me?"

"Because Matthew is Cain's only hope, kid," said Woof solemnly. "And you're Matthew's."

Chapter 33

*M*atthew, waiting in the wings, was alarmed to see Cain walking toward him. The rock star was not alone. The demon roadies were on his heels, as was his makeup artist, dabbing his sweating face with a cloth, and security guards. Natalia was not with him. Matthew didn't know whether to be glad or alarmed. He could only hope that Kimo was doing his job.

Matthew withdrew deeper into the shadows of the curtains, clasping his hand over the golden crucifix so that it would not catch the light and reveal him.

He needn't have bothered. Cain walked with his head held high, his gaze straight ahead, but he wasn't actually seeing his surroundings. Matthew was reminded of a line from a movie Hannah had forced him to watch one night.

Dead man walking.

Cain knew he was being drawn to his doom, but he couldn't help himself. He was too weak, too frightened to defy his masters.

The curtain was still closed. The audience was stamping their feet rhythmically, clapping their hands, shouting for Cain. He came to a halt in the wings, standing so close that Matthew could have reached out and touched him. His entourage, including the demon roadies, were forced to stay back. This was Cain's moment, and he was alone, just as the devil had planned.

Cain had been forced to fire the band and get rid of Kimo and Al. Cain had been goaded into alienating Natalia— or trying to. Matthew guessed that she wouldn't alienate that easily. She would cling loyally to her wretched friend, trying until the very last moment to convince him to turn away from the darkness.

He kept standing there, and Matthew suddenly realized that Cain had stage fright. It occurred to the angel that Cain had probably never before been onstage alone. He'd had the band with him, backing him up. He'd had Natalia, smiling and encouraging. Now he had no one.

The audience was starting to get restless and so were Burl and John. Burl came up to Cain, said something to him. Cain paled visibly. He licked his lips, glanced fearfully at Burl, then walked slowly out onto the stage.

The elaborate stage set, which had been designed to feature the band, had been scrapped. There hadn't been time to design and build anything new. Natalia had suggested that instead of trying hastily to throw something together, which would have looked as if it had been thrown together hastily, they go for simplicity. A single tall stool stood alone on the empty stage. Cain's guitar (not the demon guitar, that was saved for the last act), stood beside it.

As Cain walked onto the stage, the houselights went down, the curtain went up. A single spotlight hit him. The audience cheered wildly to see him, but their cheers faltered, changing to uneasy murmurs.

Cain hadn't acknowledged them. He wasn't paying any attention to them. He walked over to stand in front of the stool. He reached down to pick up his guitar. He clasped hold of it thankfully, as a drowning man might clasp hold of his rescuer. Then Cain turned to face his audience.

Bathed in the spotlight, he stared out at them in the darkness, not able to see them, but able to hear them, feel them. He lifted the guitar over his head in a gesture of triumph. The audience yelled and shouted.

Then Cain sat on the stool, keeping one leg extended, booted foot on the floor, and began to play.

Matthew had assumed Cain's performance was going to be an unmitigated disaster. Demons were waiting in the wings to make sure he fulfilled his part of the contract. Hundreds of innocent kids and teenagers were waiting out there in the darkness, soon to be driven to murder. Cain himself would probably be dead shortly after. Satan wouldn't want the trouble of dealing with someone so high maintenance.

Cain knew all of this. Matthew could see it in his face. And now he could hear it in his music.

Cain wasn't playing for the audience. He was playing for himself, playing for what he knew would be the last time. He was pouring his soul into the music.

At first the audience didn't know what to make of this change. They missed the hard-driving beat of the drums and the bass guitar. A few jeered, but they were quickly silenced. They knew they were witnessing an extraordinary performance even if they didn't know why. They sat hushed, mesmerized.

As Matthew listened, he realized that Cain was telling the story of his life. An unhappy, unattractive child, he finds solace from his loneliness in music. He goes to concerts, watches the stars, and longs to be one of them. He begins to realize that he's good enough to be one of them. He just needs a break. He forms a band, meets Natalia, and they go on the road. They play one dive after another, not making much money, but becoming a family, doing what they love. The happiest time of Cain's life.

But it's not enough for him. He waits for his break, but it doesn't come. No producer comes to him after the show to offer him a multimillion-dollar contract. He's gaining a small following, playing better venues. He wants more, and he doesn't want to wait. He opens himself up to the powers of darkness. He's tempted. He falls.

He's now a success, but it's empty, hollow. He has everything he's always wanted, but it has cost him everything he's ever loved including—and this was the bitter irony— his music.

At this point in the act, Cain would normally take a break, then return for his final number, "Possession." He did stop playing. He sat in silence on the stool. The audience was hushed, still not making a sound, for the most part, though someone could be heard sobbing.

Matthew himself was moved. He had grown bitter and cynical over the years, caring about nothing and nobody, not even himself. Then he'd encountered Grace. He had fondly imagined he'd saved her, but now he realized she'd saved him. He had come to feel again, to care again, to love again. He owed God something. Matthew determined he was going to fight for Cain, fight with all the strength he had.

He waited for Cain to leave the stage, but Cain continued to sit there. The demon roadies were not liking this.

"We're losing him," John growled in Burl's ear.

The demon guitar materialized in Burl's hands. He walked out onstage and held it out to Cain. The audience was startled; this wasn't what they were expecting, but then the entire concert had not been what they expected. They waited to see what would happen.

Cain held on to his guitar, made no move to take the demon guitar. His face was a ghastly white in the lights. The black eye makeup made him look like a death's head. His hands clenched. He shuddered and bit clear through his lip. A trickle of blood ran down his chin.

This was not Matthew's cue, but he decided it was time to make his entrance. Holding his Bible in one hand and the relic in the other, Father Gallow walked out onto the stage.

"I'll take that!" he called in calm, measured tones, and held out his hand for the guitar.

The amazed and confounded expression on Burl's face as he gave a start and whipped around to see Matthew was almost worth the inflated price of a ticket. Cain looked dazed, and a tiny flicker of hope shone in the dark desolation of his eyes. Satan doesn't give up easily, however.

Burl lifted his free hand and pointed at Matthew. A jet of flame flared from his palm and struck Matthew in the chest. The crucifix shone with an angry white light, saving Matthew from the searing flame, but the force of the blow blasted him across the stage. Matthew landed heavily on his back and lay there for a moment, half-blinded, hurting from the fall. He thought he had probably broken a rib. He gasped for air and groaned as pain tore through him.

The audience was cheering what they thought were special effects. They began to cheer even louder when Burl, the roadie, dropped his disguise and began to shift to his true form.

His face twisted into ugliness. Fangs glistened. His eyes glowed red. His body hunched. Wings sprouted from his back. Long, sharp claws jutted from his fingers and toes. He shot another jet of flame at the guitar Cain held in his hands. The guitar was consumed, leaving Cain holding nothing but ashes.

How fitting, thought Matthew.

The fiend thrust the demon guitar into Cain's hands.

The audience whooped and yelled, loving this, thinking it all part of the act.

Gulping, sweating, Cain took hold of the guitar. He hesitated. The fiend snarled something and Cain paled. His hand trembling, he struck the opening chords to the song "Possession." The audience members leaped to their feet, yelling and screaming.

The last chord of this song was the trigger that would send kids the world over on a murderous rampage. And the song lasted only seven minutes.

Matthew gritted his teeth and rose to his feet.

"God, give me strength to endure this," he prayed, and he remembered suddenly making that same prayer before.

The day he'd died.

Matthew advanced on the demon, who stood between him and Cain. Matthew raised his voice, began his prayer, the prayer that he'd used before in a hundred phony battles against evil and in one very real one.

"'Saint Michael the Archangel, defend us in battle,'" he cried loudly, and as he walked, he raised the crucifix and held it front of him. "'Be our defense against the wickedness and snares of the devil. May God rebuke him, we humbly pray. And do thou, O prince of the heavenly host, by the power of God thrust into hell Satan and all evil spirits who prowl about the world seeking the ruin of souls. Amen.'"

Cain's hands were shaking. He was hitting wrong notes, making mistakes. His mouth was dry. He couldn't sing the words, he mumbled them. He cast a desperate, pleading glance at Matthew, and a fearful glance at the fiend standing at his elbow. The audience booed Father Gallow, shouted for him to leave Cain alone.

The archfiend turned to face Matthew. Its mouth twisted in a hideous grin.

"Call down Heaven's wrath all you want, Father," the fiend told him. "Cain's ours. He's not possessed. He came to us willingly. We gave him what he asked for. Now it's his turn to serve us."

"Satan pleading for fair treatment," Matthew remarked, coming closer and closer to Cain. "I'll bet that's a first. The kid didn't know what he was signing. I'm guessing you boys didn't bother to tell him the whole truth."

"We told him the truth. He didn't want to hear it." The fiend shrugged. "That's not our fault."

Cain ceased playing. His hand went limp, fell from the guitar strings. The fiend dug his claws into Cain's back, and Cain cried out in agony. He hunched over the guitar with the laughing demon's face, and played and sang.

The audience cheered wildly, thinking this was still part of the act. Cain gazed at them in a kind of horror. They were cheering his pain, cheering his destruction. They couldn't know that, of course. To them, it was make-believe, an act. But perhaps it didn't make any difference. Perhaps they would have cheered even if they'd known the truth. Cain gave a low moan. Tears trickled down his cheeks, grotesquely smearing his black eye makeup.

Matthew took another step nearer to Cain. He was within arm's reach now. The fiend grinned, did nothing to try to stop him. Matthew found this disquieting. He wondered why. And then he had his answer.

"Take a look stage right, Father," said fiend.

Natalia stood in the wings. Her face was pale, but she was bravely smiling. John, the other roadie, stood beside her. He was in his human form, but Matthew could see the dark wings spreading out, enfolding Natalia.

Cain kept singing, goaded on by demons without and within. The song was nearing its terrible end.

John's attention was fixed on Cain. The demon roadie

was grinning hugely. Natalia's lips tightened, and she suddenly drove her elbow with all her might deep in John's gut. The roadie doubled over with a groan and, as he did so, Natalia smashed her knee into his face. He crumpled in a heap to the floor.

Like Matthew, the demon was immortal. John stirred, his bloodied face twisted in rage, and was about to rise when Kimo appeared, emerging from the shadows. The big man slammed his foot into the demon's back. John collapsed with a grunt. Kimo placed his other foot on the demon and stood calmly on top of him. The demon floundered beneath the big man, clawing and scratching, but Kimo didn't budge, and the demon couldn't free himself. Kimo nodded solemnly at Matthew, telling him silently to proceed.

Natalia looked at Matthew, looked only at Matthew. "I love you," she said.

He couldn't hear her, with the demon guitar screeching in his ears and the audience hooting like demons themselves, and Cain pitifully forced to sing a song that was now a horror to him, a song about the joys of serving Satan. But Matthew knew what she said. He heard her words in his heart.

"I love you," he said back, words he had not said to anyone in a long, long time.

Love, he'd told William. *Some crap like that.*

"Trouble's waiting in the wings," Matthew told the fiend hovering near Cain. "Stage right."

The fiend glanced in that direction. He saw his partner squashed like a bug beneath the feet of the stolid Kimo. The fiend's face contorted in rage. The fiend looked back at Matthew almost immediately. The song was within three words of reaching its conclusion, but that split second of inattention was all Matthew needed.

He raised his voice and shouted, *"'Ab omni hoste visibili et invisibili et ubíque in hoc sáeculo liberetur.* From every enemy both visible and invisible and everywhere in this lifetime be freed,'"* and he lunged at Cain. The fiend moved swiftly to intercept Matthew, but missed.

For Matthew did not try to save Cain, drag him away or lay his hands on him, as the fiend had anticipated. Matthew took hold of the demon guitar.

"Let go!" Cain cried wildly, trying to wrest the guitar from Matthew's grip. "I have to play! You don't understand! I have to play!"

"I do understand," said Matthew firmly. "What's more important, God understands!"

In the silence left by the absence of the music, his voice rebounded throughout the theater. The audience hushed, sank into an awed, breath-holding silence.

"Let go," Matthew said softly to Cain. "Let go of fear, let go of unhappiness, let go of guilt. . . ."

Cain shook his head frantically and moaned and gripped the guitar.

"I can't! I gave away my soul! The devil owns me."

"He doesn't! Your soul is still your own. Ask for God's help, ask for God's forgiveness!"

Cain hesitated. "But if I do, I'll be . . . ordinary."

"The one time in your life when you were happy," Matthew said quietly.

Cain stared at him, then he shut his eyes and gave a shuddering sob. His arms went limp, his hands flaccid. He started to let go of the guitar.

Dark wings folded about Cain. Dark claws dug into him. Hideous fiery red eyes glared at Matthew.

Cain's hand moved on the strings, poised to play the final note.

"Take me!" Matthew cried suddenly. "My soul for his!"

He took hold of the crucifix and yanked it from around his neck. Matthew threw it on the floor.

A bright white spotlight slanted through the darkness and struck the demon guitar. The audience gasped. They thought the spot came from the lights in the theater.

Matthew knew better.

Guitar strings twanged discordantly, as if it were crying out in rage. The demon guitar burst into flame.

Hellfire swirled around Matthew, burning him, and he was back in his nightmare, struggling to escape the fire. *But there was no escape. The flames licked the soles of his feet. The pain was excruciating, and it would get worse. Matthew tried to keep from screaming. He wouldn't give his tormentors the satisfaction. He began to pray, but his flesh was roasting now, and he couldn't help himself. He screamed and screamed and kept screaming as the stench from his own burning flesh filled his nostrils . . .*

Matthew gasped and opened his eyes. He was not on fire, though he could still feel the pain of the burning. He found himself in a darkness so complete it was as if all light everywhere had been obliterated, had never existed.

All around him he could hear voices crying out in despair and unendurable sorrow.

He recognized them.

The cries of the damned.

Yet, somewhere in the distance, he could hear other voices, living voices. They were hissing and booing, demanding their money back.

Matthew smiled.

"Congratulations, Matthew Gallow," growled a voice like a thunderclap. "You've ruined my plans, cost me years of wasted time and effort."

Claws dug into Matthew's flesh, ripping at him, tearing the cassock to black ribbons. He cried out and sank to his knees.

"I can use a man like you in my organization," the voice continued. "A fallen angel. You're charming, a fast talker. You know a lot about the ploys of the enemy. I won't keep you down here. I'll send you back to the world. You'll have everything you ever wanted.

"Just sign on the line. . . ."

Chapter 34

$\mathcal{H}$is room was basic: two double beds, one window, Venetian blinds to shut out the lights of the parking lot, a curtain, two towels, a shower, TV, and phone. Matthew went through the usual routine. He found the remote, turned on the TV. He always turned on the TV. He didn't like the quiet. He tossed his suitcase onto the bed and opened it. The suitcase was empty, except for the flask.

The suitcase was always empty, except for the flask.

The TV talked, though it never made any sense. He stretched out on the bed.

Another night in the Inn-B-Tween motel.

Night after night after night. Forever and always.

He opened the flask, poured the bourbon in a glass, added ice. There was always ice in the ice bucket. Just one of the little services provided.

He went back, lay down on the bed, watched the TV, though he couldn't ever understand anything anyone said or make sense of the pictures. He took a drink . . .

A knock came on the door.

Matthew froze. His hand, holding the glass, jerked, spilling the bourbon.

There weren't supposed to be knockings on these doors.

"Hey, Matthew!" called a voice, "open up!"

"Natalia!" Matthew whispered. He closed his eyes, the pain of loss and loneliness jabbing through the bourbon fog.

This was a dream. Not like the nightmares. This was a good dream, though it hurt him so much it might well have been torment.

"Matthew!" she cried again, sounding exasperated. "All right. Well, you asked for it. All right, Rat, do your thing."

The door swung open. Natalia stood framed in the doorway. She was wearing a white blouse and blue jeans, her long, now-chestnut-colored hair shimmered in the sunlight.

Matthew sat up, staring at her dumbly, in disbelief.

Natalia entered the room. She looked around, made a face, then came over and sat down on the bed beside him.

"What are you doing here?" he asked, finally finding his voice.

"Did you ever hear the story of Orpheus and Eurydice?" she asked.

"I don't know," Matthew said, more bewildered than ever. "I suppose so . . ." He shook his head. "I don't understand—"

"Orpheus was the ancient Greeks' version of a rock star," Natalia said, settling herself comfortably on the bed, legs crossed. "He could play so beautifully that he charmed all the wild beasts in the mosh pits. He had a wife named Eurydice. He loved her dearly, and she loved him. One night she was dancing in the forest and stepped into a nest of snakes. The snakes bit her and she died. Do you mind if I turn this off?"

Natalia grabbed the remote and silenced the TV.

"Poor Orpheus was grief-stricken. He poured his sorrow out in his music, and it was so sad that even the gods wept. He went down to the Underworld and played his music for Hades, who was moved to tears. Orpheus begged the gods to give Eurydice back to him. Hades agreed, on one condition. That Orpheus could not look back at her until they reached the world. He had to have faith in love.

"Orpheus agreed. He left the Underworld, and Eurydice followed him. But he began to doubt. He feared she wasn't coming. He turned around and looked for her.

"He saw her," Natalia finished softly, "but only as she was waving good-bye forever . . ."

Matthew listened in silence. He had begun to dare to hope, and he was afraid to speak now lest his hope be shattered.

"I have a friend of yours with me," Natalia said. She drew out a battered hat, opened it up. Arthur lay curled up, asleep. "Father William gave the dormouse to me. He figured I might need him. He said you were stubborn."

Natalia looked at him, her eyes, with the golden flecks, shimmered. "He told me what you did. How you 'went to Heaven and threw yourself off.'"

"Another quote?" Matthew asked huskily.

Natalia nodded, unable to speak herself for a moment. "Father William said you refused to sign the contract."

"I had already signed one contract," Matthew said with a smile. "I didn't want you to sue me."

Natalia laughed, then she shrugged. "That contract's null and void now that the band is gone."

"What happened to Cain?" Matthew asked.

"You mean Rupert?" Natalia shook her head. "His last concert was a bust. The fans soon forgot him. He went back to school. I heard he was planning to major in history. He's happy, I guess. I don't hear from him anymore."

Matthew reached out and took hold of Natalia's hand. She was warm, flesh and blood, not a dream.

"And Ms. Ashley?" he said. "What's she doing?"

"Like Billy Joel says, 'It's still rock-and-roll to me.' Jordan and Mike and Ryan have formed a new band. I'm their manager. We'll never hit platinum or even gold, but we're having a good time."

"And Kimo?"

"He's our bus driver now, since Al went back to be with his family. Kimo and Woof brought me here. Oh, Woof says to say 'hi' by the way. He was sorry he couldn't hang around to see you, but he heard that Jerry Garcia's forming a band, and he went to see if he could join."

"So Woof finally made it to Heaven," Matthew remarked.

"If that's where Jerry Garcia is, I guess so," Natalia said. "And now it's your turn, Matthew Gallow. Only I hope you're not planning on returning to Heaven too soon. I want you to spend some time with me first."

Natalia rose to her feet. "I'm going to walk out that door. And I'm not looking back."

She leaned down and gave him a kiss.

"We'll have breakfast at Denny's," she said softly.

Natalia turned and walked toward the door. She didn't look back.

Matthew sat on the bed. He didn't deserve this chance for redemption.

But then, if we all got what we deserved, Hell would be filled to the rafters.

And besides, if there was ever a way for him to get to Heaven, it would be with Natalia.

Matthew stood up and walked out the door after her.

Next month, don't miss these exciting new love stories only from **Avon Books**

Never Dare a Duke by Gayle Callen
Christopher Cabot is the perfect duke. His family's penchant for scandal has proven to him the need to suppress his recklessness and instead focus on leading an exemplary life. But the unexpected appearance of a meddlesome yet beautiful woman at his house party may undo all his hard work—especially if she succeeds in uncovering his one secret.

Bedtime for Bonsai by Elaine Fox
An Avon Contemporary Romance
Pottery artist Dylan is starting a new life when he opens up his own shop across the street from Penelope's store. While the chemistry between them may be heating up, neither has any illusions about the other: They are from different worlds. Until Mr. Darcy, Penelope's mischievous dog, suddenly forges an unbreakable connection between them.

The Abduction of Julia by Karen Hawkins
An Avon Romance
Julia Frant has secretly loved Alec MacLean, the wild Viscount Hunterston, from afar. So when he accidentally snatches her instead of her lovely, scheming cousin for an elopement to Gretna Green, Julia leaps at the chance to make her passionate dreams come true.

A Bride for His Convenience by Edith Layton
An Avon Romance
Lord Ian Sutcombe has no choice but to seek a marriage of convenience and sets his sights on Hannah Leeds, a newly wealthy merchant's daughter. They wed, and soon learn that passion and desire and a commonality of interests force them to know each other, yet their pride may prevent them from discovering a once-in-a-lifetime love.

REL 1108

At Avon Books, we know your passion for romance—once you finish one of our novels, you find yourself wanting more.

May we tempt you with . . .

- **Excerpts** from our upcoming releases.

- Entertaining **extras**, including authors' personal photo albums and book lists.

- Behind-the-scenes **scoop** on your favorite characters and series.

- **Sweepstakes** for the chance to win free books, romantic getaways, and other fun prizes.

- Writing **tips** from our authors and editors.

- **Blog** with our authors and find out why they love to write romance.

- **Exclusive content** that's not contained within the pages of our novels.

Join us at
www.avonbooks.com

AVON

An Imprint of HarperCollins*Publishers*
www.avonromance.com